Praise for Jam

'Powerful… There are echoes of D...
This slim, punchy book is extra...

'Yorkston's new novel is a dark and desperate odyssey' – *Scotsman*

'Funny and touching… beautifully told' – *Herald*

'I absolutely love this book. A brilliant evocation of a child's view of the world. The story flows effortlessly… An unsentimental and unflinching miracle of remembrance' – **Jarvis Cocker**

'Funny, affectionate… The acclaimed folk singer's jewel of a novel follows a penniless poet dragging his young sons across Ireland' – *Telegraph*

'There's no denying that this is a novel in a minor key, and yet its rhythms and cadences are constantly evolving, drawing the reader closer. Listen out for it and you'll even hear a note that might be described as poetic' – *Observer*

'His prose has tremendous rhythm and a rambunctious energy… delightful to read' – *National*

'Assured, funny and tragic all at once. Brilliantly captures the quirks and paradoxes of small town Scottish life' – **Doug Johnstone**

'A rural take on *Trainspotting* themes, this book is funny and tragic all at once' – *Scots Magazine*

'A beautiful book about being on the road: brilliantly funny, unsentimentally poignant and shot through with the clear-eyed honesty that James Yorkston brings to his music-making… Unmissable' – **John Burnside**

TOMMY THE BRUCE

JAMES YORKSTON

Oldcastle Books

First published in 2025 by Oldcastle Books Ltd.,
Harpenden, Herts, UK

oldcastlebooks.co.uk
@OldcastleBooks

ISBN
978-0-85730-594-7 (Paperback)
978-0-85730-595-4 (eBook)

2 4 6 8 10 9 7 5 3 1

Typeset 11 on 13.35pt Adobe Garamond Pro
by Avocet Typeset, Bideford, Devon, UK
Printed and bound in Great Britain by
CPI Group (UK) Ltd, Croydon CR0 4YY

MIX
Paper | Supporting
responsible forestry
FSC® C171272
FSC
www.fsc.org

For Hamish

When I was a child, my father used to drive me around rural Scotland, stopping off at these grand Victorian hotels that would occasionally rise out of the landscape. The thought of what happened in these places, in and out of season, always fascinated me. Here is one such imagining.

Pitsneddon, Perthshire, Two-thousand and something.

Part I

1

I BEND DOWN TO reach the strawberry jam supplies, grab a wee bairn's portion-sized pot and stand back up, banging my head the instant I do and crying out – *FUCK* – that super-sharp skelp of pain rushing right through me, scurrying my hangover this way and that, my poor scalp having shards of ice pushed within, eyes closed, the blood red and the stars... I lose my balance and topple over backwards, landing on that old sweeping brush and pan, cracking the handle of it, sitting straight down in the dust and stour of last night, last week, last month, last year – but no further noises, nothing falls on my head, nothing else collapses around me.

There's maybe three seconds of peace, peace I value, before I hear – *Tommy! Tommy! Are you ok in there, Tommy? Listen, don't you worry about the jam. If that's going to cause you any problems, the missus and I will be perfectly happy with just some butter. Or perhaps some olive oil. Have you any olive oil, Tommy? It's perfectly wonderful drizzled on toast, Tommy. Perhaps with some banana? Have you any of those, Tommy? Any bananas? To go with the olive oil, I mean. On the toast. Oh – and about the toast, Tommy. Your toaster machine has popped up. I heard it. Would you like me to fetch the toast for you? It'd be no bother...*

I make to stand, but every ounce of me is calling, pleading for me to remain where I am and sleep. A fine bed, right here, this back cellar. Friendly mustards, vinegars, kitchen rolls, cereals, bottled water, cat food, tins of tomatoes... All this silent, wonderful company would not disturb my sleep. But no – I need to get up and out before that beloved customer, that beloved, bothersome customer, makes his way into the kitchen and sees just what a sty his breakfast is being

11

prepared in. I inhale. I sneeze, a minor sneeze, and then I arise, being aye super careful not to dunt my head once more. All the way up, all the way up to my six foot two inches of height, blood pouring back down to ma toes or wherever it goes when it leaves the head, but concentration on full, steadying myself and then – *No, it'll be fine, Mr Grayson. You sit yourself back down and I'll get you your breakfast. You're my guest, Mr Grayson, and I like to make my guests comfortable.*

Mr Grayson is waiting for me as I emerge – *Um – Tommy, are you ok? There's a bit of... blood...*

I raise my hand to my head and yes, indeed, there is a bit of blood. Fuck. *Oh – aye, I, um – I banged my head. Just... Just give me a moment. Here – here's your jam –* I hand over a tiny pot of raspberry jam – *Made in the Highlands of Scotland by McShoogle and Sons –* and make my way back into the kitchen.

This place. This fucking place. Stour everywhere. Mouse droppings, even. Awkward to hoover up, mouse droppings. If you go in when they're still fresh you can scoosh them around the floor, but if you leave them – well, then you've got mouse shite everywhere. I got a cat for it, you know, for the problem – I am aware of the problem – but the cat turned out to be more a problem than the mouse. When the Health and Safety people arrived, they weren't happy to see a cat in the kitchen, and I guess I could have – should have, even – told them – *But aye, it's for getting the mice?* But in a way, I'm glad I didn't. No point pointing out the gaps in the cleanliness, if I can avoid it. I got enough bother off them anyhow – the bins, the cludgie, the fire escape, the back exit, the food preparation area... they said I was *Lucky To Keep My Licence* and gave me a severe warning, a week's notice...

Well, in that week I gave the place the best cleaning I could muster, a sweep AND a hoover, wiped the surfaces, bleached the bogs... And there you go, we passed, with a Two out of Five – *Major Improvements Needed –* and the lucky punters o' The Inn of Pitsneddon can still get their toast and jam or whatever other luxury they choose from our extensive menu of frozen foods.

I walk to the sink, the mirror, check my reflection and lo, there certainly is blood, though it's curdling now, or whatever it is blood does, congealing maybe, a wee solid crimson splatch right where my hair's possibly receding, slowly making its way off my head, abandoning ship.

Tommy – Tommy – do you need any help?

What a demanding guest this auld boy is. I tell you, he can drink and talk for Scotland. If I had any memory I'd know all his business, but I cannot recall a scooby of what was said past – oh, I don't know – 1:00 am? Up until then he'd been talking to me about property prices in Edinburgh. You can't blame me for switching off.

He's a university guy, I mind that. Hillwalker, tourist. We get a few of them this time of year.

Aye, Mr Grayson, I'll be right back out, almost done here.

I'm splashing frozen-cold water out of the tap onto my red-raw hands, easing the blood off of me with a rough blue cleaning rag, rinsing it down the plughole until there's no more red to be seen, hanging the rag back to dry, giving my hands one more frozen scoosh – then tap off and oot.

So, Mr Grayson – what was it you're after again?

2

I't's all I've known, this place. We rarely took holidays, even. I grew up here, heck, was almost born here – in emergency, the way Auld Jock talks about the drama of it, Jock being almost as old as the village itself, it seems, and our most regular and easy guest... My father, well, he loved the place. Mother didn't, as far as I can remember... but she took the big flit good and early – I can't blame her, after my brother John died so wee. There were too many reasons for her to jump ship and too few not to. And I guess my father and I weren't enough of an anchor to keep her onboard.

That bites a fair bit.

So, my father struggled through. He enjoyed it, though. He loved village life still, saw his profession as a service to the community. The community who'd rallied around him when he needed them. And he built up a pretty good reputation, I think, here amongst the hills and the fir trees, the deer, the winter snows, the spring frosts... He provided a warm welcome. Basic, but warm. Heck, he'd not recognise any of these daft beers that the brewery thrusts upon us now. *Real Ales*. Same old shite, just tastes soor and awfy. I mean, I'm not an ale drinker anyhow, but I cannot keep them tasting good. I pour away as much as I sell, barely get them in now, even. Also, I've found that if all I have on tap is Tennent's and McEwan's, that's what folk will drink. Folk are too lazy to do anything else. And it's not as though I have any competition, nearest bar being, what... well, probably way over in Aberfeldy, anyhow, so a good half-hour's drive... And house wine. Fucking house wine! Co-op wine. It's their wine. I'm just the guardian. £5.99 a bottle to buy, £15.99 to sell. Easy business, this business. If only everyone drank wine.

14

I was never a natural with the hotel, not the way my father was, and now, now I can see how much work he put into it and how much of that work was just being friendly and polite and not telling folk to fuck off too hard, even if they DID need to fuck off, due to the drink or whatever. Now, after all this time alone here, I love it even less. Just a long, slow drag, heaving this auld building behind me to my death. Can't sell it. I've looked into it. After costs, I'd be lucky to get just enough for a two-bed semi in Dundee, which I do not fancy one bit. Plus, what else would I do? At least here I have the trees, the hills and the quiet, the snow, when it comes, the owls, the wildlife. And the connection, you know, to my childhood.

Pretty much all my school pals left the area as soon as they could. Off to Glasgow, bar work, call-centre work, into a mortgage on a tiny two-bed cheuk-coop place... The young farm boys are still around, mind, but they work hard. I'll seldom see them in here, more likely hoiking about in their double-cab things, wrapped up in those tartan fleece jackets. They'll be in for a funeral or such and we can shoot the breeze then, however awkward the funerals can be. Knowing most of the folk around here, I don't feel right charging what I should, what I could... Some old guy will put a £50 note behind the bar, thinking that'll last all night, but – well, you'll know yourself, £50 can go on a round or two these days. So, I'll let it go for a while, before being the bastard asking for money, being seen as making money from a wake, despite the fact I'm losing out. Them lot complaining about the sandwiches I provide, a low murmur of disapproval, but fuck it, if they only give me £30 for a hundred sandwiches, aye, they're going to be tiny fuckers filled with nothing but corned beef. And jam. Jam for the weans, keep them from whining, screeching, greeting away.

My father's was the worst of those funerals, of course – me somehow deciding to open and hold the bar, serve the regulars, his old pals... Maybe three-dozen people were in then. All insisting on paying, shoving tens, twenties at me – *Keep the change, keep the change...* Back when tens and twenties had a reasonable value. I was glad of the bar between us, the normality of it, but also the distance it kept me from well-meaning hugs. In the end, the numbers got swelled even further by a hillwalking crew, and them figuring it was a wake they'd just entered – everyone dressed in their black and white – and asking ME whose funeral it was... Well, that was enough for me, but Auld Jock, well, he saw it and came round to my side and tended bar, all evening, let me squirrel myself away in the bar snug, do the public grieving in semi-private, at least... I'll always remember Jock for doing that, always grateful.

There were a load of regulars then – we had the older farmers, certainly every weekend, if only until 10:00 pm or so, early starts calling them away... That Gillian lassie from the shop and Lang Johnny Moore, the teacher... Freddie Jackson, the butcher – before he got done for selling poached venison, of course – and that elderly gay couple who pretended they were brothers.

One by one, though, they dropped off. Not all died, I mean, though some have, but – well, I guess my hangdog, grieving, miserable pus wasn't as inviting as my jolly-cheeked father's.

Ach, I miss my dad. What a poor run he had.

We can do ok still, though – I say *we*, but I mean *me* – if one of those tour buses pulls up unannounced. I'll spy it straight off and turn the coffee on. Warm up the auld stuff, no matter how auld, get the aroma out, then straight back to the kitchen and flick the oven switches.

Can you do food for twenty?

Aye, I certainly can, just sit yourselves down and I'll take your order.

And I certainly cannot, but once they've placed their food order and got their drinks, they're a captive audience, prisoners, almost... One thing I do reasonably well is keep the freezer stocked, so chips, chips, chips, and beans and sausage and all that crap that a'body loves.

Do you not have someone helping you? You could really do with some staff.

Aye, I've got two staff members, but one's in hospital about to give birth and the other's off sick, but I couldn't just give their jobs away – I wouldn't do that, I'm loyal to MY staff – so I'm just doing my best here myself, I'm sure you understand.

It's a' shite, of course. But this way I get excused for lazy management and the mess, and I get tips, tips for my effort.

And what clan are you? I'm McDonald. My family emigrated from here in 1802.

Ah, good folk, the McDonalds. I've known many a McDonald in my time. No – my clan's Bruce, I'm a direct descendant of Sir Robert himself. We got gifted this land, in fact, for loyalty. There's been a staging post here for the coaches and horses since way back then…

Mair shite, mair shite.

And if I'm lucky, a few of them might stay at the bar and spraff, getting picked up when their coach arrives back from whichever tartan wonderland it's been visiting. We'll be doing fine left to ourselves. Doing fine unless themselves offer me a drink, in which case it becomes fifty-fifty, but more like seventy-thirty or worse as soon I'll be drinking myself and, well, they'll see me a little scooshed and do their best to take advantage, of both my good nature and my bad arithmetic. Heck, what's 20p between pals, eh?

3

A ND HERE'S ANOTHER day, another morning.
If I should cough, my skull will shoogle my brain to such a
point that it shakes me out of my bed and into the cauld, the damp,
the whatever time of year.

Another hangover, another unwelcome surprise that comes as no
surprise at all.

A pint of warm tap water to start things off and then I tell myself
– Give it ten minutes and if you STILL need painkillers, then so
be it – and ten minutes later I do need them, so I'm at the cabinet,
picking through the half-empty plastic and foil packets of whatever
pills remain.

Down the stairs and clearing up, looking for last night's guests in the
check-in book and seeing just the two, a couple from Hastings, down
in England. Normally ok, the English, not prone to complaining, just
after a cheap room. I scout the bar, picking up debris, thanking God
for the glowing ashes of the open fire that I can chuck the burnables
in. Thanking God too for the dishwasher I bought myself with that
money I found in that wallet a Geordie guy left three or four years
ago. Stacking it all in, plates and glasses and knives and beer towels
and whatever the fuck needs cleaned that'll fit inside. Wiping the
tables, the bar, as quick as I can, finding that doing it this way means
it gets done – leaving it until after my breakfast means nothing at all
gets done and a whole morning is spent grinding my teeth, trying to
rattle myself into sweeping the kitchen or paying a bill or checking
the bookings or washing the sheets...

And just as I'm finished, the footfall thumps on the stairs and last
night's guests are here –

Oh, good morning to you. Will you be having breakfast?

Oh, good MORNING to YOU, Tommy. Two fine full English breakfasts, please.

And a nudge in the ribs from his lady friend –

Oh – forgive me – full SCOTCH breakfasts, please. Now then – wherever shall we sit?

I wave my hands in a biblical fashion, offering them the scope of the entire room. Just not the bar, please. That means full-on conversation. Who'd have a bar meal breakfast? Well, some folk do, believe it or not.

But not these twa, these twa are right up against the window, and I can imagine the shiver coming off it so I make a big song and dance about stoking the fire. I should have cleaned that out, lit it, first thing. Just too many things to do. I need a wee mannie to do all this. Folk say there are no jobs, but I'd pay someone a tenner a day to come in and scurry the ash away, build a new fire, clean the bar, clean the sheets and get folk breakfasts, for sure I would.

Pile the firelighters on, keen to not look amateur, to look like the king of the fire makers – *Shouldn't you clean that out?* – the man asks, but fuck it, it'll light if there's enough of these wee beauties scattered around. I give the whole thing a rattle and a poke and a load of ash falls, a cloud of it lightly snowing the bar floor. I can sweep the rest of the ash away easy now. To give any new fire a wee bit of breathing space, pile the sticks on top of the firelighters, the coal on top of the sticks and then a muckle big log on top of the whole gang, light it and stand back. No real heat will come off it until the breakfasters are gone, but I've shown willing, and the flicker of the flame might convince them they're warmer than they are, or at least waft an element of romance into their day.

Now then. Full Scottish, was it?

It was – and two coffees, if you please.

I can grin at that with ease as the two coffees will come first and making three is just as easy as two, so I'll have a strong black coffee myself, to hold in my hand whilst I fry whatever I can find and serve it up as a full Scottish, or a Perthshire full Scottish if they should complain and ask why there's courgette in there instead of mushroom or whatever. Ach, all most folk want is the sausage, egg, bacon and bread, and as I said, I'm awfy good at keeping the freezer full.

I just chuck it all in, heat the oil up and fry it to fuck. Make it black and crumbly. Zap the toast, big scoop of mustard. Aye, looks good enough to eat.

Deliverance to the troops and retreat, retreat before they can question, demand, query…

The guests have left. There's a scraping on the door and it'll be the cat. I pour some dry food into a flowery tea mug and offer it over. The podgy young thing will nibble on those before taking its place by the fire, bringing with it charm and warmth and an old-school welcome that I cannot master no matter how hard I smile. If the day is quiet and I've cleared up the unfinished breakfasts and made my Tesco delivery order, I'll pull up a chair beside the cat, beside the now taken and aflame fire, and the cat will jump to me, muster upon my knee. I'll have a Dick Gaughan CD on the machine, perhaps, and I'll snooze. And you know, that's the happiest part of my day…

…Until the door opens with a clatter as the brass bell my father installed hollers through to where I am. If my snooze is deep, I've learned to slither down from my perch to the fireplace and poke at the fire until I've awoken, to put off any questions, any requests until I'm at least semi-conscious. Work out: How many beds are made? Can I be ersed to make lunch, or is the *chef* off today?

I jump down to stoke the fire. The cat makes off with a startled sprint.

Hang on a sec, I'll be right wi' you…

Christ, I'm dizzy.

There are no voices, just a light shuffle – could've just been the postie, but more likely someone *caught-short*, desperate for the cludgie –

Aye, the toilets are just beyond the bar, way over –

I gesture behind me, not so accurate, but granting permission to whoever it is to go for their business and get out of my life. Fuck. I forgot I've got to clean those toilets…

Oh, hi, Tommy, I was just wondering…

I turn around and spy a lassie, jeans and trainers, blue puffer-coat bomber-jacket thing, smiling, tight brown hair… She's bonny, familiar, a bit, not sure who, but someone I remember, vaguely, maybe a semi-regular or a guest from long ago, her clothing suggesting she hasn't come far…

I make to stand, knowing fine to grab hold of the hearth, steady myself, prepare for the pain as the blood rushes from my head to my feet.

Upright now, and although the room is still spinning, I can see her face is flushed, as though she's been out running herself or is deeply embarrassed. I still cannot place her…

Can I get a gin and tonic, Tommy?

I rub my face, three days of beard sprouting through, causing a satisfying pull, encouraging, teasing the blood to circulate, wake me up.

Umm, aye – sure thing.

I make my way round to the bar, stumbling slightly as my legs come to life. The Gaughan CD has long since finished. How long was I out for? I glance at the clock – 3:00 pm. A good couple of hours.

Is it… Is it… Gordon's?

I'm sorry?

Is it Gordon's gin you're after? And tonic? Schweppes? Slimline?

She's looking at me as though she clearly doesn't give a fuck. I say no more and scoosh her the cheapo mixer on top of a measure of the house gin. The Co-op gin.

Now, I'm no' one of those barmen that expects to be entertained. I won't hand over a pint and wait, wait for the explanation, the story of your day. Nope. I'll hand over the drink and back off. Heck, I've less interest in your day than almost any other thing.

But before I've even cashed the fee, she's asking for another –

Same again, Tommy.

We see these – I see them. It's common for someone or other to find themselves with a question to which the only answer is alcohol. And that person, more than often, will come into a bar to get things going. If they're lucky, they'll find the answer in those first few drams and not have to take home a six pack or a bottle of supermarket spirit.

I prepare another gin and tonic. This one, I garnish with ice and lemon. Ane o' her five a day.

This one, she sips.

I make my way to the other side of the bar and begin the process of unloading the dishwashing machine. I hear a laugh and look up. She's peering over the bar –

You put your dishcloths in the dishwasher?

How does one answer that? I continue to empty.

Aye, lass, I do. It's just soapy water. Disnae bother it, what it's washing. Dishcloth's never complained yet, either.

There's no follow up, she backs off and continues with her sipping. I'm not keen to speak more, not showy with my work. There's no pride to be shared in finding places to hang sodden bar cloths.

I press play and the Gaughan CD jumps back into life. Some company for her. Something to concentrate on that isn't me.

She takes the hint, vacates the bar stool and makes her way to the fire. I watch her walk – what is she – mid-twenties? She's bonny, for sure.

But none of my business who she is, just how much she drinks. If I have to hang around for her, I can tidy things up and pretend to be professional.

I see outside that a light snow is falling. That can grow easily enough round here. I wonder if this lass is driving. Ach, not my job to question folk's sobriety.

Once this lassie goes, if no one else comes in, I'll close up for a couple of hours. Maybe go out for a walk up the hills. Wrap up well, try and find life's answers somewhere, try and work out what the questions are, at least. My father's stout boots are still good, his jacket still warm. Experienced walkers grin when they see me, wearing old, battered but good-quality clothing, obviously a man of much experience, not some weekend walker, but it's all a sham, a sham. I'm just a big man in hand-me-downs... I love the view from up there, watching the village from up high, avoiding the dog walkers, taking the smaller paths, keeping an eye out for roe deer. Sometimes I can feel rich, if even just for a moment; I can hypnotise myself into some kind of comfort, some kind of forever. What is it I feel up in the hills? What are they giving me? A memory? The peace and the quiet? Or is it just the calm smell of the pines?

And there are times I just want to keep on walking. Up, further up, into the cold and the lost and the no escape, with nothing but a flask in my pocket to lose any remaining sense.

But enough about that.

4

A GOOD FEW HOURS pass, me in the kitchen, wasting time, dicking about, cleaning, returning to see my sole customer still here, after an occasional refill, always the same, gin and tonic. She makes no complaint whether there's lemon or no', ice or whatever. Picks the drink up, her long woollen jumper helping grasp the glass, then over to the fire. On a few occasions, I note her placing a new log down, keeping the flames fine. *That's fine*, I say, but she pays no heed. What was I going to do, after all? Take the wood back off the fire?

Thirsty now myself, 6:00 pm almost. I go off out back, can't be seen drinking alone. The curse of the bar owner, all this majestic drink, free to the touch, every which way I look. I cannot stand McEwan's so take a carryout tin of that, hoping the sour pinch will put me off, slow me down. I've a wee storm porch and stand there, my father's old coat wrapped on, forever stashed nearby for this exact job. Staring out into the low orange glow of the back yard, taking in the snow settling, the cold, the light going low. In theory, this time of evening is when the bar should begin getting busy, but any shan weather of note always puts people off.

I sup the drap at the foot of the tin, pitch it into the recycling bin and wonder who sorts a' *that* shite out.

Back inside and towards the bar, I can hear voices. American, I think. So much for my plans. I keep the coat on, an excuse for my absence – I can make out I was changing the oil or chasing off a deer or securing the back gates from the weather. Anything vaguely outdoorsy usually does the trick. Just don't tell them I was drinking the blues away, flirting with the idea of walking north until I could walk no more.

I squeeze through the entrance door and see the lassie is behind the bar, pulling a pint of Tennent's. She notices me – *Oh, hi, Tommy, these guys were after a pint, and I couldnae see you. Hope this is ok?*

She shows me the pint: a small, lightly frothed head, well poured. *Sure,* I nod.

Oh – and they're after a room. Is there a room free?

Fuck, last thing I need. Hmm. Well, there's fourteen rooms. At least one should be ready. Or clean, at least.

I put on my happy hotelier face – *Let me just take a look. Is it a double you're after or a twin?*

5

THESE STAIRS. How many times have I heaved this body of mine up these stairs? A good bit of wood on the banister, you wouldn't get a carved bit of wood like this now, would cost far too much. The carpet is worn but not yet through, the good and the bad of the number of guests I get – any more and it'd be threadbare, but I might also have the money to replace it... Ach. I like the swirls in the carpet, I like the barely discoloured far edges, the hidden corners, untouched by sunlight or footfall. I played with my toy cars on this carpet, the edging providing a racecourse, a slalom for the brave Matchbox heroes. I don't want to lose that, either, that connection...

The floorboards creak. If ever I am reminded of my need to get fit, reminded of my slow age into life, reminded of my parents, it is when pulling myself up these fucking stairs.

I am greeted, as ever, by a statuette of a stag, perched proudly on a mahogany table, lord of all it surveys. I put that there in an effort to appease the tourists, sell the faded grandeur. There's a three-light chandelier above it, with one shade missing and one shade held together by Sellotape. I had it down and in soapy water, cracking twa of the shades together, one totally lost, the other repairable, just. You can see the light bulbs protruding and each one is different – one of those curly-wurly eco things, a 240W bulb that has somehow survived since the 1980s and a lesser, quieter light, perhaps a bulb for a kids' nightlight or whatever. It sums this hotel up, though, that one chandelier – it's old and fucked and bric-a-bracked, but I could also probably fix it if I could only make the effort. There's always tomorrow.

First three doors are open. They'll have been used. I don't even look in. The sight of an unmade bed depresses me. Plus, if there's anything really unpleasant within – a condom, a coffee-stained carpet, food on the floor, keich stains in the bog – well, who needs it?

Fourth room is closed and locked. I struggle with the key, shunt the door with my shoulder, and in. It looks clean, clean enough, anyhow. It smells a wee bit, but that can't be helped. To be honest, it was better when folk smoked, it hid the other aromas. There's a chill, so I bend down and switch on the white convection heater, which clicks to life straightaway, burning any dust that has settled. I walk around the bed – a double, a good size – and inspect the bathroom – no shower, just a bath. A cause of concern for some folk, but I had the showers removed after one dowp too many flooded the floor below, granting me a light rainfall in the bar…

Anyway, the soap's out, a new one. I open the lid of the cludgie and it seems clean – not a deep inspection, but enough. A glance. Who'd be a plumber, eh? Give it a flush, anyhow.

Ach, this room will do. Maybe I'll try and get those folk to down another pint afore giving them their key. If I can get them over the drink-driving limit, they'll have to stay, after all. Or walk.

Back downstairs and the young lassie is at the fire, chatting away to the guests. I nod as I walk in, take my place at the position of power behind the bar. *Aye, that's the fire on in your room. Warm it up a bit.*

Oh – is it an open fire? How quaint!

Shite.

Um… no. It's a heater. On the wall. A wall heater. Still warm, though.

I see the blood leaping to her face, blushing now, and within a second I'm doing the same. I turn away and make to polish a glass. Wipe a surface. Adjust an optic. Ach, right enough, who'd want one of those awfy wee heaters in their bedroom? It's a disaster of a thing, all the romance of bedding down in the corridor of a call centre.

They're getting on fine, the lassie and the American couple. Odd-looking together, the guy a good six-foot-four-inches tall and mighty wide, the lady a plump wee mouse beside him, the shape of one of those woollen bobble snowba' things we'd make as kids. Funny how the Americans who come through here always have shiny faces. The women, anyhow. I guess it's the moisturiser, slathered on. They always seem to be of that age – fifty-five to sixty-five. Maybe their last hurrah, last exploration, a journey they always wanted to undertake. Perhaps, maybe, I am making things easier for them, showing Scotland for what it is, patchwork and bodged, rather than the romantic dream they've been harbouring since hearing of their Scottish roots. We'll hear, soon enough, from these twa. What they've got under their bonnet, a percentage of German, a slither of Scandinavian…

No, no, I'm from these parts, I went to the school just up the way…

It's the lassie speaking. That'll be why I recognise her, then.

Aye, my brother Robert was at school with Tommy here. That's how I know him. Isn't that right, Tommy?

Eh? Oh, aye, lass, sure enough. Robert. Rab. Good fellow, Rab. How is he?

Well… he died. Do you no' remember?

No, I don't. Of course I fucking don't. I wouldn't have asked. She's looking over at me, accusatory.

Ah – no – I remember fine, o' course. Sorry, I was in a dwam. Very sad.

Aye. A good while ago now, but.

Aye. I half nod. I know not what I am nodding for. I wonder who Rab was?

She stops looking at me and continues her talk – *And these hills here, aye, they're fu' of history. Plenty of wildlife…*

Are there any golden eagles?

It's the guy now. Deep voiced, authoritative. It's always the golden eagles they ask for, but there's none here I'm aware of.

A few, but really – the lassie continues – *really you'd have to go further north…*

FURTHER north?

Aye, there's a bit tae go yet!

Looking outside, with the snow now piling down, I can see how they'd feel they were already somewhere quite remote. And I guess they are.

We have American bald eagles. Do you know them? He looks to me.

I nod. *Aye. Big auld birds, them fuckers.*

I regret swearing immediately. The company seem shocked, but maybe, hopefully, disbelieving, questioning their ears. Quickly, I follow things up – *Um, will you be having some food?*

It's not a hard sell, just a distraction.

The chef isn't in, but I can get you something basic, right enough.

Always works. No chef, so it's my effort, just for stodge. Be grateful and thankful for the stodge, the burger, the beans, the chips. Praise me. Heck, I might even chop a tomato, if I can find one.

Ah, ok, well, we can certainly see what you have. We were thinking of maybe taking a drive along to Auchterglen and trying the fish restaurant there – unless you have fish?

Kind of. I raise my eyebrows and make my best offer – *Fingers?*

I'm lucky. They see it as a joke and laugh. I laugh along and soon enough the wee lassie is joining in.

Ma name's Fi. You dinnae mind me, do you? Or ma brother?

She's telling me now, the guests having driven off to their fish place. She's a wee bitty drunk, but on the whole has held the alcohol reasonably well.

Oh aye... Fi, eh? Fiona was my mother's name.

Silence. For a second, her eyes flicker to mine, but I cut them off. Instead, I examine a crisp packet.

Robert was ma brother. He was in your year, I think.

I still cannot place a Robert. And I mean, well, my class was small enough –

Robert? You mean – Jim?

No. I mean Robert. Shuggy.

Ah. Fucking... Shuggy? What a dick that boy was. Two years above me, in fact. Maybe three. So long ago now, though.

Shuggy Mclean?

Aye, that was him. Do you mind him now?

I do, aye. I sup on my pint. How can I say something positive? The boy was a thug. *I mind he had that thatch o' ginger hair. Like a bird was in it.*

She laughs.

Aye. You probably knew him better than me. He died just over ten years ago. I was only fourteen. Never kent him as an adult, just a big brother. She stares into the fire. *He was SO kind.*

Kind of a prick, she must mean. A bully, a shit-thick dullard.

Did you – did you play wi' him?

He played with me, until I got so big and lang he'd leave me alone.

No. I didn't really. You know – aye – we werenae the best o' pals. He could be…

She looks at me, expectant.

He could be a bit – rough.

She squirms, aware, then makes to defend – *Ach, that wisnae really him. That was that arsehole o' a friend he had, that Jim Blair. Now HE was a fucking eejit if ever I knew one, everything we heard…* She trails off.

You know, my father caught them once, Jim Blair and some other dowp, creeping in the back door o' the hotel, trying tae steal alcohol – he reckons they'd done it a few times; he'd noticed the odd mistake in the stocktaking – but this one time, he bumbled intae them and chased them out.

Fuck.

Aye – it got worse, tho' – they turned on him, began throwing stones – at him, at the windows. He was pretty shaken up. I can mind that well, them boys just a few years above me at school…

She's quiet, then, accusatory, almost – *And – do you think – do you reckon that was Robert? Wi' him, I mean? Is that what you're saying?*

Ach, I'd never thought… It probably was. I mean, I didn't see it. Dad didn't say… *Eh? No… I doubt he'd do that. Even if it was him, Dad said the Blair boy was the ringleader. I mean – he went on tae big-league crap, did he no'? He was aye a'ways trouble.*

She tuts, she squirms, she mumbles – *Aye, that whole family is trouble.*

And then she's up, off the seat, stomping over to the lassies' cludgie. I seldom venture in there, finding lassies a cleaner sort o' beast than the menfolk, tidying after themselves, saving me a job. Two minutes later, she's not out, and I suspect she'll be taking a keich so I'm off behind the bar once more, finding something to wipe down, checking the mixers, changing the music, putting on some Altan. Irish, I know, but I like it enough, and all the diddly stuff is the same to the tourists. As if there would be anyone in on a night like this…

The brass bell clangs again and I look over – just to see those American tourists returning, snow-dunked and frosted.

The bridge was closed! Can you believe it? We drove all that way and the bridge was closed. Why couldn't they have told us?

I wonder which bridge she means, for there's no bridge between here and Auchterglen. *Which, um, which way did you go?* I set up two glasses. What was it? Tennent's and vodka orange?

No more of that lager. If we're staying here, I can take a whisky. I'll have a – what have you got? He peers in at my meagre selection of malts – *I'll have a Glencuddich.* He pronounces it Glen-coody-itch.

Good choice, I lie. It's surely the most sugary of all the malts. Heck, I only ever use it in coffee, and even then, just the instant coffee. *Ice?*

Ice! No. Who do you think I am? I'm as Scottish as you, son. No ice in my whisky, thank you very much.

I smile. Well. Since I'm up there anyway, I might as well tak' a dram for myself. Not Glencuddich for me, though, oh no, I go for Talisker. A far classier scoop. I don't wish to offend, so when he's not looking, I quietly give myself twa cubes of ice.

A few hours later and we're all sat hugging the fire, sausages and chips all round. I did my best to cook them reasonably, aware from the moment those folk trooped downstairs from the room that I wasn't exactly popular.

Is that… your best room?

They're all… much the same.

Huh. No wonder there's no one here.

It's true. I cannot argue, indeed. I raise my eyebrows and grin, nod in agreement.

So how on earth do you keep this place running?

Shrug – *Well, I do my best. When the bypass was built, we lost a lot of business. It's hard to justify any further investment...*

This is the line I tell anyone who wants something to believe in. It usually derails folk, puts them back on the polite track. No one wants to talk about the awkward stuff, surely?

It does the trick. They quieten. They quieten and munch.

Good sausage, though, it has to be said. Are these local?

They are, aye.

From the local Co-op, anyhow. Who knows what nationality of beast the meat came from.

And the snow fell and the bar kept quiet, the awfulness of the room keeping the tourists downstairs, the awfulness of my job keeping me with them, and, well, what kept the Fi lassie here, I do not know... But the drink kept flowing, the anecdotes kept coming: Oor Yank, Graeme Kilbride, it seems, had led a hard life up until now, a soldier in Korea, but brushed past that, no more than a mention, the rest of his life spent selling cars, trucks, diggers, tyres – putting the work in, long hours of self-employment, never making it big in rural Minnesota but getting by, putting their kid through college, with one eye on retirement the moment he hit sixty. His wife, Bridie – Irish family, but as American-voiced as Graeme – keeping it all going alongside him, her stories full of sewing bees and rural thieves and bears in the back yard, of migratory drifters freezing to death in the thick snow and being discovered in the thaw...

And finally, here they both are, still alive, still together. It made me feel guilty, hearing of the adventure of their lives and having nothing to add myself, no luxury to reward them, doing my best to come out of Host mode and become Tommy, myself – though I've long forgotten who he is, not really using him much, not many conversations had in recent years about anything other than the hotel business and the weather...

And Fi still here, joining in, explaining they'd gone *the old way* to Auchterglen – *No one uses that bridge anymore except the coos* – us both laughing, but gently, I hope. Fi seeming as sheets to the wind as I am myself, but not turning lairy or shouty, handling herself with grace, just happy for the warmth inside her, the shield from the world that alcohol brings, the ability to hide from whatever she came in to escape, the company she does not know, the chat, the banter...

...And Auld Jock arriving, on time for his usual half, a settler for his bed, perhaps, the American couple delighted with the auld buzzard. He soon relieves me of any responsibility I might have felt for keeping the conversation flowing, and now I can relax, sit back, only speak when I've actually something to say...

...And the whisky is brought down from behind the bar, and I even remember trekking upstairs to my own supply, bringing down a seventeen-year-old Lagavulin and trying to convince Graeme of the beauty of the peatier, earthier whiskies whilst also attempting to rein in my dislike of the sweet and Irish whiskey, but failing, no doubt. Over-talking about music, using Bridie's Irish blood as an excuse to play Planxty, aware I'm losing my guests now, who seemingly don't give a fig about music but nod politely since I lost my off-switch around three drams back...

And at some point, that's it – muddled senseless – we're gone.

6

THE PAIN WAKES me, as ever. The pain of the hangover, an angry goose pecking inside my head, but nowhere near as amusing as that sounds. I lie dead still to see how bad the pain is. I try to remember what I drank, to gauge what I should expect. I wonder if I had any guests who I have to rise and serve? As the answers settle in, none of them are pleasant. I cannot remember going to bed, yet I can remember half-falling down the stairs whilst collecting my whisky. I remember I have guests. Americans. I remember I ate something, which isn't always the case and should help…

I can only take the shortest of breaths, for any deeper and I seem to be alerting my stomach to the possibility of the luxury of expelling whatever is left within, swiftly, via my gullet. And Christ, I hate being sick. I fight it away. I attempt to focus. My head is hanging out of the bed, and I open my eyes and attempt to focus on something, to stop the spinning. There's a sock on the floor, that'll do, but then – there's another sock – and whose sock is *that* sock? And, more importantly, whose shoes?

Ah, shite.

It's not common. It happens, you know. But it's not common.

I listen intently, hoping to hear the sound of sleep. Of one person sleeping. I do not want to have awoken beside an elderly American couple.

That is even less common. I'd go as far as to say it never happens.

There's a light, snuffling snore – clearly still asleep, whoever it is. I mean, it has to be that lassie – Fi, right? Unless someone else turned up… I'm curious, but the shrieking in my skull is demanding I stay

34

stock-still, and my seasick stomach is agreeing, anchoring me tight to the bed.

I look for the clock but cannot see. My field of vision is hampered somewhat by the duvet that is clawing over my forehead. I have to move, and after one... two... three... I collapse my head back onto the bed, pointing my eyes at my ever-faithful, always-there bedside clock, which is declaring impatiently:

08:04

Which is an almighty terror of a time for one to wake up when one is in charge of preparing a hotel for the day.

I lop my head up, my neck doing all the work, glance down and see it is indeed Fi lying beside me. Well I never.

She sounds deep, fast asleep.

I'm thinking, I am. I cannot remember a thing.

I hoik my legs out, quietly, for I know that nothing gets better from me staying in bed. Once I'm awake, I need to be out, and, well, I'm supposed to be serving breakfast from 7:30 am.

I stand, I sway, I lean against the wall. I look at Fi, her hair loose now, draped over her cheek... She's snuggled right in, and I cannot blame her, for the room is as cauld as a penguin's wingtip.

I am pleased she is there, for I shared warmth with a fellow human being and maybe later on I may feel more human myself, despite having no recollection of any *event*.

I bluster, stagger into the bathroom, the mottled window covered by snow, little light making it into the room, but I have no desire to turn on the bare bulb that harasses me every morning. The tiny cabinet light will do – I pull the switch and delve inside, reaching the paracetamol and taking two down as quickly as I can, no water required with these slip-shelled beauties, but filling my trusted bathroom pint glass nonetheless and drinking down as much of a pint as I can manage.

And I need a shower, oh, yes.

Once inside the claustrophobic shell of cheap frosted plastic, I nearly fall asleep a good half-dozen times. The dark, the warmth, the feel of the water patting my back, snaking down my legs. My head riddling me, demanding an early bedtime, a closing at lunchtime, a snooze behind the bar, a *what-the-fuck went on...* I stretch my shoulders down, I raise my neck, attempt some recovery. Eventually, the heat and the steam become too much and I emerge, skin shrivelled. I have been hiding, hiding from this Fi lass, knowing the shower would wake her and wondering now how to greet her, though very aware I have to go straight downstairs once dressed and rescue any illusion of being a hotelier.

But as I make my way through to the bedroom, the collapsed duvet quickly informs me that she has gone, and my heart – though it has invested nothing in our friendship that I'm aware of – well, my heart sinks like a stone.

7

My skin is searching for ease. I can feel it moving, like junk on a thick, slow river, attempting to find a peaceful haven just around the next corner. I cannot hear a thing beyond my own movement, the snow enveloping and snatching any sound from outside. The corridor to the hotel proper is frozen cold, ice on the inside of the windows. I consider gloves, but surge straight through to the bar, aware that stopping my march for romantic views of the notions of winter will only let my temperature descend further.

Upon entering the bar, I can see out of the corner of my eye that the table closest to the fire is packed high with all sorts of debris, but I dare not focus on it and begin to – need to – examine the fire. The poker has been left inside, sticking out like the one arm of a puggy, there are no sparks, barely any warmth… To shovel, to clean out the ashes now would be the daftest of moves as deep inside, somewhere, there could easily be a nugget of glowing ember, ember that could leap and burn my arm, the carpet, whatever…

There's a soft nudge on my arm and there's the cat. Did I put it out? Is this it just in? I know better than to confuse his nudge with affection. No, he's just placing his breakfast order, same as any of the other guests would be if they were down.

I carefully shoogle the grate, releasing the majority of the ash, scaring the cat. Then, using the thick black horsehair brush, I harry the ash onto the side, hide it behind the log basket. There's still a fair bit of fire debris left over, and this is where any of the good stuff will be. I delve into the logs and pick up any smaller, thinner lengths, twigs if there are any, and begin to pile them up, one by one. And a bodging firelighter, as ever. Squeeze it, poke it underneath, then light with a Bluebell and retreat. Ach, it'll take or it won't.

And the table – on the table… Cripes. We fair drank a few, it seems. The worst thing to see is that we, or perhaps I, finished two of my good bottles of whisky. I'd be amazed if I charged for them, so that'll have been the generous drunk in me emerging, gifting his best friends. Fuck that guy, he most certainly doesn't pay the bills.

Four plates of tomato-based slime, lightly dotted with discarded edges of chips.

Fourteen bags of crisps.

No, not fourteen. Six, maybe. Just scattered, ripped.

Ten, twelve glasses, ranging from pint to wine to shot.

No mugs. No one was sensible. No 3:00 am tea was drunk.

A mess, but there's no sick. Nothing broken. There's been worse mornings. The cat returns and nudges my leg. Time to get moving. If I can get that cat fed quickly, I can get some coffee on and maybe even eat before my guests make their own similarly daunting trek downstairs.

I put on a Billie Holiday CD. Her voice croaks through the bar but my precious, brittle hangover stops me from singing along.

It's all cleared up by the time they stir. The guy's massive frame clumping down the stairs, alerting me to their impending arrival, then them grunting at me for breakfast. All I have to offer is the same they'd had the night before. Well, they liked the sausage well enough then.

They're not keen on chatting, making wee snipes about their room being dry, what with that wall heater taking any moisture, so I bring them a pitcher of water, trying to bring them round, remind them I'm human and not just that damned guy with the shite hotel.

For a moment, I consider reusing their same dirty plates.

No sign of Fi this morning?

Eh? No. She left early. Not sure what she's up to.

Or who she is, really. Just the hint of a spark of a maybe. Ach, she'll've only stayed because of the snow, because of the drink... Who am I kidding?

Food and coffee in, the guests warm back up.

You know, it's as we said, you could really fix this place up, with a bit of elbow grease.

I nod, but I know it's all I can do to keep it as it is. Too many roofs. Too many scabby rooms, too much damp. Too many debts. Too many scuffed walls, worn carpets. Where to start? Ideally, at some point I'd close for a month, but I do not have the money for that and am no carpenter, am no painter, no builder. Heck, I can bodge things for Scotland, but there's little point in that.

So I run around in circles doing nothing. I fiddle as the crisp packets burn.

Time comes and I wave the jolly Americans off. I hope I haven't ruined their dream of Scotland. Mair folk, in and out of my life quick, never to be seen again.

8

FI TURNS UP.

My eye was on the door the moment the bell sounded, of course. But I wasn't expecting her. Not really. She'd woken up in the bed of a shell of a man with no' many prospects. Who'd expect her to return?

That was fun.

I have no reply. I'm blushing. What an eejit. I smile and hide underneath the bar, under the pretence I'm looking for something.

But a man cannot remain crouched behind a bar all his life. Aside from anything, afore too long my knees began to ache. I grab something – anything – a tin of lemonade – and stand back up, even more red-faced and dizzy now from this sudden movement.

I continue my vague grin, looking, no doubt, like a prize chump.

Is that for your hangover? You were fair far gone last night.

I look at the tin in my hand. Christ, I hate this sticky, sweet stuff.

Um, aye – no – I'm no' so hungover.

As I am a real man who feels no pain.

I'm no' so hungover, just a bit…

Shoogled. I open the juice and take a swig. Yowsers, it's as bad as I remember. A sour, room-temperature acid lightly tickles, its accompanying sugar clogging my throat.

Good stuff. Cough.

Have they… have they left?

This I can handle. Shop talk. Normality.

Aye, they were fair quick tae go. I reckon – I reckon they'd had quite a scoop.

And how about you?

Aye – well. Me too, I guess.

We watch each other for a moment. I note she's carrying two shopping bags.

What's, er –

Oh, I got the stuff we spoke about… She makes her way towards the bar.

Ah, cool.

I wonder what it is? My eyes cannot hide the curiosity.

Do you no' mind?

Um… Kinda.

I'm hoping it's chocolate. Bags and bags of chocolate. Chocolate liqueurs. And more painkillers. And a fry-up, made by a successful chef who has happened to open a travelling pop-up kitchen in my car park.

But the first thing she pulls out suggests it's none of them. It's a paintbrush. Followed by a roller, a pot of white paint and a black plastic tray. These items wound my eyes and trouble my soul.

What's…

Mind last night? When the Americans were complaining about the room? You said you'd no' got the time tae get stuff in. I offered tae get you the paint from the hardware store and you – she produces a receipt *– you said aye.* She reads. *And that's £33.19, please.*

I scratch my neck in dismay. Ach, I wisnae…

I was thinking – nae pressure like, but if you fancied – well, you could get started today?

Eh?

Aye – and I could watch the bar… Gie you a break, even? You were saying…

I have no idea what I was saying, but it's true enough, the walls of this place close in on me a'most every morning I'm down there.

No' today, tho', eh? Ma head's aching.

Ah, come on now, Tommy. It'll do you good. Look – at least get started, then you can see where you are, eh?

An hour later, though, and it's – *What the fuck am I doing?*

Fi's downstairs and I've just cleared a bedroom of anything I

41

figured I should give a hoot about and stacked it in the bedroom next door. There's a fair amount o' clutter, doddy wee bedside tables – fine, but three of them? One under the window, even. Take the curtains down, pull them off their wee plastic hook things... Stinking. Fu' o' transparent spiders, daft enough to spin their webs in *this* hotel. Then down and under the double bed, months – years, even – of no hoovering, of socks, prophylactic wrappers, coins... Fucking hell.

This is the last thing I want to be up to. I want to be outside, wrapped up warm. Or downstairs, by the fire. Tackling a room like this – well, there's a very good reason why they've seldom been touched since my father passed...

Ach. Fuck this.

You ok, Tommy? – I've brought you – I've brought you some tea.

I emerge from my angry burrowing, arse in air, crawling backwards – *Eh?*

Just some tea – I wisnae sure how you liked it, so I, um, I made it sweet.

My head is pounding, the blood scooshing this way and that, the hangover...

Aye – sweet's fine.

Fucking... sweet tea is the worst and as soon as she leaves it'll be flushed down the cludgie – but she doesn't leave, just stands about, motioning me this way and that, encouraging me to remove a lampshade, empty the bin, strip the sheets...

But I shouldn't have stripped the sheets as, Jesus, the mess awaiting me on the mattress was just a horror, all green and brown stains, as though people had been throwing coffee on the thing, then climbing all over with grass on their boots, jumping up and down, even...

Oh Tommy – you can't keep... that –

And then –

I hope – I hope YOUR mattress is cleaner than that...

But my mattress is an old hotel mattress, so if anything, it's worse. I mean, maybe I've turned it, once or twice?

*

So, now I have to struggle down the stairs with this giant double mattress, but thankfully Fi is helping, and the smells coming from it – the dust, the history, the dung of the thing – well, it makes us laugh, for there's little else we can do, other than dry boak. Out the front, as we won't get through and behind the bar with this, then across the snow before dumping it against the verge near the bins. I tell Fi – *I'll move it as soon as* – but with every fleck of snow that falls upon it, the mattress is making itself more and more at home, and in the back of my mind I just think – Well, how am I going tae move THAT fucker now? Twice as heavy, soaked through…

The reek of the paint, the window wide open now, the freezing air crawling inside.

Double-jumpered. For once feeling – *I'll've earned a pint*. A long wait still, mind.

We have lunch together. At one point, whilst remembering the tourists attempting to drive the auld route to Auchterglen the night before, she touches my hand. Naturally, mistakenly. Friendly, even. But I recoil. I bring my hand back to the safety of me with the speed of a striking snake. We spend then the next minute in embarrassed silence before I gather the courage to speak. Well, to clear my throat. She says – *I didn't…*

And I say – *No, it's cool – I was just…*

We don't drink. Alcohol, I mean. She makes some more tea, which I ignore, opting instead for some fizzy water.

We talk about the weather. The snow. The Americans, the hotel. About Auld Jock, his history, us both filling in blanks the other hadn't known – for no reason, just for the sake of discussing something safe, off topic. But then she asks – *Did Jock know your brother John well, then?*

It takes me aback, surprises me, I'll admit. I'm not a great talker of my past, certainly THIS bit of my past.

How? What did he say?

Eh?

About… About John.

Jock? He didnae say onything – you telt me last night.

I don't remember that. I search for a flicker of a memory, but there's nothing there – I'm just, well, curious, confused. *John – John died young…*

I ken, aye.

Oh. Right. I don't remember… I don't remember talking about… him.

I'm flustered, uncomfortable.

It's ok – we dinnae have tae. I was just… asking. It was just – funny – that's a'. Well, no' funny ha-ha, but strange. You know – I telt you about ma brother dying, and then, well, efter a while, you telt me aboot John.

I'm not in the habit of talking about John, but if she says I did, I guess I did. I wonder if there were tears. There must have been. Ach, well.

I wouldn't say I'm enjoying the work, but it does some good. Even just being away from the bar – a different view, you know? I have the radio on – the Gaelic station. The babbling that's occurring goes right over my head, but I can imagine myself in their company, and the not-understanding keeps my mind active and whirring away. It helps. I think of Fi, of course, and of John.

And there's her talking about her own brother dying… Ach. If only I could dredge that delicate info up. Would be awkward, asking again now…

I hoik up the edge of the carpet and a nail jumps up, hitting me square on that squidgy bit at the front of the nose. It's nippy as fuck, albeit only briefly. My eyes water and I blink it all back in.

Fi moseys into the room to say goodbye and I am relieved to be kneeling almost as far from her as I could be – avoiding the embarrassment of an awkward hug, a kiss, a whatever.

Bye, then.

Aye – cheers, hen.

Fucking *'cheers, hen?'* Who says that? Pa Broon?

I'll lock up behind me for now, but you'll be needing tae go down.

Aye. Sure – I'll wash up and go. Cheers, doll.

Christ. *'Doll?'*

She waits – a second – a second longer – and then she's off.

The minute she goes, when I can actually hear her walking outside, I head back downstairs. I'd love to say it was to man the bar, get things ready for the evening, but no, it's to pour myself a pint, empty my head and sit in peace.

9

SLOWLY, THE BAR begins to fill. It can, sometimes. On seemingly random occasions, as though the village suffers a community-wide hallucination and has an unyielding desire to pay over the odds for some crap lager.

It's the company they seek, I know that. Not mine, necessarily.

I tried group nights in the past – a quiz night, dominoes – but only three scant teams came for the quiz, them barely drinking and me grudgingly having to hand a £12 crate of Tennent's over to the winners… And the dominoes? Well, that was quieter still – just me and Jock. Some evening, there.

One group o' folk, plus Auld Jock, is kind of, almost, usual. Two groups, plus Auld Jock, of course, is a good night. But here, now – well, there's five individual groups.

Plus Auld Jock.

Busy enough, Tommy.

Indeedy, Jock.

Some kind o' rugby on, was it?

In the olden days, with the school team, a victory would, on occasion, send the fathers of the players into the bar, where they'd meet with my father, who'd listen with apparent fascination as they described the mud bath win over some cheuchter school nearby.

Dinnae think so – these guys look mair… mountainous.

Middle-aged fellows, light waterproofs, owl glasses, tightly cut curly hair – all suggesting *grown-up day jobs*.

My good man, please inform me what ales you have on this evening?

Well, there's only two taps on, Tennent's Lager and McEwan's Eighty Shilling.

There's no ale?

What?

There's no ale.

He frowns, his schoolmaster spectacles creeping down his nose.

I had it delivered this morning, but there was something up with it. I won't sell bad ale in the bar, me.

It's a lie, of course, there was no ale, but here I am, pushing myself forward as the Real Ale Hero, saving others from the indignity of a sour pint, a returned scoop.

Ah – fine fellow… fine fellow, that's what I like to hear – quality control – it's what the world needs…

Can I… Um… Can I get you a Tennent's? It's a Scottish lager. Quite, um, fruity…

Fruity?

No, son, I'll stick with whatever my companion got me last round – the Eighty Shilling. A further four pints of that and another lemonade shandy for our designated driver.

One of the advantages of not having a TV – and it's no plan, just a side effect of my stinginess, laziness, lack of concern – is that folk do tend to talk more and drink more. There's no light sipping, staring up at the screen, the only words shared – *Ooooohhhh* – or – *Goooaaalllll!!!* When the bar is like this, half full, I don't tend to put any music on, preferring the rhythm of the voices, allowing fellows to bellow their accented opinions out, perhaps encouraging interaction. It amuses and interests me. Plus, it gives Jock and me something to talk about on the many, many quieter nights –

Mind that time that guy said that thing?

Aye.

I pull an endless flow of lager, no room for chat, Jock grinning over at the room – *It's like the auld days, eh, Tommy?*

Aye… Hey, Jock – mind that Fi lassie?

Whit – from last night? Aye, o' course I do…

Aye – but do you mind her family? Her brother?

Och, that fellow… Bad news, he was. Part o' that whole gang, was he not? I mean, he wisnae – he wisnae the worst. He was a bit – no' saft in the heid, that's no' right – but, well – easily led, ken? I mind young Fi at the funeral, in her school uniform, greetin' her eyes oot…

How did he die?

Can you no' remember?. He lowers his eyes. *He drowned, sorry to say, Tommy.*

Ah. Him and John both. That's right, I mind that's what Fi told me, now. So yep, tears would have been spilt.

Jock sees my expression. He's apologetic, uncomfortable.

Aye – bit o' a strange ane. Open verdict, I think. But here – that Jim Blair, that was the last time I saw him – onyone saw him, I reckon…

How do you mean?

Well – he was at the funeral, but was a' dressed up tae the nines, good suit, clean shaved –

Aye well – it was a funeral –

No, no – beyond that. He was a scruffy fucker, that Blair boy. And here he was, looking like he'd won the lottery…

Right.

But – no – thing is – that was the last time I saw him. Last time anyone saw him… afore he died in that car crash, mind?

I do, aye. They found some flash motor the Blair boy had bought, all burned out, Jim Blair himself inside. I remember very clearly thinking that I'd no' miss him.

There's a table of local ladies, mothers on their night out, perhaps, squawking away. One of them I vaguely know waddles to the bar, asking for prosecco, but me having none so her being happy with a pitcher o' white wine and fizzy water, a wee dram of vodka to spruce it up. *Whit's it ca'ed, Tommy, this cocktail?*

Um… Oh, it's like a kinda – champagne substitute – it's called um…

Then Jock butting in, pleased to be talking of less delicate affairs – *It's ca'ed Auld Jock's Lum. It's a local delicacy…*

And she laughs, in the swing of things us all, and her knowing Jock at least half her life, no doubt.

Busy tonight, Tommy!
Aye, it is that. Good tae see.
Aye, cheers, then…
And she potters off carefully, out of practice in her heels.

Later, Fi comes in, and I'm pleased. Relieved. I didn't realise how much I'd been waiting, keeping an eye… It somehow made me proud for her to see the bar so full, however supernatural the event might be. She's on her lonesome but pulls up beside Jock and the pair of them begin chatting away, Jock shooting me raised eyebrows and the occasional grin.

There's a table of young lads talking loudly about football, no war to fight so swearing their allegiances to some team or another… It's seldom serious here, none of that Glasgow religious pish… Heck, there's so few folk around that you'd be daft to fall out with them that are.

A pint o' lager, please, Tommy.

This one not knowing me but knowing my name. He could be at school, he looks so young, not shaving, lowering his voice as he orders – *And a bag o' nuts* – as though he's in for his supper after his hard day's work. I'm not sending him home, though, not me. I read somewhere that, as a bar owner, I get one official warning about under-agers before I get fined, and well, I've had no warning, so this boy gets his lager and his nuts and I get his pocket money, just hoping none of the other tables are polis on a night off.

I go to change a barrel, an awkward thing involving lifting and cursing, Fi nipping round to take the bar, pleased to be asked. Maybe just pleased to be away from Auld Jock and his reek of pipe, mind you, but I can hope, and when I return, it means I can sit with a pint myself – the first from the barrel, ken, just testing it out, clearing the foam away.

I peek round at the company, good-humoured all, one guy balancing a guitar on his knee, digging up the confidence to play, now he has enough alcohol in his belly.

He strums, exploratory, not one person quieting, then begins to sing –

Oh! Ireland…

Oh, Jesus.

I love you…

Auld Jock shakes his head – *Here we go.*

But it's not bad. He can sing, a bit, this guitar fellow. Lord knows I've heard worse, pitching up here singing 'Brown Eyed Girl' and such. I'd say this guy's in his mid-thirties. He's got some classy clothes on – designer-looking, thick cords, new walking boots… It suggests he's moneyed, a lawyer, perhaps, or a stock exchange fellow. He has that confidence that a wallet full of money will bring.

And the table o' lassies, well, they join in, the table of cheuks, they just talk louder, and the table of climbers – well, I suppose for them this is some auld-time Scottish hospitality as they lap it up, applaud furiously, clap along, buying round after round…

As I see the money going into the till, I think – *There's a new mattress, right there.*

She stays, again, Fi. I lie beside her, frozen, too feart to touch the beautiful, generous human deigning to lie beside me, amazed at the warmth and the skipping of my heart, and only my fatigue finally chasing me to sleep.

10

AND AFTER THAT, after that… Well, it's not every night she stays, but most… Three out of five, if I were counting. I wonder at this alcohol-inflated body I am carrying around. Heck, I wouldn't happily show it to a doctor, let alone a lassie… When she's awa' I do my best to tidy up the midden that is my bedroom. I open the window, air it out, change the sheets.

Broon sheets?
    Fuck. *Aye, it was all I had clean…*
    But – BROON sheets? Where did ye even buy them? Who thinks tae themsel', 'Ah ken what'll sell well – broon sheets'?
    We laugh. But the next morn, I change the sheets again.

A week later and I've finished decorating the first room. One room. And it's pretty shoddy, but not as bad as I'd feared, and I'm a wee bitty proud. I've even got ane o' those skips in ma step that folk talk about.
    You've no' finished – there's plenty mair tae go. She sees I've left the heater attached to the wa' and raises an eyebrow. *Tak' that oot. Get that cardboard aff the mantle and get the auld fire working. Go on, Tommy – make a thing o' it. A feature. Premium room. When folk come, you can at least offer them one good room. Then, if they complain you can say – 'Aye, but you chose the basic room'.*
    Ach. She's right, and I'm lazy. I've not finished the room at all. I've bodged it. I bite the bullet and, using the claw hammer, tease, then rip, the fleck-wallpaper-covered chipboard from the fireplace, revealing a small mountain of soot, grit and feathers and the bones of

51

a small bird. Beneath that, though, beyond the dirt, there's a decent wee fireplace, with tiled sides and an iron frontage.

I remove the old radiator myself, but it emphasises the slack of my paint effort: once it's gone, there's a rectangle of old paint on display. Between that and the exposed fireplace, I'm near back to square one.

Fi's been looking after the bar. Without asking, she orders actual fresh food for down below. I have my worries, but I look at the stour I'm raising up here and bite my lip. Plenty for me to be doing.

It's good. A positive. Overwhelming, almost. I'm so pleased she's here, so keen she stays.

This is great. I'll pay you —
I know, Tommy, I know.

She's learned her way around the bar. I look on in awe. Folk are in, chatting to her. Mainly aulder men, but folk her age too. Takings go up. I just dunce around in my painting overalls, chatting to the plumber I get in for the leaking shower, the electrician I ask to tidy the wires...

Is this yer gaff?
Aye.
Whit — the whole 'hing?
A-ha.
Doing it up, likes?
Aye. I guess.

And I'm feeling great. Energised. Alive. I needed this kick up the erse... Fi and I, we have a laugh — a real laugh. But then I remember how shy I am and I always back right down...

She'll just grin — *Oh, Tommy! Tommy... Who are you in there, eh?*

There's more between us than against us, I can see that. And I'm loving being away from that sodding bar. It's like a holiday. It IS a holiday. I find myself whistling, even. She asks if she can get a different ale in — *A 'guest' ale, something tae write on the blackboard.* I'd forgotten there even was a blackboard.

52

*

There are moments, though. If I surprise her, blunder into the bar or wherever she's resting, she'll seldom be looking happy, content. And there's her phone calls… I can't ignore them, though I'm fairly sure any raised voice is not aimed at me. I hear her, though, from upstairs, doing that whisper-shout thing into her phone, no doubt arguing wi' some young cheuk…

But so what? What's that to me? She's seemingly happy here, and not so somewhere else… That's good for me, right?

I mean, my eyes are wide open.

I pay her. Just usual wages. A wee bit above minimum wage, which is good going for round here. She counts it out and smiles. She's paying for herself, the business she's bringing. Seems folk like bonny, friendly lassies behind the bar more than crabbit, auld-afore-their-time, drink-addled buggers like me.

She kisses me goodnight, places her arm on mine, her hand on my shoulder. But still I lie there, a lummox, well aware and feart of the fluttering and the hope. No' wanting to scuttle any applecart.

And after a few weeks, after a night drinking the courage in – weeks drinking the courage in – we embrace, we kiss and we… Well, we finally, eventually, fuck.

I apologise for my belly, my nerves, my hands, my general shiteness, but she, she helps, she guides me through. It's been a long time, and I cannot pretend it was majestic, I cannot pretend I was a Hollywood stallion, a Burt Reynolds, a Six Million Dollar Man, but she was still there in the morning, which was some kind of victory. And as for me, I was now well and truly hooked.

11

O NE MORNING, ONE morning. Cleaning the fire out, sweeping the floor, rearranging and straightening the tourist flyers, coffee on bar, music on – Lizzie Higgins, unaccompanied, sweet songs – me humming away, out of tune but happy. Fi away, not sure where, one of her wee disappearances, cannot ask her, as though a jealous husband... Ach, imagine she had no life away from here, that'd surely be worse? Christ, she'd get right nippy. I need my space too...

There's a clatter at the door – someone after the cludgie, I imagine, caught short on a morning drive. I look over and my thoughts are confirmed: a coiffured, manicured, camel-coated, tangerine-skinned lady –

Is it the lavatory you're after, love? Just carry on through...

But she does not. Instead, she walks towards me – not to the bar, to me – stopping just a few feet from me –

What are YOU doing wi' ma Fiona?

Who's this, then? Fi's mother? Come to see who this is, the man who's blindsided her daughter with his romance, flowing locks and dashing good looks? If so, Christ. Judging by her tone, when she saw this big lump I'd say she nearly fainted with fricht.

I suck my belly in, pull my neck up.

I'm just – she's, um –

She looks me up. And down. I'm aware I don't add up to much in front of a lady appearing so Glasgow Posh.

Aye, I ken fine whit yer up tae. She's half yer fucking age, ye auld perve –

Well, maybe not that posh.

Eh? She's no' half ma age, it's just six or seven years between us, mebbe...

54

Seven? Dinnae talk shite. Look at you – you must be… FIFTY!

The worst number she can think of, but I am not. She's way off. Christ, I don't look that bad, do I?

Excuse me – I'm…

But she rants on, her eyes roaming around the bar, the fittings. Close up, the unusual colouring of her skin, the pitch-black, painted-on eyebrows… An ootae-season, ootae-bottle, all-year tan.

By the way – this place looks a total shitehole from the ootside.

Why, thank you. The compliments are flowing. True enough, though. The ceremoniously dumped mattress hasn't helped. Got to remember to move that…

I mind this place. I've been in here plenty. When it was something. Somewhere. Ye know, I kent yer da.

I smile – *Aye, so did I.*

You've let him down, letting this place… go.

Truth hurts, truth hurts.

I couldnae believe it when I heard – no' from Fi, no chance o' her telling me onything – just from the gossip – that Fi had moved on – tae you! Tae this! Christ. She disnae tak' lang, that lass…

She slows, considers, turns 360 degrees once, then twice. Taking in the building. She walks to the fireplace and removes an old brass car horn from the display above. She examines but thankfully doesn't sound the klaxon –

Is it just yours, then, noo?

What – that horn?

No. No' the fucking horn. The hotel.

Aye, it's mine. Of course.

Is it no' the bank's? No', no' – no' some brewery owning it now?

No. It's just mine.

She replaces the horn, watchful it doesn't roll onto the floor as it wobbles to rest, then turns to me –

Well. Right, then. Mark ma words – you be careful wi' ma young Fiona. She wags her finger – *Or I'll puir fucking skelp ye.*

Her piece said, she's off and out.

*

55

I think I handled that well enough? And if that's where Fi's been escaping to, well, I won't be following her too often. And if that's what she's escaping from, well, I can't blame her. Fifty, though? I seek a mirror – there's one in the gents, but the coarse, attacking aroma puts me off. I've got to clean it, got to clean it…

A clang of the door and Fi arrives.

Hey – how's it going?

She smiles. *Hey.*

She walks over and puts some shopping bags down on the bar. Jings, what's she been buying now?

Your mother was in earlier.

She stares at me.

Ma mother? Here? Christ. You're joking? What did she say?

Well, she swore a lot…

Heh. Aye, she wouldae…

Fi makes to unpack. Bleach. Soap. Bog roll. Where to look, presented with such fineries?

Aye, she um… She warned me off hurting you.

Fi stops unpacking, stares –

She whit?

I carry on – *Aye. She said I'd let ma da down, the way I had this place… which I guess is true…*

Ach, I'm sorry, Tommy, just ignore her. She's nothing but trouble. What do they say? Ye cannae choose yer family…?

She tuts.

Aha. She's something, eh?

She certainly is, Tommy. In the way dug shite is something… Did she say onything else?

She did, aye. She asked if I owned this place. If it was mine… No' the bank's…

And that does it, aye. Fi shakes her head and whispers – *Fucking cow* – slamming yet further bottles of cleaning fluid onto the table. *I'm sorry, Tommy.*

She's not looking at me. If anything, she's talking to that bag she's just emptied.

How do you mean?

Well, ye ken whit she was – implying – right, Tommy?

Eh?

I do, though, of course I do.

Well, I'm no' after this fucking... place.

No – I dinnae think she was implying that, she's just... nosey?

Aye, she's that, but mair. And you... Do you think I am...? After this place, I mean?

Fi's not angry at me, it's her mother, I know that, but her eyebrows have crept up and she's shaking her head. I almost expect *her* to wag *her* finger.

What? No. I don't. It honestly hadn't crossed my mind – I mean, this hotel – it's a – it's a fucking liability. Who'd want it? I don't... I don't... I don't think that's why you're here.

The thought has ridden over my mind a few dozen times, though, of course it has, amongst a barrel-load of other thoughts, ideas, panics and insecurities. Why else would she be here? I'm just thankful for the company, the warmth. Grateful for her intrusion in my life. And life's about give and take, no? I give her this place, she gives me... solace. Company. Love?

Fi's winding herself up, cursing under her breath. She takes her anger out on the now empty shopping bag, scrunching it up and throwing it on the fire, where it melts into a small, scurrying black ball, sending out that artificial smell of burning plastic. She looks at me once more and growls – *I'm gonnae go see her* – before turning, making for the door and aff, aff she goes.

12

FI DOESN'T STAY, or even visit, that night.

Alone in the evening, I try smiling at the punters as I stand behind the bar. Being friendly. But, as of old, people stay for one drink then leave me to myself, which will eventually lead me to the whisky.

In an attempt to sway a potential overnight customer, I prance upstairs like a jolly laird, showing him my plans for the new room, but they're of no interest. He takes one look at what's available now – the cauld, the damp, the depressing murk of the room – and departs for the more welcoming climes of Aberfeldy. And who can blame him?

I watch out of the window, for five, ten minutes. No one.

I wipe a clean glass with a greasy rag, over and over.

The bell goes and my ears jump and my heart pricks. But it's just a guy after use of the cludgie. I smile and show him the way, waiting behind the bar should his conscience force him into buying even just a coffee. It doesn't, and he scuttles out with no more than a distant *thank you!*

Eventually, Auld Jock arrives with a cough, slowly making his way through the door and down towards the bar.

Hey, Tommy. Get that fire roaring, will ye? I'm cauld a' the way through.

Sure, Jock, no worries. Usual?

Of course, of course.

I set the drink pouring, leave it to settle, then nip out round the back for some firewood, a little wet, but it goes straight on the fire and there's steam coming off it soon after.

Cauld out.

Aye. Been worse, but... Nae sna', at least. Quiet tonight, eh?

Aye, Jock, as ever, it seems...

Hey – did I ever tell ye aboot the time me and yer father put up here for an entire week?

Hmm?

Aye – when ye were wee. Yer mother was awa' somewhere south with you and your brother John, leaving just me and yer da. It was snawing a bit, no' too much, just a scattering, and I was in here as ever, keeping warm, keeping counsel wi' yer da... But that evening, well, the weather fair sped up and the sna' came doon so heavy... I mean, there was no one else in the bar, just the twa o' us talking rot, so we barely saw it landing, settling... but, well, come midnight or whenever, I couldnae even open the door, a wee sna' drift had lodged us in...

Really?

Aye, God's truth. And yer da – well, he tried the back door and that was fine, but it'd have meant me climbing through past the bin yard then scurrying up the hill and the like, so he said, 'Just stay o'er, Jock, there's naebody in the hotel, seems daft you getting wet...' I mean, we were a bit pished, it seemed sensible, and I bided here fae time tae time, onyhows... So, I ended up staying o'er and that night – well, the storm was brutal. Come the morns, power was doon, nae light but candles, nae heating coming through fae that auld boiler thing he had... Yer da gave me breakfast fae the gas cooker, and we relit the fire there, cleared up the bar a wee bit, had a mid-morning ale, looking ootside ontae the sna'...

Heh.

Aye. A pretty fun time, ken? We got on well, yer da and me... But onyway, come the afternoon, a polis guy came chapping at the windae asking if there was onyone in and such... We ca'ed oot saying aye, it was us, and how we were fine and he was no' tae worry, and he was like, 'It's no' YOU I'm worried aboot...' And behind him there was this wee camel train o' tired, cauld-looking folk, so we were like, 'Aye, well, ye better come in, come in,' and it was a' these families, foreign folk, ken? The polisman like, 'Aye, they need somewhere warm tae stay, eh, their tourist bus is stuck here, the route south is closed with the sna',' but we're saying, 'Well, it's no' o'er warm in here...' but he looks o'er ma shodder, sees the fire, saying, 'It'll do, it'll do, just tae get them somewhere inside, ootae the sna' and that…' And we're like, 'Who are they? Are they needing fed? Who'll pay for that, then?' But the polis guy's saying they're Frenchies, o'er for some big wedding thing in Glasgow, up here on a day oot and caught in the weather and, well, we were tae do oor bit…

Wow – so what happened?

Well, yer da put them a' up, didn't he! A'most the only time I've ever seen this place a' fu'. Those diddy wee fire grates in the rooms – well, we had them a' lit, no' just the ane doon here. Barely ony hot water, ken, but they werenae seeming bothered wi' that – and what wi' no lecky, the freezer started melting and a' the food in there was gonnae go aff onyhow, so we fed them that – big hunks o' beef, lamb shanks… Man, good times.

How so?

Well, it's odd, but ye ken – me and yer pa – together, working side by side. I couldnae get tae MA work, so I had tae pitch in, ken? And we were laughing awa' and eating a' this amazing meat yer da had stored…

Oh, aye.

And in the evening, us twa and a' these auld French lads, just drinking awa', fair demolishing the whisky, them paying yer da with their own money – nae use here, mind, but a' they had – and yer da no' kenning the value o' it either, but taking it nonetheless. Nae sure whit he did wi' it, mind. Mebbe he changed it… Onyway. I ended up staying for a week – best part, onyhow, even tho' those French folks left efter – whit – just twa nights? Ma wee cottage still had nae electricity… It was like that, back then, ken? Ye just got used tae it… So, I stayed and helped yer da clear up, change the beds an' that, but come the end o' the week it was just getting daft – I was fair reeking and we were running well low on the good food – we'd resorted tae just eating tins o' carrots and stale crisps.

I laugh – *That's still my diet now. Minus the carrots, mind.*

Aye, somehow that disnae surprise me, Tommy. Still. There ye go. Some place, this place. Some memories. He sups on his drink. *Aye. I miss yer da.*

When he leaves, I haul the hotel dehumidifier into an untouched guest room, turn the dial, let it begin its low whirring drone. I watch for a moment, then, in a fit of optimism, depart for the store cupboard, return and hammer a nail right above the bed, then hang up a picture – a print of a watercolour of a proud, erect stag. I move the mug of teabags, sweeteners and milk portions from one side of the box telly to the other. I lean down and sweep clean the bed covers where my boots had been, clearing flakes of mud, flattening auld ripples, creating ripples anew. I switch on the electric heater, which joins in the whirring of the dehumidifier with its own slow creaks and clicks. If someone visits now, at least the room will be warm.

Would Fi approve? Would Jock? Who knows. Wha' kens.

At night, my bed feels huge. Huge and cold.

I dream. I'm up in the hills once more. There's a sun breaking through the tops of the trees, and I've turned so it's burning, warming, my tightly jacketed back. I'm staring down at a green moss that has completely covered over some windfall piece of branch. I can hear singing, perhaps. I stay still and attempt to pinpoint where it's coming from, but there's nothing further. I raise my head, look around – no.

The meltwater is slow, appearing almost considered as it drips off the leaves.

13

NEXT MORNING, FI returns. I have bags like gowf ba's under my eyes and my hangover is unforgiving. I pay her a wage a few days early, for the ease of the contact, the chance of a talk, and she takes the envelope, stuffing it in her tight jeans. *There's this too —* and hands me a receipt. I glance at it, open the till and peel out the last of the notes within. She's looking at me, but I can't read what she's after, what response, contact, she needs... She's been crying, I think — her eyes are red, anyhow. Ach, maybe she's just as hungover as I am? Or been out on the lash wi' some young, thin guy... She's no' for talking, though, and spends the morning clumping around, working out what needs ordered, replaced.

Did you sell nothing?

Accusatory.

Not much. It was quiet.

I spy a cabbage that needs thrown out. Six soft tomatoes that can go, too.

Fuck, I've left that heater on in the guest room...

What about the ale?

No. It was just Jock, and even he didnae hang around beyond a second.

I nip up the stair to turn off the heater, leaving the door open to let some fresher air back in. I move the dehumidifier back to its broom-cupboard cell and return down the back stair. As I approach the kitchen, I'm aware Fi's just outside the back door, talking to someone. I stop still and listen in — of course, I do — and she's upset, clearly. But I can't make anything out.

Ach, it'll be her mother, mebbe.

I'm hoping for lunch with Fi, an attempt to straighten things out, but silently she gathers her coat, her scarf and her hat, and she leaves. I watch from the window as she trudges through the remains of the snow. There's a wee hatchback thing waiting in the car park, engine on, smoke chuffing out. She opens the door and climbs in without invitation.

There's no goodbye, and it's as though she does not care about me at all.

I wonder – is she blind to this? To me?

The car stutters off and, matters worse, matters worse, as they pull out, a minibus of tourists pulls in, so I can't even wallow in the mystery and the misery of my stupid, teased heart.

14

A BRAVEHEART-LOOKING CHARACTER CLIMBS down from the bus. Long black hair tied behind his head. He's kilted up, but he's wearing no sporran. I can never get my head round that look – surely the sporran hides a multitude of bulges? It's cold out, and he's hurrying his passengers off the vehicle whilst jumping up and down, keeping warm.

As the last passenger clambers off, he stomps in front of them all and quickly leads them to the hotel door before bursting in from the cold.

Aright, mate.

He offers a broad grin.

Aye, welcome in.

Straightaway, he's peering over my shoulder, into the bar – *Can these ladies get some food here, mate? Maybe use the – the conveniences?*

Aye, of course. Toilet's that way. Food's fine, but chef's away. Got a broken tooth. I can sort it, though...

I count them in – eight, plus driver. Not bad.

Thanks for bringing them in. Appreciate it. I nod and smile at the soon-to-be customers as they stream by me on the way to the cludgie. Older ladies, most of them in their sixties, I'd hazard, clutching handbags, fur coats buttoned up tight.

Oh, that's no problem, mate.

He's English, this dude. Birmingham or its surrounds, at a guess.

Here, is that an English tartan?

Hey hey – well spotted. No, I'm, eh – not your typical Scottish tour guide... ok – GOOD NEWS, WE'LL GET FOOD HERE,

64

GOOD TRADITIONAL SCOTTISH GRUB – What's your name, mate?

Tommy.

Tommy. What can you get them, if the chef's not in, mate?

Ach – a good plateful. Sausage. Local. Beans and chips. It's um… quality scran.

Ok. Hmm… LISTEN UP – TOMMY HERE'S GOING TO TAKE YOUR ORDER, BUT THE CHEF IS OFF, SO IT'S A LITTLE LIMITED, BUT LOCALLY PRODUCED. ALL GOOD, MAKE YOURSELF AT HOME… Here, can you stoke that fire a bit, mate, make it a bit more welcoming, keep the punters happy and all that?

Sure, sure.

And with that, he bounds himself off to the cludgie.

It's a financial bonanza. More than a half-dozen folk, and they all have the chips, the beans, the sausage. A few even asking for salad.

Salad? No' here, ma love.

But then I remember those auld tomatoes, retrieve them from the bin, rinse and slice them thinly, losing any bad bits, spreading them around.

Quite a business, preparing nine plates of chips, sausages and beans, garnished with Real Ground Black Pepper. I almost feel as though I've achieved something. Whilst the ladies are still all sat down and eating, a few of them risking half pints of the real ale Fi got in, the driver approaches the bar. He's wolfed his food down and presents me with a tomato-stained plate, grinning like a toddler expecting praise.

Is this your place, then?

'Tis, aye.

It's not… not the busiest. Decent scran, but – I hope you don't mind me being honest – it's a bit… a bit… scabby?

Eh?

What, the food? Scabby? How?

No – the food was fine, for basic stuff… But, well, those gents toilets… Christ almighty – they could do with a bleach, know what I mean? I see a lot of these places, up and down the country… You need to be top of the game, mate, top of the game. Top of the game to stay in the game, you know? I took a chance coming here… And as soon as I saw that mattress outside, well, I considered turning around. But – well. To be honest, I needed a wazz. Badly. Know what I mean, mate?

I laugh – *Well, I'm sorry to let you down – we're actually just beginning a refurbishment – but here, pal – mind you're a' dressed up in your finery driving a wee party of auld German wifies around. You're hardly businessman o' the year, are you?*

He sups at his flask of coffee – *Fair enough. I'm only observing, mate.*

Aye well. Pint down, cloth out, bar wiped. *Can I ask – if you don't mind – Where's your sporran? And that kilt – why's it down below your knees? You ken how most folk wear it, aye?*

Heheh, yep, but too chilly on a day like this, driving that bus, the wind ripping in through those crappy automatic doors – I cover up as much as I can, mate, know what I mean heheh?

He winks.

Sure. Yep. Here, you want a real drink? I mean, something fresh? Not from a flask?

I'm ok, mate. I'm picky about my coffee.

He's peering around, taking in the decor. I follow his gaze, making a mental note to sweep the cobwebs, clean the windows, wipe the tables…

Is it good work here? I mean, my lot aside, you're quiet, mate, if you don't mind me saying. I guess it busies up at night? At weekends, maybe?

Aye. Perhaps.

He's up and off his stool, walking around the tables, talking to his audience, flirting with the grannies, them giggling away at whatever he's saying. There's a few thumbs-ups, him smiling, nodding, then he's back.

They seem happy.

They do, they do, mate. Good food, they're saying. But here – there's not a chance you've got a chef.

Eh? How do you mean?

Well – this place... For a start, there's no one in. I mean, we've been here almost an hour – but not a soul's come in. Phone's not rang. Nothing. You couldn't afford a chef on this business, surely? That and the – the smell of the place –

The smell now, is it?

The smell of the place and the general muck – I'm guessing this place is... pretty quiet, right?

There's no denying that... but – muck?

My friends have a place like this, you know. Back home. They exist on a tipping and bribing economy. Gotten so bad they're stalking the undertakers, pushing their business cards onto them, going for the post-cremation crowd...

I shrug – *Aye, we're no' that bad...*

Are you, you know, declaring everything? The folk I know, they end up doing all sorts – buying cheaper lager but selling it as the premium. Adding a pound a pint. A pound a pint can't be sniffed at. Got to be clever, mate... They cut their own chips too, you know – potatoes are cheap – just needs a bit of forethought... You can do it watching telly, you know?

Well...

You know, maybe I could help you out? – He leans in – *See, all MY work is tip based. I'm on minimum wage here – but I make it work since the crew –* he gestures behind him – *the crew tip me. Sometimes I do ok. Like last week, last Thursday, I think, mate, I had twenty people onboard. A full house. But today – well, I only have eight people. I'll be lucky to get forty quid from them...*

I sup my early afternoon glass of ale. It is sour. I mean, ale always is, right? But this is sour-plum sour. The joy of the barman, though, sampling all o' life's varied delights.

I mean, I don't want to speak out of turn, but how's about – if I'm carrying a small team – like today... I mean, many more and you couldn't handle it... But if I come in here and we get food, it's good for you, so how's about – how's about we make a deal that you make it good for me? Then I could bring people in more often... I have this place, a place up in Inverness, and they, well, they'll tip me for bringing a crew in…

I wasn't really listening to his gibbering, I was mainly contemplating the complexities of the ale, but I think I got the gist of it –

So, you want me to…

Well, as they say in the movies – 'You scratch my back' – I mean, only if you wanna – I CAN take this lot up to Arndour House, I'm always well received there, always plenty of other coach drivers to chat to, catch the gossip, you know, but that place is corporate. Staff on wages, they don't give a hoot how many folk are in…

It makes a little sense. I can see Fi being happy with it, perhaps. And some gossip to tell Auld Jock.

Um… How much would you want?

His mouth widens, gaps between his teeth, teeth stained with coffee – *Well, you know – how about three quid a head?*

Three quid, eh? How much do I make on a plate of food? Easily a fiver – so, multiply any remainder by eight, add on any potential ale sales… I scratch my head.

Hmm. Two quid… mebbe? A wee bit easier for me.

And… a plate of food for the driver?

Heh. Sure. Two quid a head and a plate of food for the driver.

He's grinning. He extends his hand and we shake.

An hour later and I'm beginning the tidying of the plates, the party stopping inside a while longer, so pulling the pints also, fire fed, doing my best to harvest, to be polite and genial. This load of auldies seemingly content with the basic facilities on offer. I cannot speak a word of German, but that suits me, allowing me more time to get it all done. Another couple o' folk have arrived, walkers in from the weather, happy with pipe-gun scooshed cola and nuts, all income, all good.

Thinking about my business deal, I never enjoy being this busy and would probably pay the guy his sixteen quid to keep away, but I cannot say that now for I know before too long the bar will be empty, this brief clutch of business will disband and any hint of a reasonable mood I have will crash once more. I keep up the façade and long, long, long for more, for many happy returns of the Englishman in the kilt.

As they finish up, the door goes repeatedly, the punters making their way out and in, last cludgie call, proclaiming their accented *thank yous*. I feel ok. Good, nearly. I mean, there's a hell of a mess to clear, but the fire's still burning, I can get some music playing and there's worse ways to spend an afternoon than this. Again, the door chimes. But I don't turn.

Looks busy!

It's Fi. Now I turn, for my spirits are up and it's easy to continue the smile for her.

My arms are full of sticky bean-juice-orange plates. In my heightened state, I'm tempted to hoik them in the air and juggle them, but I'm aware they'd crash immediately to the floor and I'd seem nothing but a lunatic throwing plates about.

Aye, busy, Fi. Good to see you.

I stand there, motionless, awaiting a reply.

Well, get tidied. Here – I'll help –

She turns away and removes her coat, one of those thick cotton things a' fu' o' feathers, fake fur trim on hood. I watch for a while before I realise I'm *watching* and make to move on, stacking the plates on the counter, ready for me to collect on the other side and get washed.

Here – I've something to tell you – the guy, the guy who brought these customers in… Did you see him just there?

I'm walking round to the other side of the bar, out of eyesight, so calling louder –

Aye, he reckons, the kilted guy, he can bring folk round every now and then in exchange for a wee tip. No' a bad idea, eh?

Seeking her praise, like I would've my father's. Pleased to have something to talk about, something solid, not emotional, not trying.

So, I reckon – I hope – we'll…

Note the *we'll*. My way of saying – *I pure need you here, my love…*

Hae a few more busy lunches. Can't be bad, eh?

As I reach the other side, Fi is waiting. She's piled a few more plates but isn't off anywhere.

I've something tae tell you, Tommy.

Ah.

The way she's standing, shoulders tight, eyes down, barely looking at me – not good.

The bar is a thick, wide mahogany thing. Single bit of wood, well-polished. Fifteen feet long, mebbe. I cover it, as much as I can, so there's only one wee six-foot spot where I actually place drinks. Crisps. Water. The fizzy lager taps and real ale beer pumps and their accompanying drainers, there to catch the slop from a messily drawn pint. Cardboard-cutout adverts for nuts I no longer sell. A sign – *No Football Colours.* This way, I only have a small serving window to worry about; folk can't come at me from all angles with requests…

I said, I've something tae tell you –

…Just means I can get a bit of peace, if it gets busy. A'body kens their place. Plus, it doesn't overcomplicate things, no' too many orders at once.

Tommy –

Ach, the music's stopped. I need to change it – *Haud on, Fi…*

Tommy – stop pissing about.

I stop. I leave the CD quiet, unspinning. I brace myself.

Thing is… The thing is…

I look at her, my face steeled, ready for the blow. I shall not flinch.

The thing is… Well – I'm pregnant, Tommy.

15

INSIDE, I COLLAPSE.

My mind races forwards – she doesn't love me, she's pregnant to some young dude, she can no longer work here, we can remain friends, except we inevitably won't and I'll probably never see her again, end of story.

Well, that's that. The heart burrowing Fi out of my life. I make my way to the edge of the bar and peek out of the window beyond, look out at the hills, the remains of the snow and ice, up now to the sky, to prepare for what's coming next. Steel myself. Bite my lip. Chase the ludicrously premature, but very much gathering, water from my eyes.

Did you hear me?

Fuck it. I'm thirty-fucking-two years old. Stop behaving like a bairn.

I say – *You fucking tricked me, you fucking tricked ma heart* – except I don't say that, I don't say that, of course not.

I turn and glare at her, cannot stop myself giving her that look, of disappointment and upset, a broken spirit, a sad look of *Well, fuck you*, a look of *Why me?*

I understand now, I understand why she was here. She's messed up. Whoever she's been talking to all this time – they're both messed up. Messed up youngsters. I'm just a bit part in their story, I ken that. Ach. I make to say – *It's cool, dinnae you worry about me* – but whatever it is inside, that hurt and frustration, emerges first and I spit out that daftest of things, that cruellest of double meanings –

Well, good for you.

And then – *You and… whoever. I hope you'll both be very happy.*

I add an exaggerated, theatrical wink.

I'm sure I'll see you around. Yer welcome here... any fucking time.

Pointed and sharp and full of regret.

Straightaway, she's greetin'. Tears coming out fast, herself dabbing them away. *Fuck you, fuck you, Tommy Bruce.*

And she's off away from the bar, towards her coat, and the sight of her movement throws me to my senses, the sight of her leaving once more – *Fi* – and I make to catch her, around the bar – *Fi* – quick as I can, out to the bar front – *Fi, Fi – I didnae mean it like that – I just got...*

Quick, Tommy, get something out.

I've just gotten used tae having you here and, ken. I like you, and we work well, and I was just disappointed about that room and oor plans and...

What the fuck? That fucking room? You – you fucking eejit. You're just another TOTAL cunt, my mother was right...

But...

And how the fuck am I getting flack for this?

Look – you stayed here! I didn't ask you...

She stops dead and stares at me.

Whit the fuck has that got tae do wi' it? Eh? You were aye part o' it, you – at least – went through wi' it, did ye no? Aye, we were drunk, the pair o' us, but ye cannae fucking get away wi' it just like that, Tommy Bruce. Nae fucking chance. No fucking way.

It's her turn to glare.

Look, Fi, you can work here as long as you want – I'm happy for you tae stay until, until...

Until whit? Oor bairn arrives? Well, thanks very much.

Eh?

What? How do you mean – 'oor' bairn?

And she looks at me then, as though I am a thick-skulled, dim-witted loon.

Well, who the fuck do ye think is the father, Tommy? Whit kind o' lass do ye think I am?

And I cannot answer that, and I cannot believe it. Basic arithmetic I excel at, and the basic arithmetic looks dodgy to me...

I'm shaking my head. She peels off and stomps out, tears in her eyes, feet skeeting across the ice, somehow managing to stay upright.

I think – *I should salt that car park.*

But I think little else. I am numbed. Oh, for the simplicity of a stocktake, a sweep of the fire, a wipe of the bar.

16

ALL AFTERNOON, MY thoughts flit to my father, to my mother, my brother John… Who now can I talk to? That Birmingham guy? Auld Jock? I'm a man alone here. If I ever needed a brother, a family, it's now.

And maybe, well – maybe this is my chance to have a family.

Listen. I know it's not my child. If there IS even a child. I know it's not mine. I ken it's no'. I'm no' daft, or saft. Well, a wee bit o' both, but no mair than the next man. It's all about – percentages, you know?

For – Fi has brought – colour. Life. Light. There's that word again: light.

Against… Fuck it. It's only someone else's bairn, eh? I can grow to love it. Like a dog. Or a good, reliable oven. Heh. I mean – it's not The Devil. If she'd already had the kid, would it have made a difference? No. I don't believe it would have.

And I think, you know, I love her – I love Fi. Do I? Do I love her? Maybe I do. Say it out loud, then…

I can't. Even to the crisp bags and optics.

Fucking hell.

I'd hate to lose her.

So, it's all for good, right? Right? We've decided?

17

AFTERNOON DRIFTS INTO evening, and no one else in at all. I feed the fire; I clean, kind of, there still being tables to wipe from lunchtime... I listen to Van Morrison. He should know the answers – but, no, he doesn't, he just prattles on the way he does... Maybe after a few drams he will, tho'. I take one dram. My stomach churns, from the ale, from the news, from the busy lunchtime, from the grease of the clean-up...

Nah, it's from the news.

The cat riddles around my legs, demanding food. I go to its bowl and see it has totally ignored the butt ends of the leftover chips and sausages, covered as they are in tomato sauce. The cat bowl just a pitstop for this discarded food on its way to the bin proper.

Watching out of the window, dark now, fresh white snow illuminated by the orange streetlights. I turn on the outside light, the light that illuminates the building, makes the hotel, makes me, as inviting as possible. I spy Auld Jock making his way down the scooping path towards the bar, but there's too much snow and even he turns after just a few slippery footsteps, carefully heading back the way he came.

Ach, I could have done with *some* company, other than that cat... I should salt that car park, that path.

The silence, the still.

Come on. Shift your body, Tommy. Get it done. Move on.

I make my way out, coat on, full bucket in hand, snow tickling down my neck. Throwing the salt, feeding the invisible geese, powdering my path, letting it do its work unattended, moving on, up the slope, the snow melting through my hair, onto my scalp, slipping down my nose...

I loved this weather, this snow, as a kid, but now it's just an almighty pain. Stops me in. As if I go anywhere particular... But if I wanted to, I couldn't. Brings the powerlines down, on occasion. Freezes the water, bursts the pipes; my decrepit four-by-four struggles to get out of the car park. I look back and see the lights of the hotel. I need a light on the chimney stack, subtly illuminating the ascending smoke, calling in anyone duped by the romance of an open fire. I turn, again, and continue up the hill, scattering, scattering...

I reach the brow of the hill and am there, on the high street now. Well, some high street – a wee Co-op-Post Office hybrid, a few scattered crafty shops and, far along the street, the now closed *Rab's Bar*, once my sole competition. There're no cars; the road's gritted, but fresh snow over fresh snow over that grit and there's not much use it's serving now.

I should have worn a hat.

I should have sold up when my father died.

Who wants to live in a ditch by the side of a B-road?

But the quiet is tight and precious, the hill's looking michty, those giant black shadows keeping the worst of the wind out but the snow in, the saddled trees moving slowly, giving the shadows life and a slow, thick fur. I chuck the last of the salt and turn back towards the hotel.

Even with the salt just fresh, every step is a skid.

Making my way down slowly, I catch sight of that mattress, completely covered in snow now, off down by the michty bins the local cooncil force me to use, since the hotel is, in theory, a *food establishment*. In the summer, sober folk use those bins as a place for their dugs tae shite and drunk folk are often to be seen scuttering down there for a piss or a joint or a fuck. I tried to put them off, put up signs – *Nae Dug Shite* or whatever – but I guess dugs can't read and their owners don't care. I even directed a light at the spot until I saw how bad it looked from the road, as though I were advertising the fact I had massive, overflowing bins. If anything, it just encouraged people, showed them the way down to piss anarchy heaven.

I carry on heading below, my eye on the path, but spying a wee movement to the side so keeping an eye too on the trail down to the bins, seeing if something's there now. Maybe it'll jump out, so I'm getting ready for the fricht of a fox or whatever, no' wanting to skid on ma bahookie.

Hello? Who's there?

I whistle.

No reply. There's nothing there. Something scarpered, maybe. A fox or badger? A stag, even? Then I think – *I bet it's a tramp.* And that thought shivers me a bit – a slowly freezing tramp, in the dark, in a keich-y cubby hole? That's no' for me. I'll get back inside.

But as I turn, I hear movement again, not enough to call me back, but enough to stop me where I am. I listen, for the rustle, the scamper – but nothing. Ach, it's way too cold for this bother.

And two-foot, three-foot, four-foot away, I hear a voice.

Tommy.

And, and, and – well, there we are, and there she is.

I turn, and emerging into the light is Fi, my Fi. My heart calls, my eyes melt... I wait, breathe, focus, then walk slowly, carefully towards her, offer her my arm for protection from the skite of the snow and take her in.

18

I SAW YOU COMING *out. I didn't know where tae go. Wisnae sure –*
wisnae sure you'd want tae see me...

She's shivering, her coat now a darker blue, soaked through as it is.
I've been, I've just been walking around...

On the way to the fire now, her coat peeling off, her jumper below
almost as wet –

Hang on, I'll get you the towel.

THE towel. As if I only have one, one that I trust.

I hoik up the stairs, three at a time, quick, run down the corridor
to the flat, open my unlocked door and grab the thing, smelling it as
I jog back – damp and used but not off-putting, I hope.

Jings, what a prize for my princess.

She takes it and begins to rub her hair – *Tommy, can I get a rum?*

I go, but then – *Is that, um, is that – sensible...*

Ah, fuck.

Aye. Fuck.

Oh well. Just a tea. Ane o' those raspberry and passionfruit I bought,
please.

That's her hippy tea. It smells awfy, like an auld ladies' loo.

Sure.

At least – at least I ken you care! A shake in her voice from the cold.

Heh.

I jump round the bar, quickly reach for the tea, boil the water...

Do you – do you take milk, in this? In this fruity stuff?

What – no. Of course no'...

I make the tea, deliver the tea. The purple of the bag quickly
seeping out into the water.

Thank you. It's puir baltic oot there.

She sips. One, two.

So... where were you off to?

She shakes her head.

Tommy – I don't know... I telt ma mother. This afternoon, when I found out... She – she kicked up such a fuss. Said I was a 'stupit wee lassie' and you were a 'pervy auld man'. Then I came tae you – and you – you – you what? Offered me a job? Fuck's sake, Tommy.

Aye, it was just – it was just – well, we only, we only – you know, umm... Ah just fucking say it, Tommy – get it out in the open – We only just did it – slept together, whatever – like, three weeks ago?

She peers, perplexed – *What? Tommy – How about that first night. Do ye no' mind?*

Ah. What? But no, I don't remember. I cannae mind shite about *that* night.

And now I don't know what to believe: this bonny lassie who's brought light into my daft heid or that daft heid itself – a heid that cannae even mind what happened, so why should I believe it? I'm either daft for believing my own scunnered heid or daft for believing her.

It's – it's no' I cannae mind, it's just... Well. I suppose it is. I just cannae mind!

And I laugh. It's a gamble. But she smiles. In relief? Relief I hadn't just turned her down? Relief I'm just a balloon-headed clown? Relief she's no' ootside in the cauld?

And as for the thought, the lie, the worry – well, I'll just chase that away. For now, at least.

In for a penny, eh?

19

FI TELLS ME about her parents, about how her Glaswegian mother had been brought up by her own single mother in Maryhill but had somehow hooked herself a farmer boy from these parts, a laird almost, rich and landed to look at, but that same land crippling him. A shy, hard worker, too much time spent begging the fields to produce and not enough wi' other folk, easily blinded by Fi's mother's good looks and promises, not worried by the bairn – Robert – she'd had young to another man. So, they got married, and Fi's ma persuaded him to use his dwindling savings so she could open a handbag shop – *follow her dream* – but the shop failing, of course, because – *who wants a fucking £100 handbag around here?* – and them splitting up soon after, the reality of a damp Perthshire farmhouse too much for Fi's ma and the stress of the collapsing finances too much for Fi's da. He took to the drink in a more serious fashion, took up loans for these new shortfalls, those loans becoming out of hand, so the bank stepping in and eventually him losing it all, his family's land for however many generations. No support, no family now, just an absent wife.

A farmer with no farm who couldn't even see his kid and going on, well, to swing from the beams in the barn.

And every word hitting me straight in the heart as I remember my father explaining to me where *my* mother had gone and *how* exactly she'd got there. I bite my lip, hard.

Fi doesn't remember her father at all. There are photos she's found, hidden away in the house she was brought up in, a house bought with the remainder of the money, once the debts had been cleared.

He looks – big. Tall. Scared o' the camera. Ma mother standing beside him like a beauty queen. Wee Robert scooting, hiding between their legs.

I know the house, of course, a daft turreted thing at the top of the back brae. Not big, but with presence. We used to walk past it as kids, on the way up to the waterfall, always wary of Fi's brother Shuggy – well, half-brother, I guess – seeing us and giving us grief. No wonder that Shuggy boy was so messed up, twa fathers at least by the age of ten and one of them found hanging.

But it was a' a bit... especially after ma da died. Well, ma mother – she wasnae a'ways around then, ken? There was a lot o' drink, tho' I didnae ken what it was at first, of course, just thought I'd pissed her aff somehow. Ended up a few complaints at school, I mind that, me going in no' properly clothed or hungry or wi' a bruise or two... So, well, I spent, well, a lot of ma childhood wi' ma gran, back o'er in Maryhill. Gran was SO different, loving, warm, happy tae have me. I think she felt bad that ma da had left so early, I don't know... Whatever, that's where I was, until ma would sober up and demand me back, so I'd have tae pack and wave goodbye tae ma pals 'for guid this time', but it never was... never for the good, and never forever.

20

IT'S 2:00 AM, maybe 3:00 AM – a week later, anyhow – and we're sat at the bar, her the lady o' the bar, me the customer. She's plying me with drink and generous with her crisps, this bonny wee bar lass, generous with *my* crisps. She's bought four different types of wine from the wholesaler and we're going through them, one by one, though she's only sipping, of course... I'll be honest, after a' the alcohol o' the day and now a' the crisps we've had, the wines all taste of salt and the threat of a major hangover. She's blind-tasting me, this wee hostess, a sup o' each wine, a dishcloth tied round ma heid so I cannae see the colours, as if that'd make a difference right noo, and it actually making matters worse with the smell o' the onion and bleach coming off it. The fifth wine is the best. *What! Tommy! That's water!* I remove the mask and lo – it is indeed water. She's laughing, goes and changes the music – *Here, what's that you were playing earlier, that auld guy – grumbly voice?*

Oh, that was John Strachan. Aberdeenshire singer.

Oh aye. No, did ye see folk leaving when that came on?

Umm...

Aye. They did. We cannae afford that. Where's the CD and I'll bin it...

Will ye fuck –

And she's got a CD in her hand, threatening to frisbee it over the bar, so I try to jump over the bar myself and wrestle it off her, but my legs catch the pumps and I roll down, onto and over the sink, down onto the floor, taking a bottle of the wine, however many crisps, some Co-op own-brand cleaning stuff, a scouring pad, a shattering pint glass and heaven knows what else, in slow motion by the end, my left leg taking an age to dislodge from behind a pipe.

TOMMY THE BRUCE

And all the time, the twa o' us giggling like school kids.

From my position of great strength and dignity, I admonish her —
There'll be nae throwing awa' ma music, eh?

Happy, lying there in amongst the glass and the stour and the wine and the crisps, looking up at my joyful tormentor.

21

Fi's in, she moves in, properly, almost, and it's good. We relax, or she relaxes and I kind of join in. It seems a fantasy, this bairn thing, and we ignore it at first, don't really discuss much, the whole situation taking a good while to adjust to without this third unknown being waiting in the wings.

We get on with the rooms, finish one, then two, then three. Fi waits the bar and, as simple as that, folk stay longer, return more often. Even Auld Jock makes it past his usual. She changes the music, Fi, and I hate it, this new stuff she puts on, a sort of bagpipe-techno thing that makes me feel ill, but no one else seems to mind, to notice, even.

Fi's ma calls by.

Tommy – ye've met my mother – Migrit.

Migrit glances at Fi, then turns to me –

Margaret. Pleased tae see you again.

She looks anything but. She holds out her hand yet somehow simultaneously withdraws her arm, her engoldened wrist resting on her hip as though she's sporting a six-shooter.

I nod – *Hey.*

She seems not much older than me. You know how some folk try and dress young and some folk just don't gie a fuck, so perhaps look a wee bit messy and such? Aye, well, that's her and me, respectively. Although I'd say her orange-lotion soiled face is actually aging her more than she realises.

I try to chat, bring her in, but Fi is so cold and short with *Migrit* that there's no chance of a real conversation, of getting to know her, at least not right now. Best I can do is to not offend, be polite, smile.

I note the twinkle in Margaret's eye as she drinks her free coffee and keeks at the underside of the tables, perhaps adding up their value.

She doesn't stay long, though, and when she leaves, Fi whispers to me – *See when she's in? See when Migrit is in? Turn the decent music aff and put the auld Aberdeenshire droners back on – then turn them right up, until she leaves.*

Folk ask Fi how come she's no' drinking, and at first she says she *disnae while she's working* but that doesn't sit so well when I'm there beside her taking a scoop, supposedly working but drinking any profit away. It's all a bit of a headfuck for me. Folk ken we're together now, of course, but her pals will come by and stare at me as though I'm a bull at an auction; they'll sit whispering to each other, pointing, almost. Fuck, my tumbling belly is there, I ken that, but I hold the weight well, I think, my big frame disguising the worst of it. I feel obliged to try chatting to Fi's pals – beyond bar talk, I mean – and eventually the odd word about something other than the weather is exchanged. It's hard work.

Fi and myself, though, well, we're past that now. We're laughing more than no' and regularly just chatting away, and I tell you this – we work together well. I don't know what she was needing in her life, but Fi was aye what I needed and she's slotted straight in.

And then we go for the three-month scan and the technician asks if I'm Fi's father.

Cheeky cow –

Tommy! Shut it.

I guess… I guess… Well, I tell myself I look auld and michty for my age, and Fi looks young and sleek. I can be proud of that.

There's seven years between us. Eight, during that wee bit when I've had my birthday and she's no' had hers… But eight years, even? That's nothing. Ach.

The scan comes out looking braw, and that's the important thing. And it's a boy, we're told, and that night we're sat late after the bar, me a wine or two down, perhaps a nip. We're going through the names; I'm wanting Ivor straightaway but Fi's giving it — *Ye cannae call a wee lad Ivor — Nae chance. Too old fashioned. We should call him Robert — after my brother...*

Robert Bruce? Dinnae be daft, Fi... But in my head I'm thinking — she's taking my name, should we get merrit for that? IS she after getting merrit?

Ok — then how aboot efter my father, George? Wee Georgie Bruce?

How about after MY father? James Bruce. Jamesie. Wee Jimmy Bruce.

She screws up her face.

Nah. I hate Jimmy. It's... like Taff. Or Paddy.

Heh. Who'd've kent I'd be here, three months back? With a lassie of my own, a bairn on the way, someone to share my after hours with. It's just — it feels unreal. Amazing. I don't know if it's the whisky talking or some daft elation, but — *So, if it's to be a Bruce — Should we get, um, married?*

And the bubble sweetly pops.

Eh? No. There's nae point, Tommy, is there? Whit use is marriage? There's nae safety there. You ken that as well as me. She's calm, though. She locks eyes with me, then trails off — *Besides, you dinnae want tae be joined tae MA family...*

22

I MAKE IT UP the hill, alone. We're at the other side of winter now, so still cauld, but spring is most definitely here. Snowdrops have been out a long while, a'most dead now, in fact. Everything seems different. Got a home now. A partner. A kid on the way… It tears me up to think the wean *probably* isn't mine, but what can I do? I push that thought away, push it far away.

My name will be on the certificate.

There's a warmth I'm feeling from Fi – we're getting on well. I don't know what she sees in me, but there's something, and I'm happy to go along, disbelieving or not. I don't believe she's after the building; I believe she wants away from her mother, and I believe she wants a father for the bairn. I can do that. I've done the emotional sums, time after time after time – it's worth it for me. This is worth it. So long as I don't allow myself to become attached, become a lovesick fool – but, of course, it's hard not to move towards the warmth, after so long stumbling around bewildered. You know what else she brings? Sense. Common sense. I'm getting things done. WE'RE getting things done, Fi and me, me and Fi.

I wonder at the locals, as they hear the news, do their own arithmetic, raise their eyebrows.

Auld Jock – *Good on ye, Tommy. Yer da'd be proud.* And he winks.

As ever, there's little mention of my own mother or brother John, they've been filed away by one and all as *Unspeakable / Forgotten / The Past / He's Gotten Over It* – but have I shite. Every single day I think of them both, play the same short memories back and forth, each time highlighting and erasing, caricaturing.

And the youngsters – they perhaps think Fi's gone mad or just been very sly. Hooking up with an older loon… Some are jealous, sure. No' much to do around these parts. Bit time jobs in the Co-op, farm work, get pregnant… And Fi's got herself a man who willnae run, willnae batter her, can feed her, give her something to do, clothe her bairn…

And she's got a hoose now. A hoose with wide stairs. Lady o' the manse, almost.

I scramble up a wee steep bit, the sun slowly setting now, that strange orange glow arriving, colouring the trees in ochre, still just reaching the scattered forest floor.

There's still those phone calls. At first I thought it was to her mother, but no. One time Fi'd just put the phone away as her mother trooped into the bar, bringing twa of her purple-haired pals, talking a' posh – *Oh, come in, Tracy, come in, Linda – well, here we are – and this is practically my daughter's place now, she's done wonders – it's literally unrecognisable, on its way up. You should have seen it! Oh, you wouldn't have believed the state…*

Only to meet crabbit-pus me at the bar, and I'm surprised to see her so soon, thinking as I had been that she was somewhere out of the way, on the phone to Fi…

But, no, and soon snapping out of it – *Oh, hello, Migrit. Delighted to see you.*

Her lips flatlining.

Oh, Thomas – turning to her pals, whispering – *This is the guy I told you about* – then back – *Thomas, would you fetch us some food? Be a good man.*

And me, in a good mood, just thinking fuck it and playing with her – *Sure, I've something for you here* – and chucking her a bag of Ready Salted crisps from a box I was clearing. *They're ootae date, mind, but that willnae bother you, will it, mither?*

And her replying – *Well, it didnae bother ma daughter, did it?*

And the cackling of the mother hens rings out, shrill and cruel and again me just wishing my own mother was here to knock her gums out.

I back into the kitchen, Fi standing there, the pregnancy showing, no' just the bump or whatever, but her skin looking flusher, somehow, healthier. Ach, maybe it's just she's no' wearing as much make-up. I asked – *Who – who was that on the phone?*

Ach… it was ma gran. She's peely-wally.

Her gran.

Fi shakes her head before cursing at the sound of her mother's voice – *As if SHE gives a fuck* – and making her way through, just calling back at me – *Here, go empty that dishwasher. Get the glasses stacked afore the evening.*

And there's me, a troubled bar hand, riding the shoogly bike o' life.

I climb another ten feet or so, perhaps a sighting of a deer, but elusive creatures and far off. I've seldom startled them, but on occasion I'll spy two or three, thirty or fifty or a hundred feet away. I wonder at the folk who go out hunting these beasts. City folk, mostly. Moneyed, of course. Stupid buggers.

She doesn't like me drinking, Fi. I mean, I had a fair idea I was drinking too much, you know, compared to what those government doctors recommend, but surely those limits don't apply to bar hands and hotel staff? It's a perk of the job, surely? Do I no' get some kind o' free health pass? But no. I need *nights aff*. Well then. Imagine that. Getting through one of these days and not even being allowed a wee drink. And mind – she was no angel, she's been well-swallied on many an occasion since I've known her… And jings, that first night, mind?

Ach. Who am I to say that. I cannae recall much about that night, myself… And I've thought back – believe you me.

I step over the branch of a broken-down tree, the ground around it thick with pine needles, softening my footsteps. I turn and examine the view. Good enough, well above the village. Smoke is rising from a few chimneys, being dispersed by the wind, as light as that wind is.

It's too high up where I am for all but the most dedicated of dog walkers or weans – weans intent on misbehaving, sniffing glue, fucking... This'll do. I reach into my pocket and bring my flask out, a flask of decent whisky, Talisker. In the past, on occasion, I'd put the hotel mixer whisky in, but would always curse myself at this point for doing so. Sure, it'd save a few quid, but what's the point of rewarding a walk if the reward makes you curse, makes you boak?

I remove a glove and feel the fallen tree – dry, it seems – then sit myself down. It's solid; no movement. Above, there's a catch of the sunlight left, but it's only hitting the top tree branches now, nowhere near me. So, you see, I need this whisky – it keeps me warm. I'd be foolish to come up here without it. I pop the clasp and take a swig. It's good.

This was my father's flask. I wonder if I'll pass it down to the wean? I look at the flask's dull, scratched surface, the dints it arrived with, dints that my thumb has polished countless times. This is the sort of object that means the world to one person and one person alone. The rest of humanity would throw it away as junk without a thought.

23

I'M DRIVING THROUGH a tired wee village, signs everywhere reading *20* but me going at, well, sixty, to be honest, approaching seventy. I am looking out for obstacles, of course, as it's 2:00 am and the only folk about now would be drunks, quite capable of falling in the path of my four-by-four. Fi is screaming beside me – *I cannae feel the heartbeat, I cannae feel the heartbeat* – and she's *sure* they have but to be honest doesn't quite know if her waters have broken or not – *Is this it? Is this it?* Which I guess means they haven't, but well, here we are, and I cannae look and see now, can I? Just fucking swerve by that van – who'd fucking park a van half oot in the road like that? *Fucking cunt*, and me almost sober, almost sober for a month now, except the odd drink here and there, some nights, most nights, but cutting down, just taking the edge off things, but no doubt four or five times over the limit, the limit being SO small here – what, half a pint? So, don't read this and conclude, *Well, he's a drunk driver*, as in the auld days I'd've been fine. And anyway, vodka-drunk seems to be different from my preferred whisky-drunk as vodka-drunk only really gets the front of your head, doesn't it? And then we're out of the village and I can speed up along the A9, thank Christ, and eventually get us to the maternity hospital, and we're lucky there's a parking space right out front – it says *Ambulances Only* but fuck if this isn't an emergency I wouldn't know what is, and thinking *Fuck it*, they can burn the car, tow it away, push it down the hill, I dinnae gie a hoot, just got to get Fi inside, get Fi inside, get that baby oot… And pouring her into the hospital, opening the doors like a puir expert, us both knowing the way having been here a good half-dozen times, wasting our evenings talking bairns wi' the nursing staff, blues and pinks and reds…

And Fi is welcomed, me phoning ahead the right thing to do, despite not being allowed to phone whilst driving but, well, fuck it, we did it and it only took a minute and no-one jumped in the way of the car during that minute, so all good… the nurse lass taking Fi, knowing me as the da', me seeing her as a younger lassie even than Fi, all of a sudden my wean's life in her hands. Last night she was probably oot pished wi' some laddie and here she is now, that look in her eyes – I see it as laughing at lummox old me, but maybe it's excitement for another birth to witness…

Go and move the car, go and move the car – now!

And it's like Fi doesn't want me there – but no, she does, we've spoken about it, but – *Do you no' want me here?*

Fuck off, Tommy, o' course I want you here, dinnae start wi' that pish, just go and move the fucking car fae the ambulance bay –

And have you any clothes with you, Fiona?

The nurse, slow and calm.

Aye, there's a bag. Grab the bag, Tommy…

Then they're off round the corner, up to the wee birthing suite bit, where we've planned for a water birth, but who knows what'll happen now, with the panic and commotion.

I dart back outside, passing an advert for reusable nappies, thinking *fuck that*, passing a couple of young new mothers at the entrance, looking worn out, sack eyed, pale, smoking away on their cigarettes, watching me as I pile into the car, start up and move, lights off, then lights on and down into the treelined car park to try and find a space.

These last minutes of freedom, I flick the CD player on, some Shetland fiddle coming out, playing a slow, sad air. Space found, car in, engine off, but key remaining, letting the music play on. Thump back into the headrest and deep breath…

Flask out. A quick nip. Two, three, short, thrown gulps. I pull the sunshield down and look at myself in its mirror – bleary-eyed, bearded, auld but no way the auldest. Not young. To be a father now, though – imagine that a year ago.

But this self-dramatisation is not for long. Out, out of the car, open the boot, grab the bag, look for anything else Fi might have placed – my wellington boots? No – the emergency triangle? No. Just the bag. Slam the boot shut, walk off at pace, turning and locking the car with the electronic key, the car clicking and flashing in response, then quick, hurry inside.

I pass the young crones, back up the stairs, along the corridor – *Mr Bruce? This way, please* – and within a minute I'm back by Fi's side. She's grinning wide and takes my hand.

They found the pulse. It's fine. It's a' fine.

And it's what the fuck what the fuck thank FUCK for that.

Two, three, four hours later, we're still here. Fi tired now, in pain, taking the air thing but – *It does fuck all, fuck all* – so the young nurse lassies offer her pain relief, but no, Fi, champion Fi, says – *No, it'll get tae the bairn* – and just squeezes my hand tae shite, saying – *Stop it, Tommy, that hurts* – the minute I squeeze hers back, and well, what's a guy to do here?

Do you want the music? The music you asked for?

No – fucking – No.

And I thank Christ for that, though I am not a religious man, as she'd chosen some awful, autotuned American bubble-throat, and I'd hate any child of mine to be welcomed to the world by a sound like that.

And the baby's pulse drops, weakens, and all thoughts of natural birth and the glory of nature and Mother Earth go out the window. It takes the longest three minutes of my life, but they have a space in *theatre* for us, and we're ushered out of one room and into two more: one for Fi, that's the important room, with a good half-dozen folk inside, and one for me, and that, well, that's a changing room, where I have to remove all my clothing bar my scants and dress in some suit made of the same material, it seems, as supermarket Christmas cracker crowns. I put on the largest size available but my shins are exposed to the world and the tiny wee rubber shoes they offer are a squeeze, so me now looking as though I'm in some crap holiday gear, long shorts and sandals. Wash my hands, double wash my hands and shown through – *This is the father*. A few hellos, one lady advising – *Best to stand back* – but Fi holds out her hand for me, so I take it. They set a tent up just below Fi's breasts and that's us, her and me, shut out from the action.

I could peek, if I wanted. But I don't.

There's blood, there's fast talk, there's my future in the hands of complete strangers who I'll never see again – *Is everything…?* Smiles and – *Don't you worry* – concentrating, concerned faces, Fi looking exhausted but smiling up, up at me, and down, seeing how far she can see, but nothing beyond the tent, the theatre.

And suddenly we hear the bairn cry.

We hear him before we see him. Moments later, he rests with Fi, for all too short a time – what, ten seconds? Before he's eased away – *Where's he going? Is everything ok?*

Oh yes, he just needs to be weighed and checked, don't worry.

Fi to me now – *Is he ok?*

Aye, I think so. He looks fine…

I mean, he's covered from head to toe in who-knows-what, but, well, he's making enough noise…

Is he – is he ok, Tommy?

Christ, how long does it take to weigh a baby? He's just wee…

And he returns. Wiped and wrapped in thick white towelling. Fi releases my hand and takes hold.

We'll ca' him… We'll ca' him George. George. Ok?

Hours later and Fi is shaking, her teeth chattering as though frozen, but it's the adrenaline, the adrenaline, I'm told. Beside her lies – well, it's – he's George, fast asleep. Every type of emotion I've ever known is ridiculed and rushes through and over me – any teenage crush, the love of my father, the loss of my mother and brother John, anything I might feel for Fi or any music or that barn of a hotel or anything else I've ever thought I might have loved – it's all overridden. Dismissed. This is deeper, more personal, shot through, a natural drug more powerful than any alcohol I've experienced, a sensation more intense than any hurt I've felt, higher

than the depth of any despair, beyond any longing, any regret...
Pure, clean, absolute.

I tower above the bed, beaming with pride, both Fi and bairn
George looking tiny, spent and worn.

24

Fi's MOTHER NEVER visited during those next few days, though Fi got a text reply –

Congrats x

But Fi's grandmother did, and, well, she was a fine lady. Not much higher than she was wide, perhaps just four foot three inches of her, wobbling from side to side, a slight smell of damp coming off her, fat calf muscles bandaged up and covered with coffee-coloured tights. I'd say she was a wee bit dottled, judging by the nonsense that was spouting from her mouth, but she was here, at least – *Oooh, Fi, ma wee lamb, there ye are with a wee lamb o' yer own, oh, isn't she sweet – He? Oh! A wee boy, how lovely, whit ye gonnae ca' him? Here, I think Liberace would be an awfy bonny name for a boy, he was some piano player, that fella – oh, noo – is this the father? Well, Fi has telt me a' aboot ye – jings, yer a big fellow, aren't ye? I mind yer da fae that hotel, richt enough, he was a big yin, yer ma too, tho' she was a slip. Here – I got ma pal Seamus tae drive me o'er, I remember the way, o' course – we stopped at auld Betty Maclean's on Sturrock Farm, had a cup o' tea wi' her, sure hadnae seen her for thirty years, but she remembered me richt awa' – 'Oh, it's you, Sheena, good to see you, come in, come in, I'm just taking a cup of tea…' So, me and Seamus go in but she's asking, 'Are you twa merrit then noo?' and me and Seamus blushing like weans, 'No, we are not!', Seamus being a good ten year younger than me, but being a good neighbour, as you ken, a'ways helping me up the stair wi' ma messages. Here, did I tell you Seamus found oot his grandfather was a Frenchie? Aye, he did that Da-En-A tracing thing, like a wool pattern except wi' the names o' his relatives and such – his grandfather was ca'ed Zhaaack, which is French for Seamus, believe it or no' – onyway, he's parked ootside – tak' a look…*

Fi's laughing, basking in the humour and love of her grandmother, which is what you need on these occasions – family around to tell you you're special, part of the clan, part of a line... Fi and I are doing our own bonding, creating our own family. I swear to masel', right there and then, we cannot have this wean growing up as lost as we've both been. His life's going to be good, he won't be abandoned or laughed at or hit. He'll be here, with us, as long as he needs us. With all our love and with everything we can provide.

25

THAT EVENING, I return, almighty and shattered. I have been up and awake for around thirty-six hours and within that time I have eaten mostly chocolate and crisps, become vodka-drunk then vodka-hungover, sugar-peaked and sugar-crashed, and most importantly – I'd attended the birth of a child. My child.

My mind feels as though molten sap is running through it, my shoulders begging to be rested, my legs merely aching.

We'd not taken bookings for the hotel, the chance of having guests and having to run out on them was too much. And to be fair, we were both appreciating the quiet, the anticipation.

The bar was open, though. Had to see things long term. Keep the now regulars happy. Maybe show off a bit...

When Georgie was on his way, we had, on occasion – when Fi was being scanned and prodded – been forced to leave *Migrit* in charge. *Nae fucking chance*, Fi told me to start with, but it seemed very obvious that we didn't have many choices: it was Margaret, Auld Jock or a closed door.

Fi had told her which hospital the birth was to be in, should she appear unexpectedly, but no, she was more interested in the bar, in the natter, the gossip. She was enjoying the role of expectant grandmother, just perhaps less interested in the follow-up act of actual grandmother.

So, yesterday eve, when Fi's waters broke, we left her behind the bar. She grabbed the keys with enthusiasm and refused to take instructions on anything – the till, the dishwasher, the music, the beer pumps, the alarm... Nah. She knew it all.

But upon entering the car park now, I am surprised to see there are no cars here whatsoever, and upon entering the building, it becomes clear too that the bar is mostly empty, though the door is open and the light is on.

I hear voices: Margaret's own shrill cackle, but an audience also, joining in, laugh-coughing. And I smell burning – cigarettes – so very easy to smell now that smoking indoors is banned. Looking through the glass door to the bar, I see Margaret, indeed, and two of her pals, sat around one of the small circular tables, a wine bucket between them with three bottle heads popping out, at least one of them open. I back off so I cannot see or be seen, but can still hear the louder, more exuberant proclamations:

He's a total nugget…
No, no, Mary, no' in a place like THIS…
But Migrit, but Migrit… the mother? Do ye no' mind?
Oh, ye should've seen her PUS…
Fucking cow – HERE, HERE – LISTEN, NOW SHE…
Aye, Jenny, just fucking help yersel', and get me ane also…
A fucking BEAST o' a man…
Oh, aye, I mind fine…

This wrench of my heart is unfair; this should be the happiest day in my life. Why I have returned to such cack and disaster is beyond me. I could confront them, eject them all, provide more gossip and ammunition… But instead I slowly turn to the front door and change the wee cardboard sign from *OPEN* to *CLOSED*, quietly flick the snib to stop anyone else from entering and slowly, cautiously, take the backstairs up to my bed, the cackling following, chasing me until I close my bedroom door and they're finally, blissfully out of earshot.

Part II

26

THERE'S NAE SLEEP. Straightaway, there's nae sleep. She's breastfeeding, Fi, despite her ma banging on about it being selfish and how naebody likes to hear a wean screaming 'cause they can't latch on...

And the hotel has busied up. That Birmingham dude has been back and forth, back and forth, eager for his tip, and when I see him pull his minibus up I curse, as I know then I am caught between the de'il and the deep blue sea – or, more accurately, the Birmingham guy's incessant rambling and Georgie's high-pitched wail.

The money is good, though. My account is actually going up rather than down. It's an unusual occurrence and always requires a bleary-eyed double take, when those statements flop through the letterbox.

Fi looks awfy. Spent, shot through, exhausted. Hair limp, eyes deep in skull, body thinning. I always thought folk got bigger after having a wean, but not my Fi. Maybe it's the food she's taking or the stress of the feeding or the lack of sleep...

And I can't even attempt sleep beside Fi and Georgie, they're up two, three times a night. One evening, after I've chased the last o' the drinkers out, I collapse on the armchair by the fire and that's me, sleeping like a bairn until I get awoken by the cat.

Heh. Sleeping like a bairn. Well, that's no' true, is it?

Fi has introduced a total ban on any alcohol consumption for herself and myself, so I'm having to take a nip on the sly. It's all I can do, though. I'm so exhausted that my humour for guests has long since waned. It's either take a dram to take the edge off things or lamp some poor sod who's had the temerity to ask for a bag of crisps.

And there's water in one of the new bedrooms, a burst fucking pipe just, but enough damage done to need a complete redecoration. Or close the door for good.

And the four-by-four limps through its MOT, but not before initially failing on twenty-six points. *Twenty-six!* Fucking hell.

I scowl at the man and hand over eight hundred fucking pounds.

And I forget to pay the brewery, wi' some nippy wee man phoning me up – *Ah, Mr Bruce, nyim nyim nyim…*

And some young dowp from a satellite TV company comes round demanding money for our viewing of his football matches, but it's in front of a good dozen o' Birmingham boy's tourist folk, folk I've been running after for the last two hours and all I can do is point at the wall where any sensible publican would have placed a TV and shout above the general ramble – *Well, where is this fucking telly, then, eh? Show me the fucking telly!* And him starting tae greet wi' the shock of the shout and then he's apologising and saying *It's just routine, it's just routine* and a' the auld grannies that Birmingham boy has brought in looking at me black affronted, or whatever that'd be in Dutch or wherever they're from and me then seeing the satellite TV boy for what he is, just a wee lad out of school in a cheap suit and a tiny car driving around the Trossachs on minimum wage trying to catch publican folk out, so I'm then apologising, making him a cup o' tea, giving him a biscuit and a hanky…

And Georgie doesn't sleep. Night after night after night.

The whole thing is close to torture.

And Fi's body language says just one thing – *Fuck off, Tommy.* As if I'd have the energy for a lumber.

So, I take a sup, night after night after night.

27

MOST NIGHTS NOW, I attempt sleep downstairs. I stoke the fire, add a log or two, a scoop of coal. I get the dog blanket Fi and I decided fit for this very purpose and my eyes slam shut. In an instant, I'm remembering back when the hotel was falling awry and I was happy with the lack of footfall. I was drifting downstream, into what? Into bankruptcy, alcoholism, depression…

And then, moments later, I'll be out cold.

5:00 am, the fire long gone out, I'm awoken by the snot of my slight-cold freezing and biting my nose. I can hear George, still crying, but in waves now, for he too must be worn out. I stand, pouring the cat – who is delighted with these sleeping arrangements – off me, make my way behind the bar, boil the kettle, put some coffee in the plunger, listen to a minute more of George's complaint, then head upstairs to relieve Fi, if she's ready, mug of coffee in my hand.

I bring Georgie downstairs and place him in front of the fire, my dog blanket curled around him like a doughnut. I stoke the fire, relighting it, the flames and his upright position distracting him, somehow comforting him.

Come 9:00 am, I take Georgie in the pram, in the cauld, wrap him up, shove the pram up the hill like a zombie with a shopping cart, shoogle it, gently shake it left and right, get the wee fella sleeping. His eye will catch the light in a window and follow it for a second, silencing him, before the whatever-it-is kicks him off again and I must redouble my efforts, double my speed, double my exhausted smiles at glaring, questioning, accusatory passers-by.

He needs his Mammie, that's all.
I grit my teeth.
He needs fed.
I smile.
Och, he shouldnae be oot in this cauld…

A few doctor visits later and it turns out Georgie has a thing called *reflux* and that's why he's no' sleeping. His throat is getting all the acid from his stomach. *Not too serious*, the doctor tells us, but we were so fatigued we could barely focus on the doctor's mouth as he was speaking and, of course, forgot to ask the dozen questions we'd considered asking afore we went in…

Fi will leave me with George and demand her time behind the bar. *A change is as good as a rest.* She looks ravaged, exhausted, angry, without her makeup, without her sleep, and suddenly I am the more attractive proposition behind the bar, her ghostly state putting off the punters, certainly the ones who don't know her. And she makes exhausted mistake after exhausted mistake, addition, stocktaking, pouring pints… All I can do is take George out of earshot, so I do just that.

Throughout it all, Fi's mother is nowhere to be seen, thank Christ, though now we'd probably be desperate or foolish enough to take up an offer of help should she make it. Don't get me wrong, she did turn up on occasion, for the young granny photo-op, but when wee George wouldn't stop crying, well, it put her off a wee bit. Back then, of course, we laughed that it was just good taste on George's part, getting away from the *Migrit beast* as soon as he could.

And even in my escape, I'm no' far from grief. Even Auld Jock's laughing, telling me – *Aye, young Fi'll never be the same again noo. Turns them intae their mothers, sucks the fun oot o' them, spits it intae their bairns…* I'm hoping it's just humour landing badly. I mutter under my breath – *Fucking prick* – shake my head and call last orders, 10:30 pm on the dot.

Time to go, folks. Time to go, right now.

I shake any punters out. Broom and sweep them out. Fill the glass washer. I turn the music off, but Georgie's crying seeps into the silence – my silence – so I turn the music back on. I swig from a vodka bottle, swig again, and one more for luck, crawl under the dog blanket and mentally collapse.

I wonder who the da is. Of course I do. But I can't ask, as we're pretending I'm the da, right? So I wonder, but I push it away. Does me no good.

It never really goes, though. How could it? Every time I see a young cheuk in the village, every time her phone goes off…

It'd just be best to know, maybe. Possibly.

Ach. I need rest.

28

BUT THE MORNINGS continue to arrive. I cannot halt them nor the flow of punters, however small that flow might be.

One afternoon, I spy the Birmingham guy's bus and curse the coming workload, but it's only him who jumps out. I squint and examine the bus's windows, but it seems empty – and before I know it he's inside. He looks at me curiously – *A'right mate? Mind if I just...* then he's in the cludgie, seemingly keen.

I go back behind the bar and commence with the never-ending tidying, the rearranging.

A minute later, he bounds over, rubbing his hands against his kilt – *Ah, no way, man, so happy to see you were open.*

Eh?

Well, I've been by a few times since, you know, you shouted at that TV guy? You've been closed?

Really? Ah. Yeah. Mebbe. We've had a few days – doctor's appointments, you know? For the wean? He's no' sleeping.

Ah. He shakes his head. *I don't know anything about that, sorry mate.* His innocent expression flares his nostrils – *It's a foreign language to me, mate, babies... Here – could I get a coffee? My flask is empty...*

Sure.

I guess he's not so fussy today. I turn and begin the process. But nothing decent, just the supermarket version of the Nescafé – *Where's your wagonload?*

Eh? What's that?

I grab a mug, give it a swish of hot water, rinse it out.

Tourists...

Ah – No, not today. I just dropped a load off in Aberfeldy, but they were climbers, out all day. I'll be back for them this evening, but I had stuff to do in Edinburgh... I, um... I got caught short. Needed to use the lav, you know?

Nae worries. You're welcome here.

I stir the mug, a few brown dods of coffee refusing to dissolve, to conform, still floating on the surface. The teaspoon jingling on the edge as I hand it all over.

So... all good with the baby, then? Is everything ok? That last time...

Eh? No. Been a fucking nightmare, to be honest. I mean – no' the wean, no' Georgie, but, well, he's no' sleeping, you know? And the nearest GP is in Aberfeldy – hence the bar being closed...

Ah. Right. The hazards of living somewhere so remote, mate.

Exactly.

Silence. I have nothing to offer, too exhausted to present an entry point, no gossip. He sups at the coffee, visibly recoiling from the taste of it.

Fuck's sake.

Heh. Aye, sorry. Terrible stuff, isn't it? Instant shite.

Yeah... Thanks. He raises an eyebrow.

Heh.

Pretty quiet, these parts. I mean, it's lovely, so beautiful and scenic, but, you know, no doctor, just the one bar... I often think about it when I'm driving through, how it's so peaceful, but the good and the bad that the peace brings –

Aye, it can do your nut in, to be honest...

But still, it IS beautiful and – well – the advantages you guys have –

Like, you don't get any of the shitebags we get in the city...

My head is hanging low, my eyes struggling to focus, brain trying to engage, be polite. – *Aye, well, you know, we have our fair share of chumps.*

How do you mean?

Ach, you know, just local... dowps. Eejits. Wee groups of troublemakers. Kids mostly. You know, I think they get shipped out here from the cities. Restraining orders, a' that shite. The smaller community somehow containing their worst excesses... care in the community and a' that.

Do you get trouble here?

Sometimes. I shrug. *There was one family, when I was younger... The Blairs. Bunch of total pricks. Gave my father a lot of grief. You know — nothing to do around here, so the kids gravitate towards anywhere with a light on and pick away at it, seeing what they can get away with...*

Ah right. No need to explain, mate. I grew up on an estate. Same there. One bad apple ruins the whole cart, the whole block, in my case...

I nod. I cannot offer much more than that, though. I begin to dry some glasses, slowly, carefully. No rush.

He sits up, suddenly animated — *Here — I'll tell you a story. Cheer you up?*

I glance over, weary but friendly.

Here — you know where these tour buses park, right? At night, I mean?

No. No, I don't.

No, of course, you don't... Well, look — they're all parked together, in a group, right? Down in Edinburgh?

Ok?

Yep. It's in a yard — I mean, it's behind a fence and stuff, but kind of out in the open. Got it?

Sure.

Well, every now and then, somebody will climb over the fence and prise a door of a bus open then use it as a place to sleep, you know?

Who's that, then?

Well, we don't know, but we reckon it'll be a homeless guy, or maybe just a drunk who's missed the night bus home, know what I mean? I mean, these electric folding doors are so easy to open. They never really lock, as such, just... close.

I nod.

Well, a couple of nights ago — remember it was really cold? Well, next morning — yesterday morning — there were signs someone had been in the yard, but we checked the buses and there was no one in them — never is, they always clear off good and early...

Ok...

110

Yeah – but – thing is, we didn't check the buses enough, know what I mean?

What, so there was a guy inside?

No. Not a guy – worse than that – heh… Thing is, those buses get really cold, and I mean REALLY cold, and it was frozen overnight, but well, there was no one in the bus. I got the keys, so I just climbed in, scanned the seats for litter and drove off, up to the hotel who'd booked us…

Who was that?

Just an Edinburgh place close by – The Fir Trees, I think it was. Do you know it?

No.

Well. Anyway, that's not the story – the thing is, when I got there, I picked up a whole load of Italian ladies – all gold bracelets, fur coats, that sort of thing –

Ah.

Aye, and they got in, no problem – I mean, we were only driving to St Andrews. It was just a half-dayer, I wasn't due past here –

Right…

But, by the time I'd reached the hotel, well, the engine had warmed, you know?

Sure.

So I could heat the back.

Ok…

Well, as I drove off with the group, I whacked the heat right up because I figured…

They'd be cauld?

Exactly. Italians, not used to the cold. Pretty cold in Scotland. People tend to forget that. Anyway, so the heating went right up, but after a while – you know the Forth Road Bridge?

Of course.

Well, by the time we'd gotten there, there was this AWFUL smell – I mean terrible…

I stop wiping, mid-glass

I mean, it got worse and worse, I had to open my window, all this freezing air coming in – heh. These women were complaining, wafting their noses, shouting at me – as if I could understand a word of it – but one of them screaming and then shouting at me in English, 'Halt the bus! Halt the bus.' And I thought, fuck, one of them's ill or something, perhaps they'd had a stroke – I've had that before, a different time, with a big Canadian fella, but anyway... I pulled over, and the woman was right up front in the cab beside me and wafting her nose, gibbering away at me, saying, 'There is a mess, there is a mess.' And I thought, well, I'd checked the seats... But pulling in and – I've never seen a bus empty so quickly, all these grand old ladies jumping out like the bus itself was on fire. By then, this awful smell started appearing, smelled like the inside of a loo – worse than that, even. And me – well, it was my responsibility, as driver, as captain, so I had to go back inside, holding my nose... And see when I got in the back, the stench got worse and worse, and there, right at the very back, was a coiled turd. A human dump. A poo.

He looks at me for a reaction. *Fuck.*

Yeah and – guess what had happened?

I – I have no idea...

Well. I figured it. One of the homeless guys had broken in and taken a dump, but then left it. I mean, it makes sense – who'd sleep in a bus with a dump in the back? And then, the – you know – the poo – had frozen, right, with the temperature. Understand?

I do.

But then, as we drove off, as I was pumping warm air into the passenger compartment, well, slowly it started to thaw and release its odour. Get it?

I laugh. Or maybe not a laugh. A single chuckle. *Jesus. Shit.*

Exactly.

He winks at me, triumphant.

I can't really react with any great theatre. It does make me smile, though. I try to laugh, to give him the response he wants.

Heh.

I look at him, for more, perhaps, then carry on with the wiping.

Ah well...

We're quiet now. I guess that was his big story, his shot fired. He

112

laughs to himself quietly, then turns and looks outside – *Here, it's dark early.*

Aye, a'ways is. The trees surrounding this stretch mean we get even less daylight than just a few miles up the road.

Look, I better get going. Here, take this back, I can't drink it. It's awful, mate, it really is.

I laugh now, properly – *Aye, I ken. It's awfy stuff.*

Anyway. Thanks for letting me use the bog. I was desperate.

I nod.

Here, I'm glad you're back open. Reckon you're in an ok place to take the odd busload?

Dread creeps over me, but I smile –

Sure. So long as their van is clean. I mean, service might be a wee bit slower than usual, but – well, it's never been fast food here, has it?

Heh – not one bit. Ok. Cool man. I'll see you around. You take care, ok?

Sure. Listen… Thanks for popping in. I appreciate it.

He winks. *No worries, mate. I'll see you next time.*

29

There's a wean wobbling behind the bar near the hatch to the cellar and I'm thinking – *I kent this was a bad idea* – and leaping over, rescuing him, placing him on the bar and shouting – *Who's is this? No weans behind the bar!* – with a friendly wink, half barman, half polis man, half father.

Georgie is one year old now, and I have to say this party has been a relief to get to. It's the end of a busy summer and the pub should be open on a Sunday, bringing in the money that'll tide us through the winter, but Fi was insistent we should have the party here, so that was that. She's got some creepy dowp in with an inflatable castle and a disco, the music blaring way too loud, but the kids seeming hypnotised by the noise and the flashing lights. There are older brothers and sisters jumping on the castle, bouncing the infants off, being cocks o' the north, flirting, showing off, stomping around like cowboys. Who brings teenagers to a kid's first birthday party? Crisps, crisps, free crisps and tins of coke, scooshed lemonade, dozens of ham sandwiches collapsing, ignored, while the cupcakes Fi bought are almost all gone. Ah well, ham sandwiches for tea, then, and supper, maybe breakfast. A few o' the dads are at the bar, getting a wee scoop in, but I cannae charge them as, well, gottae be kind, can't be seen making money from a kid's party, so losing money instead. But I'm no' daft – *Sorry, pal, only the real ale is on, I havenae cleaned the lager pipes.* Shite, of course, but at least it means I'm only losing an ale that was selling so badly that it was going off anyhows.

Fi's working the party, moving from mother to mother, hovering around, taking gifts, stacking them up. She's had her hair done and is looking right happy. Georgie began to sleep through the night just two months back, but what a relief it was for her and for me, me back upstairs now. I tell you, I'd had enough of that armchair, that dog blanket, my back aching, the cat jumping on me for warmth then hissing with anger any time I moved... Of course, Fi'd eventually said – *Why don't you just take one of the spare rooms?* – and it was like a light turned on in my head – *Ya eejit* – but by then I was used to kipping downstairs and there was a part of me – odd as this sounds – a part of me that thought – *Well, if Fi's suffering, so should I be...* Daft, eh?

And you can't beat sleeping in front of a real fire.

That DJ fellow is playing the worst music imaginable, all robot vocals and massive bass drum kicks – and the lyrics! Jings. Not in any way suitable for bairns, though I doubt they can make them out amongst their own screams and tears, the chattering mothers, the stench of nappies...

One of the dads is right by me, sticking close, glued to the bar. He's older than me and – get this – he's a minister, a church guy.

SO – he's shouting, in ma lug – *HOW DID YOU MEET YOUNG FIONA?* It's none of his business, of course, but here I am in double-friendly mode, father of the wean, owner of the bar, twice as much shite to soak up.

Right here.

HERE?

I nod.

His wife's a big lassie, three kids they've got with them now, two older ones squirrelled at home. I can't imagine what it'd be like, being a vicar, being some kind of morality polis, always polite and right and forgiving. Still, a nice hoose they've got. Maybe it's worth the effort just for that. I mean, what work does he actually do beyond being smiley and friendly? Reading people stories on a Sunday? Easy money.

YOU KNOW, THOMAS, I NEVER SEE YOU OR YOUR FAMILY IN CHURCH. YOU'D BE VERY WELCOME.

I laugh – *Aye, and I never see you here. Get yourself in one night. I'd make you welcome* – I wink – *I'd mebbe pour you a wee dram.*

Of something cheap. But I don't mention that bit.

TOUCHÉ! TOUCHÉ!

He lightly fist-taps my arm, suggesting brotherhood and affection. He's good at his job, this guy, I want to hug him already.

We watch the party a little longer, kids colliding, drinks spilling, cat briefly appearing, having its tail pulled, then scarpering...

YOU KNOW, I KNEW FI'S FATHER. HE WAS A GOOD MAN. A HARD WORKER.

Aye. She talks about him a lot.

A wee boy – not mine – bursts a balloon, his face briefly stretching with shock, as though he's being a statue, then collapsing into tears. A ripple of *Ahhhs* emanates from the mother collective.

WELL, IT WAS GOOD, WHAT YOU DID FOR HER, THOMAS.

How do you mean?

He glances towards me –

TAKING HER IN. A LOT O' FOLK – WELL...

What? Georgie's mine – you know?

OH – THOMAS – THAT'S NOT WHAT I'M SAYING – BUT YOU HAVE TO ADMIT... WORD IS YOU HADN'T BEEN TOGETHER LONG... YOU WOULDN'T HAVE BEEN THE FIRST FATHER TO LET A LADY DOWN... DO YOU KNOW WHAT I MEAN? I SEE A LOT OF SINGLE MOTHERS, THOMAS.

And looking around the room, I can only agree with him.

Christ, though, he knows the gossip, this one.

Is this what folk think? That I rescued Fi from a cooncil flat and a giro? Ach. Mebbe they're right... I can pretend, though, can't I? I can pretend it's a' good... Thing is, most o' the time, before Georgie mucked up his sleeping, it WAS good. And it felt right. Fuck what folk think.

It's all just noise, commotion.

I nod at my heavenly new pal and leave the bar, for a break, really, but under the pretext of getting more crisps. As I move into the kitchen, I surprise a few of the teenagers. They look at me, stock-still, then bolt out of the back door.

As if I won't recognise them two minutes later in front of the bar, the loons.

I walk over to where they were and see they've opened a bottle of the cooking whisky – I mean the *local malt* – and have been pouring it, I'd guess, into their coke cans. Nothing ever changes, eh?

I close and lock the back door.

Great party, Fi.

Wee Georgie weighs a bit now, and his eyes follow mine, up and down, up and down, as I hold him high, his bendy wee legs kicking away at nothing.

Aye. Thanks, Tommy.

Have we recovered? I don't know if we have. The only period of normality was so short – with George coming so soon – sometimes I feel we barely know each other. It's like being on a rollercoaster with a stranger. I mean, I know what she's like in the peaks and the troughs, but what about life's normal pace? The straight, clear road?

Were ye drinking?

Um… I had a glass of the ale.

A disapproving look.

With the vicar guy.

As if that'd make a difference, somehow turning it into holy water, holy ale.

Oh, and I had a swig o' the cooking whisky. I don't mention that, though. Who would?

That night, when I stagger up, the day long finished, night well started, dark now even though it's summer… well, Fi is asleep, and there's no comfort, no holding, little warmth.

30

I JUST FUCKING –
You have tae stop, Tommy. You're killing yourself – can you no' see that?

Fucking – that's a bit –

But she's holding a quarter bottle of vodka up – she found it in the cistern of the upstairs loo – I mean, I put it there ages ago, but still, she's off –

I mean, WHAT THE FUCK, TOMMY? You've a bairn now.

She slams it into the glass bin, where it clangs against the dozens of spent lager and spirit bottles before quickly settling –

Fuck. FUCK'S SAKE. I cannae have this, Tommy. I cannae have this for George. He needs a proper, decent father.

She marches out of the room, back upstairs, where a screaming George has awoken.

I try, I do. Auld Jock asks why I'm no' drinking –
Well, I'm aff it the noo.

He scowls – *Well, guid luck* – and drains his glass.

Aye, I'll need that, I'll need that luck.

I get beyond 10:00 pm sober and to celebrate open a tomato juice and pour it over some ice. On the rocks. But it's so easy and obvious and ingrained now to hold it to an optic that I do just that, once, twice, thrice. I then feel guilty and down it immediately.

Guilty. I look at the evidence and pour myself another tomato juice.

I hate tomato juice. Fucking cold soup, just. So it sits there, at the bar, haunting me. Next round of glasses, I gather it up and pour it down the drain.

Jock doesn't judge, just watches, grimly. Perhaps he's fought this battle himself a few times.

31

*Y*E *NEED TAE clean this car, it's a disgrace. I'm no' having no grandson o' mine in this car.*

She's smiling, though. Why hello, Granny. Where were you when we needed you? She aye visits now Georgie is a more controllable beast. Cute, without the screaming, the writhing...

Last night she overheard me telling Fi that I have to do the Perth run, get to the cash and carry there, pick up the basic bar detritus, the crisps and nuts, cheap frozen chips, all that guff. Saving a few pound from the supermarket, but worth the effort? Hmm. Anyway, her ears pricked up and she wanted to accompany me. Who'd've thunk it.

It'll be lovely to spend some time with you, Migrit.

She couldn't work out if I was taking the piss. Which I kinda was, kinda wasn't. She looked at me for signs of it, willing me to crack a smile.

I was, and am, too tired to smile, though.

Hmm. Now, you'll be needing tae take me tae McGregor's, understand?

Yep. Sure. What's that, the bakers? Are ye after a bridie?

No! It's no' a bloody bakers. It's the auction house. Very well-to-do, I'll have you know.

And now she's here, pursing her lips.

I start the car and slowly, carefully, pull up the hill and out onto the main drag.

Ah. Cool. I didn't know you were interested in antiques...

Well, I am. I'm very interested.

120

Really? What's your… what's your thing?

Aye, well – You know – I like… She looks around her, surveys the passing street – *I like lights… And coats.*

Lights and coats. Cool.

There's that Shetland fiddle compilation CD in the player, whirring away. Aly Bain's on the now, playing a well-kent, much-loved air: 'Neil Gow's Lament for the Death of his Second Wife'. We're quiet, Margaret and I, slowing out of the backroads, approaching the far busier A9. We're sharing a moment, the beautiful scenery, the music, the glorious weather…

What is this awfy, glaikit music? It sounds… SO miserable.

She lurches over and sticks the radio on, moving straight off the Gaelic station I stay tuned to until she finds something she considers listenable. Some light, well-polished country music. Why this kind of glib awfulness has been so embraced by Scotland is beyond me.

Oh, I love this… Now, this is REAL music… And she sings along – *Oh, yer heart and mine, cheek to cheek on the dance floor, how I lang for those days, before ye went away…*

She has a good voice. I mean, it's not my thing, her voice, she puts that warble on the end of every note, but she hits every note, has the timing right – she's karaoke, that level. I sing along –

For the best things in life are a faithful husband and a buxom wife…

She stops singing – *What the fuck ye doing?*

Eh? I glance at her but keep my eyes on the road, mostly – *I was just singing along…*

Well, dinnae. Yer putting me aff. Wi' yer fucking… nonsense.

I laugh. What else can I do?

So, are you an' Fiona gonnae get merrit?

I shake my head. No chance.

I wouldn't say so, Migrit. She's awfy, um…

Awfy what?

Looking for cracks. For ammunition.

Well, she's no' keen on marriage, it seems.

She grins. Relief?

Heh. I ken that. Aye, she's had her chances…

I do not bite.

She tries again – *She wisnae keen on marrying that Blair boy…*

Eh? A Blair boy? Which one? No' that fucking Jim Blair clown, surely…

An overtaking car jumps right ahead of me, pulling in quick to avoid being hit by oncoming traffic. I break and swerve before slowing to give the guy distance, flashing my lights at him, straightening up and resuming.

Jim Blair, eh?

I calm myself, no' showing any sign of weakness, then speak, as controlled as I can – *You don't mean Jim Blair? Auld fellow? Aulder than me?*

No! No' him, thank Christ, no' that gangster. His wee brother, Simon. Aye, they were thegither just afore you got involved. Ye'd've kent that tho', eh?

My hands tighten on the wheel. I knew there was someone, of course, but for the name to be named, become real…

Aye, they were a right pair, them pair, but then he got caught – up tae nae guid. Now, he's up at Castle Huntly…

The prison.

What was he, was he… What were they –

Ach, he was done for threatening that boy Kevin Hardy who was selling the motors up Crieff way. You'll remember a' this…

I don't.

It was in a' the papers? A'body was talking about it?

Well, I wasn't talking about it.

I shake my head.

And here's a new emotion, as I try to digest it all. A name for a face. A name for… What? My baby's face? Is this what she's telling me?

Aye, they had an argument and that Simon ended up wi' a knife tae the boy's throat, telt him he wisnae paying for some auld tyres or something, and the Hardy boy's lassie got puir feart up and telt the polis. So, word gets around that Hardy's a grass and Simon was picked up and released and then, well, the garage went up in flames one night and that daft Simon was caught on the CUTV and wi' a petrol can in the back o' his car and that was that.

But I'm not really listening to her natter. I'll be honest, that's not really the bit I was interested in. I leave it a minute, don't want to flag up any tension, then – *So, were Fi and him…*

Aye, they were thegither a'most a year that final time, a'ways breaking up, getting back, breaking up. School pals, ken?

I'm silent, but my heart has surely begun jumping. I feel sick.

I was surprised she hopped intae bed wi' you so quick, right enough.

You know, I could swear she knows what she is doing…

But then, I guess you're providing everything he wisnae – a hoose, security… A father for the wean…

I cannot keep up the pretence of peace any longer. I glare at her, then eyes ahead. I spot a lay-by, swerve to the side, pulling up over the grass, onto the emerging hard shoulder, finally rolling through to a truck stop.

Fuck's sake, Tommy! You've got passengers! You DO NOT drive like that.

But I'm not listening. Inside, I'm uncontrollably fuming. Fuming at masel', at Fi, even at wee Georgie, wi' his screaming and non-stop attention, and I knew fine he wisnae mine, but to hear it so black and white – *my* secret, common knowledge, out loud – and to find out he's the child o' ane o' those Blair dowps just makes it worse…

I get out of the car, slam the door shut and march away.

But where the fuck am I marching to? It's too cold to be out. The moving cars are feet away, charging past me, the wind reaching down my neck… Behind me –

Tommy! TOMMY!

I walk on.

Up ahead, in the middle of this piddling truck stop, there's a wee caravanette thing with a sign: *HOT SANDRA'S HOT PIES.*

I stomp towards it. Fuck this.

A guy's walking towards me, tea in hand, on the way back to his stationary car – *Hey?*

I look up.

He points towards Margaret, now half-hanging out of the car – *Yer wife wants ye!*

She's no' ma fucking wife, pal.

He stops, mouth agape, but I don't, I hoik off, away from Margaret and her bruising words.

Deep breaths, deep breaths, calm down. I knew it all, I knew the most of it. Best to know the all of it, Tommy. Had to know at some point. Had to be someone, had to be someone… Margaret's done you a favour… but fucking Fi. She should've told me… I knew it. I fucking knew it.

I arrive, scowling, at Sandra's. I could have done with another few hundred yards to cool down, calm myself.

A'right, mate.

Hot Sandra, it seems, is a fat, bald bloke in his mid-forties, wearing that most erotic of outfits, the tartan fleece.

Can I help ye?

I welcome this distraction.

Umm… Where's Hot Sandra?

She's in bed wi' the flu. I'm her husband. Jack's ma name. Now. Can I help youse or no'?

Hot Jack.

Aye, Jack. I'll have ane o' those beef pies. And a cup o' tea, please. Actually… aye, make it two… That's it – six sugars in the one. Grand.

Six?

Aye. Six.

Fucking beef pie.

I'm calming down, taking the time it takes Jack to serve it all up to relax, plan, think. I'll just ask Fi right out. No harm there. Keep things mellow. I mean, if her and wee Georgie move out, so be it. I'll still see him around town, see him grow up, walking to school, coming into the bar…

At least, I've got that to look forward to.

And, at least, I've got those fucking rooms done up.

A fucking lifetime alone to look forward to.

I'll be taking a drink tonight, that's for sure.

How's yer day going then, buddy? Dinnae recognise you, yer no' a regular —

Eh? No — not a regular. I normally eat at home, I'll be honest. I'm not a great one for truck stops…

He looks at me with suspicion.

Sauce?

Eh? Aye. I exhale. *Wallop it on.*

Boiled onions?

Something like that, mate, something like that.

I return to the car, balancing my goods, adamant not to lose my cool. Margaret's out now, by her half-open door, shouting, nae shame — *Where've ye been? It's fucking freezing oot here!*

I glare at her — *Get in the fucking car, then.*

The tone of my voice shuts her up. I'm clearly riled. She tries to regain the high ground, still shouting, but less so, softer — *You shouldn't have walked off like that, you cannot leave a lady alone in a car in a place like this —*

But I'm not listening. I get in the car and sit myself down, not replying, not waiting for her. Her door opens and she clambers in, her daft posh shoes now speckled with the mud of the lay-by. She's muttering but straightens herself up and plugs in her seatbelt, winding herself up for another tirade. I'm having none of it, though.

Here — I shove the pie in her general direction — *stick that in yer gob.*

Start the car and off, skidding out of the truck stop and straight up to the speed of a busy A9.

She finishes the pie and begins the natter. I pass her tea.

She finishes her tea. I pass her the next ane.

Whit ye trying tae do? Drown me?

32

FOR THE THIRD time, I drive right past the cash and carry, where I need to go. Margaret hasn't a scooby where this auction house is. She repeatedly says – *I think it's up here* – or – *How about down there?* – but she's guessing, and her guesses are wildly wrong. We've driven into a school, a recycling plant, half-a-dozen car parks…

Fuck's sake.

She's quiet, aware my mood isn't good and not up to the fight.

Look, Tommy, here's someone we could ask –

I pull in, winding down the window, no delicate electric mechanism, more work…

Excuse me pal, would ye ken where McGregor's auction house is?

An auld fella. Baseball cap declaring *Champion!*, bottle-thick glasses, coat pulled up around his neck, some kind of wee dug on a lead, mebbe half spaniel, half Jack Russell.

Ah, right. Whaur they're filming – is that whit yer efter? Yon BBC folk? Aye, I was just there, they wouldnae let me in wi' the dug but I saw that guy wi' the flowery jacket – whit's his pus… Thingy, ken? Queer-looking fellow…

Aye. Aye, that sounds like it. D'ye ken the way from here?

I do, son, aye, just heid along tae the end there, then up Argyle Road, tap o' there, then doon past Broon's, then at the back o' the auld cinema there's a wee car park and third fae the left o' there is the church, which is richt opposite the lane whaur McGregor's is.

I nod. *Aye, got it.* Close enough. *Thanks.*

Nae worries, enjoy yersel's. He peeks into the car and taps his cap to Margaret. I drive off.

*

Filming, eh?

Oh, are they? I didnae ken that…

Rot. I see now: her lipstick, her hair all done, her posh shoes, this trip to Perth… She's aff living the Hollywood dream wi' daytime TV.

I clatter round the cash and carry, still simmering, hurling things onto my platform cart. Bin bags. Bog roll. The cheap stuff, to annoy Fi. Bleach. Pre-diluted paint. Crisps. I scowl at anyone and everything, swear I'm driving home without Margaret. I buy sixteen bottles of the cheapest whisky there is – Loch Charlie, aged four years in *genuine laminate tanks*, coloured with *caramel*…

Beans. Forty-eight tins of beans for £15. Own brand.

Bacon. Non-organic. Water-engorged.

Lemonade. 3p a litre.

Frozen, long-life white bread.

Tomato-flavoured sauce.

Salt-flavoured crisps.

I load the car and make my way over to a wee coffee shop nearby, awaiting the 4:00 pm collection time Margaret had insisted upon.

Just a coffee, please. Eh? Aye, large. Milk. No, nae sugar… And one o' those cake things – no – no – aye, that one. Lemon drizzle? Sure. Umm… just a wee slice.

Fuck it.

No – make it large, eh. I've no' had ma lunch.

This place seems human and personal, after the cash and carry warehouse of anonymity and shame I've just been trekking around. On the wall, there are posters for local events, concerts, yoga, rallies…

I sit at the window and observe. There's only maybe half-a-dozen folk in, but I'm the only one here without a phone, the only one not studying my palm.

My order arrives. I sup at the coffee before picking up a local newspaper. The headline is about the local MP who's been caught fooling around with his opposition member. In the report, he's quoted saying that it won't affect his work and such, that he can *keep impartial*. I imagine the twa o' them in bed, *keeping it impartial*.

Chase the bed thoughts away, Tommy.

There are other stories – a missing lollypop man, a dug that's been put down for nipping at a wean, a wee lassie who's won some poetry award. I remember reading about that Jim Blair in a paper like this. It wasn't every week, but he was no stranger to the front page, some photo of him skulking out of the courtroom or whatever. Petty thievery at first, but I mind it escalating – some drugs charge, that sort of thing.

And I mind him dying, the big headlines – *Local Criminal in Fatal Accident*. No picture of the car, but a description – *Burned out, corpse unrecognisable…*

Jock and I discussed it, of course, but I was in such a drunken, lonesome gloop back then, the man's death barely registered. Just willing Jock on to take another half, pay for the coal I'd put on the fire, keep me company, save me from my thoughts…

Aye, it was worse without Fi, I mind that. Far, far worse.

Just fucking lap it up, Tommy lad. Keep the peace, keep young Fi…

And surely knowing the father is better than thinking every man I see might be him? That procession of ghosts wasn't much fun.

I stare out of the window, the rain on now and an auld couple walking by, dragging an unimpressed-looking dug behind them. For a second, the dug's eyes dart my way, and it looks longingly at the inside, the warmth, the cake, before being hoiked further along the street.

And it is good cake, I can't complain there.

33

I PARK OUTSIDE THE auction house, the rain peeling down now, a BBC caravan at the back door, thick leads and wires running in and out of the building. I am not in the least bit bothered about catching this TV thing and greatly appreciate the soporific rhythm of the rain. Before too long, I spy Margaret, her wee heid popping out from behind a door, as though she's looking for something, then back inside, then out again, over and over. I watch a few repetitions, then succumb to the inevitable and flash my lights, alerting her to my presence, my position. She peers, stretching her neck, hand sheltering eyes, focusing, stills, then waves me over, calling – *THOMAS! THOMAS! THIS WAY!*

A wee mannie hurries out of the BBC van and very visually motions her to keep quiet, pushing his hands down towards the floor. I get out of the car and run over to her, the rain catching me straight away, speeding me up – *Ok, Migrit, you ready to go?*

What are you doing here? You'll be needing tae bring the car over!

She nudges me, pointing back towards the car.

Eh, c'mon, Migrit, just come over through the rain, it's only a bit o' wet...

No, no, ye dinnae understand. Ye see, I've bought something...

She's giving me a look I've never experienced from her before: it's sort of snake-like yet apologetic, childlike and questioning. Fuck – is she flirting, even? Euch. Whatever it is, I am suspicious of her motives.

What have you bought, Migrit?

Well...

129

And she makes to take my hand. I shake her off but follow her through the building's door.

It's a room full of junk, as far as I can see. Typewriters. Fridges. DVDs. Shelves of books, boxes of LPs.

Margaret's standing at the head of a table, grinning. Has she bought a table? How the fuck is that going to fit into the car?

But no. She hasn't bought a table.

She moves aside and flows her arms, presenting, as though on a seventies TV show, a three-foot crystal eagle, wings outstretched, salmon in claws.

Heh.

I shake my head. Junk.

Whatever. C'mon, let's get going.

Tommy – can you carry it? It's ower heavy for me…

Sure.

Fucking hell, what a monstrosity. Up close, it's even worse. Basic, moulded. No skill involved. Is it even crystal? Plastic, maybe? I lift it. There's no weight at all. I'll bet it's hollow.

I thought we – you could hae it. On the bar?

What!? No fucking chance –

She doesn't look hurt. She can't do. It is puir, cheap tourist shite and any eejit can see that. Still, though, she has face to gain –

Well, I know Fi would like it –

Would she fuck – c'mon, Migrit, it's awfy.

Well, I've paid for it.

Oh, Christ.

How much was it?

Her eyes widen – *It was EIGHTEEN pounds, Tommy.*

It sits on her lap, the whole way home.

What on earth made you buy that?

It was ane o' the teams, Tommy.

Teams?

Aye. On the telly. They have twa teams, buying and selling antiques…

That's no antique.

… They're trying tae make money, see, and no one was buying this. I felt sorry for them, that's a'.

I don't say a word. She can see I'm not impressed. Interested, even. She tries her final pitch —

Plus, I'll be on the telly now. She humphs. *It's good advertising. For the hotel, I mean.*

I watch the busy road ahead and will the car in front of me to crash, hopefully taking us with it.

34

I DID MY BEST, of course I did. I'm not an eejit. I could mind fine what life was like pre-Fi. But this was a new – and in a lot of ways, worse, more uncomfortable – weight on my shoulders. So many aspects: Who knew? Everyone? Jock? Would Georgie eventually know? Should we bring him up in the full knowledge? Should we let the dowp into his life early on? Surely, that'd be what anyone would do if they actually loved the wean, right? They'd open their hearts and become love itself, accepting, forgiving…

Fi, still on my case about the alcohol, but being younger and without experience of dealing with such a manly issue, counsels me with shouts and threats. I'm not having a go at her, no way. She's doing her best. She just sees a lummox of a man picking up her bairn and worries that if that lummox were drunk or hungover, he'd collapse on the wean and squash him like a bug or take him out on an alcohol-fuelled joyride, drive into a tractor. Or mebbe just worries he'd be a bad influence on him…

And I remember, of course, that her own father was a drinker, and I remember, of course, that Fi partially blames that for *his* fleeing the coop early.

So many fears.

I often take wee George up the hill, thinking – he'll no' remember this, he's just a wean, but I will, for better or for worse. Strapped onto my chest, secure, but Fi comes and checks, tightening the straps, going in for a kiss goodbye but not motivated by emotion, of that I'm sure, just checking my breath.

It's wonderful, young Georgie sitting at my chest, me bouncing him up and down, up and down, his eyes three inches from mine, him laughing, gurgling, eventually sleeping, and then his peerie head falling into my neck. I'm the happiest man alive, taking in the smell of him, the closeness, the warmth... No one can take him from me then, I know that. High in the trees, high above the village, feeling so at home. I love the chill of the wind coming in, tucking Georgie in, making sure he's warm, him awake now and looking every which way and up at me, slowly, curiously. He feels safe, I know that. His cheeks go peach-red with the cold and I guard his ears, one more minute alone, one more minute up here, away from the fire of reality below.

How could I give this up? I could not. Only a fool would.

35

I WILL ALWAYS REMEMBER this day.

Fi calls me through, out of the bar. There's no one in, a quiet lunchtime, sometimes a blessing, always plenty of other things to do to keep the place running.

We're close to the bar still, just in the kitchens, an eye and an ear open for visitors, onlookers. And perhaps, probably, Fi wanted it that way. She wanted to keep me in check, a chance for a potential diffusion.

I wander through, scuffing my arm on the doorway, clutching it from the abrasion, expecting maybe a talk about crisps or mixers or menus. Who knows?

Ok?

Hi. So — I've just had some news. She's cradling a sleeping Georgie.

Ok? I have a bar cloth in my hand and am lazily polishing, wiping the kitchen table, sending crumbs flying onto the floor. They'll need swept.

Umm, a friend of mine is, um, coming by and they need a place tae stay for a while. And a job.

Hmm? I smile, raise my eyebrows, eager to please, willing this relationship to work, doing my best, working out quickly in my head — well, another young lassie to help clean, change the sheets, et cetera, to give me time with Georgie, plus if we can pay them with accommodation, well, that won't come to much... You know, it sounds ok to me, I'm sold already.

Ok, that sounds fine — who...

Thing is — she interrupts — *they're just coming out o' prison. Well...*
That cools things.

134

This is KIND o' what helps them out: if we can offer them a job, it really helps wi' an early release...

Ah, shite. I know, I know, I know what's coming, who's coming, but one last hope, one last chance –

Who is she?

Who?

The lassie you want to work here?

Her face is down, her eyes almost hiding within themselves, not looking up, not at me, anyhow. And here it comes now –

It's no' a lassie. It's no' a lassie. It's an auld pal o' mine...

My blood freezes.

Simon Blair.

I swallow. She peeks up at me, awaiting my reaction. And me, well, I just can't help myself. The knowledge of it all, of her wanting wee Georgie's da to be moving in here. And me, well – who will I be? The fucking eejit, that's who, the cuckooed and supplanted. It'll be me getting kicked, forced out of the nest, I can see that... No fucking way. No fucking chance.

No way, Fi. I shake my head, eyes welling with tears. *No fucking way...*

Did she not know I knew? Is she treating me with even more disdain than I'd thought? Like I'm a fucking stray, flea-ridden dog or something. This is my place, my hotel, my land. What is she thinking?

I've not met him. At least, not that I'm aware of. I might have chased him out of the bar when he was fifteen or so, but those years are, well, cloudy memories. I was chasing anyone out of the bar back then; I was lost, in a dwam. Not now, though. No way.

You cannae ask me that, Fi. Your mother... she told me all about you twa...

And Fi, to her credit, keeps things calm – *Ah, Tommy... I thought you'd've known all along. And I was worried you'd be like this, so I understand, I do – but look – aye, I was with Simon, but that was ages ago. And he's a good lad. He was just in a bad family. Give the guy a chance. His brother was a bad influence, I know, but I've been, I've been...*

135

You've been whit?

I've been helping him out. Speaking to him. Talking to his lawyer, his social worker. They've gotten him out early because I could offer him secure work, somewhere tae stay...

No chance, Fi. I'm no' having him here. I cannae, can you no' see that?

I don't say – *George is mine now. I'm no' handing him over. I cannae hand him over. I will fight to keep him with all my being* – But that is how I am feeling.

Besides, besides, we cannae afford another staff member. Christ, I could barely afford you when you came in –

That's shite, Tommy, I've mair than paid ma way, and ye ken it fine. This place is a' fu' every weekend. Who was it afore I came? You and Auld Jock, talking shite about farms...

Fucking hell, I don't want this to be about me and her. Fi has been wonderful, and George – George is my everything.

Fi... I'm just – I'm just crying, that's what I'm doing. Before I know it, I'm weeping.

She moves towards me, Georgie over her shoulder, sleeping still despite the drama. With her one free hand, Fi takes my own. Her small, white fingers clasp around my scalded red clumps.

Tommy, I cannae let ma pals down. You took me in, and I tell you – I love you for it. I really do.

I blink at her through the tears.

But I cannae let Simon down. I've kent him a' ma life, a'most. He's ok. Deep down. Inside. It's just... his family were shite. You helped me, Tommy, and now I have tae help him.

My heart is grinding.

You can't, Fi, we can't have HIM here.

She shakes her head – *I've signed the forms, Tommy. And he's out. He's out tomorrow.*

Tomorrow? Fi – what...

She squeezes my fingers. George gurgles, awakening. Fi places both hands on him, lifts him off her shoulder and slowly, carefully, passes him to me. He smiles, his tiny wee hands clawing at my cheeks.

Tommy the Bruce

*

I'm skulking around the hotel, feeling almost as drookit, sullied, heavy and weathered as when my father passed. I need something, I need some kind of control. I told her, I told her – *He cannae sleep in the flat. He'll have tae stay in the hotel. In one of the auld rooms.* And she'd looked at me as if I was soft in the head – *What? Of course, not – why would he sleep in the flat?*

There's no mention of *her and him* or *him and George.* No mention of *fatherhood.* I couldn't bear to utter such words out loud. But that night, I do not come upstairs once the bar is cleared. I sit once more in front of the fire, trying to work out what is what, where my place is. And I take a drink, of course I do. I slug back wine glasses of whisky, one after the other, until my mind quietens and drags, knocks me to sleep.

36

A ND COMETH THE morn, Fi's fury is unleashed – *Don't you start drinking, Tommy. I cannae be daen wi' that.*

The cat spits off in a sprint. I've got years on Fi and she's shouting at me like I'M the wean.

I've had enough o' that, Tommy Bruce. I've SEEN what that does.

But I'm not listening. I agree with everything she's saying, I'm just – I'm just aware and wary of the very near future. I am sick with nerves, nerves and anger.

I will NOT have George growing up around that – do you hear me? DO YOU HEAR ME? You are NOT using THIS as an excuse.

I nod. I do, but it's all I can do not to shout back – *How fucking dare you?*

The comfort, the pleasure of the hangover. The compressed skull, the aches, the dry mouth and dwammed head. An old friend returning. Fi goes, rants on, and I tune her out, concentrating on the rub of my hands up and down my face, listening in to the flick of every hair, the scratch of callous on eyebrow. Her deception, her inviting of this prick into MY house, more than justifies my drinking.

Lunchtime arrives, and he's in, like a dream, a mid-afternoon TV drama, and, of course, he's a wee shite. A gobby wee erse. A muppet. A prick. Whippet thin, greased black hair, cultivated spikes, pencilled stubble, tracksuit zipped right up his neck to his chin. I can see why Fi didn't tell me. At least the wait, the dread, was mercifully short-lived.

And he laughs like a kookaburra. Like a sheep's bleat – *Heheh, a'right, pal. Ahm Simon. Thanks, like. Thanks as fuck for having me here. Ah fucking puir appreciate it.*

138

He makes to shake my hand and when we make contact, his palm is so oily and wet that it's like grabbing a fish.

Heheh, sorry, pal – just hair gel, ken whit ah mean?

At Fi's suggestion, we have a big welcoming meal. Well, as big as it can be here, what with our responsibilities to our regulars.

To get to know each other.

We shut up shop from 5:00 pm to 6:00 pm. Fi insists we all sit in the flat, in the pokey wee living room area, surrounded by boxes of cheap toilet roll, napkins, plastic cutlery, paper plates, party balloons, disposable tablecloths, toughened pint glasses, individually wrapped instant coffee portions, soap, recovered magazines and other general detritus.

I don't use this room often. Fi has been in and tidied, but even she gave up. It's a midden, I guess. Or a storeroom, at best.

Fi's cooked, kind of. It's pizza, from the Co-op, via the oven to our plates – *Aye, he disnae… disnae eat much variety* – she tells me. *Be up there at 5:00 pm. Dinnae be late. First impressions, you know?*

But my first impressions have been made, you know?

There are so many things to be done all of a sudden. Open new boxes of crisps. Check the pressure on the gas pumps. Do a stocktake. Bleach the cat, feed the floor, wash the windows, sweep the fire out…

Come 5:00 pm she's down to find me and dragging me upstairs. I don't want to go, I resist, but clever young Fi, she has me with – *It's just him and Georgie up there, c'mon!*

So up, up we go.

As we approach, Fi suddenly darts back downstairs – *I forgot something – you carry on* – leaving me mere feet away from the mottle-glazed door. I can't stop here, a shadow visible to all, so I turn the handle and walk in.

He's on the phone, a Budweiser in the other hand. On the table, I see a half-dozen more, unopened. Fi's pushing the boat out.

Heh – Aye – No – Right – Aye, wi' Fi, ken? Aye. Seems a'right… Big fellow. Heheh. Easy – too right. Eh? Nae chance. Fuck that… Aye

– right – see ye – aye – see ye then. Then turning to me – *A'right, pal, ah'll just be a minute, eh.*

I make to speak, but before I can he's off again, another call made – *Aye, I'm oot, that's me, free as a bird, Tonto... Sure, come by... Eh? In that pub, eh? – No – Fi, mind? Aye... A wean, noo...*

I stand, I stare. I look around. Georgie's not here at all. Fi just used him to shoehorn me in.

I move a box. I adjust a chair. I listen in –

Heheh. Fucking right! Fucking right!... Straight up! Straight up, big man!

I feel such a clutz, standing here on ceremony, not even having the gall to sit down, feeling as though I should wait, be the grown-up, do the polite thing. But my blood starts rushing, my mind begins to panic, and before I know it, I've turned and walked to the door...

Hang on – Hang on, Johnny –

Is he talking to me? I look over – he is – he's calling me over, beckoning with his palm – *Hang around, Johnny, ah willnae be long.*

Who the fuck is Johnny? Does he mean my brother? No... Coincidence. This is my gaff. My howff. He can't even get my name right.

C'mon, c'mon – ah've something tae show ye –

I slowly, cautiously, make my way over. There's no rush, as he's still bantering away to someone else –

Heheh – aye – puir crazy man. Fucking – auld times, eh. New times now... Plans, ma brother, plans... Aye, ah'll tell you a' about it – look – aye – ah gottae go – aye, just... Right. Bye now, ya cunt.

And finally, finally, he holds the phone clear and out in his palm, pressing the red dot and ending the conversation.

Heheh. A'right, pal, sorry about that. Here, check this, by the way...

And he hands me the phone; the screen's black. I'm no' a phone guy, not sure what he's up to.

Swipe it. Swipe it. Go on!

I rub the screen with my thumb and, that very instant, I regret it, for there on his phone is a photograph of a half-naked Fi, stood in her jeans, bare from the waist up. She's in a room I don't recognise and looks younger, how she was pre-Georgie. What the fuck?

Heheh. There she is, man. That photo – mair too, eh – got me through prison – heheh.

He awaits my reaction, but there's nothing. I'm just shocked, agape, then –

You and I – we've both worn the same mitten, eh? Ken what I mean?

I can guess. What the fuck? Is this him getting to know me?

Dada… Dada…

We turn and through the door comes Fi, holding young Georgie. *Oh, hi, boys. Glad tae see you two talking. Getting along ok? Tommy – the pizzas are ready if you want tae go and get them out?*

I'm dazed, though, from the wonderful introduction.

Eh? Sure. Sure.

I hand him his phone back. *My name's Tommy. No' Johnny. John was ma brother.*

Ouch.

That's him telt, good and proper. I walk past Fi, tickle Georgie's chin and make my way to the kitchen, my face, my lugs bright red with embarrassment.

What a wee shite. He must have thought I didn't know… Was trying to get a dig in, make things clear… What's his fucking game, then?

I consider spitting on his pizza.

Funny thing, being clubbed around the head like that, then shifting from the scene so quickly. It's almost hard to believe the event happened at all. I begin to gather the pizzas and within a minute am so desperate to get back upstairs, to confront, if confrontation is needed, to query, to read his eyes…

Two pizzas at a time, though. His and hers. Me the dumb waiter.

As I reverse through the living room door, I turn to see young Georgie crawling, Fi and Simon beside him, beckoning him this way and that –

Go on, Georgie, go on, go tae Simon.

Heheh – here wee fella, eh – heheh –

But Fi, to her credit, when she sees me – *And there's yer da, look, in he comes…*

I don't throw the pizzas down, but I could have been more accurate. He – HE – Simon, that is, has to rearrange, adjust the plate, move it an inch or two when he sits down. Small victories, eh?

I do my best to smile a neutral, untroubled smile at Fi and Georgie. I raise my eyebrows. I catch sight of myself in the mirror and note that I look as though I'm constipated.

I nip back out to the corridor – *I'll no' be kicked outae my own house. No fucking chance* – straight down to the kitchen, gathering MY pizza, then straight back up, no stocktaking this time, no time for those twa thegither, no catching up, getting to know each other once more…

Upon my return, Simon has started eating. Eating and chatting.

Aye, it was something, like. Got taught a' sorts – bit o' joinery…

Fi's arranged the chairs so Georgie is between the pair of us and Simon's on the other side of the table. A clear divide, and one I am pleased to see.

… even some eejit wi' a guitar, eh. Coming in, trying tae get us tae write sangs aboot shite.

And did you?

Nah. Did ah fuck, man. Some o' the boys did, tho', eh – that Coco Gillespie cunt wrote ane ca'ed 'My Whole House Is Blue' but he got a fucking good kicking for it efterwards, ken. A' the boys giein' it, 'Oooh! My WHOLE house is BLUE', singing like dafties, winding him up. Aye, naebody wrote ony'hing efter that, eh, heheh.

Simon… Could you – Could you mebbe not swear so much in front of the bairn, eh?

Eh? How? He cannae even speak yet. He's just a wean…

Simon – I'm just asking you – dinnae swear in front o' George, ok? This is ma house. Ma rules. Got it?

There's a look, just then, of utter disdain, from him to me. Then he speaks – calmly.

Dinnae fucking tell me ony'hing, fatman.

I stand – to do what, I'm not sure.

Ok, ok, boys, calm down – I'm sure – I'm sure Simon will be mair careful, won't you, Simon?

I look at him – *Ya fucking wee prick.*

Simon, still seated, calmly continues eating his pizza before slowly saying – *Hey, Tommy. Nae swearing in front o' the wean, eh?*

I'm left standing there alone, upright, the other two eating away, ignoring me. What can I do? I sit back down. Fi leans over and rubs my knee –

So, what were you two chatting about, eh?

I look over at Simon, who smirks. *Och, I was just showing Tommy some photaes, eh? Ken, just the local wildlife? Eh, Tommy?*

What a prick, what a prick.

I lift a slice of pizza. There's little else joy here.

Ah cannae be working, Fi. Ah've got stuff tae sort oot.

But you said – You said, you could learn a trade here, that's what we agreed, that's what we signed – get you some hospitality experience, then you can move on and find work – proper work.

There's nae fucking chance –

Simon!

There's nae chance ahm working here. NAE chance. Ah've been inside for a'most two fucking years! Ah need ma freedom, ken?

Simon, there's nae arguing here – this is whit we agreed. If ye dinnae do yer bit, I'll just tick the box saying yer no' responding well and ye'll be back inside wi' yer pals. Is that what you want?

No, ye willnae.

He looks at her whilst chewing his pizza. He leans over and pops open another Budweiser, slurping it down, yellow liquid dripping onto the plate.

Aye, ah missed this.

But it's not Fi he's talking about, and there's some relief to be had there.

37

IN THE DAYS that follow, he's threatening, every movement a challenge – *Ahm no' cleaning that room, it's their fucking mess.*

Aye, but they're guests and they've gone, now it's your job…

How's it MA job? You do it. Whit YOU daen? Sitting at the bar having a sly half? Ah can do that…

So me having to call Fi every time, her telling him over and over – *It's part o' yer conditions, Simon. Ye ken ye have tae do it.*

Aye, fuck, it got me oot, but ahm oot noo, and fuck it if ahm cleaning folks' pish up. Fuck that. Ahm aff oot masel'.

And he pegs off outside, his ludicrous, attitude-ridden walk, hopping like a cowboy who's pished his kecks.

I'm just pleased to see the fucker go. It's easier to leave him be than to argue about every footstep he takes.

Give him time, Tommy, give him time. We shouldn't have been pushing him so hard on his first week. He'll come round.

Fi, he's a fucking wee prick. An absolute fucking dough-heid, and you know it.

And the one good thing throughout it all is I can see there's no spark between Fi and himself, and, thank Christ, there's not been one look from him to George. It's as though Fi's grown up and Simon, well, Simon's grown down. He's twenty-eight going on fourteen. For the first few weeks, he's barely there, really, off out enjoying his freedom. It's only when that freedom begins to tire that he starts looking closer to home for entertainment and finding, of course, a soft belly here. Free drinks? Free food?

He kicks up such an almighty fuss whenever I say no. I mean, he can have a pint, sure. And food – ok. I don't mind giving him £1.26's worth of beans and chips or whatever, but he's been reacquainting himself with his pals, pals who are in awe of his time inside, his experience – and am I feeding these pals? Na. Nae chance.

In they come, though, stenching the place out with cheap aftershave and a seeming lack of awareness of how to shower. *Pint o' Tennent's.*

Sure, that's a pound eighty.

Eh? Ahm wi' Simon, eh.

Sure. That's a pound eighty.

And the change slapped onto the bar, thrown down for me to count, bit by bit.

Auld Jock gets rattled, nudged, laughed at. He's not comfortable here, and our occasional hotel guests, they don't appreciate this local colour, the language, the volume.

Fi regrets it all, sure. She says, once – *At least George can be nappy trained.*

38

I PUSH SIMON. I continue to ask him to do jobs, the most menial of jobs. Vacuuming the corridors. Cleaning the gents'. He responds by running a mile. I know what I'm doing. I'm doing my best to be rid of the fucker.

Fi fills in that first report for the social worker, and she fills it in honestly, saying that he's *not helping*, is *drinking, associating with known troublemakers, disturbing the customer base, making no effort to fit in...*

I don't feel guilty. I continue. Ask him to clean the windows, replace the bog rolls. He sneers, walks out, chuckling.

But maybe I go too far. I do. For when Simon has a meeting with his social worker he learns there's a real threat that he might have to go and finish his sentence inside. Fi was sitting with him, doing her concerned parent bit, trying to be firm but giving him another chance, one last chance, one more opportunity...

And his priorities visibly change. His priority now is staying Oot. But not by working, not by fulfilling his obligations, his promises. No, by getting the right boxes ticked. He needs someone on his side, sees Fi and me and decides, quite rightly, that Fi is his route to that, his safety net. Sure, I'd kick him out on a cold winter night and not lose any sleep at all.

So, he does the bare minimum. He'll empty a bin or pick up a crisp packet, but it'll take him three hours to do so.

All the time his wee pals come by, sitting in the snug with him, drinking pishy instant-scooshed Diet Coke, laughing at me, taunting me – *Ah'll change yer beds, dinnae you worry, big man* – before turning right back around, audibly cursing – *Fucking clown*.

146

*

But he's no' daft and he knows he needs more security if he's to stay Oot.

First up: he blatantly flirts with Fi. Not sure if this is for my benefit or for hers, but sure it is for his. He sees it riles me and he continues to do it, mentions trips they've been on, tattoos he's had – *Mind when ah got THAT ane done, eh, Fi?* And she glances at me, blushing.

And then there's the touching – not Fi, at first, but me. A slap on my shoulders, a condescending pat on the back... I'm twice the cheuk's size, but there it is. Sapping my power, testing the ground, entering my space.

I'm not a fighter. I'm no tough guy, no saloon hustler. I'm big, sure, but that's just the ill luck of birth. I mean, I could be a bouncer at a church tea, mebbe, but I take up, inhabit the space rather than use it as a threat. I've spent my life trying to keep out of the way; I could never clout anyone. I know it. He knows it.

Fi, to her credit, pushes him away, talks him down. And not just when I'm there. I hear her – *No. No, Simon. Back aff. Get aff me...* And we talk of it, of course, but the bottom line is always the same – *Only a few mair months, Tommy, then he can fuck off away. He'll be out of our lives, but, at least I'll hae done MA bit. As a friend.*

39

One day, Simon inexplicably takes notice of George. It wasn't planned – at least I don't think so. George was just in his highchair, sitting in the bar, having his lunch. I had to jump up and serve an unexpected customer, but I had my eyes on George the whole time – we plan it like this, we're no' daft.

George dropped his wee plastic *Fireman Sam* spoon and began to wail.

I'd just begun pouring a pint and I heard George cry, sure, but I was helpless, tied to the pump by the mid-stream and my own politeness. And I think it was just the racket he was making – I can't see it being sympathy or empathy – but Simon, well, Simon, he walked over from where he'd been sitting playing with his phone, picked up the spoon and placed it back beside George... Now, why I reacted as follows, I do not know, but I did.

Get the fuck away fae him.

The customer looked at me agape, as did Simon. At first, interestingly, he was shocked and stood back from George. But then that snakelike confidence of his uncoiled and he grinned at me – *Ah was only helping wee Georgie out now, wasn't I wee Georgie, eh?* And then, that fateful moment, he leant towards George, my George... and stroked his hair.

I placed the sloshing pint down and made my way through from behind the bar –

Don't YOU fucking touch him, Simon.

Oh, aye? Smiling. *Or whit? Ahm just being friendly...* And then a moment, a thought, a tide of realisation. Slowly, he turns, grinning. *Well... and how auld is George now? Ah...*

And then the fucker winks.
Gotcha.

40

I'M THROTTLING THE wee bastard, but he's got way more experience than me and afore I know it he's away and picked a stool from the floor and hammered me over the head with it, the wooden leg clattering against my ear with a pain I've never felt, with blood running, but no, no blood, then tears running, and aye, real tears, nae blood, real tears. And wee Georgie, well, he's screaming now, and the customer is looking on amazed but calling to us – *Heysht – fucking – you twa!* And finally, FINALLY, Fi runs in and screams out – *STOP IT! SIMON, STOP IT.* And he lets go for a moment, long enough for one errant hand of mine, mid swing, to catch him round the nose and whack it. There's a crack and a bloody split.

TOMMY! Get aff him!

Simon is now on the floor, busted nose, busted pus, blood spurting out seemingly at random. A lucky hit. Feels good, though, sending the fucker down. But he doesn't appear bothered. He's just lying on his side with his upper body raised, like a mermaid. All laughing, though. The pain doesn't seem to register; there's just an impish glint in both his eyes. He turns and looks up at Georgie, then back to me, then up to Georgie and then to Fi – *He hit me first, mammy.*

The customer, well, he left when Fi arrived. Who can blame him? Not the place for a quiet afternoon pint, this place.

Fi gathers a towel for oor wounded hero and helps him to his feet, her arms around his, sitting him down. He shakes his head, but us – he and I, for there surely is a he and I now – our relationship has clearly moved into new territory.

*

Fi and I are in the kitchen, moving things about for no reason other than to share a talking space and work out what just happened.

He started it!

Ye sound like a bairn. GEORGE was there, for God's sake. And that customer…

My hand has swollen up. She sees me testing it –

Would serve you right, Thomas Bruce, if that hand is busted…

It's not. It's just sore, bruised. I can flex it, though, there's no pain, really. It's just – nippy.

You hit him first, Tommy.

Aye, but he's been pushing up to it – he…

There's NAE but, Tommy. If we want him outae prison, he cannae be haen fights.

What? I don't gie a shite if he's in prison or no'. I wish he was! He was – I shake my head in disbelief – *He was stroking George's hair, Fi!*

It doesn't shock her, but she takes it in. It calms her, if only a little – *Ach, Tommy, you just – You just have tae fucking leave it. You CAN NOT be fighting in front o' George. If I wanted tae be wi' a fighter, I'd've…*

You'd've what?

You ken fine well, Tommy Bruce. She continues to clear up, to move things from here to there and back again.

Fi, that wee shite has been pushing it fae the moment he arrived. You know – You know what he showed me, that very first day – a picture of you, half-fucking naked.

Whit?

I shake my head. *Aye… Just you, like…* I throw my arms up and I bite my lip. *It's just a' too much, Fi. He's… a fucking virus. We need rid o' him.*

Och, Tommy. Tommy, I'm so sorry… She takes my hand. *He was a decent boy at school, Tommy. I cannae forget that. He's had a shite run in life… His brother – his brother was a complete dick, but that's no' Simon's fault. I ken it's no'.*

I don't think she believes it anymore. How many chances has she given him now? On and off the pitch? In and out of bed?

Let's just… let's just sit tight. He'll be ootae oor hair soon enough.

*

It's hard to sit tight when there's a snake in the grass. That evening, that very evening, I'd been serving behind a quiet bar with my almost-busted hand, balancing Auld Jock's pint glass against my bandaged paw. Just as I'd chased the last straggler home, just as I was about to lock up, well, here's oor Simon after being out all day since the incident, quietly knocking at the glass door, as if he knows not to alert Fi to his homecoming, giving her no chance to arrive and give him grief.

I let him in. After all, I have the upper hand, no? Having gubbed the bastard?

I attempt a smirk, a knowing grin of the type he has shot me so many times, but with my kind, soft eyes it is useless and he bats it off, dismissive.

Heh.

He goes to shake my hand, but I pull it away, out of fear of the pain as much as distaste at the attempted handshake.

Sore, eh? He grins. *Check this oot.* He stretches, tiptoes, moves his nose close, closer to my own. *Ye see? Ye broke it.* His smile is so wide, teeth showing. *Aye, yer a cunt, right enough.* Then he darts up to kiss me, to peck my lips, and I flush, pull back, duck away. *Heh heh. Let's tak' a drink, Tommy boy. Talk this through.*

And I think – *Why the fuck not?*

My only experience of such situations is from movies, or from trying to ridicule Auld Jock when he comes out with some crackpot theory or other. I suppose it's like chess, and again, I've no experience there. So, what use was I? I tried to knock things away, but I suppose my… my poker face gave me away. But then I've never played poker, so my poker face is shite.

At every mention of Georgie, I slip. I blink. My breathing deepens, my answers shorten, my eyes twitch, my drink is supped quicker. And aye, Simon, he notices that. He will have picked up on Fi nagging me about the alcohol, although we tried – with everything, not just this – to be discrete, especially around him. So, Simon mentions

Georgie, watches me drink more, fills up my glass, and on and on. He's brewing something up, seeing how far he can take it.

Do ye think you and Fi'll get merrit, then?

Aye, mebbe.

A show of strength on my part.

Ah doubt it. She's no' the marrying type. Ah ken that.

I don't flinch. It's just guff. I know there's no chance he'd've asked her, and very little chance she'd have said yes, anyhow. But he continues —

Loads o' folk ken that, tae be honest.

He watches for a reaction, but there is none, I hope, I hope.

Aye, she's been around, oor Fi has.

I smile. A broad, fake smile. *Aye, well, so've we all, mate.*

Heh. Where've you been around? Around HERE disnae count. He gestures at the bar, the kitchens beyond. *Ah mean, oor Fi — she's...*

I ken what you mean. I'm no' a wean.

My insides are scrunched. The only place I've been around is the cash and carry. I mean, I wasn't a virgin afore Fi, but I wasn't far off. He's testing, looking for my weaknesses, I know that.

Heh.

He drinks his syrupy cola and tops it up with a slap of house vodka. The overall colouring gets lighter and lighter. Then, brazen, he sloshes a dram, maybe more, into my lager.

That stuff's pish, eh. Gie it some body, man.

I move my palm over my drink, protecting it. *There's body enough in there.* And as an excuse — *I'VE got work tomorrow.* I take a shot — *Some o' us work, ken? You should try it.*

But it misses. He doesn't give a fuck about work.

Oor Fi — she was a hot thing, eh? Shame you wrecked her, eh? What wi' young Georgie and a'...

My teeth, they are grit.

Aye, folk a' aboot giein' it, 'She'll never be the same, shame for us...' He watches for a reaction. *Never mind, we a' had a go on her, we've a' got the memories...*

I'm blazing, tensing inside. But what can I do? I can act the hardman – *Cheeky cunt, eh…*

It's weak, it slips out, but he stops smiling. *Watch yer language, pal. Aye, ye got me wi' a lucky punch, but ye ken fine yer no' match.* He stands. *Yer too saft. A saft underbelly. And aye – ah ahm a cheeky cunt, but ye'd better watch oot –* he finishes his drink, but clearly, deliberately, leaves the bottle of vodka right beside me – *as this cheeky cunt might just take that George far, far away fae you. He's MA blood. We both know that. And all I need to do is flick that switch, eh?*

He watches, waits for a reaction, but I cannot even make eye contact. I stare at the vodka bottle, willing my tears away. I hear – *Heh.* And then – *Just leave me be, dobber, and I'll mebbe leave YOU be.*

I don't finish the vodka, I just sip through what I have, tidy up and make my way upstairs to bed. I crawl in and quietly sob, weep into my pillow. And Fi, well, she slowly curls over, putting her arms around me.

41

THEY'RE IN THE next morn. Almost to the minute Fi leaves wi' Georgie to a playdate, Simon and a whole gang o' the shell-suited wee bawbags arrive, loud and swearing, cocks o' the north, pricks o' the Trossachs. What with their finery and bravado, it's amazing they even go outside to smoke.

I can't leave them. I stay at the bar, trying not to watch but watching nonetheless. When they see I'm not leaving, they slowly quieten.

I ask – *Can I help you guys?*

Eh? Nah.

C'mon, Simon, this is a business I've got here. Ye cannae just take up space and no' have anything –

Simon looks at me and smirks. *Aye, Tommy. Bring me some crisps. And lemonade.*

Then back to the whispering, the chatting.

I pour out the lemonades, bring over a variety of crisps.

That'll be three eighty, please.

Eh?

You heard me.

He shakes his head. *Tommy, fuck off.*

EH?

YOU heard ME. Now, fuck off.

The blood drains from my face. To their credit, the little cheuks stay silent, make no movement, no attempt to join in.

And Tommy?

Aye?

Get that fire going, eh. It's cauld as fuck in here.

*

They're not causing any trouble. They're quiet enough. I can leave them. Ach, what's crisps and juice? How long's he here for now? A couple more months, just? I can put up with that; I mean, it's not as though the bar's busy…

A car full of walkers arrives. Four lads my sort of age, burly – rugby players, perhaps. Simon and his gang depart in an instant. A blessing. Maybe there is still some respect there?

But that evening, when Fi and Georgie are safe upstairs, Simon returns alone. He stands by the fire, warming his hands, his legs. I will his tracksuit to burst into flames and burn him to a crisp, but to no avail, my telekinetic powers a sham.

Aside from Simon, Auld Jock's the only one in. The moment Jock makes for the cludgie, Simon's at the bar –

Get us a vodka, eh, Tommy?

I grimace, collect a small glass and deposit within it a solitary dram. Barely a dribble.

Heh.

He stares at it, then looks up.

Ah need that side room tomorrow.

Eh?

You ken. That wee room. I've got a meeting, and I cannae hae folk disturbing us.

A meeting, eh? Well, that was some high-level meeting he had earlier, sure enough…

I smile – *The snug? Fine, but so long as yer wee pals make space if there's a bus at lunchtime.*

Heh. He shakes his head. *Naw. You're no' listening. Ah need that side room. The snug. Tomorrow. A' day. Nae grannies, nae tourists, nae wee nippy dugs. Nae you. Ah'll sort folk oot for hospitality.*

Dinnae be daft, Simon. I cannae just – what if I need it? If a busload arrives, that's a big part of the income for the week…

He shakes his head — *Ah dinnae gie a fuck. Just keep oot. Well, clean it up the night, then keep the fuck oot tomorrow. Ok? Look… ahm trying tae sort things oot. Start a wee business. Then — then, Tommy boy, ah'll be ootae yer hair. This is for the both o' us, ken? It's for a' o' us, ken what I mean?*

The smirk on the boy.

I don't answer, but that's answer enough. He grins, then leaves for his room upstairs before I can gather strength to argue, debate, request. Midway across the room, he slows and launches a gob of phlegm directly into the fire.

I pour his unfinished vodka into the sink, wiping the bar where the glass had been sitting.

Auld Jock returns and slowly, carefully, makes his way back to the bar.

Where did that wee laddie go, eh?

I motion upstairs.

He's trouble, that yin. His whole family.

Aye, I'm beginning tae see that.

Dinnae you put up wi' ony shite, Tommy. This is your bar, and your father's afore ye. It'll pass on tae your wean, nae doubt. His type — he motions to the stair — *are nothing but dirt. Keep well ootae it, Tommy.*

42

Simon's down beforehand, meeting me in the kitchen, putting a few slices of bread into the toaster. He seems nervous, pacing, drumming his fingers. He ejects the bread long before it has toasted, scrapes on snails of the hotel butter and eats it, long before the butter has melted. I'm not openly watching, I'm doing some basic cleaning and organising, refreshing the crisps and such, jobs that require little thought. But with him there, jiggering up and down, there's plenty to think about.

Mind, leave us alone. End of.

He winks at me whilst simultaneously making a gunshot motion. I'm not sure if it's meant to be friendly or threatening, but certainly if anyone else had done it I'd've thought they were a game show host.

Sure. Just keep it down. Discreet.

A finger in the dam.

I have no idea what they'll be up to. Maybe he's just using it as a gang hut? A nervous chuckle escapes me at the thought. Maybe it'll be scuddy mags and cheap cider. Or a book group? Scalextrics? I doubt it, I doubt it…

I make my way through to the room in question and clear the tables. Well, wipe any crumbs onto the floor, straighten the chairs. I wonder if he'll want the fire lit?

I can't help but peek when his associates arrive. Some of them I recognise: scruffy wee shites from the area, usual post-school uniform of cacky-brown tartan and shell suits. This lot practically fall over themselves to get into the snug, pushing, mounting, almost, like bullocks in a pen. And they're rowdy once sat, their murmurs and squeals very audible in the bar itself, as though they're drunk at a wedding, a celebration.

Simon, though, he's barely in the room. I spy him popping out, popping back in. There's one guy with him, a lang guy, wee bit older than me, perhaps, completely dressed in denim – jeans, shirt and jacket. Almost an old man compared to the nylon-adorned cheuks in the snug.

In the main bar, I clatter glasses, gather beer mats, vacuum the carpet, wipe the windows, empty the ash from the fire, lay a new one, polish the pictures, straighten the tables. Jings, my nosiness is giving the bar a facelift, its first proper clean since God knows when. It's rewarded, though, as mebbe half an hour later, a car pulls up. A wee hatchback, not new, I'd guess, darkened windows, lowered wheels… A young schemie guy jumps out of the driver's seat. I can't make out who climbs out the other side, but one thing's for sure, it's no' Auld Jock.

Simon darts out of the snug and looks at me, warning me away, then hops out into the car park, his denim-clad accomplice with him.

For whatever reason, I choose this moment to back off. I don't want to be keeking through the window like an auld wifey behind net curtains. I retire to the fire, bending down as if to light it and only just, just turning around to see two, no, three folk alongside Simon and the denim guy.

The snug instantly quietens. Football terrace turned library. Filling the silence, the crackle of the infant fire, far, far too loud for me now as my ears strain to hear what's going on. Within a minute, though, there's clumping, dragging, doors opening, closing, muttering. I stand to see and, well, all of the youngsters, the local posse, they've been dismissed, herded out into the car park. I watch for a moment as they light cigarettes, puff themselves up, try to work out why THEY have been dismissed, but before too long, certainly less than half the length of a smoke, Simon storms out and yells at them – *Go on! Fuck off. Ah'll be in touch*. Doesn't even await their replies, almost runs back to the snug, shaking his head.

The boys, the kids, the juniors, they silence, stay their ground for a breath, then slowly turn and walk away, cursing, spitting, gesticulating.

And then, quiet. I polish the bar over and over.

A while later, Fi returns from some infant group thing, Georgie cradled close. I walk around to the front of the bar and kiss her, taking Georgie, who's asleep.

Who are a' those guys?

I shake my head – *I've no idea. Simon just… Well, he just brought them in.*

Fuck's sake.

Aye.

She places down her michty collection of bags – her handbag, a nappy-changing thing, a bag of toys and cardboard books. *Were ye drinking last night, Tommy?*

Eh? No. I mean, I had a last beer after Auld Jock left, but no more. Look – I motion around at the bar, as spotless as it's ever been – *I've got a' this done.*

Because I couldn't do that if I were hungover.

She raises an eyebrow as if to say – *You should be cleaning to this basic level every day, Tommy*. It's almost as though I were ridiculing myself. She looks at the fire, unusually well going for a room empty aside from Fi, George and me.

Have we a busload coming in?

Oh, I haven't heard. I've been – I nod towards the snug – *keeping an eye on things. Do you know – do you have any idea what Simon's up to?*

No. Nae idea. I can have a word…?

But no, that's the last thing I want, him with her. *Them* with her. I want Simon out. I want Fi with me. Her and George with me.

Nah, dinnae bother, it'll just be… it'll blow through, whatever. We'd be best… keeping out of it.

*

There is a busload, tho'. And this doesn't please Simon. Birmingham dude, never the quietest of folk, bursting through the front doors, giving his Scottish history lessons to his tourists at the top of his hollering voice, opening the snug door, seeing the assembled crew and loudly apologising – *OH, SORRY GUYS, DIDN'T SEE YOU THERE* – then away, leading the tourists – a mixed group, mostly Japanese, this time – straight through to the bar – *HELLO, TOMMY! Ok, you fellows sit down there.* Once everyone's seated, he turns to me –

Ah, you've cleaned up, thanks for that, Tommy, helps everyone, that does. Good fire you've got going. Now, are the ovens all warmed up? He's rubbing his hands together.

They are, yep.

They are not.

Right then! Let's get the menus out and the orders in. Full house today, Tommy. What did we agree again? Two quid a head? That's £36 I'll be due – just make it a straight forty, I won't complain. Here, you two, you two…

A pair of elderly tourists are straying back into the corridor, arm in arm –

He beckons them back – *Toilet's this way, this way…*

This is a fine posse he's raised.

I nip back into the kitchen and quickly turn the ovens on. They take an age to heat, these blasted old things. Maybe I'll pre-microwave everything, speed the process up. Heck, Birmingham dude doesn't care, so long as he gets his moolah, and these guys are hardly locals, returning custom, are they? Fuck 'em, I've got plenty of other things to worry about.

The orders come in. Sausage, sausage, sausage. How many fucking sausages does one man have to cook in his life? I wonder when I'll cook my final sausage? Hopefully forty, fifty years from now. And not in here. In some wonderful, spacious apartment in southern Spain. Somewhere warm. Fi and George at my side, mebbe. George an auld guy himself then…

Looking just like Simon.

Heh.

I dismiss the thought, open can after can of cheap beans, add a bit of salt and pepper, a scoosh of tomato puree and garlic paste to thicken them up. Awfy things, these beans, like rabbit droppings in dishwater soup.

A mountain of frozen chips, spread them, even them out on the first baking tray, then the next. Shove them straight in, the oven barely warm, let alone hot. Ach. It'll mean more drink, more crisps selt. The fire's lit, everyone's comfortable...

I wonder if Simon's guys would want some chips?

I knock on the snug door and enter, without waiting for an invitation.

All five heads turn and look directly at me. None of them looks particularly friendly. In fact, I'd say Simon, although scowling, seems the friendliest of them all.

Umm, do you guys... want some chips?

As one, the four other folk turn their glares to Simon, who speaks –

Whit? No. We dinnae want any fucking chips. Clear aff. He flicks his hand as though swatting a fly.

Ok, ok. I'm tempted, though, so tempted and – aye, why not –

How about a sausage? I put on a Butlin's smile, but Simon stands, which I take as a NO. *Ah, ok, lads. Well, you know where I am.* I wink. *Enjoy your morning.*

43

A H, THE CONFIDENCE of youth. He has me square up against the kitchen wall and is brandishing a small but very sharp-looking Lino knife.

Fucking 'ENJOY YER MORNING'? Ah TELT ye tae stay OOT. Ye fucking stupid, TOTAL CUNT.

The bar's empty, Fi and Georgie away...

All ah fucking asked was quiet... and you – and those eejit tourists, popping their heads in, fucking Chinese, asking for the bogs or some shite...

Japanese.

Eh?

Japanese, I think?

Fuck's that got tae do wi' it?

I don't know. Just...

Ah tell you, if you've fucked things up, you're fucking getting it. This place – THIS PLACE is fucking getting it. And ah dinnae gie a shite WHO'S inside when it happens. You understand?

I nod – *Aye, aye, I do.* I don't, but it's a threat, I recognise that, a threat and a knife.

And see that daft English cunt? Keep him well awa'. Fucking blurting in and talking about buses and shite – as if ah gie a fuck about his fucking bus! Did you send him in, eh? Did you?

Ah shite, I didn't realise that – *No, no, o' course no'. He's just a bit – friendly –* and then – *You know, that's not a bad thing.*

I learned then not to wind up a man with a knife. He shakes his head.

Dinnae be a fucking prick, Tommy boy. Next time. Next time... He turns to leave, then stops, returns and quickly raises the Lino knife right to my face and, with a little flick, he cuts my lip.

I collapse, crouching to the floor.

Aya – fucking…

Heh.

My hand's to my mouth and there's blood, not a huge amount, but blood.

Aye, you fucking stay doon there, Tommy Bruce. Learn yer fucking place.

I look up, expecting a kick, perhaps, but Simon just leers down at me, tips his baseball cap and leaves.

I hold myself together pretty well for Fi, but when she comes in, she's altogether somewhere else –

Tommy, I've had some news. I'm gonnae have tae – but then seeing my busted pus – *Oh! Tommy! What the fuck happened tae yer lip?*

She's fearing the worst, fearing Simon, I know it, though neither of us say it.

Ach, it was a broken glass. Didnae spot it. Glass o' lemonade cut my lip.

Was it? Was it, Tommy?

I have a bar towel held against it. The bleeding is slowing. I'll give Simon this, if all he intended was a small nick and the fear that follows, well, his aim was true.

Ye cannae – dinnae… She circles round me, looking up, taking the bar towel away. *A bar towel, Tommy? C'mon. At least fucking put a… a bandage on it.*

Ach, it'll heal.

Listen, Tommy, I've had word fae Gran's pal. Gran's had a fall… Are you sure this was a glass, Tommy? It disnae look like a glass cut.

It was a glass. I was there, I remember. I smile. Then try to change tack – *What's happened to your gran? Is it bad?*

I've no' idea, but she's in hospital and I need tae head on over…

Can – can yer ma no' go?

Stupid question.

Fi's dabbing at my lip as we talk, the cut scabbing but still slowly weeping blood.

I dinnae think they're coming back, by the way. Simon didn't, um, seem to think this was a suitable venue.

No?

No.

Good.

Aye. Ouch! It stings, I tell you that. Fi says sorry and backs off, but it wasn't her; maybe there was some auld vinegar or garlic on the towel and it's gotten inside the cut… She throws the tissue away and quickly wets another before holding it up to my mouth.

You know, I – I blame masel' for Simon and whit's happened. He needed ma help, Tommy. I wisnae there for him when he needed me. Simple. I shouldae been. But he was… too much. Too much.

I pull my head away from her, from the sting of the cut.

Sorry, Tommy.

Nae worries.

Slowly, slowly, the blood congeals, the flow crawls, then stops. I appreciate this intimacy, the love of Fi's hands.

So, um, when are you off – to see your gran?

She dabs her final dab. *Pretty much now, Tommy. And I'll take wee Georgie, if you don't mind. There's space for us both at Gran's. I'll stay over there a night or two, it'll save me driving back and forth tae the hospital and –* she's finished, leans back to admire her handiwork *– there's too much going on around here.*

Ok. I nod. *That makes sense.*

I just want George far away from Simon. That's my concern, more so than what Simon could try or do with me, though I've nerves enough about that.

I'm handed Georgie while she packs. I bounce him around, I drill my eyes into his, I smile, he smiles, I feel the love, I warm… I balance him on the bar, he giggles. I lie on the floor and he slides down my belly, sooking on my finger, hugging my neck… It's all too quick, too short, before she's back downstairs and gathering him up, kissing my cheek. I help load the car, strapping him in, keeping him safe, I hope.

And the moment they pull off in our wee four-by-four… Well, at that very moment I retreat to the bar to sample the new ale.

44

EVENING, 8:00 PM: the rain is falling and the bar is empty, except for the cat, myself and the ever-reliable Auld Jock. His easy, undemanding company soothes me into a relaxed mooch, and we can quickly settle back into our old groove of little shared interest except company and alcohol. We slowly sup away, discussing the weather, the rugby – as if I have a real care for that, but I know enough to chatter on, or at least to listen to his chatter. There's no mention of Fi, but there's a look in his eye throughout, as though he's trying to read me or let me know he's willing to talk, should I need...

My lip, it throbs. Auld Jock glances but doesn't ask. Glances again...

I used to feel as though I were Jock's counsellor, the only guy he'd speak to all day, before the realisation hit me that he was probably feeling the exact same way about me. Perhaps he'd promised my father he'd keep an eye on things.

When there's no talk, we relax, no problem, no first-date nerves keeping us yapping. I turn the music up a wee bit, Planxty on now, a welcome change from the mystical-highlands, reverb-laden, tartan-socks stuff Fi puts on.

Jock disappears with a guttural – *A'right* – his signal that he's off for a cigarette, or perhaps to the cludgie. A minute later, and there's the clink of the front door. I automatically look over, expecting, perhaps, Jock to be leaving and preparing to wave my goodbyes. But no, it's the older guy who was with Simon earlier, on the edge of drookit from the rain but instantly recognisable in his denim outfit. He approaches the bar, pulling wet hair from his face, and smiles. He looks vaguely familiar, in the way faces around here always do, the gene pool boiled for many a generation before folk began making their ins and outs to and from places as exotic as Edinburgh or Glasgow.

He offers a friendly – *Hello, I saw ye earlier, mind.* He sits at the bar, takes Auld Jock's place, but quickly moves when Jock arrives back moments later, coughing to announce his return. He even apologises – *Just warming yer seat, auld timer.*

Jock ignores our guest. *Another half please, Tommy.*

Ah'll get it, here – And denim boy hands over a tenner enough for both him and Auld Jock's drinks.

No. I dinnae want yer money, Billy. I'll get ma own, thanks very much.

Billy, eh? Well, this Billy's not bothered by Jock's refusal, just carries on the charm, smiling and rubbing his stubble. I begin to place him, take some years off his face, reimagine him as I might have known him…

Billy… Billy… Were you no' pals wi' Simon's brother – that Jim Blair?

Ah was indeed. Known him all ma life. He winks and sups, shoogling on his chair as though pleased I know, as though it's saved him introducing himself, his past strengths, accomplishments.

So… so what you doing round here now then? I thought – did I no' hear you'd moved…

Or been moved. Was he not moved into one of Her Majesty's more secure hotels? I never kept too tight a rein on that type of gossip…

Aye, ah had. But ah moved back. Twelve months early. He grins then, as though he's played the trump card. *Nice place, this. Ah mind it fine fae when we were younger. Yer da ran this place well, Tommy.*

Did you drink here, then?

Hmm. No. Yer da wisnae so keen on ma lot!

Aye, so he was part of that crew that my father hated so. Why would he boast about that? Or even let me know? What a fud. I don't reply. Not sure entirely what this dowp wants, but a reply is certainly part of it. I make to clean, to wipe, to restock…

He tries again.

Ye ken, this is a nice wee business again, Tommy. Guid tae see ye daen it up. Young Fi —

My chest tightens.

Aye, I can see why young Fi would feel at hame here — ah mean, obviously wi' yersel, a man o' charm and virtue. A fine figure o' a man. Ah mean — ye've obviously kept yersel fit...

He laughs, overly loud, looking to Jock for support, but Jock, bless him, is visibly creeped by this Billy guy.

I wonder to myself — *Mebbe I should become a fighter? Mebbe life would be easier if I could just clobber these clowns? Put all this weight to good use...*

What's your point, Billy?

Och — his head's chicken-pecking, roving around as though it's dancing to some inaudible music — *nothing, just making small talk.* A pause. Then — *Simon was reckoning someone could do well wi' a place like this...*

I wipe the bar for the thirtieth time. There's a small chuggy stain from long since past, and I push at it, over and over.

Someone could... well, run a guid business fae here.

Aye. And somebody does run a good business here — me.

Ha! Aye, nice ane, Tommy, nice ane.

Jock's been silent, but he beckons to his glass — *Fill me up, Tommy.* It's a rare third drink for the Jockster. He's keeping me company, keeping an eye on things. If I were less charitable, I'd say he's fishing for fresh gossip, but that's not Jock's style at all.

Sure thing, Jock. I shift my body his way, purposefully ignoring Billy. *What do you reckon to this ale, then?* It's called 'Yellow-Spot Gold', a meaningless phrase that no doubt originated in a marketing meeting somewhere.

Heh. It's as soor as that last lot ye got in...

I laugh — *Aye, they're curious beasts, these real ales...*

Billy seems unhappy at this breaking of his spell, his removal from the limelight. He speaks once more — *Ye ken... See oot yonder —* he beckons to the car park — *ah lost ma virginity oot there.*

Fuck's sake. I shake my head and Jock grunts his fatigue, his disapproval. Billy reads it all as contempt but reacts as though it's banter –

Ha. No, seriously, though. See, before ye got those big bins in? Mind, when it was that auld half-shed thingy?

I remember. It was like a bus shelter, supposed to protect the bins from the elements, and the visitors from the scruff of the bins. Pretty soon it became amuck with grease and sodden food wrappers, and a fate worse than death was being asked to clean it out.

Aye, well – get this – ah fucked that Louise McColl lassie behind there. Mind her? Richt dirty cow...

He laughs – noticeably alone – then laughs again, attempting to hook us in, but Jock and I are embarrassed and silent. I'm looking at Billy with curiosity, but I am not embracing this banter, indulging this false camaraderie. Jock neither, so it seems –

Ye ken how I minded Billy here, Tommy?

I shake my head – *No, no Jock.*

Well, it was quite the thing. See, Billy here has the... maist peculiar o' nicknames, don't ye, son?

Eh? Ah – fucking leave it, Jock. That was years back... He straightens himself. *Nae cunt ca's me that now – nae cunt DARES, ha!*

Ah. There we go. Here comes the hard mouth – but, no, it wisnae the mouth that I was thinking o' –

Shut the fuck up, Jock. Shut. The. Fuck. Up.

Heh. Ye dinnae scare me, Billy. Ye see, I was there when ye got that nickname –

My memory's ticking, trying to dredge the name up, but I can't quite remember – *What nickname, Jock?*

Well, when he was – what – fourteen years auld, Billy? Him and that Jim Blair were done for lifting items fae the Co-op there, tho' it was an independent back then... And Billy here –

Shut it, Jock, ahm warning ye –

Well, Billy here had an accident in his troosers, didn't ye, son? When the polis came? Whit is it they ca'ed ye efter that? Billy the Keich, was it?

That's it! Billy the Keich – what a dobber...

Ah, fuck off... It wisnae keich, it was just a wee bit o'... Ye think –

ye think ah willnae fucking batter ye, ye auld cunt? Yer a saft fucking target, grandad. Ah'd watch yer fucking step if ah were you.

He's furious, embarrassed, red-faced, flustered. Came in here the King of Cool, ooted as a feart wee shiter.

Ach, calm doon, Billy. It's just banter, eh? I'm just letting Tommy ken, just in case...

Just in case what?

Just in case he draps a glass and you kek yer breeks in fright!

And that's it, this blue-clad fool grabs elderly Jock – who looks genuinely shocked at the pace of the escalation – and pulls him off the stool and onto the ground.

Get aff me, ya clarty wee bastard – Jock's calling out and I'm round the front of the bar as fast as I can, pulling this Billy guy from Jock, who's now an undignified, dishevelled mess on the floor, his combover awry, one brown shoe off, exposing a filthy yellow sock.

Ah fucking telt ye, grandad! Ah fucking warned ye – tell me ah didnae, eh? Tell me ah didnae!

Jock slowly shifts his weight to his elbows, then he's sitting up, a small trail of blood seeping from his mouth. He uses a finger to delve inside, examine. *Heh. Heh. Well. Well done, Billy. Yer father would be proud: ye've knocked a very auld tooth fae the mouth o' a very auld man. Congratulations.* My arms are still wrapped around Billy as Jock slowly pulls his way up using the bar stool, then the bar itself. Jock's breathing is now loud and fast, and that's no wonder, his heart must be working double-speed. *Heh, Billy, Billy... Well, ye telt me guid and proper. Whit a HARD man.*

Billy is quiet. He should be ashamed. He's given up any fight with me, his arms loose, shoulders down. I lessen my grip but keep hold of his jacket sleeves.

Jock straightens himself out, pats down his clothing, adjusts his shirt, walks to the fire and spits a glob of phlegm and blood into it before hand-combing his hair and putting on his cap, making it very obvious he's leaving. *Aye, Billy the Fucking Keich. Once a coward, a'ways a coward. If I were twenty years younger... I'll see ye the morra, Tommy. I hope the stench will hae left the building by then.* He looks at

Billy once more, up and down, up and down, disapproving, revolted, then he's off, no looking back.

He'll have tears, no doubt, when he gets outside. The shock of it. We watch him depart before I release my grip from Billy and quickly move away, out of such close proximity. I pick up Jock's stool, which is still scuttled on the floor, and finally speak – *Fuck do you think yer doing, Billy? He's an auld man, just.* I shake my head.

He fucking had it coming, ye ken he did.

Eh, dinnae bring me intae it. Fuck you doing here, anyway? C'mon – finish up. I'm going to close the doors. This place has lost its appeal this evening.

Eh? Hold on, hold on. We still need to sort something out, Tommy. You and I.

I look at him, my disgust still evident – *If you've got any apologising to do, you need to say it to Jock there, no' me. Fucking fighting an auld man over a bit of banter...*

He's quiet. Then – *Thing is, Tommy, we'll need the bar tomorrow again, eh.*

What? – *Who? Who's 'we'?*

Me. And Simon. Simon, he needs it.

Here we go... I play it cool, relaxed – *The snug, you mean?*

He shakes his head. *No. The whole bar. Well, this room and the snug. Thing is, Tommy, we dinnae even need the bar, the snug is fine – it's just... we cannae hae folk haw-hawing intae the snug while we're discussing business, ken? We've got PROPER folk coming the morra. We need – peace. Guaranteed.*

I laugh – *There's no way I'm closing the bar. There'll be a busload turning up and that's all that keeps this place afloat. Fi's no' for renting the rooms out whilst Simon's up there, so – no – we need the bar open a' day. You can see – I gesture to the empty bar – that's it. Auld Jock taking his half pint willnae even pay for the cat food.*

He sooks his teeth – *Aye, ah was worried ye might think that but – well, it'd be guid for us, ken, if the bar was empty...*

How good?

Eh?

172

How much good? Are you talking hiring the bar? 'Cause, you know, I've done it before, for weddings and that…

I know he's not. He knows he's not. But we can play that game for a while, sure.

Well, Tommy. Whit do ye reckon? Mebbe we could talk about value… Whit's the glass in a' these windaes worth, for example? His arm's back behind him, pointing to the pub's windows, but he is very much facing me. It is very much a threat.

But I laugh it off as though it's a game – *Fuck off, Billy…*

Eh?

C'mon, Billy, fuck off. Yer no' scaring anyone. I'm no' a fucking auld man. I'm no' Jock. This is shite, you and wee fucking Simon wi' yer 'business' bullshit. What is it? Some government start-up scheme for repeat offenders? Just… meet them up the road. In the bus shelter, mebbe?

Tommy, Tommy… Yer no' listening.

He reaches into his pocket and slowly, proudly, removes a packet of cigarettes. He delves a tarred, yellowing finger in and pulls a fresh cigarette out, holding it to his lips, mimicking smoking, watching for my reaction.

Ye ken, Tommy, sometimes yer best – he pulls out a lighter, a Zippo emblazoned with the Rangers Football Club crest, and sparks the flint, lights the flame – *just tae do as yer asked.*

And he lights the cigarette.

And what's a boy to do? *C'mon. you can't smoke here…* Ah, Fuck it. *You know – I've had enough – Just – get the fuck out of my bar, eh?*

He wipes his nose, looks at his pint, pulls on his cigarette, ponders his reply, then slowly, calmly speaks– *Fuck aff, is it? Oh. Ah didnae realise ah was dealing wi' a HARD man. Well, that changes everything, changes everything. See, ah've met a few hardmen… Ye could say that ahm mair comfortable wi' them than you would be, Tommy.*

Listen up, Billy, this is my life right here and I'm no' moving out. No' for a day, no' even for a moment. You understand? And then *Do you understand eh?*

He blows the front of his cigarette, the way one would do to keep a joint alight, but there's no need here other than for the show of it, the drama.

You fucking prick… Well, ye've asked for it, so here's whit we'll do, Tommy. Tomorrow morn, you leave the door unlatched so we can get in. We'll close the bar. If ye dinnae – then… If yer around, daen this 'hardman' thing, or getting in the way – or seen, even – if yer so much as seen cleaning the bar, Tommy boy – then, well. We'll see aboot who gets tae fuck aff, we'll see who's the fucking hardman. Oh – and one thing, Tommy? Ye'll be needing tae change yer optics –

He motions behind me towards the vodka, the whiskies, the rum. I turn, momentarily surprised at this change in tone, this neighbourly stocktaking advice, but as I face away, I spy in the bar mirror Billy raising his glass then throwing it, straight at me. I duck, but it skelfs off ma heid and smacks into the surface where I cut the lemons for the drinks, shattering glass all over the plastic mixer bottles, the lemons themselves. I automatically sink into a crouching position, down like a wean, hands over my head, waiting for the rain of glass to end.

Aye, yer some hardman, Tommy Bruce. That's that sorted, then – ah'll no' be seeing ye the morra… Agreed?

I don't reply. I cannot see him, perched way down here, but I am sure as fuck that at this point he would have winked.

And ane mair thing: if ye ever, EVER ca' me Billy the Keich again, ah'll carve yer fucking face aff. Got it?

The exit door opens, then closes. I wait a moment, a moment longer, then I'm up and straight over to that same door. I open it wide, and I shout into the gloom –

I'll be here tomorrow. I'll be here a' day. Ye dinnae frighten me, Billy. Billy the Fucking Keich!

A second, a second longer, then – silence.

Close the door. Lock the door. Slide the double lock.

Fuck's sake.

I return to the bar and begin to pick up the broken glass, sweep the mess, restore the dignity of this old place. There's a michty nervous shake in my hand for which I prescribe myself a whisky. Billy left his cigarette to burn, and it goes straight onto the fire. The place now holds the odour of cigarette, and although it's unlikely the polis – or anyone – will drop by now, at this hour, I scour around for any further evidence of the illegality and equally for anything I can throw on the fire that might disguise the smell – auld crisp packets, sodden beer mats...

Fucking Billy...

I stoke the fire, raise some flame.

Who'd run a hotel, eh?

Fuck, I feel sick. The nerves, no doubt.

I laugh to myself – *Choose somewhere else, bozos, for the sheriff here is surely too fierce.*

Stubborn, fat and drunk.

A sickness is swelling in my stomach.

Fucking Billy. And that fucking cunt Simon.

My heart is racing.

This is the loneliest hour, even without the drama. This is what Fi was so good at, accompanying me through this twilight zone, distracting me from the questions, the worries, the fears. She'd always leave the place looking braw, and the continual shock of arriving downstairs to a bar that was *tidy* and *welcoming* was never tiring.

I do my best. I straighten chairs.

Fuck it, there's no one else coming in, is there? What am I tidying for? More to cleanse my thoughts of Billy than anything else. Out of sight, out of mind and all that.

Fuck's sake.

I switch off the music.

What to do? What to do?

Just the silence of the bar, the crackle of the fire. Embrace it, Tommy boy, love it. Remember it for when Fi is here, share it, though alone now. Think of Georgie, think of next week, think of anything other than the here and the now.

And that Billy. Don't think of that Billy.

I wonder if Simon will be staying here tonight, even. He's so rarely in it's almost pointless him being registered here with the social worker folk, especially with Fi being away too – how exactly are we supposed to be helping him?

Empty the bins, lock up, last whisky, sleep. Ok? And, well, maybe some food. Crisps? I couldn't stomach a burger. Sheesh. Call it a diet. A fricht diet. Losing weight by raising blood pressure.

Back behind the bar, sweep up any missed debris, dispose of the lemons, cut or not, lift any bar towels caught in the area of the glass shower, put them all, all this crap, straight into a thick black bin bag.

Some council dowp was round a few years back about recycling and such, but the multicoloured bins are rarely adhered to by me, especially at this time of night. Whichever's emptiest, they get the bulk of it. Who'd be picking apple cores from loo-roll holders? Ach.

Hoik the sack out of the bin, heavy enough now, with a few days' discarded food, beer mats, dead lemons, melted ice cubes – that'd be water – and paper towels. I lift and observe, just for a moment, weary from past experience of bin bag leakage, but nothing, so up – up and onto my back, an off-season Santa now, bringing my sack of gifts to the rats. Back to the front of the bar, on my way outside.

Unlock the door. Listen for that Billy.

There's a shard of cardboard within the bag, digging into my lower back. I'm guessing it's that old crisp box that I threw out, first stamping on it, ripping it where I could, breaking it down – but still an irritant, something to hurry me out, into the cold.

No sign of anyone, no one at all. Not that I'm scared, not me.

Maybe another time, if I'd been more together, had less to drink, I'd have worn a coat, but it's such a short walk to the bins. Putting this bag down, dressing up for it seems such a hassle. Never mind, I'll be cold, then, but for less than a minute. I shove the door further open with my foot and squeeze out, the belly on my front and the litter on my back causing some friction, but done many a time and eventually I'm out and, ok, straight over to where I know the bins are, not waiting for my eyes to adjust to the darkness, my body noticing the light snowfall, the sharp bite of the cold. I trudge further into the dark, weary now, keen for the warmth of my bed, wishing I'd called Fi earlier, wondering how her gran is, more how Georgie is, if he misses me...

I slowly lower the bag down among the others in one of the bins, aware that any quick movements could split the thing and spread more rubbish around this already beastie-ridden haven of filth.

Job done, I relax, I stretch, arch my back and look up to the stars, a few visible through the cloud. I wonder about Fi and where she is now. I smile. For all the effort, she's worth it. Fi's worth it. And what a gift Georgie is, eh? Despite it all, despite it all.

The next sensation I feel is a colossal thump on the back of my neck and, within a second, I'm overcome by a deep, warm, black rush of blood to the head, and there I am, face down in the muck, the grease, the stench and then – oot.

Part III

45

I COULD SAY I woke up, but it didn't feel like any wake up I'd ever experienced. It felt more like coming to in a muffled world, a sensory hell. All the comfort of a morning awakening was gone: no peace, no bird call, no warmth, no Georgie, no Fi... Just pitch black, my face being repeatedly lifted and shunted back onto a gritty, cold floor... And the noise, as though my head were just about to be inserted into a woodchipper. But overriding it all, overriding this cacophony of pain and confusion, was a sharp, screaming complaint from the back of my neck and the realisation that I could move neither my arms nor my legs. I could breathe, though – that's one thing...

This isn't a hangover. This cannot be a hangover.

Am I lying on a stone? I lift my head and try to turn, to adjust my body, but a stabbing in my chest keeps me where I am, the movement pressing, pushing onto this pressure point. Just another pain to be aware of, not the worst, but there. And it's not a stone, no. I'm in some kind of vehicle, for sure, and we're most definitely moving.

I take a long, deep breath but taste nothing but thick stour. My head falls, and I can feel the various sharp aches throbbing, communicating to one another. I wonder how my body's going to look after all this? The to-ing and fro-ing of the adrenaline and the noise, the confusion... The vehicle leaps – and for one split second I brace myself for the pain of the landing, for how it will affect my face, my ribs, my torn arm muscles – but when my head collides once more with the flat, hard, surface, it's worse than I could possibly have imagined and the strength of it all momentarily knocks me straight back out.

Tommy the Bruce

*

After this, I learn my lesson. Each time I come to, I do my best to stay still or safe, to stay conscious, awake – after all, I cannot move, cannot control anything else... My blood is coursing round me as though in gangs, huge clusters of warmth flooding to my shoulders, pumping into my head, aching into my neck. My aching ribs? Well, now they seem to be an afterthought. Another bump in the road and my head slams down hard once more.

46

THE DINGHY IS not much bigger than I am, and I am too young to be sitting in it. I mean, it's ok for hunting for crabs, sitting two or three feet in the water, but here, out amongst the rocks, a good sixty feet from the shoreline, well, it feels very insecure. As though John and I are on a sheet of cardboard that has been fashioned into a boat for dolls by following the instructions of a bairn's television programme.

Bright, bright orange dinghy; my skin pale blue-pink; the hairs on our arms sticking right out from fear and attempting to capture some warmth; our terrible, baggy swimming costumes soaking wet and freezing cold. The water is a deep green. I haven't been able to see the bottom for quite some time and, although we are in a natural harbour, just beyond that is the open sea, a sea whose waves are entering now, blustering us up and down, small exploratory splashes entering the side of our vessel, intruding, testing my response...

John is grabbing me, crying, jumping. *Stay still! Stay still!*

My response is to scream, of course. To stand then fall quickly, as I cannot stand on a flimsy bit of plastic. But scream I can, and I do, but every lurch, every wave of my arms destabilises my situation once more. And I am no swimmer, no lithe hero, ready to race ashore and save myself, save John...

A chocolate wrapper floats by surrounded by grey bubbles, sitting on the slipstream, on its way to the sea. There are a dozen seagulls watching me, or so it seems. Perhaps waiting for me to fall? I've seen them taking ducklings; I doubt they'd have any qualms pecking my ears or nipping the skin loose on the base of my back. I scream once more – *Mummy! Mummy!*

John's wet himself. His face is bright red from the fear and the shame. He joins in, kicking the base of the dinghy, panicking, panicking – *Mummy! Mummy!*

Surely someone sees us? I can see them all, back on the safe haven of the golden beach – and I am shouting, waving my paddle, John is screeching in my ear... I am terrified. Surely, Mum can feel our terror from there? She doesn't even need to hear us, does she?

There's a crack from within my chest and that particular rib is surely broken in two now. That earlier sensation was mere child's play. THIS is the pain, right here. The shriek from my neck is muffled, the dead arms long forgotten as my nervous system makes way for the Champion Huckster, the Lord of All Pain, the repeatedly battered cracked rib with its dizzying threats of Punctured Lung and Internal Bleeding. Come, come and witness that all is lost, all is gone, as we swim amongst the endorphins and the – have no doubt – tears...

And I clasp the paddle to the rocks and I sit wee John down but he's not for quietening so I hold him up, I hold him close to me, the retreating tide pulling, tempting us, the gulls encouraging, and the rock – the rock's slipping from under the paddle, allowing us our leave. We're just two more living beings, mere flecks in a rock's existence, flecks to be ignored, and we swirl off, facing away from it now. We attempt to turn but lose balance once more, we freeze dead still, but John or me or both of us too close to the edge now and the water rushes over the side, the dam burst, and just, just over John's head I can see Mummy standing, jumping, and it's her turn to scream now.

I'm being shaken from side to side as though within a cement mixer. I count the beats but there's no regular rhythm – it's more like a free jazz wig-out than a four-on-the-floor ceilidh dance. To the discordant, pattern-free clatter, I find myself mouthing, whispering a song my father would sometimes softly sing:

The waves they do grow high ah the waves they grow so green,
The day is past and gone, my love, that you and I have seen.
It's a cold winter's night, my love, when I must bide alone,
For my bonny boy is young but a-growing.

And just at that moment, it all stops.

47

ALTHOUGH THE MOVEMENT and the clattering, tormenting bedrock of noise have ceased, my blood seems to lift me, as though I am still afloat. My ears fill the silence with a high-pitched ringing and a sound not unlike uncooked rice being emptied onto a drum, over and over, less then more, less then more – a tide? Waves? Or – rain? There's an ache in there and when I move my head there's a most peculiar sensation, as though somebody is emptying a bucket of water into my ear canal, every time I move, every time I move... And my stomach suddenly heaves but the rib pushes it back, reminding it of its place, until the stomach aggresses once more and my body pushes, convulses, and though there's no purchase for my arms, no way of shunting my legs either this way or that, the vomit comes out anyway it can – my nose, my throat, my eyes themselves stinging as though some thin strand of stomach lining has pushed its way through them... And before long, I am the one who is drowning, gulping for air, fearful of breathing in the non-existent salt water, instead breathing in the just-expelled sick, its warmth and texture and acidic bite... I choke, I cough, I inhale, shards of who-knows-what ripping against my throat. My body kicks against them, coughing them out, but my ribs fight every cough, neutralising, weakening.

I find a compromise: a soft, short wheeze. The breath creeping in, but used the very moment it arrives and quickly dispelled. Exhaustion seems a funny thing. You'd think that with me lying here in this – motor? – sleeping – well, not being fully conscious, but lying down... You'd think I'd be full of the joys of spring upon waking. But here I am, not too joyous and with no spring in my step at all.

I am lucid enough now, I think, to realise that perhaps, right now, I, Tommy Bruce, could be somewhere close to death.

I've never rescued anyone. Never been in that situation again. Never been the failed hero since. I don't have that burden. I never rescued John. I couldn't have, I was told – I was just a bairn myself. What could I be expected to do, except cling on, panicking?

I rip at my bonds, but the weights pushing my hands together are not for moving and with every jag, every hoik, I become aware that my hands must be bound together using, I'm guessing, cheese wire. Every attempt is halted by the pain I am feeling, not the strength of the bonds. And my legs, well, I've long since given up on them, crammed as they are, bent at the knee and shoved behind me, wedging me in to this… wherever I am. But I can hear – it's rain, I know that now, and the occasional buffeting of the vehicle I am in. And I can hear, just, footsteps and forced, urgent, whispering.

I never saw him go down. I looked the other way. Next time I saw him, he was lying on the beach. I kept on expecting him to get up and come and play, but he didn't. He just… lay there. I scooted off behind some rocks and poured sand into a small rock pool, causing a hermit crab to scamper away somewhere less eventful.

There's a loud *clank* and a change in air pressure as a door opens… But no light floods in, no answers, just a different type of noise brought in by a cold, long, icy blast of air sweeping in and the van – for it must be a van – the van lifting, as though it's ready to fly off with this new force. I feel my legs being grabbed, and I'm roughly pulled, heaved, shuddered out of the van and collapse onto the wet ground outside. A light comes on – a torch, must be – and shines straight into my face. I have no defence from this glare, what with my hands so firmly wrenched behind my back, but my eyelids cram shut. A moment later, a thick, warm hand and thumb clamp down my cheek and pull my eyes open. For a second, my eyeball contracts, my eyelids close, attempting to escape the intensity of the light and that must be enough of a result for my tormentor, for he lets go of me completely and allows me to crash-land onto the sodden ground. I cry out, of course I do – defenceless as I am, it's the only thing I can do. But there's no helping hand, just the sound of a van door being slammed shut by the wind, and I fear, I fear I am being left here by my tormentor.

Then the door is opened, the air flooded with audible curses – *Fucking cunt* – and my face is grabbed once more, but this time my mouth is the prey. He – for it must be a he, with a voice as low and coarse as that – grabs and presses my cheeks close together and then rams something into my mouth. It smashes against my teeth, then fluid pools into my mouth. I can but swallow, and I recognise the taste immediately as *cheap vodka*. It keeps coming, it keeps coming, despite my coughs and attempts to move my head this way and that. His grip becomes firmer; at one point he changes position and vices my head between two sodden thighs, the vodka slightly diluted by rainfall but nothing else. It becomes obvious that to reach the precious air I so seek, I am going to need to swallow all this muck. I attempt to do that, but still it is reaching my airways and being coughed out, my body desperate to avoid drowning by vodka.

My head is dropped and, at the exact moment I hit the floor, I hear the clank of the discarded, empty bottle.

I open my eyes to a low crimson glow, from the lights on the back of the van, no doubt, and then a large clouded shadow looms above me once more. I curl as much as I can curl, I await a kick in the stomach, a fist to the head, but there's none of that, just a strange warmth emerging, flowing over me, my face, my neck, as though a bottle of warm water is being poured upon me. But there's laughter and – *Who's pissed himsel' NOW, eh, Tommy Boy? Tommy the fucking pish!*

And I thank the rain for diluting whatever has just occurred.

I wasn't allowed to go to John's funeral. I was taken up the side of the mountain by my father. He and my mother had been shouting a lot, since John had… Just tears. My mother wouldn't cry herself to sleep, it'd be more a scream, a howl. My father would drink, and I would play with whatever I could. Sometimes with John's toys, with John himself the other side of my game, John my left hand, me my right, his soft toys talking, dancing, swimming, screaming at each other. And every time I got in the bath, I couldn't help but look for John at the other end, his end. Every single time, even now, even now…

Now, Tommy, there's a sign back there that says there's a bothy close enough. You get tae it and you stay there. Or, you go wherever the fuck you want. But just stay the fuck away fae the hotel.

His hand moves behind me and jerks me over, my face now stuck tight in the earth. There's a sudden freedom as my hands are pulled right up behind my back – almost dislocating at my shoulders – then dropped, as though sacks of sand, either side of me. Loose. My legs are next, but are equally stunned and useless once freed. I lie there, my blood surprised, then confused, then excited, rushing to these now available areas of my body. I hear the sound of a door closing, an engine revving, a vehicle leaving.

Before my mother died, we'd visit John's grave each and every day. Father would say not to take me; there'd be arguments, talks, begging, but I seemed needed, as though I was a conduit between Mother and John. She'd say – *Tell him I love him* – and endlessly, it seemed – *Tell him I'm sorry.* And I, confused, just a wean, repeated the words – *She loves, she's sorry* – but just wanted to leave, thinking not of John but of my toy digger at home, of how I shall use it to dig a pit like the pit John is in. Why did they put him in the ground? Why are all these other people in the ground?

He'd still visit me, in my dreams, for years and years. I had to shut him out, in the end, as I became a teenager. I couldn't have this ghost-child haranguing me. But still he'd come, calling out, arms outstretched… But when I was drunk, well, he would stay away. It was as though he'd seen me take that step towards becoming an adult, further away from him, our past, our childhood.

He was beautiful and it hurt so much, closing that door on him, on his memory.

And when Mum decided she'd finally had enough, well, that was that. She went with him. She joined him. They went together, and the visits to me stopped completely.

The thing that woke me, the event that probably saved me, was snowfall. You wouldn't think that. You'd imagine the snow would cover me and I'd slowly freeze, but that wasn't the case. Lying there, open-mouthed, the cold of the snow tap, tap, tapped me awake, curling my tongue and forcing me to swallow. At a certain point, there was too much, and I choked, once, twice, before finally coughing myself conscious. And then, I thought only of Georgie, and how I could not die here, leaving him alone.

Bolt upright, arms outstretched, I resemble an out-of-season, lazy scarecrow. The thought of this makes me laugh, and the laugh, though sharpening my ribs and shunting at my ear, awakens me also, pushes the blood around, gives me a sense of myself, of clarity. I attempt to open my eyes but then become aware that they are already open and that I can only see nothing because here, wherever I am, well, it is so dark, that there is nothing to be seen.

I try to stand. I move onto all fours, a shard of pain piercing through the numbness of my hands, another sign that I am alive, as I slowly, carefully, push myself upright, unsteady, blown by the wind, bent knees to steady myself, balance shot by the whatever in my ear, but upright, surfing on the grass to keep balanced, scanning the horizon for this *bothy*, seeing, maybe, a field of lights, a town, but a town a good distance away, too far to walk – the distance? Oh, I don't know – a hundred miles? A hundred sodden miles? But behind me, towards the wind – as one's natural inclination is, of course, to turn from such a bitter blast – behind I can see nothing other than a huge black shape that I recognise to be a mountain as above the matte black there is a slight and staggered deep blue, the night sky creeping over the mountain's peaks.

But there is a something within the black. A tiny shard. A reflection, just. But of what?

I grimace at the thought of walking away from the town, but this light, it must surely be the bothy, right? Or was that just nonsense from Billy? Part of some plan?

Idiot hillwalker, unfit, unprepared and drunk, found dead on hillside. Mountain Rescue insist again that more is done to alert people to the danger of the wilderness. 'Deaths like this can be so easily avoided,' says Inspector Jackson of Police Scotland.

Nah. Could Billy even have a plan? He's thick as mince... Although, he is in a nice, warm van whereas I am not...

I begin. I batter my arms, flap them against my sides. I attempt to curl my toes in and out, in and out with every footfall. I can move my fingers and do so, keeping a rhythm going. I stumble, of course, but raise myself instantly every time, though these sodden gullies do somehow seem like wonderful places to rest. I need to continue, to keep up, to walk until the sun rises, one foot at a time.

And at least this rain is rinsing my clothes.

You know, I once heard my father shouting that HE could have swam it, HE could have got Johnny in time, but my father was no more a swimmer than myself. What did he think? That he'd suddenly become some Olympic champion?

I am suddenly held where I am and lash out as though Billy has returned, but soon realise by the sharp, piercing sensation on my thighs that I have stumbled onto some barbed wire. I reach my hands out and slowly, carefully, place them on two spike-free zones, resting my body, assessing my situation. I've been walking for – well, five minutes? But it could be an hour... Turning, the mountain seems just as close as it ever was, but don't let that fool you, Tommy boy, mountains are big auld beasts.

I can still see the pale, very pale yellow-orange light. Or is it a figment, a defect of my eye? It seems to remain, if I can keep my shivering head still, the glow seems to remain...

It has to be something to head towards, right?

Oh, Georgie, Georgie, Georgie...

Oh, Johnny, Johnny, Johnny…

I cannot scale this short wall of wire, can I? Can I even try, what with my legs having creaked shut during this short, luxurious rest? No. I have one further choice, one further option, and I go with it: I will my body forward, peeling, toppling over the wire and landing headfirst, then neck, then body on the ground beyond the fence. Somehow keeping that momentum, I stand, I move one foot, then the other, then one foot, then the other, then Georgie, then John, then Fi, then Mother, then onwards, a short push, a stagger – and the light, the hope is still there. I cannot move these arms, I cannot abide these frozen jeans, but the good thing is my body feels so warm now – from the motion, I'm guessing – and I want to remove my clothing, but somewhere deep within a memory warns me – *Dinnae do that, Tommy boy, keep on, keep on* – so I keep on – *Mother, Father, Georgie, Johnny, Mother, Father, Georgie, Johnny, Johnny, Johnny… Fi.*

And my teeth, they chatter like a cartoon fearty.

The light is definitely growing closer. I can see – steps? The sound of my footfall changes, from the soft squelch of the sunken grass to the crunch of a hard, brittle gravel. I tear this gravel behind me with every motion, the toes of my feet dragging long slithers behind them. The light is visible and all too real and just there, just here, almost – a stone building? But not modern, a light inside, flickering but there, a yard to cover now, and even the weight of the mountain pushing me on, the wind giving me that last bit of strength, Johnny and Georgie holding hands, watching from the sidelines as I finally reach the steps – one, two, three – push the door – it doesn't open. I slam my shoulder against it, but again, no, and that is it, there is no more, my mind is made up, I shall fall here, and just as I do, just as my body begins its collapse, there's a *click*, and rather than falling straight down, I fall forward, within, deep within.

48

I AWAKE, I AWAKE.
I am warm.

There's water and touch and commotion, but it's very different this time.

Someone is wiping my brow – or something is brushing repeatedly against my brow. From my recent experiences, I know that this is something I need to avoid – I pull away – but my rib reminds me – *Do Not Pull.* I jerk my head, but my earache kicks in. Then, a lady's voice – *Keep your head still.*

I obey.

He smells –

For God's sake, Brendan. He's clearly in a bad shape. It's not his fault...

Sure, but he could be a fucking nutjob when he wakes up – like – like some bus-station crazy, or, or a drug mule –

Brendan, look at him. How crazy could he go? Having a bath would be crazy for him right now. Besides, there's something...

What do you mean, something?

Well... Why would he be out here with no coat? We're in the middle of nowhere here.

I think... I think him being so close to the fire isn't good. It's like... it's like we're cooking the piss smell. Baking it.

Leave over. He's frozen solid, poor man. Here – look through his pockets!

Are you kidding me? I'm never looking through some jakey's pockets – what if I – what if I brush his... donger?

Well – what if I brush his donger? Here, you look. Look now, see if we can find out who he is...

When Mother died, Father shut the hotel. Mothballed it. He wouldn't even open the kitchens, preferring to cook in the upstairs galley using just a microwave. We lived off of noodles and beans, from memory. No fruit but bananas, them things he was always eating. When I asked him about it – years later – he said it was them that kept him off the drink. But this was rubbish. He drank more than anyone I've ever met. Maybe the bananas slowed the drinking, for only those thirty seconds it took to eat one.

Ugh... fucking Nora...
Brendan! Brendan! Wake up – he's awake – he's coming to!
Ah fuck, so he is. Hold on, I'll grab this just in case...
What?! Put that down, you are not going to brain him with a kettle, the poor soul –
No... I meant I'll boil some tea up...
Did you fuck, Brendan Moore, did you fuck.

All my strength to open my eyelids.

Once open and peering into this new world, it is as though watching television, so unreal and different it seems. For neither of them, the two stars of my new favourite sitcom, seems to be in any anguish whatsoever, except they have a worry – about a dog, perhaps, or a new born. As the screen flickers on and off – oddly, with the timing of the shard that is piercing my chest – they blur in and out of focus, the lady coming closer, the gentleman more distant. He has a hairy face, I note, like a Western version of Christ. And he has a large bluebottle living on his cheek and a kettle for a hand.

Why the shiver? I'd awaken and there'd be ice on the windows, on the inside. I'd be so cold I'd get dressed under the covers. My father slept with the windows open, and sometimes that seemed wise, for sure it was warmer out than in on occasion. But that wasn't the reason. He'd open his life to random events as he needed something, anything to distract him from the loss of first his son and now his wife. He'd drive without a seatbelt but – get this – make sure I had mine on. As if I wasn't feeling any loss. Auld Jock, younger then, of course, came down with us on a trip to Perth once, me in the back of the car, wondering why this man was sitting in mother's seat. I remember Jock asking Father – *Are ye no' wearing yer belt, then?* – and my father replying – *No. I'm a coward wi' a knife or a rope. This would be quick.* And only years later did I realise that Jock probably didn't need a lift at all. He was just keeping an eye on things, as though he somehow had some responsibility.

Look, shall I go and try to find a phone? To get an ambulance?

What? He's not that bad, surely… There's no way you're leaving me with… him. And anyway – look – look outside. The snow's way too deep. Sure, the main road is a hike in itself.

Well, you go then, Brendan. I'll be fine here…

I'm not leaving you with, with – this. No chance. He could – he could…

He can barely move. He won't do anything. I'm worried about him, Brendan. And you know, he doesn't look like a tramp, when you really look…

There's a liquid placed against my lips and I swallow it down.

I remember the funeral, the second one. I was dressed in a suit for some reason, a tie. Looking my best for Mother, but I couldn't see Mother anywhere; I was expecting her to be at the church, but she wasn't. That suit, that suit, it stayed with me. It was kept wrapped in plastic at the back of the wardrobe, but slowly, slowly, I grew out of it – it shrank, seemingly – and I wondered at the size of the arms that had fitted in those sleeves, the slenderness of the legs that had filled those trousers…

It seems like a different lifetime. I don't know. Sometimes, I don't even know what I'm here for, when everyone I loved has gone.

So, when Georgie arrives, I'm warmed but conflicted. My love for him is real but it is reserved. I am terrified of its removal. For he is not me, he is not mine... And Fi? Well, she too is not me, she is not mine, she is just another soul, and how can I trust another soul to stay now?

Here, we can't stay in much longer. We'll have to make a break. Look, we only had food for a few nights and we've been here three, and now this fella's here –

He's coming along, it's ok. I can see it. He's breathing deeper now. Besides, we can't get far when it's snowing like this unless we leave him here, and even then... Just one more night, Brendan, one more night.

When I open my eyes, there's nothing to be seen except a dull flicker of light, out of focus, maybe seven, ten feet away? My teeth begin their chatter and I instinctively feel for and pull over a cover, a blanket, woollen, I'd guess, warm enough just. I stare, stare over at this light show, aware of a hunger within but mostly mentally testing every inch of my body for feeling, usability, working out where the pain is coming from and how best to position myself to avoid it. I can hear movement: the crackle of a fire and light snoring. I smell food of some type and it draws me, but the cold air and my bodily discomfort advise I stay just where I am, just where I'm lying. Am I on a bare wooden floor? No – there's something below me. A cloth? A towel, maybe? Whatever it is, it's providing scant comfort, failing to support my weight and bruising my bones as I sleep. I make to move, to turn to the other side and, well, we're fine for a head turn, a weight shift, a slight roll, but then the rib pangs and this time I address it – *Ah, you fucking... Ah, you... Ah, fuck* – before collapsing once more. This time I remain conscious and I listen to the light padding on the roof – rain or snow? Snow, I'd guess, then, slowly, I remember my walk – *Holy fuck* – and then that Billy guy, the journey – all these aches become clear now – and... Oh Heavenly Father up above – what is this smell? Am I lying in a pigsty? But the shape of the room, the walls I can make out, the breathing of sleeping others – no, it's that building… The bothy. I made it to the bothy.

Billy's fucking bothy.

I smile, and I cough a small celebratory laugh, just for myself. Staring upwards now, I watch the light on the ceiling. Although I cannot see it, I can guess the fire must just be embers now. Certainly, I am not warm, and I believe I am right beside it. I make another effort to move but am supremely wary of my anguishes, so slowly I adjust, test an arm, bend a leg. Sure, they *ache*, but there's no pain to stop me there. Using my right arm like a jack under a car, I begin to lift my body, by centimetres at first, waiting for more reminders, some wound I'd forgotten about. My head swells, the blood draining from it, leaving nothing but a hollow, agonising cold – but my body is rising, is coming up, is sitting now, leaning back on both arms and the movement, well it starts me wheezing, coughing and that sound – like a young crow's caw, actually – well, it silences the snoring as their own ears twitch alert. A dark shadow rises, a female voice – *Brendan! Get up!* – and I think – *Who's that lassie?* And *Who's this Brendan?*

Hello?

In response, I make the crow noise again, but this time it's a more adult sound – *Arrch* – then – *Arhh* – and next – *Urghh* – before finally finishing with – *Ooough.*

Shit, he's awake – get a light on…

There's no light, calm down. Just light a fucking candle, Brendan. Sir – sir – are you ok there? Are you choking?

There's a rush, splintering my arms. Pins and needles, cramping the muscles. *Arh… Aye. Ahm… Where? Fuck…* I tell you something funny: my head actually feels as though it's two feet to the left of my body, somehow floating off on its own accord.

There's a light now, not blinding. A single flame just, but enough to bring some colour into my vision. I see that Christ-like figure from earlier – but it's just a bloke. He looks wary, scared. I wonder what of?

Are you – have you – can I get – hey –

SHUT UP, Brendan.

The second shadow moves before me. It's female, covered from head to feet by a fat, bloated coat and a sheep's worth of woolly accessories – scarf, hat and gloves. *Here, maybe you should lean against the wall, look...*

I hear a scrape and a clatter behind me; she's moving things away. Then she's back in my view and next to where they'd been sleeping, rolling something up –

Hey, I'm using that! I'll be cold now.

Oh, man up, Brendan. Put some fucking wood on the fire.

Then she's back behind me and – *Give me a hand, Brendan.* Then he's down also and the two of them are taking me under the arms and slowly dragging me to the wall. I realise what's happening and attempt to help, to scoot myself along.

Even in this twilight, my shoes look fucked. Ripped, loose, flared. My breeks no better, filthy brown mud from the crotch down, flared now also, possibly. Flapping, anyhow. I'm aware I am wearing some kind of fleece, but I'm not sure I recognise it. I don't like fleeces, not my bag at all.

Where – Hi! – Who...

I'm Martha. This eejit is Brendan. You're in a bothy. You've been – WE'VE been here for two nights now. Well, three including the night you arrived. The snow's too thick to leave and our phones have got no reception, so, well, here we are!

They're Irish. I look over at Brendan, who's breaking and burning a small wooden crate. He looks back at me – *There's no more coal. Just this firewood.*

The strips of crate provide further, flickering, jumping light.

Am I... Am I in Ireland, then?

Martha answers – *What? Don't be daft. We're in Scotland. We're near Spean Bridge.*

Spean Bridge?

Of course. Where did you think we were?

Well... I was in Perthshire. This is – wait – the Highlands?

'Tis.

Fuck.

Billy. That van...

We'll have to leave soon. We were caught by the snowstorm, but we only had enough food for a day or so. Running low now. Didn't want to leave you, though – and it's quite a walk to anywhere, truth be told. Were you... were you on a stag do or something?

I smile at the thought: the thought of Billy and me being on a stag do together, of him rupturing my eardrum, knocking me out cold and breaking my rib, then pissing on me and abandoning me to the cold. Just for a laugh, ken? Just stag-do antics between pals...

No. I very warily shake my head. *No, it wasn't a stag do. Here, have you anything to eat? Anything at all?*

They look at each other then – *Well, here's the thing...*

People leave things in these bothies, it seems. Coal they've brought but not used, matches, any food they hadn't needed. If they're on their way back to civilisation, they'll leave any spare supplies. And that's what my new friends have been eating since their own supplies ran out.

These beans were out of date. What a smell they made coming out the other end!

Brendan! Don't be a dick. She shakes her head apologetically. *There's been plenty of firewood, though, thank God. Even in decent weather, we're a good hour's walk to the nearest village and the road that goes through it. That's where our hire car is. There's been nonstop snow since we arrived – then you tumbled in – quite literally. Gave us quite the fright.*

I can remember, just, I think. I had no idea I was so fit – fit enough to survive that battering and the walk, anyhow. I guess what's helped has been all those hillside ascents with Georgie... Georgie. Fuck. How long have I been here?

How long have we been here – what's the date now?

I told you – three nights. It's the 21ˢᵗ now.

Listen, I have to get back or... *Have you a phone?* But I make to move and – *Oh, ya bastard...* I clutch at my chest, my side. I retreat, back resting once more on the wall.

We saw that — she motions to my hand, covering the painful spot. *We saw... Your shirt is ripped and you have a terrible, big bruise there. One on your neck too. I stayed up, that first night. As if there was anything we could do — but I stayed up, nonetheless.* She looks at me, expectant.

Thank you.

She smiles.

How am I going to get back? I shunt forwards, but my aching eardrum buffets me down, reminds me of my place. Fuck it. I have to move. I have to get home.

49

My food is an open-fire heated, out-of-date tin of Spaghetti Hoops. I tell you, they taste delicious. I'd've eaten three tins of the blighters, if they'd been available. I make a mental note – when I get home, when I sort out all that Billy pish – heh – once I've done that, I'll be back up here with a wee box of tins for the store cupboard. Just pub stuff, you know – cash and carry beans, that sort of thing. Nothing too dear. But aye, I needed those Hoops and am thankful for them.

The lady asks – *Are you from round here, then?*

No, no, not at all. I'm further south. Perthshire. You know it?

No. A pause.

Once it gets lighter, as soon as it's not snowing, I'm away.

What? You're wearing… What are those – pumps? Are you sure? You're wrecked altogether. We can hole up here another day. There's still a tiny bit of food – well, if you like old tins of beans.

I am grateful, but I am needing to go – *I have to. I've been away too long, I need to see my wee boy, tell Fi… Tell my lassie I'm ok. Get back to the pub…*

I have no idea what will be awaiting me. Perhaps this was just stag-do games after all. Perhaps I need to learn to laugh at myself. Or perhaps Billy will lamp me the first moment he can and put me straight back into the van for another joyride. Maybe I should take him and Simon more seriously.

Is there any more clothing here? Whose fleece is this I'm in?

Brendan pipes up – *That's mine now. But, you know… I was over-dressed, and anyway, it's…*

It's been rolled around the floor on a man who's all bloody and smells of another man's urine. I understand.

I can wash it? And send it back?

No – no – you're ok.

Aye, it'd be a poor parcel to receive, that one, no matter how many washes it'd had.

With the food, with the clearing of my thoughts, I find I can rest – or more so, I find I cannot *not* rest. I lean my splitting head against the split plasterboard of the wall, relax back into my rickety wooden kitchen chair, measuring the likelihood it should collapse beneath me by the creak it makes, but feeling confident it's strong enough. I close my eyes and sleep.

Georgie's running up to me, collapsing, falling over onto my belly, falling into a cuddle. I give it everything I've got, keen he feels loved, a father's warmth, solidity, safety. Fi is watching, smiling. Suddenly, she walks towards me and picks up a pitchfork out of nowhere, piercing my side.

I blink myself awake and change position before dozing once more.

Auld Jock now. He's just laughing at me. Or with me, perhaps. We're holding hands as crisp packets scatter all around us like snow. That Birmingham dude is haw-hawing in my face and demanding 26p as someone has used my outside lavatory. I explain I do not have an outside lavatory and go to look – and there's Billy, except he's a bairn with an adult-Billy head, and he's pissing on a building. I step forward, look closer and see that it's a model of the hotel he's pissing on – but what's that? Above? I look up and there's giant grown-up Billy, super-sized, gargantuan… pissing on us all. I turn my face, I turn my face…

My head slips on the wall, waking me up. My neck is stiff tight round to the left, as though I'm squinting to hear some private conversation. There is a small waterfall of drool dribbling from the side of my mouth.

To be honest, for the most part I preferred the first of the two dreams.

It's beautiful and clear outside. If you're going to go, well, now's the time. And sure, look – Martha gestures with two Tesco bags *– we can tie these around your slipper things. Keep your feet dry, at least. And look – we'll come with you most of the way.*

Brendan then *– What? We're going to Perth?*

I pipe up *– It's no' Perth, it's Perthshire. I'm nowhere near –*

No! We won't go the whole journey, but we'll get Tommy on his bus. Ok, Tommy?

Sure, sure. Yeah. And, um… Could you – I don't have any money. Or a wallet.

Yeah, don't worry we'll pay. What'll it be? A few quid?

Aye, something like that. Maybe a few more. I'll go in with the luggage on the bus, though. Save a few quid…

What? They do that?

No, no. It's a joke.

She smiles. *Ok.*

Great – and you can stay at my hotel on your way back down? Free of charge? And I'll pay you then?

She nods *– Yeah, sure. Your hotel.*

She means *– No.* And perhaps *– You've no fucking hotel.* I can read that in her eyes. But that's fine.

Before we leave, Martha insists upon emptying out the fire – with it still going, ashes still baking hot – before laying it once more and placing matches just above it on the fireplace, one match sticking out for easy access. Just in case, you know? In case the next person to blunder in is as frozen as I was.

What a waste of time. Come on, Martha, we've only got three more days up here. I want to explore, not babysit and then tidy up!

You're a pillock, you know that Brendan McCarthy? A pillock.

They have to take everything they brought, of course. They cannot leave any of their gear abandoned in this bothy, so when we leave we're fair laden down – though I am the biggest burden. It soon becomes apparent that I need both their shoulders to walk with or I'll be flat on my arse in the snow, clutching my rib like a wean.

Shall we not just call the air ambulance?

What with? There's little reception here, if any. And helicopters are for emergencies. Tommy here is fine. Just a little... sore.

Heh.

To our left, there's the beginning of a michty loch that extends beyond where I can actually see. Ahead, there's a gathering of huge, snow-covered peaks, outstanding in normal circumstances, but here, with me hungry and weak and lacking in sleep, they seem almost surreal. Certainly, they dwarf my favoured hillside at home.

C'mon – this way –

The three of us, bound together by my pitiful circumstances, stagger towards the loch. I can't make most of it out. The sun is so low and bright, and its reflection bounces off the snow in all directions, blinding me. My two companions are suitably sunglassed.

Did he not even bring sunglasses? Jesus...

Imagine. Though there is a pair somewhere around the bar – up with the nuts, mebbe? The lenses a bit scraped, greasy with oil... I'll look them out.

That is, of course, if I have a bar to return to. Which I must do. I need to phone Fi...

Can you see if you have any reception yet?

Good idea – have a look, Brendan.

Ah, we don't.

What? How do you know? We're out in the open now, it could well work, out of those four walls...

No, it's not that. We're out of battery.

What? How's that, now?

Umm, I used the torch last night. To get to the jacks and gather more firewood, you know?

Oh, for fuck's sake, Brendan. What was it – were you scared of the dark?

204

I say nothing. I concentrate on keeping my head steady. My arms are simultaneously protecting my chest and rib and keeping me balanced on Mr and Mrs. It's exhausting. My head is frozen as well, and my teeth are chattering before too long.

Are you ok, Tommy?

Ach, I'm just so cauld – my ears...

Ah, shite, I didn't think... You know, I could help... Here – I've got something for you.

We stop and Martha reaches into her backpack. I'm hoping for a thick woollen hat, something that'd reach down to my neck, that I could snuggle into, sleep within, almost.

But it's not that she was looking for. It's a strip of pink cloth proclaiming *Just Do It!* It's like the belt of a bairn's ballerina outfit.

Here, bend.

I lower my neck – *Aya bastard* – and she forces it on my head, as though I'm getting a too-small, crappy cloth medal for being the World's Coldest Man. Then she adjusts it – *Ah* – and I work it out: it's to cover my ears. A strip of a hat. A headband. The top of my noggin is still exposed, but my ears melt with pleasure at this sudden escape from the wind, the cold.

Wow. That's amazing. Have ye – have ye anything else in there?

She smiles. *No. I'm wearing everything else.*

My new headgear is perfumed. It smells good. Clean. Intimate. Certainly, it is one-hundred-times better than the Bodily Function Special cologne that I appear to be sporting.

Brendan looks at me – *Fuck's sake.* He shakes his head.

So, who's your wife, Tommy?

Eh – oh – ow – she's, um, just a lassie from the village – and we're no' – ow – married.

No? But you have children?

Child...

All the same. You should marry her. Make her feel secure, you know?

Aye, well...

*

And how did you meet then?

She's keeping me distracted. I appreciate it, for I am slowing, my feet are slipping every second step with these fucking plastic bags tied around them. The ground is so wet, but my feet would freeze if they got wet, I know that.

Um… She – just – came – into – the – bar…

Ha! Sounds like my kinda girl.

Brendan's eyes are on the various peaks far we can see. *That one's Càrn Mòr Dearg. I've been up there.*

Bully for you, Brendan.

How… How far to go now?

The car's about four or five miles. But the trek eases up once we find the path proper…

Four or five miles? Christ. Distraction, that's what I need. And rhythm, rhythm in my step. *And how about you two? How did you meet, then?*

Heh. We worked in a fancy shop – do you remember that, Brendan?

Course I do – how could I forget? You in the cookery section – a whole section of cookery books, can you believe it? To me, then – *This is in Dublin. Do you know Dublin? There's this ridiculous shop called Broon Tam's. Do you know it? Oh my God, it's for all the moneyed elite, the U2s and the like, the property magnates, politicians…*

I don't, I've never been over…

Well, don't go to Broon Tam's, if you do go to Dublin. It's crap. Brightly lit crap.

C'mon now, Brendan, it is not. There's plenty of amazing things in there – amazing… You're just sick for being fired…

I am not! I wouldn't have stayed another season. Guess what – guess what I was in charge of, Tommy? Go on, guess – have a go!

Give him a chance to speak, Brendan, at least…

Oh fuck. Think… Umm. What's Irish – stout? What are those wee green men they have over there…

Ties – I was in charge of ties.

Ah.

Can you imagine? A fucking rack of ties, the length of a bus, almost.

And me, just sorting, smoothing, displaying. Fucking drove me mad it did.

So, why – how did you get fired?

Ach. They didn't like me, that's all. And to be honest, Martha was partly to blame.

Don't talk rot, Brendan, I was not!

So you were, Martha. You got me drunk at lunchtime.

YOU were doing the drinking, I wasn't.

Well, whatever.

We tramp on.

But anyway, I had to do an order. And I just… Could. Not. Be. Bothered. You know what I mean, Tommy?

Aye, aye. I…

So, the thing was, I ordered a load…

Of novelty ties – they were novelty ties!

They were not! They were… for discerning gentlemen on an evening out.

Bollocks! I saw them when they came in. Snakes. Elephant trunks. One looked like a keyboard – they were for eejits! Here, one looked like a man's wotsit, you know? They couldn't have that hanging in the shop.

I laugh. It hurts.

You ok, Tommy?

Heh – I reckon.

Yeah, well. Anyway. That's where we met. In the shop.

Before too long we're skirting the side of a forest, its trees whitened by snow but impressive, providing a windbreak and their dark shadows helping negate the wince-inducing sunlight. My shoes' make-do waterproofing is ripped off by the shale the moment we leave the snow and now I just have my flappy slip-ons, looking shitey and haggard. You know when you see a pair of shoes clearly unsuitable for hillwalking abandoned on a hill path somewhere? Well, this is that situation, or it would be if I had any replacement whatsoever.

I need to rest, and on occasion we'll do just that, but there's no food, only water, and every time we stop the sweat freezes on me, beseeching me to *move on, move on*.

The lie of the land means we can see the car park for a good two miles before we actually reach it. At first, it's just another patch of ground so, so far in the distance. We can't see the car itself, and this seems to concern Brendan, but Martha reassures us – *It'll be under snow. Don't you worry Tommy here*.

There are a couple of folk marching towards us. We spot them a good distance away and them us, no doubt. As we tramp down in their direction, it gets me thinking about life outside of this trio bubble. I wonder what Georgie will be up to? I wonder if Fi's worried about me or has thought about me at all, or if they've called the polis... And the clowns. Ha. Easy to say from this distance. But, of course, I also wonder what those Billy and Simon clowns have been doing in my absence.

And Auld Jock. Was he ok, after Billy had his way? How's he got his drink? I hope I don't lose him to the Co-op buy-your-own...

There are apples in the car.

Eh?

There are apples in the car. And some chocolate.

Wow. Thank fuck for that.

My mind leaves Georgie and Fi, Simon and Billy, and fixates on the chocolate and apples.

The two bodies slowly, eventually, get closer. They are easily visible now: walking jackets, stout sticks, hats, rucksacks. They're going to think I'm a total dowp, out here in ma baffies and ma ripped trews; a borrowed, too-small fleece – a' topped off wi' a wifey's pink sock or whatever it is, coiled round ma head...

Hello!

Hello!

Hiya!

Aye.

Lovely day.

'Tis.

Beautiful.

Are you ok?

Aye, just…

Actually – have you anything…?

What – is he ok?

Yes, he's fine, he just had a fall.

Heh – I'm not surprised with shoes like that. What were you thinking?

Ah, it was a' a wee bit…

Last minute, wasn't it, Tommy?

It was. That it was.

Stag night?

Kinda…

But if you have…

Maybe a food bar for Tommy here, I know he'd appreciate it.

Of course, of course! Here, let me just root inside here…

Lovely day, isn't it?

It is.

I've been up there – Càrn Mòr Dearg, it's called.

Ah. Yes. It's Gaelic. It means 'The Great Red Peak', I believe… Gosh, what's that smell? Has a dog done its business around here? Watch your feet…

No, it's him.

Heh. Thanks, Brendan.

Ah.

Here, here's a chocolate – a Penguin. Do you like those?

I'd eat the fucking wrapper!

Ha ha ha!

Here, could you…? I've no gloves.

Open it? Sure.

Where you guys…

We were in the bothy.

I got lost. I stumbled in. Not this way, though — I don't remember a loch.

It was dark, though.

Aye.

You're a long way from anywhere here.

Aye — these two — that bothy way back — pure saved my bacon.

Well, that's what they're for — bothies, I mean.

Here now, if you're going, you should know we pretty much stripped it of supplies. We've been in for a few nights...

Ha ha! That's ok, we're only here for the day, aren't we, Andy?

We are, Gerry, that's right. Hopefully!

Here, we're going to move on. Thanks for the food. Tommy needs to get home. He's hurt his side.

Ah yes, I can see you're limping. Ok, well, good luck. You've only a mile or so to the car park now. Is that where you're headed?

It is, though I can't see our car yet.

Well, there's one there for sure, it's just under some snowfall.

That'd make sense.

Ok, bye now.

Goodbye.

Slàinte mhaith!

Aye — yer health!

Bye now.

Thanks for the chocolate.

Not a problem!

See you.

Ok.

50

W̲E̲ ̲G̲O̲T̲ ̲T̲H̲E̲ *smallest, cheapest hire car.*
  I can see that.
  Brendan wanted a four-by-four, but why bother? All the roads are well looked after. Although – she gestures – *I wasn't counting on the snow…*

I collapse in the back. The car doesn't move once started – well, it shakes erratically from side to side but is snowed and iced into place.
  But I, I am slouched in the back, worn-out. I could sleep here, easily, despite the crazed, engine-versus-nature shoogle happening around me.
  Brendan, however –
  Fuck! He jumps out. *Ok, start again… I'll push…*
  And to give him credit, he certainly does push. We go nowhere, though, just rock back and forth. Then slowly, inch by inch, we gain traction and move off. Brendan jumps in and slams his door triumphantly before quickly winding his window right down – *What is that fucking smell? Jeez, Tommy, you REEK.*
  Close the window. It's too cold.
  No, I can't. The smell is too much for me. Just – just put the heater to full, to maximum – here…
  A constant faceful of freezing cold, the occasional nuzzle of warmth and a frankly revolting smell that overrides everything. Everyone's perfect journey. I close my eyes, hand to nose, the aroma acidic even within my mouth.
  Sleep.

51

I WAVE GOODBYE TO my two best pals. I even get hugs. Sheesh, that's brave. I wouldn't hug a man with my aroma.

I offer the fleece, the ear-warmer – but no. They're mine now.

I climb aboard the bus and the driver sniffs, recoils.

I walk all the way to the back and open a window. A minute later, a fellow passenger closes the window. A minute after that, he opens it again.

And then we're off.

52

THERE'S SNOW PILED up on both sides of the road, a barricade of sorts, grey-black from the oil and diesel and filth of the road. This would be a journey to remember if one was from some metropolis: the snow, the mountains, streams cutting the snow-white fields in two, few animals out due to the weather, but all the same... Strange to think this is the same country as Glasgow or Edinburgh. And don't even bring further south into it. London, from what I see on the telly, well, it seems like a sort of Hades – the population, the filth, the traffic...

But I'd rather be heading down there than back to the hotel right now.

So, how am I going to play this? I mean, I can't stop off, recuperate. I have no means of getting a room and a wash until I arrive home. I just need to return, see the lie of the land, the lady of the land... Ha. The state of play. I need to see Georgie, for sure, but I don't want him to see me like this... but then, would he even notice? Or care?

I need a shower and a new set of clothes. Then some food. I guess it'll be evening by the time I return, so hopefully the bar will be open – if Fi's made it back. She must have, and she must have called the polis by now, eh?

If she's not there, I'll call her. First thing I'll do.

Christ, I could eat. Anything. Even the chuggy on the back of these bus seats looks tempting.

As we roll in closer to home, the hills begin to look more familiar, the farmsteads, tourist hotels, petrol stations displaying the local newspapers. My nerves rise; I tense up. I rub my neck, feel my rib, lightly bounce my head, testing my ear. It all still feels pretty fucked, to be honest. My only memory of this sort of full-body ache was when I briefly played rugby at school. I was a big lad even then so was pushed in that direction while the smaller, lithe boys were encouraged into football. Quite the employment strategy. Still, it got me out of football, which was where a' the real heid-the-ba's went. But after those games – especially when we were playing older teams – well, my body would nip and complain from scalp to foot. I wouldn't shower after the match – it was about a fifty-fifty split between the boys that would and would not. I'd just pull a tracksuit on to hide the mud and scabbing cuts and grazes, waiting until I got to the privacy of my own home, disliking the torment and overfamiliarity of the shared shower. And the random water temperatures. And the opposition dickwads who'd rifle through our clothes. The bus home would smell of Deep Heat, that muscle-ache cure-all, trusted even to us youth to dispense. Deep Heat and sweat, of course.

Back then, I'd be going home to Dad, to solitude, to my toys, to peace and quiet.

Not this time.

Whatever happens in the future, Georgie is the priority, right? He doesn't need the kind of memories I have. He'll be burdened enough when he finds out that shite Simon is his real da.

That pinches at my heart. Squeezes my stomach. What a stupid fucker I am. What a stupid fucking situation.

We're pulling into the outskirts, which soon becomes the centre, the bus stop fast approaching… I could stay on? But where to? I have nothing but the soiled clothing I am wearing, no means of supporting myself even momentarily elsewhere. The bus slows, creaks, halts. I hear the pneumatics of the door, take a breath, stand and depart.

The only welcome I get is a screeching, bitter wind that rips right through my adopted fleece. The street is iced, salted wet, snowed up. It's too cold to be out even when properly dressed, but now, dressed as an eejit from an eighties New York dance film… Well, the only thing driving me home quicker than the temperature is the embarrassment of my outfit, of being seen like this.

There's no one about; I'm the only one off the bus. A car comes creeping up the high street, its lights on, as dusk falls. There's nowhere for it to go other than onwards.

The ground is so slippy I have to creep, to slither as though an amateur roller skater lurching towards my doom. Salt to the wound.

I pass a garden fork, resting outside the all-in-one ironmongers and tourist-tat shop. Should I take it? Use it to spear some fucker? Some awaiting Billy?

I look in the window and see the owner staring out, towards the light, the snow, the street, no doubt – but now towards me, the man who is limping past her shop. She leans her head closer to the glass and attempts to work out – *Who's that oot in this weather?*

The road towards my hotel is just off the main drag, so I have a few minutes' warning, time to see that lights are on upstairs, where Fi might be with Georgie, if I am lucky.

But no one's salted this road. Of course not. That'd be down to me, and even if I'd been here, it's unlikely I'd've done it.

I look down to where the four-by-four would be, but there's no sign of it and no tracks in the snow from where it might have been. So I can presume: no Fi, no Georgie. Ach.

I grasp hold of the hedge, feet deep in snowdrift, but not slipping, not skelping my erse. This is the safest and most discreet route; I have learned that from dozens of alcohol-challenged comings and goings.

I observe through the bar window that there's not a lot going on inside. A couple of folk – Simon, probably, and that Billy guy, for sure, his denim a giveaway – but no one else, unless someone is hidden away in a corner.

And here I am, at the door. There's the familiar thump of Fi's dance-y bagpipe shite coming through and, for the first time ever, I'm pleased to hear it. I push through, as quietly as I can, careful not to set the brass bell off, head straight beyond the bar and up the backstairs. I cannot confront Simon dressed like this, looking like this. I need some kind of dignity, time to gather my thoughts, to work out where Fi and Georgie might be…

The backstairs are fairly bare. There's no carpet, no heater; a place filled only by the echo of footfall, where one can almost see one's breath, even in the height of summer. A bare bulb illuminates my journey to the frosted glass of the upstairs door. Above it, written in gold on a black metal strip, is the word *PRIVATE*.

Hello? Hello? Fi?

There's no reply, no sounds of life. I look this way… and that… nothing.

Hello?

There's not even a sound to quieten.

I gather all my strength and hobble along to our bedroom, to see what's up. Perhaps Georgie is asleep in his wee cot thing? Perhaps Fi in the bed beside him? Awaiting my return.

But peering in, first thing I see is there's nothing in the cot, not even a blanket. Further in the room, the bed is unmade, a mess – and a pair of jeans are crumpled on the floor beside it. Adult male jeans.

53

Fuck is this? I mean, there's no sign of Fi, but the mind can't help but wander, right?

No Fi, no Georgie, bedroom just the same as I left it. Except...

Someone's dirty breeks on the floor. Not mine. Not Fi's. Do I believe Fi would be sharing a bed with either of these two dowps? I do not.

But there are no answers up here, just more questions.

In the bedroom mirror, there's a filthy, broken wretch of a man who isn't going to inspire fear in anyone. Perhaps, at Halloween, it could be seen as a particularly realistic jakey costume, but that aside...

I need to clean up. Think things through. Delay the inevitable, yep, but not by long. More so, gather strength. Get things straight.

I pull a fresh towel out of the drawer that Fi has commandeered for such things, open the bathroom door and walk through to the shower. Ach. It smells like a school gym.

There's one of those shitey wee shower gels, blue in colour, Real Man or whatever the fuck it's called.

And there's nae fucking soap.

Well, I'm not using that shower gel. I look for some shampoo or other of Fi's and end up with a half bottle of conditioner. Ach, that'll do.

My skin is embracing the water, the heat, my muscles pulling in any warmth, relaxing, healing...

Fi should have Georgie in bed by now, eh?

After a minute, maybe two, the shower begins to run cold. What a junkheap this place is.

54

*G*OT TO GET *this right, Tommy boy. Keep your cool. Keep your temper.*
I dry. Quickly. Patchily.
In the mirror, I look ok. Dressed. Clean. Serious.
Dinnae you show any weaknesses, Tommy.
And now, down the stair.

55

*H*EH – WELL, *look who's here, Billy!*

Simon and Billy. Simon behind the bar, Billy sat back on Auld Jock's stool but standing the moment he sees me.

We were just talking about you. Ken whit? Ah was genuinely beginning tae worry Billy had gone a bit far...

And Billy then – *Tommy! Guid tae see you, auld pal! Last time ah saw you, you were – well, how should ah put this? A wee bit under the weather – under a shower, anyway...*

A funny cunt, eh?

Oh, come now, Tommy, let's no' be like that! We just needed a bit o' peace. Give me a hug, c'mon...

And he comes towards me, open armed, ready to embrace, but when he sees that I'm coming towards him far, far quicker, he begins to back away – but too late, as I'm head down, straight into his chest, winding him, then my arms flail around, scrapping, scratching at his face, ripping his hair. It'd be called a catfight if we were lassies. Billy recovers from the surprise of the attack and pushes at me – *Back the fuck off, Tommy.* I hit him, skelp him, anything. He grabs me in a headlock, the force grinding my sore rib down – but there's strength enough left in me to react and, from the weight of me, the two of us are soon crashing towards the fireplace, a fireplace sadly unlit...

Get affa me, ye fat cunt!

I'm fuming, though, breathing double-quick, spittle fizzling from my mouth.

Let go ma neck, ye wee shiter. Fucking coward – hitting me fae behind, eh? Think yer a big man? Fucking... Billy the Keich... Jock was right there!

All the time, hitting his thigh as hard as I can, the only part of him I can reach, but my rib is screaming in pain...

And in the background, laughing at my efforts, Simon – *Heh heh, heh heh... He's got you there, Billy. Billy the Keich, eh? Ah'd forgotten a' aboot that, heh heh...*

Simon's enjoying the show. Billy's easily getting the better of me, but I ram his back into the wall and repeatedly shove, heave, hoping there's a hook nail or something to do some damage.

Ok! Ok! Tommy, let go!

After this thirty-second scrum, I am exhausted – *You fucking let go!*

Ok! You twa – heh – Billy, let him go. Right now. RIGHT NOW.

And my neck is released. I'm fuming still, my blood flowing michty and quick. As I get free, I throw one more fist at Billy's face, but it only skelfs him, though he does let out a satisfying – *Ooya* – then backs right off me.

I stand straight and wipe my saliva-covered face. I step towards Billy once more, but Simon gets between us –

That's it, you twa. Heh, heh. Tommy – TOMMY! Listen, drop it. Calm down. Calm down... Now. Billy and me have been discussing things, and you'll be pleased tae ken we've thought o' a way you can get shot o' us for good.

And that gets my attention. I glance at him, but my main focus is still on Billy, should he come at me again. He's as shaken up as I am, and it gives me genuine pleasure to see him as red-faced and shocked as he is. Fuck him. Sure, I took him with my size and my anger and surprise just, but, well, that's enough for now.

Tommy? Did you hear me? Because we can make it happen. Come on, sit doon. Let ME get YOU a drink, for a change...

56

AH CAN SEE yer no' as saft as we thought, Tommy boy.

How's one supposed to answer that? I'm sat now, as steady as I can muster, looking in turn from Simon to Billy, hoping they'll confuse my silence for strength, impending threat. The adrenaline is such that I can barely lift the whisky Simon has poured for fear of spilling, fear of betraying my shaky hands...

I opt to keep a clear head.

Billy's stretching his back, where I hoiked him against the wall. When he catches me noticing, he winds himself back in and readopts the pose of *hardman*.

Ah can see yer angry, Tommy. But you know, we had tae — we had tae insist you leave. You'll mind we asked you at first. Politely. Will you agree with that?

I'm breathing slow and deep, trying to calm down — *You've no place to ask me to do fuck all. This is mine. That bar is mine. That whisky you just poured me — mine.*

Ok. Ok, Tommy. Ah get it. But look, we had guests coming, Tommy. Proper guests. We needed you out. We couldnae hae that English cunt busting in wi' some auld granny or you talking aboot... whit was it? Fucking sausages? Nah. We needed you out. Now, you were asked. Requested. Treated wi' respect. But Billy here — he says ye werenae up for it. Gave him lip. Is that right?

It's my fucking bar, Simon —

Aye, nae dispute. Nae dispute. But we had a disagreement, and you fucking paid the price. End of. Your responsibility, Tommy, no' mine, no' mine. A'right? He wipes his mouth. *But now we can forget about that. It's done, right?*

221

I'm no' forgetting anything...

Simon breathes in, audibly annoyed. He's trying to keep his voice level, trying to restore peace – *Say whitever ye like, Tommy. But right now, the way ah see it, we need each other, you and me.*

Eh? I shake my head. *That's no' the way I see it at all, Simon.*

Tommy, we've got the same goals, you and me. Ken whit they are?

Getting you the fuck out of my life, that's my main goal.

Heh. Exactly. And same here, pal. I'm after bigger things. Bigger things than a damp hotel, a daft wee lass and a nippy wee bairn... Whit sort o' name is George, anyhow?

He's trying to be funny, I think. Friendly. I shake my head – *You're a Class-A cunt, Simon, you know that?*

He grins, taking it as a compliment. *We have tae move on. We're businessmen, me and you. Agreed?*

I shake my head again – *Simon – just – tell me what's on your mind.*

57

I DIDNAE LIKE PRISON much. Let me tell you that. But, well, I made it work for me.

I can imagine. My heart is pounding, but I'm trying to take in what he's saying, letting him talk.

There's a' sorts in there. Eejits learning nothing. Small-time pricks... But there's also folk — folk who are keen tae make it work for them, ken? And you know, these guys — these guys operate on a different level. Ken whit I mean?

I sniff, my nose still birling from the rough and tumble.

And these are the guys AHM interested in, ken?

He awaits a reply, staring.

Ok.

See, when I was inside, there was a wee bit o' jostling for position and that... And well, ma brother's name came up once or twice. Ah found — Ah found it helped a wee bit, I'll admit it. Being — being Jim Blair's brother, well, it... raised ma profile. Gave me certain advantages, ken?

Simon's looking away as he speaks now, not wistful and romantic, just avoiding eye contact, perhaps getting things clear in his own mind.

And it was good. Folk gave me a bit o' space, bit o' respect — word got around a few o' his auld pals and ah got tae sit in wi' the big league. No' the fucking — persistent shoplifters 'n that. Wee fucking druggies. I mean, you and me ken I dinnae belong wi' them...

He exhales.

And that day — that day, when we asked ye tae leave, mind? Well, some o' Jim's auld pals were due round. And I couldnae fuck it up, Tommy. Too much at stake. Understand?

I nod. A tiny, almost imperceptible nod.

And the meeting went well, thanks very much. I got the contact, the go-ahead I needed. But here's the thing – they need tae see Jim now. For the next level. The final hurdle.

He's silent now, just looking at me expectantly.

Aye, but Simon – Jim – Jim is dead, right?

He flinches.

Heh – no, Tommy. Jim's no' deid. He's mair... lying low right now. But you ken what? I reckon – I reckon we could bring him back.

And he tells me his grand idea, and it is the most ridiculous idea I've ever heard. At first, I think he's joking and I look to Billy to see how he's reacted – but no, Billy is straight-faced, and it seems that big-businessman Simon's cunning plan to jump up to the big league is, well, he wants me to become *Big Jim Blair* for one night only. He wants *me* to meet up with these *investors*.

I'm incredulous.

Are you fucking mad?

Tommy, Tommy...

Look, I cannae do that, dinnae be saft. I'd be fucking... I'd be pissing ma breeks, but I can't say that. *Look, they'd ken me, I poked my head in the snug, mind? – one o' them will remember me.*

That wisnae them, Tommy! Ahm no' daft. They were just... fucking wee pricks fae around here and inside. They had nothing tae offer me. NOTHING. Coming on like the main men but – fuck all. Ahm after big league, Tommy. Ah've had enough o' this... shite.

But Simon, I mind yer brother – I look fuck all like him.

Same height, Tommy. Same build. He smiles. *He was a fat cunt too, mind.*

Was?

IS.

But – if he's no' deid, why don't you just ask him?

He shakes his head. *Too risky, Tommy. He's... He's got too much tae lose. He went underground for a reason.*

Aye, because he fucking died. I mind the wreck of that car crash, the whole thing...

*Look, Tommy, ma contacts, they need tae see him. Tae ken that you –
that Jim – is behind me, a' the way. They trust him. They'll believe him.
Once they see him, that's it – ahm done. WE'RE done. Ah'll be far, far
awa' fae here… Ah need this, Tommy, and you need it too. It's the next
step for me – it's big business. Proper. Tommy – this will be in and oot.
Quick. Understand?*

Sure, but if it's just that in-and-out quick – can Billy no' do it?

*No. They'll ken him. O' course they will. The window o' opportunity
is very short, ma friend. And you're the only choice, for two reasons.
Firstly, you want something ah can gie ye, right? And that's me outae yer
life. Right? Agreed?*

Aye. Sure.

*And secondly? Well, because you, my friend – ye've got it a' tae fucking
lose.*

And that sounds like a threat. *What are you saying exactly, Simon?*

*Well, Tommy. Cards on table. If you couldnae help me now, say –
well, I'd be pretty pissed aff. And I'd just be sitting around here and
getting mair pissed aff. And ye ken whit happened last time ah got pissed
aff, right?*

Aye, I mind. That garage – up in flames.

*Oh, slow down, Tommy. Slow down. I mean, I wouldnae admit
tae anything like that, but I'd hate – I'd hate tae see anything similar
happen here, Tommy. Your hotel – and what, say – say the fire spread
intae the flat – and whit if Fi was in there, mebbe wee Georgie…*

You fucking cunt.

Aye. You've got that right.

I'm furious. *No way, Simon. How about this: I just fucking tell the
polis a' your plans. You're on parole, Simon. You'll be back inside – I
click my fingers together – Like that…*

*Aye, mebbe. Thing is, tho', do ye ken why Fi let me back here? Had
me back here?*

I stare in reply, dread rising as he speaks her name, tempted to
say – *Because she's a saft wee cow* – but keeping schtum.

*See, it's no' just some daft loyalty. Naw. She was wi' me the night that
boy's place got burnt. And no' just that night, plenty o' others. Aye, she*

225

was in for a penny, then spending ma pounds... And ye see, I kept her oot. I got twa year? She'd've got something. Accessory. Driving. And see if I fucking go back in? Well, she's coming wi' me.

I keep my peace. I sit still. Who's bluffing who?

And see that wee George? Well, wha kens where he'll go. What, wi' both his ma AND his da in jail...

And that does it – I jump at him, but the bar is between us and he backs off, leaving my arms midair, as if grasping for ghosts...

He shakes his head, grinning.

It's just as I telt ye, Tommy. We need each other.

58

I WEIGH UP THE odds.
In and out. In and out.
How hard can that be?
It's only a few days away, and then Simon, Billy – they're oot o' ma hair.

Get Fi back. See Georgie. Simon has zero interest in either. I'm home free there… Things – things can calm down. Return to the norm.

Ha. It'd be worth it just to order that Billy around, if he was there – *You! Billy lad! Awa' and hae some cake and jelly. Let us men do the talking…*

I wonder how Jim would speak? I wonder if I could pull that off? A lot of *cunts* and *fucks*, I guess. Though maybe he's beyond that? Maybe, as some kind of spiritual gangster-ghost, he's grown out of swearing. Or maybe he only swears at home, when he drops a tin of beans on his bare feet, say. Or maybe he saves it for a special moment – *You! Billy! Away and buy us some fucking crisps, ya dish-faced cunt…*

Or maybe he died long, long ago and I'm being a muppet for even considering it.

One thing I know, I've got to speak to Fi, get her over, sort all that out. Make sure we're sound, we're sorted… See the wee lad. That's the thing. Hold onto Georgie once more.

*

Oh, hello – Jeannie?

No, no, it's Lizzie here, her neighbour. Is it Fiona yer efter, son?

It is, aye. It's Tommy here.

Who? Oh, Tommy, how are ye, son? She'll be pleased tae hear fae ye…
The phone goes quiet, but just, just in the background – *That'll be yer Tommy on the line. Here – I'll get the tea started – mince is it ye've got? Braw, I puir love a guid bit o' mince…*

TOMMY!

Hi! Fi! Is – are –

Where the fuck have you been, Tommy Bruce? Are you drunk?

No – I'm…

Tommy, I've called, I've called…

I was just… away.

She cannot hear about this daft business right now. Wait until I see her.

Away? Away is it? What about me? What about your bairn? You've responsibilities now, Tommy Bruce, don't you fucking give me AWAY. Where were you? Up that bloody hill this whole time?

Um… No, I was…

Where? Where was I?

I was in the highlands. I just – I just felt the need – to get away. I stayed… in a bothy.

A what!?! A fucking bothy? How come you never let me know? You could've – you could've even asked us along? You know Tommy, this may be too much for you to comprehend but Georgie may've enjoyed that – mind Georgie? Your son?

Hmm. No, no, Georgie wouldn't have enjoyed it – But…

We couldae come up, Tommy, as a family – closed the bar. Got, fucking, Simon tae look efter it. He was the only ane YOU left in charge, after a'. I cannae believe you didnae call me. Tommy Bruce – this is the last fucking time you do that. Understand? Well?

I…

And how come you didnae take yer phone? That's whit they're for. For taking. No' for leaving on the fucking freezer –

228

Aye, I dinnae really use it –

I ken that, ya – ya fucking eejit.

Look, I got snowed in – in the Highlands, I mean. I didnae mean tae stay that long…

But the line goes dead. Or, more accurately, the line goes fucking dead.

I look around me – what for, I do not know. There's a clutch of old pens in a jam jar. Last week's newspaper, a half-finished sudoku violently scrawled out. Was that Simon? I peer over it. Skill level: easy. Ha. Maybe it was that Billy…

Then the phone's alive again, ringing.

Hello.

Da-da.

I melt. *Georgie – hello, Georgie – how are you? I've missed you – have you been good tae your mum? Have you been looking after her?*

I saw duck.

You what? You saw a duck? Where, in the park?

…

Was it in the park?

… Mama.

Brushes and scrapes as the phone is handed over.

Right, Tommy, it's me –

Was it in the park?

Was what in the park, Tommy?

The duck? Did he see the duck in the park?

What fu… what duck, Tommy?

Ah fuck – never mind – now listen, I'll need you to come and watch the bar for a while…

What? Why?

Um… could you do – the next three days? Or four, mebbe?

WHAT?

I know, I know – I – I have to go somewhere. I have to do something.

What the fuck, Tommy?

I need to – I've been asked to – I've got to go and do something. I pause. *With Simon.*

She's quiet. Then, slowly – *Oh, Tommy, Tommy… dinnae get involved. Is that where ye've been? A' this time?*

Aye, Fi. It was… kinda not ma choice. Look, it's… um… I have tae do this thing – and then – then he's gone.

How do you mean, 'he's gone'?

I mean, he's going tae leave. Leave us in peace.

Oh, Tommy – what's going on? Dinnae trust him. Dinnae trust a word he says.

I – I think it'll be ok.

She exhales. *Tommy, it'll never be ok wi' him, never. Just say no. Whatever it is. Believe me.*

Fi – Fi, answer me this: were you wi' Simon when he torched that garage?

Silence, then –

Oh, Tommy… I… I'm so sorry…

Then we've got nae choice, Fi. I've – thought it through. I'll just be in and out…

She's crying now – *Oh, Tommy, what have you agreed tae?*

It's nothing, Fi, honestly. Dinnae… dinnae you worry…

Tommy, remember you've got Georgie tae bring up.

I bite my lip. *It'll be fine, Fi. It'll be fine.*

59

*F*I'S COMING BACK *right now?*

Aye – to look after the place, while I'm away – let me see Georgie…
Right. That's it. We're aff. Gather anything ye need, Tommy boy.
We're no' having a happy reunion the now. Nae chance. Billy? BILLY?
GET DOON HERE.

But Simon – I've no' seen them for a'most a week –

Aye, well, twa mair days is fuck all, then, eh. Heh.

But she'll need…

She'll need whit? Whit, Tommy? There's fuck all she needs round this
place – ony cunt can change a fucking barrel, Tommy. Wipe a fucking
table. Whit she needs – she needs YOU back safe and sound, so let's work
on that, eh?

This news, this delivery, well, it brews nothing but hate within
me.

Billy arrives – *Hey, Si.*

Dinnae ca' me fucking Si, Billy. Ah've telt ye that a thousand fucking
times. Gather yer stuff. We're aff right now.

Right now? Ah was in the middle o'…

You were in the middle o' fuck all, understand? Now, get yer car,
bring it tae the door, right now. You'll be following behind me in the
van, got it? And you'll be driving Tommy. Now – Billy – if you need a
keich or whatever – go now. We're no' stopping mid-route. Got it? And,
Tommy, listen – you cannae be wearing THAT shite when you meet
them – grab yer suit.

My what?

Yer suit. You must hae a suit, no?

Ach, Simon, I had ane years ago but, well, it widnae fit now!

Fucking hell. FUCKING HELL. Never mind. We'll get ye a fucking suit somewhere. C'mon – get a move on.

What's the rush, Simon? I just want tae see Fi and Georgie…

Ah'll tell ye whit the rush is: right now, see you and me? Our needs are mair important than yours and hers. Ahm no' having that nippy wee cow round here telling me I cannae be daen this or that. Soon as this is a' sorted, you can play happy families a' ye like. Until then, yer wi' me. Understand? It's for all of us. The best for all of us.

I use my time to scribble Fi a note and tuck it behind the bar, above the sink.

Had to go. It'll be ok. Simon says back tomorrow and all over then. Kiss Georgie for me. Love you both. X

And that's it. That's my time gone.

60

WE'RE IN A tiny wee Peugeot thing, a 306 or whatever. I'm squashed in the back, feeling like a toy gangster. Billy's got his seat reclined right back but for some reason I'm not allowed beside him in the front, so I'm scrunched up beside some Tesco bags, a dog lead, half-a-dozen old newspapers, a sandwich wrapper, some Coke cans...

This is hardly The Godfather, *eh?*

Aye, well, Tommy. We dinnae need picked up – nae polis, eh. This vehicle here – well, it fits in, right? Draws no attention...

So... is it stolen?

Eh? No. It's ma gran's, eh.

The final bit of convincing I needed.

Me and Simon – we're – we're on a different level tae you cunts. Fucking... civilians. We dinnae even THINK like you.

It's funny to think of Billy having a gran, having a family. I wonder what they make of him, with his denim outfits and murky employment record? Does he see them at all? I wonder what they know of the thug he is.

It feels like a dream, this. Not in a magical, wonderful way, but because I'm so tired that the whole absurdness of the situation seems so far in the distance, the least of my worries. I could have done with a night in my own bed. Not sure where we're heading now, but I'm fairly certain it won't be to a kicking in the middle of nowhere – for all Simon's flaws, that seems unlikely. I have my concerns, of course. But the seat, the snooze of the engine, the warmth, even the way I'm sat – half lying down, head against the window – it's all so damned soporific, and after my recent adventure, it's as though I'm being treated as royalty. It's all I can do just to stay awake, but the pain of my injuries, inflicted by the man driving this very car, means I just cannot snooze.

So, Billy… tell me about Simon's brother, then?

Eh?

You know, if I'm going to pretend to be the guy – I'll need to know a wee bit mair about him. I haven't seen him in, what, ten years?

Neither's onyone else, heh.

Aye, I get that, but – say they ask me something?

Who?

These guys we're meeting. Say they ask me about… I don't know – plans?

Fucking… I dinnae ken. Just fucking – mak' stuff up, eh?

Aye, a deep thinker, Billy. I can make stuff up. I'll tell them I'm Lex Luther. Tell them I'm working with Al Capone. For what do I know of that shite?

And jings, my head is heavy.

So… So, where are we going the now? You know, I could sleep. Last few nights –

Haha – aye, sorry aboot that, pal, but ye fucking wound me up. And ah just had tae mak' sure ye kept away. Heh. It worked, eh?

He turns to me, looking for an affirmative. Well, I guess it did work. Job done.

How did ye get back, by the way?

Eh?

Fae that field where I dropped ye?

Well, there's a story… *I got the bus, Billy. I got the bus.*

The bus eh? Right.

So… where are we going now?

Fuck knows. Ahm just following Simon up ahead, eh.

We continue in silence, me watching out of the window, taking in the surroundings…

George and Fi seem so far away. This is not dissimilar to my nights on the hill, where I'd drink myself into a dwam and become someone else, somewhere else… That feeling of detachment, of comfort, almost, it's dangerous, especially at a time like this.

This must be quite different for ye, eh, Tommy?

How do you mean?

Ah mean, a' this! A' this smoke and dagger.

Oh. Aye. I suppose...

Well, ahm well used tae it. This is ma life yer getting a wee peek intae. Aff the radar. The underworld.

Aye, it's... it's, um...

We overtake a lorry, two lorries, three lorries.

These fuckers shouldnae be on the road, eh.

What did you say?

These fucking lorries. Keep freight on the rail, eh?

Oh. Aye, sure.

The wipers dart back and forth, full speed ahead.

Fucking... hard tae see which car's Simon, eh?

So, did – did you know Jim well, then?

Did ah ken Jim? Aye. Too right. We were – we were best pals, me and Jim. Me and Jim Blair, Jim Blair and me. Partners. A' the way through school, eh. And beyond... Ken, ah wisnae – ah wisnae the best at school. Jim was smart, tho'. He helped me a wee bit. He was a clever cunt, like you, eh.

I'm flattered.

Billy's peering through the windscreen, eyes on the road, eyes on the road.

I can remember him a bit. You guys were a few years above me at school...

Aye, well – Jim left, mind. Ah followed a few months later. Jim got asked tae leave, ken. Took money fae some auld wifey's purse, eh – ane o' the dinner ladies or office wifeys. She caught him red-handed, and that was that. Jim kent, tho', even then, he kent he'd be getting mair ootae school than in. Nae flies on Jim Blair, no sir – fucking, look at this eejit – GET OUTAE THE WAY, HAMMERHEAD...

I'm leaning through the two front seats – *Watch out – watch out for that motorbike!*

Eh? Ach. They shouldnae be oot in this weather. Ah wouldnae be, ken. If that were MA bike, ah'd be on the bus, heh.

The bikes fly past us, soon out of sight.

And how did you hook up with Simon, then? Did you ken him as a wean?

Simon? Aye, a wee bit, a wee bit as a bairn just, but Jim wouldnae go near his hame for such a lang time. Ah think his da hit him and such, so ah never saw Simon grow up, eh.

Really?

Aye. Aha. Jim never spoke well o' the guy. Deid noo, mind.

Who? Jim?

Aye — well, no — no, Jim's no' deid — ah meant his da, eh? Fucking drank himsel' tae death. Jim telt me once, but he really never spoke o' it. My ma telt me a' aboot it, mostly. Big gambler, debts and that. Ah think Jim was — whit? Fifteen, mebbe? That was that.

Wow.

Aye. Wow. Happens, tho', eh.

A car pulls between us and Simon, a long Volvo thing, looking far more stable in this weather than our own grandmotherly vehicle.

Fucking — ah, c'mon…

Jim tho', eh. Well. We were daen quite nicely. A bit o' buying and selling, ken. Import and export… He took in a BIG load o' money, just afore he died — ah mean, disappeared, ken? But then, well — aye — the crash, or whitever — and that was that. Folk came looking, mind. For Jim. Or maybe the money… But Jim was too smart. Kept himsel' hidden.

Aye, hidden in the morgue. A clever cunt, Jim.

But fucking years later — years and years — Simon — fucking — he — got in touch wi' me, eh. When ah was working up at the fruit farm there, picking berries, eh.

Oh aye?

Aye — it was — well, seasonal. Cash in hand. But it was ok, if ye didnae mind red fingers, eh.

236

Heh.

Aye, but Simon, well, ah didnae even recognise him at first, just thought he was a wee Rome... Rome... Romanian lad come tae pick berries. But no', soon he was like, 'Mind me? Mind me?' And asking a' sorts aboot his brother.

Cool.

Aye. Decent bloke, like, Simon. Ah mean, YOU might no' think so – but he's no' bad.

Ha. Bosses you about a fair bit, no?

Eh? No. Well... He's no' his brother, that's the thing, eh. Jim and me? We were like THAT.

He crosses his two fingers and waves them in front of my face, for one second, two, three, until I worry about his control of the steering wheel – *ok, ok, I've got it...*

We carry on, mostly in silence, the sleet seemingly pouring directly onto the windscreen. Billy, at least, is a conscientious driver – *Fucking wish that Simon would slow doon, eh.*

Ah, here – look – seems we've arrived somewhere. Simon's pulling in.

We follow Simon's van, blinking, slowing, pulling into a large, open car park. Billy waits for Simon to stop his engine then does the same with ours. Before we know it, Simon's at our window, then sticking his head in, out of the sleet –

Tommy, Billy – you two stay put in the car. I'll sort it, then come and get you. And when it's done, Billy, you just heid straight tae the room wi' Tommy here. Nae shite at the vending machine, nae banter wi' whoever's at the counter, nae singing, nae asking for the cludgie – just straight up. Got it?

Aye, Simon. Ah've got it. Nae hanging aboot. Straight in.

Simon departs and Billy turns, raising his eyebrows at me. What a peculiar mess.

61

IT'S JUST A Travelodge. Just a room in a Travelodge, that's all.

I'm hurried through reception by Billy, who, for whatever reason, has chosen to wear a pair of wrap-around sunglasses, thus completing his Status Quo roadie look.

It seems so normal and polite here; I can barely detect any threat of danger. But in the lift I glance at Billy's shoes and I remember them kicking me down. The pain in my side is still very much there and I believe, despite my washes, that I will forever smell Billy's piss in my hair. Bring on the barber.

We pile out of the lift and make our way down the corridor, Billy not letting me know which room we're in so just herding, prodding me along. I mean, why not just say – *It's room 38, Tommy* – or whatever? Because he's a prize fud, that's why.

We arrive and it's two rooms, just one for me, though – a connecting room, a family room. Once inside, Billy straightaway pushes the spare bed close against the door to the corridor, to stop me from bailing out – unless I'm devious enough to move the bed away from the door, of course. But should I play their game, carry on, well, I'll need to go through their adjoining room to leave the building.

So, it's like I'm trapped in a crap, comfortable prison. There's a bed and a bathroom. Jings, this'll do for now. If I can close the door and take a twelve-hour sleep, I'll do just that. I can reevaluate in the morning. See just how stupid I've been to agree to this farce.

My stomach aches with hunger, and I wonder if they'll pay for room service.

The empty bed calls forth thoughts of George, but upon lifting the phone – my only way of contacting Fi – it is dead. I sit on the bed, lie back. Consider the television but can hear talk from the conjoining room through the thin plywood door and that pulls me in –

Ah cannae wait tae see Jim again.

It winnae be Jim. It'll be – him – fucking Tommy. Pretending. Get it?

Aye, o' course – but – will Jim no' be popping o'er?

No, Billy, he willnae. Why would he do that?

Ah. Silence. *So...*

Aye?

If these Irish boys dinnae believe it IS Jim – then whit?

They WILL believe. Why would they no'? They ken ahm his brother, they ken you're his pal – ah mean, you ran wi' him, back when I was wee...

Aye. Ah mind that!

So, they're BOUND tae believe. I mean, aye, it's a' bluff right enough, but that's why we have tae get it right. Understand?

62

I BATHE. I DIDN'T sleep. Of course not. 4:00 am, inner-voice wake-up call – *What the fuck are ye doing, Tommy the Bruce?*

So, I bathe.

I lock the door, to stop Billy bursting in.

I consider my options, and here's what I'm always coming back to: the prize. The prize of solitude, of Georgie and Fi.

Between here and there? Well, I can play this charade, and all being well, all shall be well.

In and oot, in and oot.

Or I can jump ship. But before I got to anywhere near safety, there'd be risks – the main one being I don't think I'd ever sleep well in that hotel again, wary and aware of Simon's fire-raising skills. And that's after the immediate kicking, the hassle of the running, the escaping...

My rib, it aches. The warmth of the bath does not soothe but amplifies, surrounds.

My ear, my neck...

I am not in tip-top fighting form. Nope.

All reminders of how brutal Billy can be.

So, I shall become scary auld Jim Blair. For however long it takes.

It's funny, wallowing here in the bath, wishing I was halfway up my hill, sitting frozen, feeling the whisky sook down my throat, warming my belly, numbing my senses. Georgie strapped on, the quietest place in the world, his little eyes wondering at the light, his cheeks against the wind, red with cold... Seems so far away, so alien. I need that back.

63

*T*OMMY! *T*OMMY!

Shite. I must have fallen asleep. The bath is now… lukewarm. A creeping cold with every movement.

Aye – who's that, then?

I know it's Billy, but the irritation of the awakening means I cannot resist this lightest of barbs.

It's me! Billy! Is that you in there, Tommy?

Aye. Of course it is.

Whit ye daen?

I'm taking a bath. How?

Just fucking… Ah thought… Never mind. Here, ah've got yous breakfast. Simon wants ye fed, eh. It's sitting here, getting cauld now. Fucking beans are setting. Ah mean, if yer no' efter it, ah'll gie it a go…

No, hang on, hang on, I'll be out in a moment…

Give me the ambush of a hangover any day over this pish.

My breakfast: a piddly wee orange juice and a spoonful or two of reheated beans slapped on two cold slices of toast. Well, hallelujah.

Right, Tommy, the barber's coming this morning, right? And we'll measure you up for that suit…

Measure? Is it – is it going to be handmade then?

Naw. There's nae time for that, sir. It'll be aff the peg. I made a call last night and, well, people are keen tae see you. Tae see Jim, that is. I suspect we'd be as well getting this o'er wi' as quick as possible, heh. But we'll get yer basic size and I'll send Billy oot tae Topshop. Buy you something fae there. No' too…

241

Shitey?

Aye. It willnae be shitey, dinnae you worry. A'most a'hing relies on you looking decent. Moneyed. We willnae put ye oot there in a crap suit, never you worry.

What about my shoes?

Eh? What about them?

Well – I gesture towards the collapsed once-white trainers I'd been wearing – *they'll no' work wi' a suit...*

Fuck. What size?

Eleven.

Ok. Billy, take a note o' that. Get him something neat. Same colour as the suit. I'm no' having folk saying they saw Jim Blair and he looked a tool. Naw, we've tae get this right. All about impressions, eh, Tommy?

I nod. It is indeed.

My stomach contracts and squeals.

I get my head back down. Simon's next door on his phone, shout-whispering, organising who knows what.

I cannot drop back off.

At one point he jostles through the door and switches my TV on – some mid-morning antiques shite – ups the volume and leaves.

The shout-whispering continues, but now against the drone of car boot sales and auctioneers. I thunder out of bed and open the window, just the four inches or so that Travelodge deem suitable to my needs, then clamber back in, pulling the covers over me, leaving just a tiny wee hole for my mouth. I attempt to rest, to sleep.

Oh, Georgie, Georgie, what tales I will have to tell when you are grown, of how we met, your mother and me, of young John, of my mother, my hard-working father... I wonder, I wonder if you'll keep the hotel, or if you'll have some drive to get away – Christ, I wish I had done enough, but it's as if my father were watching down now, keeping me in place... I wonder if you'll have a sister, or a brother... I hope you will, I dearly hope you will... Come here now, come on, we can play, climb on board, young Georgie...

*

Ok, Tommy – up, up, oot o' bed. Your servants have arrived, heh.

The light is switched on, the curtains hoiked open. I am in the comfort and sweetness of a dwam that I would pay a king's ransom to return to…

Tommy? Covers aff in three seconds –

Ok, hang on –

Three!

Haud yer weesht, I'm coming –

Two!

Fucking –

One!

And my heads out – *You cunt.*

Well, that changes things.

Watch yer language, Tommy boy. There are ladies present.

I peer out of my eyes, adjust to the light, the company. I'm bare-chested but covered still below. Two young girls – heh, young? Fi's age. Dolled up, wigs – wigs? Dyed, sculptured hair, anyhow… Identikit make-up: orange-faced, ski-slope eyeliner.

One of them speaks up –

Is this him? He'll need his hair wet. Have ye a shower here?

Aye, there's ane through there – I motion, as though this is my territory, as if I should be showing the girls around my kingdom.

C'mon, then. We've only got the ane hour for lunch.

Billy – Billy – will you pass me the dressing gown?

Eh? He considers it, but this request, the thought of HIM answering to ME, is obviously too much, especially in front of the present company, these young, impressionable ladies… He shakes his head. *Na.*

I exhale a tired, quiet laugh and throw the covers off, thankfully wearing boxer shorts of a younger vintage, and pour myself out of the bed like a seal clambering down a rock, the blubber of my stomach settling a fraction after my legs. I stand, all eyes now on my unsteady belly, walk to the robe, put it on and make my way to the shower room, slowing just to wink and say – *You got yer thrill, eh, Billy? You got yer eyeful!*

Billy's eyes quickly burn back at me and there's a notion of a lunge, but Simon laughs, genuine, defusing, cruel – *Heh, some fella Fi's found hersel', eh, Billy?* – and that distraction, that ribbing, is enough for Billy. For my place, the bottom o' the heap, is assured once more.

Whit style would ye like?

Eh?

Whit haircut ye efter? We've only brought scissors, we cannae do colouring or nothing.

Ah, ask Simon there.

Who? Oh, Mr Drummond?

Umm… I guess so. The one not wearing a denim bodysuit.

They laugh, one of them disappearing, the other turning the shower on and feeling the water's temperature.

HE's a puir eejit, by the way.

Who?

Him in the denim.

Aye, he is. I'd say you're remarkably perceptive…

Well, whitever – But he's a perv.

Is he?

Aye. Shouldae seen him in the lift, skirting his hands aboot – here, lean yer heid back…

Scoosh, scoosh, scoosh.

Here, ye've cuts a' o'er yer heid. Did ye ken that?

Aye – just – stuff.

Well, we willnae cut it too close. Keep them covered, eh.

The other lass returns, comb and scissors in hand –

He said cut it 'businesslike'.

Whit does that mean?

Dunno. Dull, I guess? Bit o' Brylcreem?

Here, shall I do it like yer da's?

Aye, why no'. He's a businessman, efter a'.

Um, what style does your father have?

Eh? Oh, dinnae you worry. It's just neat. Short. Nothing distracting. He sells carpets. Snip. Snip. Imagine that? I couldnae do THAT for a living. He aye says, 'Folk are no' in tae look at ma hair, Marjorie, keep it simple.'

Who's Marjorie?

That's me.

Oh.

Ah ken. Stupit auld name, eh. Quite like it noo though, eh. It sounds... exotic.

French.

Aye. Or fae the Spanish Riviera – oh sorry, water in yer eyes...

Never mind.

Here, sit up.

Whit do you do, then, Mr Dylan?

Mr Dylan?

Oh, sorry, did I get yer name wrong? They telt us –

No, Mr Dylan is fine.

Snip, snip, snip.

I'm a hotelier.

Ah, really? Is this place yours, then?

No – what? This place? No, I own – I own a place over in – um – Edinburgh...

Check me out, playing the undercover game.

Aye, the, um, Rose and Castle. Heard of it?

No. Haud tight the now...

Snip, snip, snip.

What a welt on yer neck! Are you ok?

Aye. I um... fell over.

At the Rose and Castle, was it?

What?

When ye fell o'er?

Aye. Something like that. On the stairs, mebbe. Or in the kitchen, perhaps.

Ok, watch yer ears...

Snip, snip, snip.

Jenny, get me a towel, will ye?

Here ye go, Marj. Here, c'mon, we'll be in trouble if we're no' back soon.

Och, I willnae be lang. Cannae leave Mr Dylan here wi' half a haircut.

She clumps my spent hair between her fingers and drops it neatly into the bathroom bin behind.

So… hae ye any bairns, Mr Dylan?

Aye… One. You?

No. No' found the right man.

Plenty o' wrong 'uns, tho'!

Shut up, Jenny. You can talk!

A towel is raised and used to buff.

A girl? A wee girl, is it?

Wee boy. George.

Ah. I like that name. Efter the prince, is it?

Hmmph. No. His ma's da.

Well, mebbe HE was named efter a different prince.

Aye, mebbe. You could be right there.

Here, put yer heid back aince mair…

She rinses, she runs her hands through my hair. It feels… good. The intimacy, the care…

Here, ye'll just need dried now. Jenny, get through here! Ye got that drier? Jen?

Oops, sorry, aye, here we go…

I perch on the edge of the bath, not the most comfortable of places, and watch in the mirror as my hair is teased and creamed and blow-dried into shape by a bonny young lass. Staring back at me: a slightly neater man than this time yesterday. Carpet salesman's haircut. No beauty, that is for sure, but ok, maybe? My face is scratched but not scarred, I'd guess, red raw, a lifetime of too much alcohol, too little sleep, bags under my eyes… Sure, I could pass for a gangster or, perhaps more likely, a shite, dim bouncer, but equally, I could pass as some patsy behind the counter of a pie shop or a depressed, sun-shy IT guy. I'm just a naebody, a random, an anonymous non-achiever. I catch a glint in my eye and smile sadly back to myself. Well, this'll be a day to remember, should I get that luxury.

When the girls leave, we relax. Billy puts his machismo back in the box. Simon's hopping about, agitated, no longer watching his words. And I – well, I no longer dream. I focus on the case in hand.

Billy has bought me a suit, as asked, and boots, as asked. But nae scants, nae socks and – get this – nae shirt. What a plum.

Ah – Ach – Where's the fucking shirt, Billy?

Ye never asked for a shirt, Simon.

But it's a fucking suit, Billy? Whit's he tae wear it wi'? A vest? He'll look like a fucking – like a jakey.

Simon's fuming now. He's freaking a wee bit, stressed out. The shirt I'd been wearing – a brewery freebie promoting the virtues of Red Cock Real Ale – isn't considered appropriate. Although I shouldn't be, I am trying to calm things, to help Simon out a bit. I scan for replacements, but Billy has a pale-blue-flecked cotton thing on, and Simon – well, Simon's half my size.

Have I no' got time tae go get ane the now?

Simon's shaking his head, furious. He looks over to me – *Ye see? Ye see what I put up wi' for ma brother?*

I raise a sympathetic eyebrow, but Billy's not so keen –

Eh, Simon? How do ye mean by that?

Billy. YOU KEN how important this meeting is, and ye cannae just think for one moment, can ye – 'Oh, it's a suit – he'll need a shirt for that.' Ye fucking… Ah, Christ!

I'm not sure how this sits for me. I do want to help, but, well, I cannot make a shirt out of a bedsheet, can I? But then – *Simon?*

Whit is it?

Ken, places like this – even in MY hotel, when Dad had staff, we'd a'ways have a spare shirt or two hung up. It's worth asking the man at the desk, no? Just tell him – tell him Billy spilt his cereal on it or something.

Fuck ye mean by that? Ahm no' a wean… Fucking spilling cereal. Tell them – tell them YOU spilt YOUR cereal…

He's pointing his finger at me, genuinely angry.

Billy, Billy – I didnae mean it like that – I was just trying a bit o' humour – calm down. What I mean is, you could go down, say I stained my shirt or something – mebbe we were fixing a car and we got oil on it? Whatever, just – just try and borrow or buy one of their spares? They'll have them, and they'll be better than nothing.

The pair of them look me over, considering.

And I can wear yesterday's scants. My auld socks. They dinnae matter a jimny, do they?

Simon is looking at me, his anger brewed, but surely not with me – this is his nerves for the meeting, his annoyance with Billy. He turns and slowly spells it out –

Billy – go – downstairs – and – ask – the – reception – for – a – shirt.

Billy breathes in and stands, looking down at me with flaring nostrils.

The shirt is cheap shite and it's too tight, but it's arrived and, well, it's an actual shirt, which is better than a pillowslip with head and arm holes. If I stand, if I stay standing, if I suck my belly in, it looks ok. Just.

The suit is *royal blue*, I'm told. I'm not sure of the material, but if I were to guess, I'd maybe say *balloon*. It's brand new, but tatty and cheap and, well, whoever has the generic body shape it was designed for, it isn't me. It fits, though – I mean, it fits around me. I need my belt, but that's the least of my problems – a scaffy belt on a rotund waste, a super-thin shirt, my nipples clearly visible, chest hair, even…

There are three buttons on the jacket and they all work. Good, as I shall need them.

The trooser legs are so long I fold them up, I tuck them in.

Shitty brown plastic shoes. Tight, inflexible, cheap. Who'd wear plastic shoes? I guess they're for weddings or whatever. One-offs. Ideal for the here and now, then.

But there's little escaping that I do not look like a gangster, unless that gangster is off to court to face some minor charge – an unpaid parking fine, not picking up dog litter, perhaps a late-returned library book.

Come lunchtime and Billy is gone.

He's just taking care o' a bit o' business for me, heh.

Simon's ordered up a couple of pizzas. Dull: cheese and tomato, just. Says a lot about someone, I think, the type of pizza they order. Where's the adventure here? It's just fat on tomato on bread. I'm glad of it, though, for the breakfast was scant enough.

Simon seems infinitely more relaxed without Billy. I suspect there's a loyalty with Billy that is invaluable, but he's the loose link in Simon's masterplan. He left me stranded, perhaps for dead. Was that on Simon's request? I really don't think so. One thing in his favour: Billy certainly gets things done. I could do with a Billy in the hotel. To clean under the fridge, that sort of thing. And that gets me thinking of Fi and Georgie, of course.

Would you mind if I called the hotel, Simon?

Eh? What for? You'll be back the nicht. A' being well.

Hmm.

No distractions, eh, Tommy. Best for a'. Clear heads.

He turns away, ending the conversation. The television is whirring away in the background, some lassie singing a dance music thing over a backing track. Sounds shite to my ears and reminds me, as ever, of Fi and the dross she plays in the bar. I need to get this day over with.

Simon's lightly nodding to the tinny, televised bass drum. Chewing his pizza to the time of the beat.

Do you – do you listen to music then, Simon?

Eh? No… Unless ahm dancing. Wi' a lassie. Even then – even then, ahm no' really listening, mair just – mair looking at the lassie. Trying tae work ma way in, ken?

I regret the subject.

Man, this pizza is fatty. Grease running down my thumb, towards my brand-new shirt. I'm getting agitated, nervous, just as feart as Billy and Simon. Of course I am.

So… are you actually confident this will work, Simon? This — me-as-Jim thing.

He looks up — *I am. And here's why: THEY want it tae work, same as us. Ma brother, see, he had — HAS a reputation. That's what they're buying intae. Quite a coup for them. These guys we're seeing — they're… big time-ish, but only in Ireland, eh. They're moneyed, ken, a'ready? But even so, this is — quite an opening for them. A new avenue for their business, on the mainland.*

I smile. I chuckle, as though I am part of Simon's gang, looking down on these part-time crooks from my great height of badness. But it's a nervous, uncomfortable mirth.

And — how did you meet them?

Well. We've no'. No' really — ach — it's through jail, eh. As I said, there were folk — folk I was happy tae have on ma side. Jim Blair this, Jim Blair that… Bought me time. And, well, folk heard about it inside, and then — and then folk heard about it outside, I guess… Thing is, folk were asking me what Jim was up tae nowadays, ken? And I mebbe said… Well, a few things. Anyway, end o' story — these folk want tae invest.

Eh? In what?

Well, in Jim Blair. But listen, Tommy — this is SERIOUS money, ken? We're no' talking sma' beans, here. This is — ootae-Scotland money. So, I formulated a wee plan. And this — this is it.

He cannot be talking about us two with our half-finished pizzas. If this was part of his plan, his attention to detail is admirable.

We climb into the car — Billy's gran's — Simon swearing at the driver's seat, having to move it forwards to fit himself in, then wiping the steering wheel — *Whit's this fucking grease here? Fucking Billy wi' his Quavers…*

I try to keep my head down, my mouth closed. The nerves are washing over me, keeping me good and queasy. Maybe that pizza wasn't a good idea, the oily taste still there in my mouth, my stomach churning. I know, I know, I should be still and quiet — but I have to ask – *Simon – Before we go – you'll be needing tae tell me where I've been – what I'm up tae – even just a name I can drop, a place – some event? Where I stay – even just the country? I cannae just make stuff up. W – what if they ask where I'm living and I say 'Dundee' and they ask whereaboots?*

Why the fuck would ye say 'Dundee'?

Simon, that's no' the point. Dundee's no' the point. The point is, I NEED something. Or else – or else I'm just a man in an ill-fitting suit. Look – I dinnae look threatening. Or – successful. I need… Give me something – just anything…

He glances towards me – *Ah ken, ah ken… Yer right. You want some information about MA brother, eh? About ma fucking brother, Jim fucking Blair… Right then – let's see – let's see… Look, yer daein well. Ye've been o'er in Spain, say –*

Spain? Simon, I'm the whitest man alive – I never see the sun, in that bar a' day.

Aye, well – Spain it is.

Fucking…

Shut it. He's no' calm, no' collected. *And the bar there tae mention is, um… the Queen and Country. Got it?*

The Queen and Country? Cool. And where is this – Queen and Country?

It's in Marbella. On the Argarve.

The what? Do you mean the Algarve? That's – I'm no' sure that's Spain, Simon…

AYE, WELL IT IS NOW. WHO GIES A FUCK? THIS ISNAE A FUCKING GEOGRAPHY LESSON, EH? THEY'RE NO' GONNAE FUCKING ASK WHERE THE FUCKING ARGARVE IS, EH?!

And there's no arguing with that. Christ. The two of us, well wound up. Give me a head fu' o' shite. I am well prepared. Well riled, anyhow.

He starts the car, a wee annoying *beep* coming from the dashboard, reminding him to put his seatbelt on – *Eh? Shut the fuck up, ya wee cunty car cunt* – before he shoves, rattles the seatbelt into its slot – *There.* He starts the car, hoiks the gear stick into place and we peel off, out of the Travelodge car park and onto the M8, the motorway that cuts through Glasgow itself.

I give him, five, ten minutes, until he appears calm.

So – and what am I – What's Jim Blair needing the money for?

Well, Tommy, it's down payment. Investment.

Aye. I get that – investment. But for what? I cannae be in there, just – floundering – if they ask and I dinnae ken. Look, Simon – I'll do this, and I'll do it well for you – and me, and Fi, and Georgie – but you know – the more I know, the better, eh? It's safer. It just means less nerves for me, less nerves for you. Steadying the ship, eh?

He turns and looks at me, reading my face, looking for the piss take, the ulterior motive. But my motive is to simply survive. In and oot, in and oot, remember?

A'right, a'right – fucking… It's drugs.

Ah, shite.

Drugs?!

Aye. You fucking heard. Heroin. Opiates. Coming up through the Channel Tunnel, up the country in vans and then – and then via me, o'er tae them.

Oh my God. Fucking Nora. That raises the stakes. I don't know what I was hoping for – maybe dodgy laptops or cigarettes, stolen cars, perhaps… But heroin? Christ.

Simon, this is way…

What?! It's the same fucking thing, man. Yer part hasnae changed ane bit. Keep it calm, eh.

He smiles. He winks. As though he is proud of the plan and this was its punchline.

I'm not proud, though. I'm keiching bricks. Thing is, though, so is he.

And where are these – these drugs, Simon?

Well, that's nane o' yer fucking business, is it, Tommy? You just mind yer place in this, eh? This'll work. Ah ken it will. Trust me, eh? Ahm no'… ahm no' a kid.

Then softer, again – *Ahm no' a kid.*

*

I think this through.

Here sits Hardman Jim, in his shiny, crappy blue suit. A suit coloured, no doubt, for a marketplace that knows nothing about taste or discretion, just knows it likes blue as its football team plays in blue.

The shirt beneath the suit is worse still, tight and sheer, the buttons strained.

Hardman Jim has a body which suggests he's done nothing but drink and eat since faking his own death a decade or so ago. Ooh. Watch as these bad Irish men flinch at the sight of such dedication.

Hardman Jim has no issues with such things as shoes that nip, cause him to limp… No, Hardman Jim is too hard for that.

Hardman Jim is accompanied by his brother, a brother who looks suspiciously nothing like Jim.

Hardman Jim has no recollection of where he's been or what he's been up to. Perhaps this hardman has had a lobotomy?

Hardman Jim is not very confident. Hardman Jim suspects he is fucked. And the pizza grease on Hardman Jim's shirt is now orange and solidified.

64

I KNOW THIS ROAD, a bit. It leads down the west coast to the docks, to where the passenger ferries come and go. Not too far as the craw flies, but the twists and turns, the amount of traffic, heavy goods vehicles, sparse wee villages... Well, the hundred miles or so take an age.

We went over once, to Northern Ireland, my dad and me. We got the train over – same route as this, mind – to see a vehicle he was after. But the guys selling it, well, they saw Dad as an easy touch, him having come all the way from Scotland, so they upped the price at the very last minute. I mean, we'd had a wee drive about and such, but all of a sudden they started talking about a higher offer from elsewhere... It was bullshit, of course, I kent that even then, and I was, what, fifteen? And Dad, well Dad was such a stubborn mule he refused to pay this extra hundred quid or whatever and ended up swearing blue murder at these guys. Then us walking and rural-fucking-bussing it back to Belfast, easily missing the last ferry sailing, and sleeping underneath some chairs in the bus station, all the time Dad whispering to himself – *Fucking pricks, fucking pricks...*

Next day, or next morning, very early, we walked a mile or so to a car lot where Dad bought an almost brand-new twin-cab pickup truck for three or four times the price of the second-hand thing we'd been to see the day before. This new one was a terrible yellow colour, but ex-showroom, smelled of leather...

The salesman couldn't believe his luck, two desperate eejits in his shop at 8:00 am, buying a custard monstrosity.

My dad, though, well, he'd won, in his eyes.

And this drive, on these long, curved roads... brings me back to that day. What Dad would think of me now, eh? I've hardly conquered the world. The hotel is only afloat because he owned it outright, so no mortgage. Well, that and Auld Jock, siphoning his pension directly into the till. What tales I'll have for Dad and the family, should there be pearly gates and should they all be there, awaiting me.

65

SIMON AND ME, me and Simon – the unlikely, unloving couple, off on our road trip, our unromantic getaway to the west coast. Simon's no doubt got a flask of soup and sandwiches; I've just got a head full of rot and confusion. The only relief about this part of the journey is that Simon's almost as nervous as me, so there's no babbling cack in my ear, the way there would be if Billy were here. No, Simon's talk is short and tense.

I make to turn the radio on, getting as far as hitting the button, but before any music or speech makes it out of the speakers, Simon slams it off.

Leave it!

So we have the silence, the engine, the occasional – *fuck* – slipping out from Simon's internal monologue. His driving's erratic: forcing the accelerator, missing gears, over-compensating with the brakes. I try to calm him, bring him back to the moment, for my immediate safety more than any concern for his nerves, for our paths are linked, of that there's no doubt –

So, have you… are you in touch wi' Jim, then, Simon?

Eh? None o' your fucking business.

Eyes straight ahead, every corner an adventure. Too many roundabouts to get by, too many vans that could be polis, too many speed cameras… and then the odd mile or so when he relaxes –

Of course ah am. He wouldnae leave me, would he? Ahm his brother.

We rumble through another depressed-looking village. The view of the sea over to Northern Ireland is quite something, and I'm a little surprised that this place isn't more populated, more sought

256

after. But then, it's so bleak and weathered. A good place to visit, maybe. Or to hide...

The snow of Perthshire had long ago turned to rain the further south we drove, the west wind now buffeting the car.

Well, why did ye no' just ask him?

Eh?

Tae meet these guys, I mean. Why take the risk with someone else? With me?

Fuck's sake —

But this time it's not me he's cursing, it's some oncoming tractor with its rear wheels doubled over, safer in the field, no doubt, almost pushing us into the kerb, the ditch...

There's nae time. And Jim wouldnae — Jim wouldnae come back — tae this... Too small a business for ma brother, heh.

I leave him be. But after a while he opens up, if only a little.

See inside? Well... No' everyone kent Jim. I mean, that'd be daft, right? I ken that. But some did. Enough did. The thing about this Irish lot, tho' — well, ah wasnae even in contact wi' them. But ane o' them heard I'd been talking about Jim and that was it — he was right curious. All over me, every detail, every plan... Nah. They'll believe us. They WANT tae believe us, and that's half the battle, eh.

And is that who we're meeting, then?

Aye, well, he'll be there. Peter's his name — he was at the hotel too — heh — that day you, um, went for yer walk, heh. But someone else will be there as well, and that's the main man. A wee Irish man wi' a pot o' gold, heh.

He accelerates suddenly, quickly overtaking a car and caravan on a short stretch of road, before pulling back in.

Listen, dinnae you worry, Tommy. I've seen it. Jim's a... a big name tae these Irish lads. A name tae look up tae, for me tae conjure wi'... He glances at me — *It's worth the gamble, Tommy boy. A 50k pot o' cash can set a man up well enough, heh. Ah'll no' be small fry then, eh? Eh, Tommy?*

Fifty thousand, eh? Fucking hell.

Ah ken, eh? Big money... Heh. But never you mind, Tommy. Heh heh. Worst case – worst case, we just run like fuck, eh!

And with such planning, I go into this adventure full of confidence.

The final ten miles, two miles, last mile, the conversation, the brief civility ceases as Simon's own nerves take hold and he tries to toughen up, reassert himself. The only responses I get now are – *Shut the fuck up* – or – *Christ's sake, just do as I say!*

I attempt humour, goodwill, empathy – there's no reward. He's building himself up, back into character. No soft underbelly to show. He needs to be the focused, threatening hardman now.

Fucking, that cunt Billy better be there...

And me, well, I'm feart almichty. I've had little hardman experience. Most I've had is the occasional fight behind the school as a teenager. I mean, I guess I've thrown a few drunks out of the hotel in ma time, but the vocal threat does ninety-five per cent of that work. Bellow my voice out and bleutered folk leave. I doubt that tactic will work today.

Without Simon to talk to, my mind can only go within, to the fear, the nerves, the sick... and to Fi and to Georgie. I tell myself – I am a father, doing his best for his family. In a day, a week, all of this will be gone. A memory. I'll be laughing with Auld Jock about Tommy's keiched jeans once more and all shall be right with the world.

66

B UT NEVER MIND all that, for when we arrive at where we are to be – which is just a wee, isolated country pub off the main route, away from anything other than sheep and hills – well, when we get there, we have company.

Simon pulls into the car park, small enough and two other cars parked within. I try to gauge who'd drive cars such as those parked there, but with little to work from: midrange, second-hand, motorway-intended cruisers.

Simon pays those vehicles no notice. Simon, he pulls in and stops the car and then – before I can say a word – he laughs that peculiar laugh of his – *Heheh* – and points something out to me – *Tommy, check it, eh.* He's pointing off, over the fields, and I'm wondering if it's some bird of prey he's spotted or the bad guys approaching, perhaps over the hill, but no, it's a vehicle... it's a van.

Is that... Billy's van?

Heh. Here, inside the glove compartment...

I open it, and there's a shiny binocular case. I hand them over to him, but he pushes back.

Nae need for me. Ah can see what AHM looking for. You – use those – check Billy oot, eh?

Billy? I wonder what's going on. I unclip the case, soft inside, definitely fake leather, flaccid and nylon, and remove the pair of binoculars. Widen them, open them out, perch them on my nose and struggle momentarily with the focus until – until...

I see Billy, waving from the driver's seat of his van. Champion fud.

But in the van, there's someone else; I play with the focus,

259

concentrate my vision on the passenger seat and – *Fi? Ah, shite. My heart, it leaps.*

I look again, steady my hold, cling to hope… No. It's her. For sure. And she has something, someone with her, which can only be, obviously, Georgie. *What the fuck is this?*

My stomach convulses, sick, but not quite – *What – what's going on? How's Fi here?*

Simon grabs the binoculars back, unable to resist a wee peek himself – *Heh, so she is. Good auld Billy. Fucking good auld, reliable Billy. Nae questions, nae bullshit. Just happy tae be telt whit tae do. Like a fucking puppy.*

But – I didn't…

Aye, well. This is where we are now. YOU ken what Billy is capable of. And YOU ken what I want YOU tae do now. Understood?

I nod – *But this wisnae…*

Ah telt ye – nae fucking buts. That there – that there on the hill is ma insurance that you willnae piddle me about. Right? There's nae turning back. Nae funny cunting. I ken you. I ken you think yer aye clever – fucking a' posh wi' yer wee hotel… Yer fuck all. Nothing. See whit ah've just done? Ah've proven ah can run rings round you. See me – me and ma brother? WE'RE different class.

He's grinning at me. What a smug fucking weasel he is. But my mind is everywhere other than here. This wasn't the way. This wasn't the way to gee me up, get me ready and onside.

Ok?

But the last thing I am is ok. Fuck – I shake my head in disbelief.

ARE WE UNDERSTANDING EACH OTHER, TOMMY LAD? EH? AFORE WE WALK INTAE THAT THERE PUB AND PLAY THE HARD CUNTS? ARE WE SORTED? ARE YOU AWARE, VERY AWARE, THAT YOU CANNAE AFFORD TAE FUCK ME OVER?

I swallow. I nod. There are tears in my eyes; I fight them back.

Sure, Simon. I'm in. I bite my lip, hard, harder still, then emphasise – *You've got me.*

But see if there was anything sharper than a butter knife sitting within reach? Well, I'd've done my best to grind it between this prick's shoulder blades.

Good man. He winks. *Well. Here we go.*

The seatbelt, the car door, the gravel, the final look at where Billy and Fi and Georgie are... Can they see me? What's Billy said to Fi to get them here? Has he... hurt her? Hurt Georgie?

My nerves have fucking trebled and I'm nowhere near relaxed or ready. That fucking Simon.

We enter the building. There's a small cobwebbed security light above the door, out-of-date CAMRA stickers on the glass windows and the place stinks of damp, mustiness, old... mouse shit, piss, a scent familiar from the storeroom of my hotel.

There's chatter in the room beyond – jovial, nervous, mebbe.

Fucking Simon.

Maybe they're shitting it as much as I am. Imagine if they're just dudes like me. Imagine if they're all just normal folk, except, of course, for Simon here.

I can smell burning.

It's clear this place is no longer used, the dust, the stour... As I look down at the carpet, I notice it's thick, barely worn. I feel sorry for whoever bought it, hopeful that their tenure in this pub would be worth the investment in a new floor covering.

But then the door opens and such luxuries as my tame, mundane thoughts are over.

67

SIMON'S IN FIRST, of course.

Aye aye.

A greeting met with silence.

All to hear now is my heart and the crackle of a fire. Well, someone's got sense, trying to get some warmth in the room.

I can feel Simon trying to drag me into the room by strength of will, by mind control. I have no desire, but my fear of the boak – of throwing up everywhere – is so inexorable that I need distraction. And the pull inside – well, there is no escape. Who am I kidding?

I walk in. There's six or seven of them. Most of them are wee radgies, I can tell from the off. Of the age who'll come into the bar on a Saturday afternoon for a bag of crisps and hang around as long as they can, soaking in the grown-up atmosphere, laughing, raising their voices, swearing... until I ask them to leave, which they inevitably do.

But these guys? Their faces are scarred. Tight, burnt red, far from childhood. One of them is half-sooking from a wee carton of orange juice – I say *half-sooking* as, well, the pace of drinking has slowed. They're looking at Simon, but they're looking beyond Simon, at me – as though I'm some pop star.

One of them speaks – *Ok, Simon?*

A young lad, early twenties, not suited like me, but not trainered-up either. Beside him, an older gentleman, a different generation – father or possibly even grandfather.

No one seems sure what to do, to say. I become aware that I am the hot potato, the object of most curiosity. Well, we cannot stay like this. In for a penny. I step out from behind Simon –

Ahm Jim Blair. Now. Who was it wanted tae see me?

68

F<small>UCKING</small> *J<small>IM</small> B<small>LAIR</small>, is it?*
The old fellow's up, towards me. I stand my ground. He's not charging, he's almost hobbling.

He nudges past Simon, visibly ignoring him, Simon allowing him this churn, granting him his pass of age – *Here now* – and soon the old fellow's looking deep into my eyes, at my hair, my suit, at one point taking my hands, seemingly looking at my nails. *Jim Blair... Jim Blair... Well, I never... I've heard a lot about you... Well then – I didn't know – wow. So – ha – so, you're a clever man, Mr Blair. A lot of people looking for you – but – ha – here you are... Let me introduce myself. My name is Jack McDonagh. You'll know that name now, I'd imagine... You'd've heard of me. No? Yes?*

I'm stoney-faced, watching his eyes skip around, up and down. I'm looking for warmth in those eyes, empathy. But there's none of that, just a dank curiosity. Finally, he releases my hands and, with one quick motion, he pats both of my pockets, removing his hands as quick as they arrived – *Ha – well, well... Jim Blair, they say, eh? Jim Blair.* Then he's looking back over his shoulder – *It's Jim Blair here, Peter. Come and say hello. Give the gentleman the credit he deserves.*

Peter jumps up, quick, rubs his hands on his trousers – he's immaculately dressed like a middle-aged man, a golfer almost, in a ridiculous 1980s Pringle jumper, a jumper even I would reject, the last choice, surely, in anybody's wardrobe. His skin – the skin on his face – he has too much of it. A very odd look – it gives him an aged, hangdog expression, but there are no wrinkles. He's more like – more like a cartoon or a television character, moisturised and coiffured to extinguish all blemishes, but when he takes my hand and smiles, open mouthed, well, the blemishes are evident straightaway: coarse, coffee-coloured teeth, pegs, just, and the smell – no garlic, no food, no alcohol nor tobacco – just undistinguishable rot, stench.

Heheheh – it's good to meet you, Jim Blair. I know your brother here – but he doesn't even point at Simon, doesn't take his eyes from me. His thick, rubbery hand is shaking mine and will not let go, as though we are politicians in a photocall, playing for the cameras. The shake continues on, on, as Simon fidgets beside us, bowing almost, back and forth, uncomfortable at the loss of his control. Peter moves further towards me, his charming breath puncturing any remaining personal space.

There's a smatter of chat and laughter from the youngsters, then McDonagh speaks –

Shh! Don't you young ones laugh in the presence of Jim Blair here. He was once – and maybe still is – someone to be reckoned with.

He has looked deep inside my soul and seen a scared, unfit mannie. Maybe he'll consider that some kind of unpredictable radge exists, my inner torment not fear but an unhinged, whirring mind. My nerves are not settling. I cannot keep this up.

McDonagh steps forward, becomes host once more – *Here, take a seat. By the fire young Fergus has lit for us all. Make yourself comfortable. Sean-Paul – Sean-Paul, get a drink for Mr Blair here. Whisky it was, I remember – you like your malt now, don't you…?*

Aye, but just –

… Just Scotch! Ha! I remember talk of that surely too. No good Scotsman drinks Irish whiskey, and the same the other way around, the same the other way around.

Fresh glasses, brought out of a Nike gym bag. A bottle of Glencuddich. A bottle of Jameson. Both newly purchased on the ferry, I'd wager.

I'm afraid we've no ice. But, Mr Blair, what is it you've brought us? Simon had – oh, such, such promises…

69

So — where've you been, Jim? All these years. We hear rumours —
I was in Spain, I was…

Ha! No. No. Were you fuck in Spain.

He smiles. He's calm.

Look at your skin colour. You're grey as paste. You've never fucking seen Spain, certainly not these last few years. Now — where were you? Tell the truth now. There's enough money involved that we deserve the truth, wouldn't you say? You're among friends now, are you not?

Ah, fuck. And Simon — he's straight in, pushing back into the limelight, grasping for control —

Heh — He's been — he's been hiding oot, eh? Hiding oot wi' me. We've got this hotel — we're — heh — running a few things through the books — heh. No' — no' sma' things — big things. No' — no' just the tourist thing, ken. Folk who need places — quiet places, eh — ootae sight and — eh — buying and selling, ken? If ye get ma drift — heh. That's, ken, that's why we're…

I interrupt this nervous, jilted flow of keich — *Shut it. Yer rambling.*

Simon looks at me, open-mouthed — how dare I? But then, perhaps, he remembers who I am supposed to be. Maybe he even agrees with me — he was rambling, giving too much away. His fist had raised, though, maybe a whole six inches, before he lowers it, giving me a look — a *just-you-wait* look.

This isn't going to Simon's ratchet-y, schoolboy plan. He's clearly spooked by his surroundings: the ned wallflowers, watching his every move; the old goat, seemingly in charge; and Peter, the one friendly face that Simon was relying on, silent, pretty much. And whose side am I on? My own, my own, of course. So, who should I root for here?

I speak as calmly as I can muster —

Listen. A' these – a' these young lads. It's – good tae see them, the next generation an' a'. But as far as the polis are concerned, I'm out of the game, and I mean to keep it that way. I'm no' saying fuck a' in front o' a' these lads. I cannae risk that.

I meet Mr McDonagh's eyes and do my best to hold his gaze. Simon is shuffling beside me, keen to keep the upper hand, of course – *Aye, and –*

But I interrupt again – *So, you see, this is a' very pleasant. But Simon here –* I swallow – *Simon and ah came here tae talk business.*

Simon draws his chin back in disgust at the thought – *Heh. Aye.*

I ignore him – *SO, what I suggest – if I may, Mr McDonagh?*

He gently raises and lowers his head, looking me all over, wondering at this wee punchline.

What I suggest is that you and I – the heid high anes – we go off ootside there for a wee wander. And WE discuss what needs be. And then – and only then – we continue this jolly. And see that – I point to the Glencuddich – *that, I wouldnae use that tae clean ma bath.*

The grin on McDonagh's face widens. He points a gnarled finger to the air and laughs – *Bravo, Jim Blair, bravo!*

Simon speaks up – *Aye, and ahm coming too! –* for Simon is clinging to the idea that he is The Big Man, the one not to be left out. But I cannot have that, and, for whatever reason, whatever slither of a thought tells me it's a good idea – for it clearly isn't – I lean towards him and kiss him squarely on the cheek – as a brother would kiss a brother – and I say – *No. You stay here, Simon. Get tae see Peter again. Get tae ken his lads.*

The moment I do it, I feel like a bad white actor playing a Native American chief, admonishing his young brave in some crappy 1960s cowboy film. The corn of it all, the cheese, the embarrassment… But that shock of the kiss, well, it momentarily stuns Simon, and that moment is all I need.

After you, Mr McDonagh.

And I tell you, whatever I have in mind had better work as Simon, well, he's just storing up the reasons to bang ma pus over and over, and I cannot be having that.

I move quickly, making my way outside after McDonagh. Simon's eyes are now as wide as twin full moons, threatening while smiling, playing the part of the dutiful younger brother, infuriated both to be left by me and to be left with the tracksuited young team, the bus stop pissers, cider drinkers, ID fakers... For surely HE is bigger than that.

He glares at the window, then at me, and then at the window, over and over, again and again, making it oh so very clear that he'll be watching my every move.

The walk through the corridor: I hold the doors open for Mr McDonagh and he says – *Thank you*. We briefly revert to normality, just two humans making their way through a small, enclosed, shared space. There's a rack of pamphlets by the front door, faded now from the sun shining in, and covered in dust. Mr McDonagh – he picks one up, for the Ulster Agricultural Museum, and shows it to me – *Heh – See this, Jim Blair? Well, it's old news. It's closed now, see?* I wonder how to reply to such a mundanity – what would Big Jim Blair say? But before I can open my mouth, the exit door is being held open and Mr McDonagh is gesturing me through, waving me outside.

We walk on, ten, fifteen feet away from the building, side by side, old pals after a game of golf, perhaps, off to discuss the scorecard. Mr McDonagh pats his sides and brings out a packet of cigarettes, the branding hidden by a photograph of a diseased body part. He offers them over – *Do you smoke, Jim Blair?*

I shake my head. He smiles, then looks away, towards the hills.

Jesus, it's cold and wild out here. Tell me, then, before we freeze – and he leans away from the worst of the wind, lighting up – *what's on your mind, Jim Blair?*

And here, here I take the plunge, I take the gamble, I offer my all and hope it lands with a grateful recipient.

70

*S*O, I'LL BE *telling you something the now and all I can ask is that you don't react – or at least no' in a way that'll spook the horses – put the frichteners on young Simon in there, who's watching us close from the window as I'm sure you've seen. Can I... Have I your word?*

McDonagh's nodding, smiling, amused, eyes half-closed from the wind, like a stoned hippy standing at the hearth, entranced by the flames of a midwinter fire.

You do, Jim Blair, you do.

I look down. I whisper, almost – *Well, ye'll ken... Ye'll ken fine... I'm no' Jim fucking Blair.*

No reaction, just a curious look, encouraging more, more.

My name is Thomas Bruce. I run a hotel in the Trossachs, and that Simon in there – he's no' pal nor brother o' mine. And... I'm no' here on my own volition. I'm here because that wee boy is a fucking wee tool and, well, he has ma family hostage and he is planning tae rip you off, Mr McDonagh – tae take yer money and tae run wi' it.

He grins, but there's no visible shock, no movement beyond a turn of the head, a raised eyebrow... And then, just a calm, conversational reply – *Ha. That's interesting. Hostage, you say? Would you care to... elaborate?*

He has my – he has my – my partner and our child. They're nearby. On the hillside. Simon there, he has, umm, a right-hand man. Billy. And Billy has them. My boy Georgie, is no' yet two. And that Billy is a cruel, fucking thick bastard. And a' the marks you can see on my face and neck are fae him, and there's many other marks you cannot see, hidden by this shite suit. And THAT is the only reason I am here. No' for yer money, or for Simon, or for Jim fucking Blair... for my family.

Hmm. He nods, amused. *This type of... deception. Well, it happens, Mr Not-Jim Blair* – he sooks on his fag – *in my line of work. And tell me again – about the money? My money?*

Ach, there's nothing... It was drugs, right? That's what Simon told me. But he's got none. He cannae have – he's no' that level – no' anywhere close. He as good as telt me he was just going tae run...

Ah. And there we have it. He chuckles. *Well then. That's funny. I'll tell you why: I knew Jim Blair. I knew him well. Jim Blair was a jumped-up chump.* He smirks at me, as though we're discussing a play or a movie we've both seen. *But – and I'll give him this – Jim Blair was convincing. And, well, he owed me. He OWES me. Jim Blair owes me, like he owes many others. And that's why I'M here.* He looks me in the eye. *See when he did his disappearing trick? That disappointed a lot of people. Do you understand?*

Sure.

So, when Son Peter told me he'd met Jim Blair's brother inside and how he was full of the talk and reckoned he could bring us all together... Well, I knew it was bullshit. I knew the real Jim Blair wouldn't come within one hundred miles of me. But, well, I was curious. Intrigued, even, and if there was even the slightest chance... Can you see that?

Of course, aye.

But you know, in amongst all this humour, the funniest bit was when I saw you walk in – a great big fucker, no offence – with that strange haircut – and Jesus Christ almighty – what the fuck is that suit?

I take the verbal licking in my stride. After all, I am well used to my body's peculiarities. I see them most mornings. And as for the suit – well, I'm no tailor, but the way the acrylic pulls on every leg hair makes it ever more obvious to me that it is not the suit of kings.

They – they got me the suit. It's pretty uncomfortable – I don't think it's umm... from –

He cuts me off – *Shut up about the suit.* He exhales a long stream of cigarette smoke, thick and visible in this cold air.

Quite the prick, this Simon seems. In there, he knew fuck all. He was spooked the moment he saw me, and that little army I have, all those kids – he couldn't handle even the pressure of them. Whatever plan he had was shat out into his drawers the moment he arrived. He's JUST like his brother that way, let me tell you – Jim wasn't some kind of fucking underworld demon-hardman. Why that boy thinks that, I have no clue... Some of the things he told Son Peter, Jesus...

He looks around, beyond me, perhaps trying to spy Billy or the vehicle, but being subtle. He's in no rush here, Mr McDonagh, despite the cold.

Well. All that information. That's quite the trust you're placing in me, Mr Not-Jim Blair.

I know. I know.

And I'm not a social worker. Are you aware of that?

I am.

See, I came here... Well, I knew it was a long shot. But if it HAD been Jim Blair, well, it would have been SO sweet to have seen him again, after all these years. I've been curious, you know? Unfinished business. He looks wistful, disappointed. *But never mind.* He shakes his head before straightening, moving on. *So, anyway. That's that. Are you wanting something from me now? For telling me this, what I already knew?*

I'm just – I'm just trying to get them – you know – away – trying to take care of ma family...

Ah. I see. Well, that's a shame, as I think I'm just going to have to leave you to the wolves, Mr Not-Jim Blair. C'mon, let's get inside.

Ah, shite. And I'm panicking, for it is true, and if Mr McDonagh were to leave now, I'd be left – the traitor – with Simon, and then Georgie and Fi would be left with Billy. I cannot have that.

Er, no – Mr McDonagh – hang on. He was trying tae make a fool of you... I stopped him.

He turns and motions towards me, like a venomous snake ready to strike – *You stopped fuck all! I knew it wasn't Jim Blair the moment you bowled in. So what exactly have you brought to the table? This commotion? I don't need commotion at my age. But don't you worry – I'll batter that little shite.*

But that is not going to be enough. I have to get Georgie safe. Long term. Beyond, behind Mr McDonagh, I can see the outline of

Billy's van. I am not looking, not drawing attention, but it is there, haunting me.

No – No, hang on – there is one thing…

He stops his walk and looks round – *One thing? Ok. I'll listen to the one thing. After all, you've been most amusing so far.*

Look… Look, they've got my kid… It's not much but – I have the hotel. I'm not sure how much this Jim Blair owed you but – you – you could mebbe – I spit it out – *USE the hotel. Like Simon said. For money – running money through the tills or having folk stay for a while if – if they – if they need tae disappear. I don't know, I mean – I just…*

I'm just fucking desperate.

I just – I can't… leave THEM to ma family.

Prostrate. Begging. Christ, there's almost tears in my eyes.

He pauses. Then –

Ok. So that's what you're offering. Now, spell it out simply and calmly, so we can get back inside, out of this cold. What exactly is it you want from me, Mr Not-Jim Blair?

All – all I'd ask is – you get HIM off my family's case. A threat. Back him off.

For good?

I swallow. I look at my feet and nod the slightest, most terrified *Yes*.

Is he disappointed? Surprised? Or does he see this kind of shite all the time? He gestures me to follow.

Well. There we are. C'mon – back inside with you.

71

THE ROOM IS silent, expectant, as we enter, and I've a feeling that not a word has been said since our departure. The animosity Simon feels about being left with the kids is clear: he's practically jumping on the spot, surely raging inside. These wee boy-men themselves are unsure how to play it, Peter still in there, keeping them grounded, in their roles.

Well now, Son Peter, we've sorted all this out now. Have you fellas been having a good talk yourselves?

Not really, Da'. He's barely said a word.

Ah, that's interesting, because this fellow – pointing to me – *well, he said quite a lot of words. He's an entertainer, you know? He's told me some amusing things. They made me laugh – tales I can tell again and again by the hearth when we get home. You – Simon – you're a lucky man to have a brother as witty as Jim here, wouldn't you say?*

Eh? Um, aye. Totally. He's fucking – class.

Right. Hmm. Peter – Peter – do you remember our old friend Jock Stewart?

And at that moment, at the mention of that name – a code, I suppose, or perhaps someone from their past, but whatever, never mind – Peter and three of the young team wrap themselves around Simon, holding him straitjacketed, covering his mouth, checking his pockets for weapons, stopping any movement. At the same time, the rest of the tracksuit boys get behind me, grabbing my arms, pushing them tight towards my neck.

It's no surprise to me and I offer scant resistance, but Simon, he isn't so happy.

Hey, get the fuck aff! Whit the fuck ye think yer daen?

273

But from McDonagh, there is no drama.

Well done, Son Peter. You know, it's as you suspected. This one – he points towards Simon – *has been telling you lies from the start. He's just a little gobshite, as his brother before him. And this man here* – he points to me again – *he's not Jim Blair. Of course he's not. Now, a few things gave him away. Firstly* – and he slowly approaches Simon, coming face to face, spittle close, only here and now injecting any emotion into his words as he bellows – *I KNEW JIM BLAIR, YOU LITTLE PIECE OF SHIT.* Then he backs off, voice quietened, restraint restored – *You think you could take me the same way your brother did? That was very fucking stupid of you.*

And there's a look, a confused, feart look in Simon's eyes that makes it clear he has no idea of the relationship between his brother and this man. Of course he didn't. Even Simon wouldn't be that bold or daft.

Simon bites the hand that covers his mouth, the hand of a foot soldier, and spits out – *Ah dinnae ken whit this fat fuck telt ye, but there was NO way ah was thinking o' ripping ye aff. Ah had plans, proper plans: the twa o' us thegither, fucking business, supply and demand, fucking blue-sky thinking – straight up! Top man! That's me.*

McDonagh watches him closely, reading his eyes, his expression – *Ah well, you see, the problem here is who to believe. And Thomas Bruce here – he's a very believable man – and you – I suspect you're just a jumped-up little prick, as my ever-perceptive Son Peter told me you were. Don't get me wrong, I WANTED to believe you. I SO wanted Jim Blair to walk through that door – mostly so I could batter him to fuck with a fire extinguisher, right enough – but this – this effort here* – he points over to me – *even if I hadn't known Jim Blair, do you think me SO stupid that I'd be fooled by THAT? Now, Peter. There's a fellow on the hill yonder in a little van. He has Thomas here's woman and child with him. Go and get them – and here, take those three lads* – he points at the three tracksuits holding me – *you might need them. This fellow here – well, you won't give us any trouble, will you?*

I shake my head.

There's a scurry as the youngsters, keen to be involved, begin their flock to the door, letting me go. My aching arms fall, but –

Now, now. Two of you are staying here with me. Sean-Paul – put a couple of those plastic wrist ties on the little prick here. Nice and tight. And Mr Not-Jim Blair?

I look up, ready.

You're in MY debt now, Mr Thomas Bruce.

72

*S*O THAT'S IT, *is it? Well, do yer worst, auld man. Ahm no' feart o' you – you're feart o' me – that's how ye turned up wi' a' these numbers…*

No, no, son. I turned up with all these numbers as I'm not a total amateur.

Aye, well, that's me tied up – how? Cause yer feart. And well, ye've nothing on me – ye've nothing tae gain fae daen fuck a' tae me, eh? Just fucking let us go and that'll be that. And leave – leave this fat fucker tae me.

No, no. You've got your uses yet, young Simon. Here – Sean-Paul?

Sean-Paul ambles over. He's eighteen, twenty at a push, still sporting his blasted acne, a shiny tracksuit, indistinguishable from the other cheuks around. Uniformed, but podgy, bloated, uncomfortable, working out his way in the world… I feel for him.

Shut him up, eh? Good lad.

Sure, boss.

And Sean-Paul's pale pink, meaty right hand flails onto Simon's face. It's quite a sight and sound, like a large fish being dropped onto a concrete floor. Simon's nose jettisons a small fountain of bogey, which quickly leads to his eyes watering and then – perhaps – tears. But there's no blood, not yet.

Shut yer gobhole, yer wee streak o' piss. I'll only hit yer again, over and over, until ye do.

Sean-Paul then nods at Simon, as if hoping they'd come to a mutual agreement – exchanged a car, perhaps.

Simon spits, coughs, shakes his head, curses – *You fat, Fenian cunt.*

And again, again the hand, less of a slap this time, more of a hit,

276

though only – what? – twenty per cent? – of Sean-Paul's full power behind it.

Simon groans, spits blood this time. He is playing the tough guy, of course, but for whom? He splutters further – *You cunt, you cunt –* before McDonagh interrupts.

Shut the fuck up now, Simon. That's the best advice I can give you. He – he can do this all day. He has done.

And now any angry words, any profanities are uttered under Simon's breath, lower, but curses just the same, through the snot and the tears and the heavy breathing – *You fucking, you fucking, you cunt…* As this wave of rage and shock lessens, Simon's breathing slows. He quietens, just shaking his head, regaining his composure. He fixes his glare on me now, perhaps the easiest target, whispering, as if in a classroom and wary of attracting the teacher's attention – *Yer deid, Tommy Bruce. These cunts willnae kill me, but AH'LL kill you… And that fucking hotel. Burned tae the ground, just as ah said… You just wait. Yer puir getting it. Just you fucking believe it…*

And I do believe it.

Is he bothering you, Thomas?

I know, I know, if I say yes then Simon will get slapped once more. On my account, my command. McDonagh's willing. But I cannot take that responsibility. I pass it over to Simon once more – *Umm, are you bothering me, Simon?*

Heh. You coward. No. Ahm no' botherin' ye. No' just yet. YOU dinnae ken whit botherin' means, pal.

But he quietens again, he does, his breathing lowers. Sean-Paul hovers close, cracking his knuckles like a 1950s B-movie baddie. I get the feeling this is the one thing Sean-Paul does well.

As the silence descends, I realise I have a more urgent need – *Can I – can I get tae the cludgie?*

McDonagh spins round from the window, through which he's been staring – *The what?*

The – um – toilet?

Go for it. A wink. *Piss for your life, Thomas Bruce.*

*

These lavatories are frozen cold, out of paper, stinking, and there's a dead pigeon on the floor – always, always. How do they get in? It appears gnawed, eaten.

Someone fitted these pipes, these stalls. Some work went into it, long ago.

There's a poster on the wall, warning of the dangers of AIDS. A cartoon syringe, a smiling condom… And an engraving – *Eck loves Jackie 1989* – surrounded by a lover's heart. I wonder if Eck still loves Jackie. Or if it was a fleeting, one-night sort of love.

I breathe. A long, slow breath. I try to focus, to bring peace, prepare for whatever is about to happen. As if I could do that, eh? As if it were that easy.

I zip up and leave. I do not expose my hands to the no doubt freezing tap water.

Get over here, Thomas. It looks as though Simon's man Billy there is giving it a good go.

And I join him, nose against the window, staring into the distance to see a figure – Billy – struggling, fighting with three, four other figures – McDonagh's wee-man army, of course. Beside them, to my horror, are tiny Fi and even smaller Georgie, animated, hunched, screaming, perhaps, audible if we were only to go into the cold of outside, if the wind were to drop… What the fuck have I brought them into? Or what has Fi brought me into?

Behind me, there's the droning murmur of Simon, a reminder that neither Fi nor myself are the problem here. We're no' the shite in the soup, that particular honour belongs to someone else entirely.

The struggle continues, but Billy seems restricted, tied now with these wee black plastic things that have got Simon shackled, I guess. He's still lunging, with his head, mebbe – and then there's a bend, as if a fist has hit the stomach; a fall, as if another has hit the side of the head. Then he's down, down on the floor, then up to his knees – but all this a surreal viewing, the distance and the misted, filthy windows providing layers of removal, like watching a 1920s silent movie of a group of boxers taking on a circus gorilla.

Billy is up and shoved into the back of the van, followed by one, then two of McDonagh's aides, Fi and Georgie motioned into the front seat. I think to myself – *They'll need a seatbelt* – but such thoughts are from another life.

As they move out of sight, I'm sickened, awaiting their presence, just to be in my vision, that'd be enough, enough. Minutes pass, nothing audible but the wind outside, the crack of the fire and Simon's shallow but husked breaths…

And the car re-emerges, silent at first, then out of sight once more, McDonagh still at the window, watching, listening. The car is then audible but not visible, growing louder, and here, here it comes, jumping into the back car park, fully into our view, the adrenaline of the driver causing a few jolts, perhaps Billy himself still loose enough inside to give grief.

On the side of the car hidden from our view, the driver's door flies open and out stomps Peter, then hauling the back doors open and pulling out Billy, who spills down to the ground. Peter's movements then suggest that he's stomping on something – Billy, I think, but what part of Billy I could not guess. Following Billy, the two young cheuks emerge, bloodied now, one holding his hand as though lame, the other, slower, opening the front passenger door to reveal Fi and Georgie. Georgie's screams now accompany Peter's shouting, Billy's retorts… But worse, far worse than that, is Fi's face, which is blackened and bloodied, and Georgie's head, face, red – blood –

Fuck!

I make to go outside, but McDonagh – though an older man than me – grabs me with a strength I'd never have thought possible in one so wiry and throws, encourages, insists, threatens me away from the door – *No. You'll only get in their way now. Go and sit back there. I'll sort this. Sean-Paul – you stay right behind the Blair boy here and make sure there is no movement whatsoever. If he gets up, then you make sure he stays down, you hear me?*

There's tension, fear, nerves in McDonagh's voice, his veneer of cool being worn through by these very obvious, primal emotions.

I hear you, boss.

Good. You – he's talking to me now – *go on, sit down.*

And I follow his advice. Just out of Simon's reach, grab, on a cushioned perch at the end of a once-comfortable snug. Simon's on a more traditional bare wooden chair; my comparative luxury is another sign of my current standing in this relationship. Simon, though, is keen as ever we communicate –

You fucking piece o' shit, ah'll fucking leather you, fucking cut you up, you and that –

A slam on the back of his head, but –

The very first moment ah get – top o' ma priorities, Tommy boy. You're ma number one concern now.

Sean-Paul's palm slaps against Simon's head again, this one quietening him, briefly. The inner doors of the bar then shunt open, then closed, then open once more and Billy, twa of the young team and Peter – the four of them are in a dog fight, an eight-legged beast flailing into vision, their language one of curses, yelps, threats.

Simon jumps up, but is held straight back down, a hefty *clump* on his right ear almost knocking him onto the floor, before he uprights and begins a verbal assault instead – *FUCKING CUNTS* – but this too is silenced by a further battering, this one a fist, not a palm, and this one knocking him onto the floor. He lies there for just a moment before Sean-Paul raises him up with one hand and plants him squarely back on the chair, his mammoth hands now keeping a dazed Simon balanced and upright more than imprisoned. McDonagh watches on before noticing there's no Fi and so leaving, returning perhaps twenty seconds later with a tearful, bloodied, distraught young woman and a burrowing toddler, clutched tight in her arms. Fi's head is back and forth, back and forth – *It's ok, Georgie, it's ok, it's ok, it's ok* – but her voice is so frantic and panicked that the last thing Georgie will be picking up is the feeling that it is indeed ok.

And I am wondering what the fuck happened to her face and whose blood that is on Georgie.

SHUT HIM UP!

I look to McDonagh, Fi too, but McDonagh's looking away from us and squarely at Billy, the churning, bundling tied arms and loose legs –

Fucking – tape his mouth. And his legs. Ah, c'mon, lads. But this unlikely modern dance quartet continues, for Billy is seemingly outside anyone's control, until – *Ah, for fuck's sake* – McDonagh's over, walking towards the commotion, reaching into his chest pocket and bringing out – I don't know what; a small cushion, perhaps? But no, this object, this black velour item, is brought down upon the back of Billy's head with a swift, sharp strike and then – all ceases, Billy's body collapses, all strength, all resistance disappearing in that instant. Peter and his two disciples step back, impressed and relieved, leaving Billy open and displayed on the floor, a skinned rug.

73

THE ROOM IS quiet. Fi calming Georgie, Simon slumped. Tied up, his right-hand man down, potentially out. Simon's plan has certainly failed. His breathing heavy, through the drool, the blood, the broken teeth.

Fi – it's no' what it looks like… Ah didnae want you and the wee man tae be here…

My gaze rests upon him. What is he thinking? Is this regret? Contrition?

That was Billy. You ken that's no' ma style…

He moves his head, catching my eye for a second, then straight back to Fi.

I still love you Fi, I do…And you know it… I KNOW you do…

And then, to me –

Tommy, pal – YOU ken ah wisnae wanting a' this, eh? It's just gone too far… I mean, c'mon… I bought you… I bought you a fucking pizza, for fuck's sake.

My mind flits to a thousand more comfortable thoughts – the quiet nights at the bar; the jokes with Jock; the long, beautiful days with Fi and Georgie… I do nothing. I say nothing. I tell myself – *He had this coming, right?*

Heh. That's it, is it Tommy boy? Just ignoring me? That's it, eh?

A glint, a smile, almost. His options slipping away.

Fi – then at least allow me tae hold the bairn… just once. Put wee… Put wee Georgie down, let him walk tae me.

She tenses – *No!*

C'mon, Fi, c'mon. If yer going tae leave me here tae... these animals... at least let Georgie come tae me – just once.

Then –

It's only fair, Fi. Ahm his fucking da, after a'. We a' know it. We a' know it, eh?

74

WHAT EVEN IS a father, these days? Any eejit can do the fun bit. In and out in a second. But the tricky bit, the FATHER bit, is the bringing up. The loving. The time spent, the long conversations, the teaching how to walk…

That's a real father.

But the word – *da* – coming from Simon's bloodied lips – it cuts me. Of course it does.

The horror upon Fi's broken face, as if she really believed I did not know. And the thumping of my heart. What the fuck is he doing? What is this last play?

Fi looks to Simon, and then to me – but I have no answer. Not to this.

McDonagh does, though. He's intrigued.

Well, well. Go on, then – put the wain down, girl. Let's see how this game plays out.

So, she does. And little Georgie, just a bairn following his curiosity, little Georgie leaves his mother's arms, free to roam these strange new surroundings. He comes tumbling towards Simon and me both, his footfall still unsteady, unsure.

Simon whispers – *C'mon – c'mon, George* – but me, I'm silent. Wondering at this humanity in Simon's voice, the softness, the plea, and however false it might – or might not – be.

Or maybe I'm just terrified. Frozen.

Here ye go – c'mon now – though Simon's arms are well tied behind him, his face in no shape for such a reunion – *George, come tae Da* – and Georgie waddling forwards, towards him now, ignoring the massive spade shape of Billy, who is stirring slightly, awakening.

284

I cannot say a word. I just watch through grieving, distraught eyes as the person I love more than any other parades towards another man, another father.

Tommy – call him – Tommy –

I look to Fi, through my tears – her nose is busted, face is flushed, but again she says – *Tommy, he's yours. Call him. Please. Please call him.*

And Georgie, well, he is looking to Simon and then to me and then to Simon – Simon, who is continuing – *C'mon, Georgie, come tae yer da.* Georgie is enjoying this game, even, us adults, us grownups, all watching, all attention on him. He's loving it.

I attempt to speak, but it is a mere cough, nothing coming out. And Simon continuing –

Heh, c'mon here now, son…

McDonagh is transfixed at the sight, obviously aware now of the complexity of our relationship, and this further layer amusing him, this infant grounding everyone here with his – well, his innocence.

There's a good lad – come tae yer da, here ah am. What's Da got behind his back, eh? A wee sweet for George, is it? Come and see.

It's like a dream. All those years I have dreamed of my own mother, this situation in reverse, my need for her calling me for one last hug, hold, comfort. And yet here I am, powerless.

Ca' him, Tommy… Please – please. He's yours. I swear it, Tommy.

And whether it's powered by Fi's tears or my own, or some stirring from within, I open my mouth and try once more, this time the words creeping out, low at first, garbled, but then coughed away and clear. My arms, not tied like Simon's, are out, imploring Georgie –

You come here. Come tae yer Daddy, wee Georgie.

And the moment I speak, his direction changes; the peculiar, questioning look he was giving Simon becomes one of want, and dare I say joy, dare I say love, and those last few yards he's only going one place – straight into my arms, where I take him and I hold him, I hug him and I kiss him. I wipe his face and see the blood is not his, only Fi's. *Only Fi's* – if you can imagine ever being happy at that, well, I was. And I stand and I walk, George held high within my arms, Simon seemingly looking for answers in the worn, stour-speckled carpet. Georgie and I head away from them all, towards the door, expecting I don't know what, to be allowed out somehow? As if this child would give me a free pass out of the damp and violence of this crappy, sad, conquered building.

75

WAIT RIGHT THERE, *Thomas Bruce.*

I stop. Of course I do.

Give the child back to his mother. You — go and clean yourself up, girl. The child too. Away into the silver car outside. Thomas will be joining you. But not quite yet. Son Peter — go with her. Make sure she doesn't do anything... stupid.

We watch, the whole gang of us, as she departs, as they depart. And then, then it is just us... men?

Well now, Thomas. We need to sort this.

I nod. I know we do.

Simon — you've one use to me now. And that is to get your brother. And even that — the wound is SO old that, well, I need not really bother. So — don't be thinking I am DESPERATE for the information, for I am not. But well — I think, for the both of us, I think you should tell me how you — how WE can contact that brother of yours.

GET TAE FUCK.

Wallop him, Sean-Paul.

And Sean-Paul, on demand, does just that. A second later, the same Sean-Paul is lifting Simon back upon his chair.

This is just how it works, Simon. It's tried and tested. If you don't tell, you get battered. Think of it as the most basic of equations.

There's no reply, unless one considers further spit, further blood dropping to the floor or the moans of an awakening Billy. I'd say that Simon is almost broken. He's lasted far longer than I would have, I'll give him that.

I don't need to witness this. There is a reason I am, of course: so I

know what McDonagh is capable of, so I know not to do anything
that'd cause me to swap places with young Simon.

I say – *Here – check his phone – mebbe – mebbe it'll have Jim Blair's
number on it.*

*Good thinking, Thomas. Though I doubt even this piece of clart
would have Jim Blair listed in black and white for all to see. Sean-Paul,
go find it –*

Sean-Paul roots through Simon's pockets, but when the phone
is retrieved, the screen is smashed, cracked, shattered – from Sean-
Paul's repeated strikes, perhaps, or, more likely, Simon's repeated
tumbles to the floor.

*How unfortunate. You know, I WILL need that number, Simon.
Heh.*

A nod to Sean-Paul, a scalp across the top of Simon's head,
bending, twisting his neck, a shout of pain...

*I'm getting tired, Simon. There's... too little at stake for me to
continue this. Do you see? Now, I won't ask again. Tell me about your
brother, or that is it. No further chances.*

A barely whispered – *Fuck you* – followed by ten seconds of quiet.

McDonagh grunts in annoyance, then turns to me – *Thomas? This
is going to have to be down to you. You know that, don't you?*

There's no reply, but my look, it says it all.

*Thomas, I am not going to ask Sean-Paul to finish your friend here.
No. It is going to have to be you who does it. You do it and I can forget
about you. As you then have a very real reason to keep quiet. I do it?
Or Sean-Paul? Well, then you are a witness, and I cannot have that.
You – your family – you need a real, serious investment in the silence we
require. Do you understand?*

I nod. I understand.

*Sean-Paul, open the holdall and give me the gun. Or should I say,
give Thomas here the gun.*

76

A ND I AM handed a gun. A real, live gun.

Black steel. Wooden handle. Used. Not new, no chance. Rusted in places.

I am surprised by the weight of it and further surprised by how much more nervous I am capable of becoming. It seems I am no cowboy, and no matter how many movies I have seen with heroic tough guys, I am not one of them, either.

I can see, within the revolving cylinder bit, a small brass bullet, and the thought of that bullet coming out of the gun and smashing Simon's head into chocolate egg pieces isn't one that thrills me. The fact that I am being asked to do the trigger-squeezing only making matters worse... and then I am sick. Automatically. Simply, quickly. All down my hideous blue trousers, my cheap plastic shoes, the worn woven carpet.

There's no comment from McDonagh or any of his cronies. I guess it's part and parcel of this initiation. Maybe they're all remembering the first time they were sick in such circumstances. Or maybe some of them are playing the hardmen themselves but are just as scared as I am, just as nauseous.

Billy, though, well, Billy is white. White except for the trickle of blood that is leaving his nose and running straight into his mouth. Billy has not said a word.

Simon, he is watching me with interest. He will have been amused to see the sick, though I didn't note his customary laugh. His eyes, though, despite being cushioned, swollen together, his eyes are on my arms, my hands, the gun.

Aim for his upper body. There'll be a lot less mess. Aim for his heart if

289

you can. Again, do it quick. Don't do a headshot or a leg shot. A leg shot will just bleed forever and he'll be howling throughout. The heart is the best place. He'll be gone in an instant.

My hands are shaking so much that such advice is almost useless. Chances are I'll hit the ceiling if I aim at the floor. How the fuck have I got a gun in my hand?

I look to Simon, shaking his head back and forth – *Nae chance. There's NAE chance you'll do THAT. You – fucking…* But there's fear in his voice too, a shake, a quiver. Obviously there is. I don't blame him; I don't see him as any less.

I remember those guys in the First World War. Conscientious objectors, possibly, sent to the front and asked to perform as firing squads, so not in the war as such, just there to execute their fellow soldiers, deserters, traitors… They got drink, did they no'? To get them through this?

Quickly now, Tommy. We want to get the early ferry. Get away from this place.

What? The fucking early ferry? Ah, c'mon.

Your family's outside – pull this trigger and you're in that car and away. Sean-Paul here will drop you off anywhere you fancy. Isn't that right, Sean-Paul?

'Tis. He nods.

I look to Sean-Paul, dizzy now – do I thank him for that? For that generosity? His eyes are wide, awaiting the shot as one would await the birth of a lamb. The miracle of life.

But the gun cannot leave my belly. My arm cannot rise.

You shoot him. You shoot him now. Or you'll leave me no option but for Sean-Paul here to shoot him and then shoot you and then – and then shoot them outside. Don't – for even a minute – think that I won't. For I know the only way to stop things unravelling is to leave them nice and neat. And that is what I am doing here, Thomas. I have two options of where to cut the cord – with Simon here – or with Georgie out there. The choice is yours now.

I am not prepared, built for this. I can stocktake, I can water down vodka, I can talk shite with tourists, I can drink slow pints with old men...

And, it seems, for all my fears, I cannot see my child threatened.

My hand rises, the gun's direction changing as I turn; first to duck is one of the young lads, then, briefly, McDonagh has a glint of *what the fuck* in his eye, before Sean-Paul jumps over to his left and the gun rests straight in front of Simon, who now, with the gun firmly facing him, has finally changed his tune.

No – no, dinnae – please, please – dinnae, dinnae shoot – ah'll tell ye – ah'll tell ye – Jim Blair – Jim is dead.

McDonagh shakes his head – *Oh, the hardman talks, does he? Well, it's too late, but never mind. You know, I strongly, strongly suspected he was dead – as you soon will be. Thank you, though, for clearing it up. That little nugget of information is what I came for.* He smiles. *Now, Tommy – shoot him.*

But I cannot see through the tears.

Shoot him. Now.

And my hands, they jump as though on electrodes.

NOW, TOMMY. NOW. Let us end this and go home.

And Simon is looking directly at me, as terrified as me, willing me to show empathy, and all I can see is a child sitting there, as he once would have been, not so long ago, a child in awe of his absent brother, a child grown up wrong and now facing a gun.

SHOOT HIM.

I can't... I can't...

THEN, SEAN-PAUL, GO OUTSIDE NOW AND BRING IN THE GIRL AND THE WAIN.

And at that moment, I pull the trigger. I close my eyes and I squeeze.

77

THERE'S AN ALMIGHTY bang, a clap, smoke.

But when the shock of that has passed, this side of the moment and hereafter – well, there's no damage, nothing visible, anyway.

Simon, tied though he was, had squirrelled himself into as much of a ball shape as he could manage. And now, still alive, he slowly begins to unravel, to peek, as if the bullet is yet to come.

McDonagh is grinning. I am not. I am astonished, shaking, confused.

McDonagh approaches Simon – but not too close, for Simon is now soaked through with urine and speckled with blood and snot, tears and spit.

Simon – Simon, can you hear me, boy?

Simon raises his head, slightly.

Did you enjoy that? Eh? Did you enjoy that, boy? I'm sorry. Sorry if I gave you a little scare – oh – have you pooped your pants? Have you pooped your pants, boy? Had a little... accident? Oh dear. Oh dear. Thomas – will you look – look at this. He's just a lad, just a youngster, scared literally shitless, ha ha. You see? There's nothing – no reason to be scared is there. Is there, Thomas? Is there, Simon? You see, Simon, I'd hate it if there WERE a reason for Thomas here to be scared, as Thomas here, well, he works for me now. He's under my protection. Do you understand that, Simon? Are we in agreement? Oh now, don't cry, don't cry, don't cry... You just bit off more than you could chew, that's all. It's a learning process. You're young still. Your pal there – hey, well, look at him – look at him slumped down. I think – I think it might be too late for him – look – but you, you're cleverer than him now. You're smart. You know never to say boo to Thomas again, or his good lady, or his...

292

or the child. Do we – do we understand each other? Eh? Speak up now. We do? Is that a yes? Good lad. I hope I won't be seeing you again, as if I do, well, Sean-Paul here will take good, proper care of you. Do you understand? You do? Good. Good. Now, we're going to leave now, son. We have a ferry to catch. T'was lovely to meet you.

McDonagh ruffles Simon's hair then stands, straightens his back, stretches and looks around. *Good, good. Sean-Paul, untie that one – or is he – is he gone, that one? No mind. Loosen this ferret, then give this man and his family a lift to wherever they want. I'll see you tomorrow. Got that?*

Ok. A-ha.

McDonagh smiles and I see the warmth that smile brings to big Sean-Paul, a boy who'll almost certainly grow considerably bigger yet.

And on your way back, Sean-Paul, pass this place once more and torch it. If these two souls are inside – well, that's up to them. Do a good job of it. Clean. Understand?

Easy. He grins, pleased and able to carry out these simplest of instructions.

78

WE SIT IN the back, Fi, Georgie and me. Georgie is sharing a seatbelt with Fi and she's holding him close. She's shivering, but quiet. Not ignoring me, but closed to the world, concentrating only on Georgie, and quite right too. Blocking out the nightmare. I have no idea how she got so bloodied, with her not answering, responding... Sean-Paul, well, he can drive as competently as he can hit folk, it seems, and although he doesn't know the Scottish geography, he has a voice in his phone telling him which way to turn – left, right, straight on.

It's Sean Connery. Did ye recognise it?

Eh?

The voice – on ma arp. It's Sean Connery. He's ma hero. We're both called Sean, see.

Ah. I slouch back, my head spinning.

Fi is near-hysterical still, shaking but somehow quiet, her idea of hell having been formed when she heard the gunshot, or maybe before, up on that hill, or whenever she got her nose crocked. Who she'd been worried about with the gun I do not know for sure, but I'm guessing it was either-or. But even just the noise of it would have been enough.

I am slowly, gently, stroking Georgie's hair. Fi allows me this. Georgie's face – the shape of it, his cheeks, his nose – they could be mine, I'm almost sure. The glow of orange streetlights peels into the car, covering, uncovering, covering, uncovering his face. Fi is watching, perhaps aware of the nature of my inspection, despite her current confusion. Perhaps she's done the same, many, many a time. I wonder what conclusion she's come to. Georgie's hands are pulling mine towards him – more attention, please, more for me, where've you been, where've you been, dada?

At the roundabout, take the third exshit.

Our Mr Connery. I wonder how he'd've reacted, had he been in my shoes.

Fi dares not catch my eye, but she speaks – *Is it – is it going tae be ok? For Georgie...* She's whispering, not sure of Sean-Paul's part in all this. Is she even asking me, addressing me? And how would I reply if she were?

It will, Fi, it will...

She doesn't look at me while I speak, but her eyes stop darting around so frantically, suggesting, at least, that she heard me.

At the roundabout, take the third exshit and shtay on the A-Sheventy-Sheven.

She's weeping, slow and constant. My body aches. The daylight is almost away now, winter's early evening well upon us. The road's still running clear, and Georgie's dropping off with the movement of the vehicle. I find myself catching a doze then jerking my head up, awake, to see Fi looking out of the window, one arm curled around a sleeping Georgie, the other up to her own neck, occasionally wiping a tear. What's she thinking? These cards she's played...

Do – do you like my suit?

Ach, I'm a fucking eejit. There's nothing in my words, no comfort, no warmth. Just a joke. I'm not an answer, I'm just... saying words, offering communication, reminding her of the mundanities.

She looks over, peers over and stares, not at the suit, at me, tears in her eyes, arm still around Georgie, holding him close and tight. Her head turns away once more, to the movement of outside.

Beware, shpeed cameras in shixty yardsh.

I look ahead to Sean-Paul, considering telling him to *turn that fucking thing off*, but too scared to do so. He's eyes-ahead, studying the road, the drive becoming trickier with rain and sleet, headlights coming towards us, over and over... My head rests back against the seat, the window, almost asleep again, almost asleep...

Is he dead?

She surprises me – I turn – *Eh?* – I try to be as loving, concerned as possible, give Fi all the attention she needs.

Is he dead? Did they... did they shoot him?

I'm thrown – *It was – no – they didn't – I fired the gun – it was...*

You? You shot Simon? Or... Billy?

I shake my head – *No, no – I shot...*

You fired the gun? You killed him?

No, no... Oh, Fi, Fi – you have no idea. I had no choice...

Oh, Tommy, oh, Tommy...

And she's turned, face to the window, her tears mirroring the raindrops running down the glass.

Sean-Paul now – *It wasn't yer man there. That Billy had it coming. See what he did to you! Don't you lose sleep on him, girl. Yer man there – he did well. But that Billy and the little fella – they needed told. People like that need told. And he got told, that's all.*

Short. Precise.

Silence once more. We drive, miles, Georgie asleep, Sean-Paul occasionally whistling something unrecognisable, Fi staring out of her window, sniffing, crying, wiping caked snot and blood from her nose. Sleet now, against the windscreen, but not loud enough to waken Georgie.

Fi – I didn't shoot anyone. Billy wasn't shot. McDonagh – the auld fellow – he hit him with something. And Simon, well, he wasn't exactly shot either. Just scared by the threat of it... He got very scared, but I think he'll be ok. I think. And I think, I think... I think he'll leave us alone, now.

There's no reply, no response. I watch her for a minute, two minutes, longer, but fatigue takes over and, before I know it, my eyes are closing and I'm on my way to sleep, sleep I so need. But just before the drop, I'm awoken as Fi reaches over and lightly takes my hand, giving it one tight squeeze. I curl my fingers around hers and open my eyes – but her head is back now, as though she herself is chasing sleep.

Part IV

79

OH TOMMY, YOU'VE collapsed into the drink.

And it's true. I have done my best, my very best, but I am at a loss as to how to respond to the events. Fi, we took her to the doctor, who looked at her busted nose, her bruised eyes, and then at me, and then at Georgie, examining him, his teeth, looking for marks, signs of violence… Fi telling them she'd *fallen down the stair* but that sounding even to me like the worst and most obvious, common excuse for if I'd battered her.

You're twice her size – is all the GP told me, when I went in myself, thinking about myself, telling him I couldn't sleep, I was drinking too much, I was having trouble leaving the hotel…

There was no sympathy; t'was as if I were a baddie. In a way, though, it's strengthened how I feel about Fi, for if she'd wanted rid of me, well, it would have taken just one little lie to do it, one little lie the social worker practically put in her mouth. Fi told me they'd asked her – *Did he hit you? Does he hit you? And George? Do you feel safe, Fiona?* – but Fi and I resolved, decided, not sure of the decision, but decision made, that we wouldn't tell a soul.

And there was no sign of Simon, no sign of McDonagh.

I was ok, at first – I was. I mean, I was in pain all over – ha – but I didn't feel struck upon or particularly involved – it was as though I was SO keen for life to return to normal that I jumped headlong in, bringing with me a whole barrel of nightmares, but I wasn't even considering them.

I'd be talking to Auld Jock, not a daft man at all, his questioning subtle, light. I mean, I'd obviously thought about Billy – when I saw a collapsed branch up the hill, fallen like Billy's abandoned body,

299

his crooked legs – and when in the shower, the welt on my neck throbbing under the heat – and plenty, plenty more – but it was only after Jock had nudged just once more that I kept the thought of Billy at the front of my mind. After sending Jock home and locking up, I'd fired up the computer and had a look to see what I could find, to see if he'd been mentioned. I found my way to the news site and there, there's a tab for Scotland, and I press that tab and there, again, there's a tab for the West of Scotland and, well, even though it was at least two weeks after the fact, straightaway there was a link for me to open and read, this one hitting the jackpot, if I could call it that.

First up, a picture of the building, the bar – burned down, but front doorway intact, even the stickers on the glass advertising Real Ale. No mistake. *A body found within – charred beyond recognition*. I retched a bit right then, squirming my mouth, turning away, then back, and the memories – hardly old – jumped out and grabbed me, throwing my head from side to side – *fucking Billy, fucking Billy* – and having to remind myself what he'd done to Fi – grabbed her, felt her up, mebbe, broke her fucking nose, the impact there forever for us to see, a tattoo on her face she cannot remove, a constant reminder of her manhandling, our day, our life, our troubles...

If there were ever a man I shouldn't have been sad to learn was *charred beyond recognition*, it should be Billy. But still, it's not a pleasant thought.

So, I drink. Of course I do. Just for the now.

Whatever I am up to, there is one ear on the front door. And when that door sounds, my pulled nerves leap up; I peer, gape round from wherever I am, to hear voices, identify – a Northern Irish burr? The efficiency and import of a polisman? Simon's cackle? Bad fears all, though which would be worse?

But no, nothing.

I did no wrong, I tell myself that. If I can chase away that image of Billy's shrunken body, thinned and charcoaled, blackened like in a Vietnam TV movie... and that thought of being responsible for Billy's death – anyone's death – I can maybe sleep. But I cannot chase it off, no matter how much I reason, repeat, explain. Drink does not help the reasoning, but it does put me to sleep. Send me to sleep. Hammer me to sleep. There's no joyful land of nod here.

Oh, George, oh, George, what hope have you got, my beautiful boy?

But the weeks grow to months. The winter passes through and leads to the thaw. Fi and I, we recover, physically. We smile without reminder of pain. We talk of the future, of vague plans, but plans, nonetheless – a holiday, Georgie's nursery, a school, even, for the wee lad.

And the bar, the bar brings in the money. It's as though this thump on the head has woken me up, woken me up to what I've got, what's worth keeping. I make an effort to keep shop, keep the place clean. We even begin decorating the rooms upstairs again.

Fi tidied Simon's room. I'd left it, left it too late, imagining she'd be leaving it too. One day I just thought – *I'll get this done now, so Fi doesn't have to* – but the room was spotless. I have no idea where his gear went. In the bin, I'd hope. Or on the fire.

But though Simon's on my mind, Billy is most definitely the one. It's funny to grieve, to grieve a man I had no love for. Just a gadge. A cunter. A fuckwit. A bully. If I hadn't been there, hadn't seen him, slumped… heck, there'd be no second thought.

I look up his family, find the address, drive past their house. I imagine his mother inside, devastated at her son's unexplainable death – *Why was he even in that place?*

I drive by again and again. On mebbe the fourth time, there's a twitch of a curtain and my heart quickens – I drive away, away.

Fi reckons about learning French – going on some course. Imagine that. Seems she thinks she was ok at it in school… and although that just makes ME think she wants us – her – them to runaway to France – well, that doesn't sound too bad, does it?

She's moving on, or at least trying to.

*

Busloads of tourists, again and again. I figure it out soon enough — no one else is bribing the Birmingham fella. All these chain places are run by managers there for six months, maybe, before a change. I'm the only sucker who's staying on. Well, it's worth every penny. If customers are coming in, then I am safe — safe from other people who might be watching for a quiet afternoon to visit, unwatched, unguarded. But I'm safe also from my thoughts, the silence an empty afternoon brings.

And I like him. Beyond any of the crooked economics. He brings news from outside this tiny cusp of a village, even if the news is precious more than tattle.

Fi and I talk of Simon a bit. She's more open now, about him, about her, about their past. She was only there on that night he torched the garage as he'd tricked her, told her they were just going to patch things up. She panicked at the flames, at the small explosions, the heat… Then when Simon was lifted, she was worried — she'd driven him away, after all, and kept quiet, not reported it…

And there was nothing else. No other time…

Do I believe her? I try to.

I know she's looking out for Simon now. How could she not be? I see her, watching through the mottled-glass windows, checking who's climbing out of vehicles, walking towards…

Oh — and I've had cameras installed. Inside and out. Auld Jock clocked them right away — *Different times, Tommy, different times.* He takes a sup before asking — *Well, they're no' for me. Mak's me wonder who they ARE for?*

I don't reply, though. Who are they for, after all? Ghosts? Gangsters? Do I believe in them, in one or the other?

80

I'M ON THE hill. Fi understanding more now, more why I need to escape. Spring up here so welcoming, so beautiful. Flowers are breaking through the forest floor debris, the cold almost gone, replaced now by an exploratory sun, testing through the trees, warming, chasing away any last remaining frost. I've lost a bit of weight – fancy that – not that you'd notice, though. I think it was just from the stress. And Fi, perhaps, buying better quality food, me not relying on bar snacks all day. I've cut down on the drink too – seriously. I mean, I'll have a pint at the end of a night, but not two or three... Well, sometimes I will. Sometimes I still need to.

Ach – I guess things just got easier, after that initial shock. They were always going to, eh? Time heals all wounds and all that. Fi's looking great again, back to her usual self, her wee dunted nose still there, but quite cute, funnily enough, with less inflammation, no stray blood... and when it's framed by a happier, healthier face, well, it's fine. Fine. I wonder how she feels about it, mind you, but I'd never ask, bring THAT parcel o' shite up.

I burned the suit. Ha. Stupid fucking thing. I never had it on again – why would I? I just fucking – one night, when Fi was up the stair with Georgie, I pulled it down from the back room and fed it to the barroom fire. A wee ceremony. At first, I was a little reverential – or I thought I'd be, at least – expecting to snip it to flammable chunks, like fabric sample size – but I couldn't find any scissors and then, when I eventually did, they were Georgie's blunt plastic things for cutting paper and such. They didn't work on clothing. I could have guessed that. Hardly worth the effort of the search.

I ripped the first sleeve off. Easy – bad workmanship. The thing came off the body of the suit with just a wee tug, a rip. I didn't even really have to try…

Fold it, bend it, roll it into a rough log shape and deposit it, jumping back as it flared up as though it'd been dunked in kerosene. Quite the sight. Caused me to look at the label and see, well, it wasn't even from Topshop, which I seem to remember Simon had requested. Lord knows where Billy bought the suit, but it had a disclaimer sown into one of the pockets – *Not to be washed or dry-cleaned.*

A wee black drip of it melted through the grate, a small dollop of a thick oily substance. Shite, that'll remain, stained on the floor, no doubt. Just another reminder.

The trousers folded neatly. I checked the pockets – habit, you know? – nothing. Threw them on the fire – no lesson learned, flames higher still, this time leaping out of the flue itself and lapping the front, singeing quickly whatever was on the mantle and in reach – a discarded flyer for a whisky distillery, some half-burnt candles. I looked up, higher above still, and saw, just emerging, a group of black speckles, oily stars on the ceiling sky, and other, heavier, spidery specks floating around the room.

So. Yeah. Fuck the suit. Long gone.

Don't know where the shoes went. I guess Fi threw them.

Georgie's gathering a wee following o' pals, pals with mothers keen on the space of the bar, the occasional free coffee, Fi's attention, bringing their weans over in the mornings, watching them a-root-scoot about the floor. Giving me a reason to sweep every night. Christ, the things folk discard from their pockets… How am I still finding cigarette butts on the floor of a no-smoking pub?

So many yellows in a forest, up a hill – the decaying pine needles, the bleached grass, the bark bitten off the trees by deer, leaving soft, exposed innards… the sun itself, creeping through…

Seeing Georgie so happy fills me with joy. And chatting to Fi's pals, getting to know them – not bad folk at all, most of them, a few brighter than me, if you can believe that. Interesting folk: some artists in there, one lassie wi' half a degree in History. Some daft hair, shaven eyebrows, orange skin, mind you. But even then, well, they're fine enough. Just nonstop, wind-up gossips, making me smile and laugh, both good things and welcome. There's an occasional father in, but they'll look at me with suspicion. They'd've kent Simon, right enough, will be wondering where he is, how Billy died; word sure spread about that. Local hero? I'm sure a few of them had been with Simon in that back room and now they're here, in the front, with me.

And Fi's mother's been round, of course. And I'm getting used to her. Kind of. She's harmless, if you swerve by her, like a pothole on a road, a road you just have to use. She's different now, towards me. Fuck, how could she not be? Her daughter all battered, Prince Billy deid, King Simon God knows where... I'm either a total fucking prick or a total fucking hard-nut hero with hidden fucking talents. I guess some kind of motherly instincts kicked in, seeing her Fi like that, a' shocked and bruised... So, she'll come in and just sit, staring at me, occasionally attempting to chat, or picking up a stray crisp packet, a bit of tidying. One time, she asked about us hosting a Bingo night, and I nodded and said I'd think it over, think it over... Ach. Fi's better to have her in her life than not, I know that.

There's a big auld tree that came down in the winter, a lang Scots pine. Got to walk a good sixty yards out of my way to bypass it. Already there are wee tunnels growing underneath it, beasts of one kind or another making their pathways...

Auld Jock's been blue, poor devil. *Last ane left* – he was telling me, after there'd been another village funeral, for that farmer fellow, Bill Mclean, from along the way, down past the stream, the old bridge. They'd all played in a rugby team together, won some cup or other, back in the 1950s or 1960s.

I'm keen to keep Jock in, keep him welcome, ask his advice on the ale or the fire or the bar in general, keep him involved. Occasionally, he'll mention my father and I'll listen more intently, or, once in a blue moon, my mother, for which I'll stop whatever I'm doing and engage fully. Never wee John, though, no. John's in Jock's eyes, though, and my own. Fi – get this – Fi had found an old photograph of the four of us – not us with Jock, I mean my parents, John and me. We were standing in some wood somewhere – mebbe even on this very hill. I'm looking shy, wrapped around my father's leg; my mother is beaming at the camera, young and beautiful, holding in her arms the bairn John, safe and close. Fi put it in a frame – a decent, handmade frame, no' some store-bought... and there they sit, upstairs in our living room, the room Fi herself had sorted and cleared, stashing away the cash and carry-bought hotel bog roll, the Christmas decorations, cardboard boxes a' fu' o' placemats, flyers, silver-plated cutlery...

And now, well. There they are: there's mother and father and John and myself, and Georgie will grow up at least knowing he had an uncle, once.

I often look into the photograph, into my mother's eyes, and wish. *Georgie's here now, mother, and you'd've loved him.*

There's a crack, behind me, mebbe thirty yards back. I look round, peer – paranoid still – but nothing's there. A deer, perhaps, though they have a stealth in the woods that means you seldom hear them, let alone see them. Ach, sometimes wood just cracks. A forest will always have its own soundtrack.

I'm hoping to get to the top, the crown, just where the trees thin out, the grass gives up and the rock begins the final ascent. A hundred yards, perhaps, to the top. It's here where the snow lies the longest, though it's gone now completely.

Strange the litter you get up here. A packet of Monster Munch crisps sits dunted into the ground before me, the wee purple monster leering up at me. These things are bulletproof, bombproof. Come the apocalypse, there'll be cockroaches and old bags of Monster Munch.

Fi didn't check my bag for whisky, but I've got none. It's early afternoon, you know? Who'd be drinking now? I've got a sarnie, some juice...

I sometimes consider asking Auld Jock to join me on these walks, I really do – he knows of me escaping like this, of course – but, no, it's one thing being good enough to ask, another thing entirely following through with the offer. Plus, I doubt he'd be able to keep up with even my limited athleticism... And then what? Hours later we'd just be sitting opposite each other in the bar.

Another *crack*.

I hear it this time, clearly, and I guess I haven't really switched off, for all the talk of Auld Jock. There's no escaping it, there's somebody behind me, getting closer. And when I think of who it could be, well, there's only one sensible answer. It's no' Jock, that's for sure; it's no' Fi, she wouldn't be so free with leaving Georgie. It's not that daft Birmingham fellow, in his half-weight kilt.

Ach, he's no' a bad guy at a', that guy. I'm just... nervous.

I keep on walking, moving, eyes ahead but ears on behind, definitely hearing the occasional rustle. I scan for a suitable stick, something stout, not rotted, strong enough to help the climb, heavy enough to frighten away any unwanted attendees.

No escaping it now, the whatever can only be twenty feet behind me, if that. I know the sound of this forest, I know the dead-length of any echo, how much the moss and soft ground absorb thump of footfall. I've been up here so many times.

There's a good bit of stick a few yards ahead, about the right size. Maybe a little long, but free, not hanging onto a trunk or sooked into some mud or tied into some moss.

Pick it up, slowly, secure it in both hands, keep moving, upwards and then – then, quickly, suddenly, I turn around.

81

*H*EH. *A'RIGHT, YA cunt.*

Immediately, I can see that this particular bogeyman has shrunk. Reverse evolved. He looks down-and-out dreadful. Unkempt, of course, but paler, adolescent-bearded, thinner, his cheeks sucked in, hollowed. His clothing is ripped, scarred with skid-stains of mud and green. I'm glad he's downwind, put it that way. If I had any fear, which I surely did have – well, seeing him now, it's gone, or at least dropped.

I hold my ground, examine, search –

Simon. I was wondering… wondering when you'd turn up. Um… you're no' – you're no' looking so wonderful…

Heh. Aye. Ah've been underground. Puir disappeared without a trace, eh. But fucking – ah've – ah've been watching you. You and Fi. You and Fi and Georgie.

His breathing is loud, streaming, whiskered.

Ok…

Aye. Ye've really got it a', have ye no'? A lucky cunt. But – ye've fucking got it coming now, Tommy boy…

He's limping. One of his legs – his left – seems bound up, somehow. No wonder I heard him peg-legging up behind me.

Simon, are you – are you ok?

Eh?

You look – You look – well, pretty rundown.

Fuck you, fuck you, Tommy Bruce.

I watch him struggle forward, slow, like an old man cautious on an icy road. I could flick him over with my little finger.

No, seriously – You look awfy. Have you – have you eaten? Do you want a scone?

A whit?

A – a scone, you know – or a sandwich?

Dinnae fucking come at me wi' a' this sandwich shite, ya cunt…

He's a ghost, a cutout, a wisp. He cannot attack me; he can barely move. He's still got the mouth, though, eh.

You just wait…

But I do not flee. Instead, I move towards him, my arm outstretched – *Here, here – let me help you. Let's get – let's get sat down, shall we?*

Eh?

C'mon.

He glares at me then struggles into one of his pockets, almost unable to delve inside before – *hold on* – eventually bringing out a tiny wee pocketknife, blade snapped at the top. From here, this distance, it looks like a tourist knife, the type you'd buy in one of the local Post Offices – a *Welcome to the Trossachs* sort of thing.

Come near me, ah'll fucking run this through ye.

I'm close enough now. Jings. Dirt-stained, tear-streaked cheeks. Filth, bits of leaf, crap in his hair. Eyes jellied up with some kind of infection – bloodshot, a bit, the left one, anyway. Tooth – or teeth – missing. And – as guessed – a stink. A pissy, sweaty stink.

Oh my God, Simon. What's happened to you? Put that – put that wee knife down, eh?

Fucking – dinnae you get a' pally wi' me. Ye ken fine well whit happened tae me – and now, now ah'll fucking have ye for it…

It's a stalemate. I feel as though I'm in a dwam: the sun poking through the canopies, the peculiar sonics of the forest, the birds above us oblivious to the drama occurring between these two eejits on the forest floor below. Simon's struggling. I don't know if it was the effort of the climb or his injury or whatever, but he's not recovering now we're stationary, not growing in strength, his breathing just as heavy. I decide to take a chance. I move an extra ten feet away and take a seat upon a long-fallen trunk, heavily mossed but dry, comfortable. I bring my rucksack round and unzip it, seemingly ignoring Simon, but not *that* stupid, keeping a keek out of the corner of my eye… but there's barely any movement, just the odd shudder and cough, the odd curse.

I bring out a sandwich, sliced in half. Prepared by Fi. Brown bread, ham, cheese, pickle, butter, some green bits – salad. This magical salad she's insisting I eat nowadays, as if a slither of some leaf could do me any good.

Here, Simon. Have some o' this. Look – ham, cheese.

He's glaring, but not at me. At my hands, the food. *You fucking cunt –*

No, come on, Simon, that's no' fair. Here – come here and sit down. We can talk about this. Have some o' this food – you look – you look a bit, um, peaky.

Bring it over.

Eh?

Ahm no' fucking sitting aside you. Bring it over.

I smile, shake my head – *Right then. You – you put that daft wee letter-opener away and I'll bring you a sandwich, right?*

He considers, then – *Dinnae you fucking try anything…*

Like what? Am I gonnae put some mustard on it on the sly? Simon, it's a fucking half-sarnie piece, that's a' it is. You look – you look shagged – Shagged! What is this, the 1980s? I try again – *You look, you know, tired. Hungry. C'mon. We've been through enough, you and me – put the knife down and I'll bring the food over.*

He sneers at me, then spits on the forest floor before placing the knife back in his pocket and hobbling, inching, towards me. *Here – did ah see a bottle o' juice in there?*

We're sat now, on the trunk.

They fucking – they fucking knocked me right down and left me in there. I was out for the count, like. Loosened the bonds, eh, ken. I found that when ah came to – but ma fucking arm just wouldnae work. Turns out – turns out it was dislocated, I think. But I didnae ken. Billy was – Billy was moaning away –

He was alive?

Eh? Oh aye. Fucking. Aye.

Jesus.

He's ripping at the food, tearing it down him, swallowing without chewing, desperate.

Nae cunt looked, Tommy. Those fucks – that fuck – whoever fucking torched the place – he never looked. Never came inside. We couldnae hear fuck a'. Too dark. Way too dark. Billy – Billy couldnae move, I was half-tied tae that shitey wee chair. Me telling Billy ah'd get him out, him greetin' like a wean, screaming… but fucking, me telling him ah'd get him out, get US out, managing tae stand, finally loosening the ties, looking for a light, nae lights – this ane fucking arm deid tae the world, ma mouth a' swelling up, bleeding – couldnae see outae ane eye at a', and what tae see in the dark, anyhow?

He's finishing the sandwich, clasping hold of the Lucozade, gibbering on –

And SO fucking cauld in there, that fireplace lang gone out. Bunch o' cunts, Tommy, them Irish cunts. Lower class o' cunts tae US cunts, ah tell ye that… And me fucking making it ootside, ken, but too cauld and where tae go anyhow? Coming back in, sitting wi' Billy, him whimpering away like a puppy, reckoning his back was broken or some shite, shouting, 'No!' when I tried tae move him…

Oh my God. I cannot hear this. He continues, shivering as he speaks –

And then me, just sitting wi' him, through the night, thinking – next morn, next morn, I could walk tae the van and get help – but before I knew it, some crashing – like the windae coming in – and looking over, forcing masel' up – and Christ, someone's only gone and thrown a petrol bomb intae the bar, it spilling out, catching light on the flame and woosh! That was it. Nae time, nae time at a'. I telt Billy, 'Get up, ya cunt! Get up, ya fucking clown!' But he wisnae – he couldnae manage or whatever, and me wi' ma one good arm, trying, pulling him up, but I couldnae see and I couldnae lift and the smell – the smell o' that fire, like the carpet was plastic or whatever, a thick black poke o' smoke quick, all around us, the foam in the seats going up and Billy crying now 'Simon!

Simon! Dinnae leave me!' – but me wi' nae fucking choice, nae chance tae save any cunt other than masel'… and me, well, me just running, running, leaving Billy in there tae scream for a minute – and then he's finally screaming, 'Mum!' – before he just – he just…

And he's crying now, Simon. He's choking – *You fucking cunt, Tommy Bruce. Why'd ye tell those Irish cunts who ye were? They were fucking – they were on ma side – we had 'em – WE HAD 'EM. You fucking – Billy died because o' you, no' me – YOU. I fucking tried tae save him. YOU killed him. YOU!*

The thought of it all, of all this, of Billy burning alive, or choking on the fumes, more likely – *That's no' – that's no' fair, Simon. I hardly had a choice, did I? And they kent fine I wasn't Jim Blair – McDonagh – he KNEW that brother o' yours. He fucking kent him fae years back. And what – what were YOU up tae, bringing Georgie and Fi there? Was that supposed to relax me? You do know Billy smashed her face up, right? Dinnae come wi' this angelic shite – you were the cunter here, Simon – or at least Billy – and you ken it fine.*

He snivels, then – *You fucking bastard* – and he turns, swings at me, but there's no weight, no strength. It's like fighting a wasted, auld granny. I grab his arm; he struggles, but there's nothing in him, just words – *Aye, well, Tommy, that wee boy is the only reason you and Fi are still alive, still around. You think I havenae seen you in that shitey wee hotel – heh – I've been IN, Tommy – IN yer hotel. It's such an easy target, an easy target, Tommy boy, but nah – that kid – MA kid – I couldnae burn him out, no' like you did wi' Billy. Ahm no' like you – so you fucking thank him for being alive…*

C'mon, Simon… Dinnae be a prick.

A prick? A prick, is it? You've fucking everything, right there – had it a' yer life – that fucking hotel – Fi – Georgie. What've I got? A deid fucking brother? A deid fucking pal? Billy screaming in ma fucking dreams every time I close ma eyes?

And with that he rises and his other arm lunges at me, crap knife out and forward, sticking straight towards my stomach. It reaches, it does, it gets inside and no doubt pierces, from the pain, the sharp yelp, the shock – but this coat, my layers of clothes, Simon's weakness and the shiteness of the knife – I'm no' in any real danger, but it's pain enough.

Then he's up and on top of me, and although I somehow say – *Watch the rucksack* – I ken right away not to worry about the rucksack and worry all about this piss-midden that is trying to stab me again. His arm's forward, towards me, but I roll out of the way and he trips, stumbles, losing any control with his daft, lame leg and falling straight onto the knife himself, his own body-weight driving it straight in, shutting him up, not instantly, for he shakes briefly, but in – three, two, one – he collapses, limp.

I wait. I wait two, three, four minutes. Almost expecting something. For it to get worse, for Simon to awaken.

But there's no further movement from Simon, no breath, even. He's deid now, that's obvious.

And breathe.

I don't feel ill. Don't feel sick, or even surprised. I feel as though a weight has been lifted. Fancy that.

I search, look around me – all the way up to the canopy of the trees high above, then down, peering left, then right, listening… There's no one to share this moment or to offer help, no other movement, no fanfare, just rook caw and a slight, tickling breeze.

That tight, raw nip on my belly… I make to untangle my jacket, easy to unzip – then my shirt – but just two buttons in, I can see that my voluminous grey shirt now has a poppy pattern, darker, though, and spreading, ever so slightly, as I watch.

Fuck. Well, that's that. I stare at Simon's arched back, his hanging legs, looking uncomfortably tangled.

What to do, what to do?

I never really asked to be here. I can't say I've made bad decisions, these last few years. I've more – more just drifted… Maybe my lack of decision-making has caused it all though, eh? I suppose that could be argued.

Another wee bite to my belly, reminding me that I've been stabbed. I have to get home.

Ah, Fi, Fi…

I'll make my way down, quick as I can, and report Simon, his body, of course I will. I'll just say I found him as he is. Won't mention the drama, the history. But I'll report him, for his family's sake.

But the polis will be bound to ask – *A coincidence, Mr Bruce, ye found him, a' the way hidden up there?* Which would be fair enough, for we're in the middle of rot here. It's a maze of trees and stumps and bracken and ditches – there are no signposts, no real landmarks. No *Turn left at the fifth stump…*

And that'd bring in a' that shite about Billy and HIS death. Do I need a' that to unravel? Does Fi?

There's no footfall up here; I doubt people would ever come across him, even if I just left him perched as he is. No one's looking for him, after all. There are no tourists, no farmers… I've seldom seen a soul in a' my ventures this high up the hill.

Mebbe Simon would – and mebbe he should – just disappear, into legend, like his brother. And mebbe he'd prefer that.

I look around me. For answers, inspiration. It's so calm, so peaceful up here. This is pretty much where I'd choose to be buried, however I died.

A cough and my stomach smarts. But there's no blood in my mouth, not like in the movies. It's just – burning sore.

Yer a wee bastard, Simon Blair.

What to do, what to do?

I grab his legs and quickly, without further thought, burl him over the trunk, onto the forest floor, just a little more out of sight. I make to kick some leaves on him, but as I do, I notice his phone is sticking almost all the way out of his pocket, fingered, reddened with blood and who knows what… I bend down, pull it out, try to fire it up, maybe phone down to the hotel, ask for help – but no, there's no fire in it, no power, just that cracked screen and cold, damp plastic. Why did he keep it? As I ease it back into his pocket, I spot a slip of something – paper, mebbe – beside it… I tease at this, curious, and see colour sneak into view, a picture of some sort, or the remainder of one… Curling it out gently, I recognise the scene almost immediately, for it's a photograph Auld Jock had taken that I'd stuck behind the bar myself, just a month or so back. It's been… cut or ripped in half, and I'm no longer fully visible, just a fleck of that daft maroon jumper I sometimes wear. But Fi is there still, and she's holding, presenting Georgie, who's staring, smiling and reaching out, straight toward the camera.

Acknowledgements

With thanks to: Linda, Theo, Esme, Jimmy Campbell, Nina, KJ, Daniel, Jaycock and Langendorf, Peter and Ullis, Jim Gill, Oldcastle Books, Bart, Domino, 46-30, John Williams, Sam Heughan, Lucy P & EYOE, Viking, Terry, Rodge Glass and Kate Lazda.

About the Author

James Yorkston is a singer-songwriter and author from the East Neuk of Fife, Scotland. Since signing to Domino Records in 2001, James has released a steady flow of highly acclaimed, multi-instrument, acoustic based albums. James' 2021 album *The Wide, Wide River* was called 'Another fascinating, curious contribution to the Scottish musician's constantly eddying catalogue' by the *Guardian*, 'A beautiful experience' by *Clash* and ‹Another career highlight› by the *Scotsman*. In 2014 Yorkston began playing with Yorkston / Thorne / Khan, a trio embracing jazz, traditional folk, krautrock, the poetry of Ivor Cutler and Indian classical music.

In his varied career, James has toured Europe, North America and India and appeared at countless festivals, both musical and literary. In 2011 James' debut book *It's Lovely to be Here – The Touring Diaries of a Scottish Gent* was published to great response by The Domino Press / Faber, and in 2016 Freight Press published James' first novel *3 Craws*, which has gone on to be studied in schools and colleges in the UK and America. His second novel, *The Book of the Gaels*, was published by Oldcastle Books in 2022. James also runs the music and poetry night 'Tae Sup wi' a Fifer', and co-hosts the podcast *46-30*, dedicated to 'Quality Music of No Fixed Abode'.

jamesyorkston.co.uk
oldcastlebooks.co.uk/James-Yorkston

Also Available from OLDCASTLE Books

Rural West Cork, Ireland. Two Kids, Joseph and Paul, and their struggling, poet father, Fraser, are battling grief and poverty. When a letter arrives with a summons to Dublin and the promise of publication, it offers a chink of light – the hope of rescue. But Dublin is a long, wet and hungry way from West Cork in the mid-70s, especially when they have no money - just the clothes they stand up in and an old, battered suitcase.

So begins an almost anti-road trip of flipsides and contradictions – dreams and nightmares, promises and disappointments, generosity and meanness, unconditional love and shocking neglect.

In simple, beautiful, lyrical prose, James Yorkston's novel takes us on that trip, as seen through the eyes of a brave and resourceful but poor and frightened child. It tells of the emptying, paralysing pain of grief and loss, tempered only by the hope of rescue and the redemption of parental love. It also tells of Fraser's love for his children's dead mother, as hidden within the battered suitcase is Fraser's heart-breaking collection of poems – *The Book of the Gaels*.

'There are echoes of Douglas Stewart's *Shuggie Bain*... This slim, punchy book is extraordinarily powerful' – *Times*

oldcastlebooks.co.uk/The-Book-of-the-Gaels

⬤LDCASTLE BOOKS

POSSIBLY THE UK'S SMALLEST
INDEPENDENT PUBLISHING GROUP

Oldcastle Books is an independent publishing company formed in 1985 dedicated to providing an eclectic range of titles with a nod to the popular culture of the day.

Imprints include our lists about the film industry, KAMERA BOOKS & CREATIVE ESSENTIALS. We have dabbled in the classics, with PULP! THE CLASSICS, taken a punt on gambling books with HIGH STAKES, provided in-depth overviews with POCKET ESSENTIALS and covered a wide range in the eponymous OLDCASTLE BOOKS list. Most recently we have welcomed two new sister imprints with THE CRIME & MYSTERY CLUB and VERVE, home to great, original, page-turning fiction.

oldcastlebooks.com

  kamera BOOKS

OLDCASTLE BOOKS	CREATIVE ESSENTIALS	THE CRIME & MYSTERY CLUB
POCKET ESSENTIALS	PULP! THE CLASSICS	VERVE BOOKS
KAMERA BOOKS	HIGHSTAKES PUBLISHING	